Stowaway

Partap Singh

SELPARIS BOOKS, SAN FRANCISCO

STOWAWAY

A Selparis Book

Visit our website at
www.selparis.com

PRINTING HISTORY
Selparis first edition / May 2014

Copyright © 2014 by Partap Singh

Book Design by Selparis Books

ISBN: 978-1-931833-38-7

SELPARIS
Selparis Books are published by Alight Publications
a division of Alight Natural Products Limited
P.O. Box 277, Live Oak, California 95953.

PRINTED IN THE UNITED STATES OF AMERICA

1

Stowaway

Confined to a cramped storage container with six cute but over-excited puppies, Fletcher felt compelled to reconsider his brilliant plan.

He had figured there was only one way to stow-away on a space ship. You couldn't simply walk on board since the entry hatch would be guarded. Sneaking in behind someone else might work in a comedy, but he would have to be the luckiest kid in the universe for it to work in real life, and he had never felt particularly lucky. Since almost all business was conducted on the station rather than inside the ship, only the crew had a reason for being on board, and the eldrandii ships used by Earth's traders and defense fleet had no more than thirty crew, so stealing a uniform and hoping the guards didn't recognize all the crew members was out of the question. A scrawny spacer kid like him would never be able to pass for one of them, anyway – the uniform would hang loose over him like a sack.

Fletcher figured that his best shot was to take the place of some of the cargo. This was a bit tricky, since he had to find a container that allowed for more than a day's worth of breathing. It also had to be opaque so no one would see him inside, so the air had to get in by some way other than a simple hole. Luckily, there was a huge demand for Earth pets on the other worlds, and the usual containers for them were exactly what Fletcher needed. These were simply the normal bulk containers with a tiny ventilation pump built in to filter out contaminants and manage conditions for perishable goods. Nobody had thought to add windows.

So, when he finally spotted a cargo crew loading some puppies into just such a container, Fletcher saw his chance. He waited for them to clear out, checked the departure schedule posted pretty much everywhere along the station's dockside to make sure the ship outside would be leaving soon, but not too soon, and got to work. Because Newport Station lacked artificial gravity, people generally didn't roam around unless they had something specific to do. Security was handled by camera and Fletcher had figured out how to hack one of those cameras through his handheld. It was a trick that would only work once, since the station's massive main computer had adaptive security second-to-none. But that one time was all he needed. He had been very careful about thinking this through, just to make sure that his one shot wasn't wasted.

Now in with the half-dozen frisky puppies, a dog food dispenser, and the vital ventilation system that he kept banging his head into as he shifted his cramped limbs, all he had to do was wait. Wait, and try not to mind the smell and the noise. He figured it was unlikely that someone would look inside until the container reached its new owner, and by then, he would be on a new world. No one would bother paying for his voyage back to Newport Station. He would be free. Marooned on an alien world without any knowledge of the local culture or how to survive in the new environment, sure – but still free.

After a few hours of being first delighted then annoyed by the puppies, and first unable to breathe in the stench then desensitized to it, Fletcher felt the container being lifted up and carried smoothly forward. An automated cargo pad was floating the crate into the ship's bay. With the day-long trip through hyperspace still ahead of him, he was already wishing his aching limbs would simply fall off, but that pain was a small price to pay. He was slight in all his dimensions, giving him just enough room to adjust himself a bit as long as he made sure to check for puppies in the way. They were about as excited as he was, bouncing all over the place. They didn't realize that they were living in captivity, and just going from one master to another.

The brief excitement while being transported by the cargo pad gave way to more boring hours sitting in the ship's bay. The ship's artificial gravity made life infinitely more uncomfortable for Fletcher. He had spent too much of his life on Newport Station. Sure, he had exercised daily as required and practiced in the rotating hall, but his muscles were still a long way from being ready for significant gravity. The puppies were fine – they were all Earth born and raised. With their natural environment restored, they frolicked everywhere, making a point to land on his sorest and most delicate spots. Their constant yapping was also getting on his nerves. The tight echo chamber magnified the volume and pained his ears, reminding him how quiet his life in space had been.

There was no chance to escape these tortures now since he couldn't open the container from the inside. He was stuck here until someone discovered him. With every minute, he thought more about how foolish this whole escape attempt was. What if these puppies were being sold to a vicious species that had puppies on the menu, and their new owner would kill him on sight as an intruder.

A rumble from outside signaled the startup sequence for the ship's antimatter engines. Shortly after, a jolt indicated the release of the station docking clamps and the ship began to use its control thrusters to gently maneuver clear. Fletcher felt even more force pushing him in unpredictable directions. As if the artificial gravity wasn't bad enough, now he was being shoved around all over the place. Finally, once the ship's maneuvering rockets got it clear of potential hazards, the antimatter engines fired, and he was thrown against his right side by the brutal reaction. Those engines produced an acceleration over that of Earth's gravity, and Fletcher couldn't even move the muscles in his face to grimace with pain. The dogs did not seem to have as much trouble, but they had become unusually quiet.

Fletcher tried to put his body's protests out of his mind, reminding himself that it was only a matter of time. Once the ship entered hyperspace, there would be no more acceleration, and the longest trip to one of Earth's trading partners wouldn't take more than two days. Since he had no choice but to hold out, he tried his best to fall asleep.

He was so tired from the anticipation and the day's activity that he probably succeeded despite his discomfort, but when a burst of illumination filled the container and brought him to his senses, it seemed like only a moment after when his last thought. The lid was off. He had been discovered. It took him a moment to register this, but he quickly deduced that they couldn't have reached their destination – he would definitely have woken up during the loading and unloading. Was the ship in hyperspace yet? If he was lucky, the haze between sleep and wakefulness had allowed some time to pass between his last thought and now. More likely, it had only been a few minutes, and in that case they had still not left Earth's sphere of influence - a shuttle could easily bring him back to the station.

Fletcher wanted to curse at the face grinning at him now, and would have if the shock hadn't robbed him of his voice. He could barely make the face out because his eyes were still unfocused, but it was a female face with short hair. And she was smiling. Why was she smiling? If someone snuck aboard his ship, he'd be furious. He would have sworn it was impossible, but she looked almost as if she had expected him to be in there.

"So, how are you doing?" she said, removing all doubt. Somehow they had seen through his cunning plan, but why hadn't they taken him out of the container on the station? Something strange was up. He stood up gingerly, pretending to be concerned about the puppies instead of his ability to do more than crawl while the ship was still accelerating. He was forced to grab the edge of the container for support. For reassurance, he used his free hand to pat his trusty computer concealed in the inner pocket of his jacket. That essential check made, he looked at the woman, but couldn't manage an answer.

Getting a good look at her now, he guessed she must be around thirty. Four men flanked her, all uniformed and standing at attention, but she was in a casual tee-shirt and cargo pants, posed as if impatient to be somewhere else. That led Fletcher to guess that she was the captain.

Without putting an edge on her tone, she said, "I don't have time for this. Get out of there and follow me. I need to be on the bridge until we get into hyperspace and I'll sort you out after that."

He nodded tentatively. Blood flowed back into his legs and at the same time drained from his head, making him dizzy and producing an embarrassing wobble when he stood in front of the captain. He tried to talk to draw attention away from his recovery, but only managed to say, "how'd you know?"

She was already making her way out of the cargo bay as she said, "no time for that now. I'll explain it all once we're in hyperspace. I've got other things to worry about. Just keep up and keep quiet."

Keeping up was a struggle. Fletcher would have asked the crewmembers who had stood beside the captain if they would help him, but they had all taken the captain's departure as a signal that they should get back to their own work. By the time he could muster himself to take a step, they were all out of sight. He struggled to keep up with the captain in a series of stops and starts, using the walls along the way for support, and despising himself for his weakness. The captain seemed understanding about his difficulty, and stopped to wait for him without comment whenever the gap between them grew more than twelve or so feet, but she was still anxious to get to the business end of the ship. Fletcher wondered why. From his father, he had heard innumerable times how boring journeys between worlds tended to be, and how all the action was planetside. There was something wrong here, and he was caught in the middle of it.

Had the captain made the decision to allow him onboard? Fletcher had never met her before. She wasn't among his father's cronies. From the dockside screens, he knew the ship was the *Azar* and recognized the name from the news, but didn't really know why it was in the news. Was it in some sort of trouble? That would be ironic.

He needed information desperately, but knew that the captain wanted to put off the long discussions for now. He had to go for the basics, then.

"What's your name?" he asked quickly.

"Captain Emily Pierce. Just 'captain' is good enough."

He jogged his memory. His father had despised a Captain Pierce, so that was a good sign, but still left the question of why he had disliked her. Fletcher couldn't remember.

Just short of the sliding doors marked 'bridge' and between heavy breaths, he asked, "Why are you in a hurry?"

Captain Pierce looked back at him with a mischievous grin, "because things get a lot more interesting when you've got something other people want."

And that was it. The computer announced "captain on the bridge," the first officer vacated the captain's seat, and Emily Pierce was all business. For a moment, Fletcher was afraid to step onto the bridge, being so badly out of place. Still needing to catch his breath after what, for him, had been a tremendous exertion, he quickly took a seat on the cold metal floor with his back up against a bare wall free of sensitive panels. He wiped the sweat from his forehead and his black hair and finally noticed that his jeans had puppy poop stains. Not only was that visually embarrassing, but it brought to mind how much he must be stinking up the place, and he shrunk even further into floor.

The grin the captain had given him was something he could never have expected from a starship captain. His father didn't have much of a sense of humor, running his own fleet of ships like clockwork purely to satisfy his pride, and the captains under his command seemed only to smile at someone else's expense.

Fletcher shook his head to clear the thoughts of his father out. He needed to focus on what was going on in the hope that he might be able to stay on this ship instead of returning to the station. What was so valuable on this ship that others would cause trouble to get it? Definitely not the puppies. And not him, no matter how mad his father was going to be. Fletcher knew that intercepting a ship in Earth space was a dangerous thing to try, criminal, and difficult since the eldrandii ships everyone used were so closely matched. Whatever this ship had, it must be insanely valuable.

Well, at least this was going to be interesting. Why would the captain want an extra teenager along for the ride when something this serious was going on? Was she just trying to give his father some trouble because they were enemies? Or did she . . . could she know why Fletcher had fled his home? That should be impossible, and why would she care, anyway?

The first officer stood at the captain's side as she took her seat and reported, "the ship we had identified in port has undocked and is in a faster orbit. Without any changes, it will be able to transfer to us and intercept within weapons range. It doesn't look like Commander Raiz bothered delaying them this time."

"Yeah, but this is going to happen every time now, right? He's the commander of the station, not our guardian angel. He likes to get us into trouble," the captain said through a forced smile. "But I think he'll approve an unusual burn for us. The preapproved exit trajectory was probably leaked days ago, which means we have ships ahead waiting for us, too."

"And they probably know your habit of using the Saturn jump point as an alternate," the first officer commented, "so that's out."

"Mars slingshot to the jump point on that side, then," the captain decided. "Let's see if Raiz will give us that much of a boost."

The first officer's eyebrows went up an inch. Clearing his throat meaningfully, he said, "Right. Comm, get Newport Station to clear burn that will take us closer to Mars so that we can get a boost to the nearest jump point to Plani." Under his breath, he added, "that will only take a slight correction – you planned this."

Pierce turned grim. "Let's just hope that the ships ahead of us aren't in a position to adjust. Raiz will probably have to approve the new vector for the ship behind us."

It took a few minutes for the message to get to Earth and back before they received clearance. To approve the new vector so quickly, the Newport Station commander must have been ready for the request.

Fletcher knew what was coming, and braced himself more firmly against the wall. The first officer finally took a seat, leaving no one on the bridge standing. The maneuvering rockets fired after a ten second warning blared throughout the ship, warning everyone to brace for the acceleration. Then the main engines fired for a few seconds. The force once again rattled Fletcher's frame and he grimaced. The rest of the crew had a bit of strain in their faces, but otherwise took it mildly. He doubted any of them had spent years of their childhood in space.

The forward view now had the plot of their Mars rendezvous and the locations of the ships in the area. The path of the one that was tailing the *Azar* was highlighted in yellow, but there was no way for Fletcher to figure out which of the other blips might be able to intercept ahead of them. Presumably, the first officer was trying to rule out ships based on their current paths to find the right ones, but there were hundreds of ships in the Martian vicinity.

The captain looked down at Fletcher, who was still seated on the cold steel. "Now they'll have to contact us and bargain," she said. "The ships that were meant to box us in and make the threat good will definitely be out of place now. We should be getting the call right about . . . ."

"Captain," the communications officer said, "there's a message from the ship tailing us."

"Great, let's see what they look like." The display now filled with a stereotypically dry plani face. Grey skinned, gaunt, and sneering, it matched in every way the cold, ruthless character that the plani cultivated. Fletcher would have been embarrassed if he so closely matched the impression other species had of humans, but the plani seemed to delight in their sociopathic reputation.

"Oh, fun," Pierce sighed.

The transmission was by regular EM, not hyperspace relay, so there was a fifteen-second delay between comments. The use of EM was required in Sol space, since it allowed Newport Station to monitor everything.

"Captain Pierce, it is pointless to evade us," the plani said matter-of-factly, "you are headed for Plani. This is foolish. Every plani conglomerate will be after the secrets you carry with you, and you will be vulnerable once you land. Why not negotiate with us now and save yourself further . . . unpleasantness. We will . . . protect you while you are on our planet."

"And I trust you why?"

"We would like to establish a partnership with you. We know

you discovered these secrets in ancient ruins, and that you know the locations of other such ruins. We know there is technology. We know that the ruins have something to do with the human past – something to do with Earth's past – and cannot risk the possibility that they are secured against non-human intrusion. So, you see, we know we need you, Pierce." The plani captain's lip curled a bit as he said this, as if he had just tasted something unpleasant.

Captain Pierce sighed, tapping her fingers on an armrest console. "Tell you what, if no one from my crew dies while we're on Plani, we'll talk." Fletcher's jaw dropped at this reply. Was Pierce really thinking about giving them what they wanted?

The message delay left the bridge in an air of suspense. It was difficult to anticipate how the plani would take Captain Pierce's brusque manner. During the pause, the captain had to be careful not to betray any sign of doubt on her face. The plani captain seemed able to express and hold exactly the desired expression without effort. He snorted in disdain and said, "Fulfill our part with so little guarantee of return? I cannot believe you are unaware of our customs, Captain Pierce. Negotiate properly. If you are trying to delay until you are ready to jump, we will continue to take whatever steps are necessary to secure whatever information you have about the hyperspace drive."

Fletcher's eye widened. So that was what this was all about. He had heard that Earth was working on the hyperdrive, cracking the most valuable secret in existence and one kept exclusively by the eldrandii. Somehow, he had stumbled onto the ship that had discovered the key. Unbelievable.

Captain Pierce continued, sounding as if she had been through all of this dozens of times before. "Of course you'll do what you can to get it. Everybody will. But let me ask you something – how do you plan to get it if you attack this ship? Do you suppose we'll eject it out so you can collect it right before we blow up? I don't have anything to give to you for your reassurance, and I'm not that interested in your protection anyway. Isn't the safety of free trading your most important custom?"

The opposing captain grinned, flashing fierce canines. "I suppose . . . there are prizes for which custom must be abandoned."

"That's a big risk, isn't it? You're the center of ISC trade because everyone knows that even though they might be cheated and robbed blind by your negotiations, they won't be harmed. That's the only reason I'm still willing to risk trading with plani when I've got a galaxy-sized target on my rear."

"There is precedence for a breach of custom, Captain," the plani retorted. "It has not occurred in eleven thousand Plani years, but the opportunity to be free of the eldrandii hyperspace monopoly – or any dependence on foreign powers for hyperspace access – will be a hundred thousand year event."

"Yeah, but eleven thousand years ago your planet was a dumping ground for fugitives. Now you're the biggest economic power in a thousand light years. I don't think you're going to throw that away so easily. That's what I told the other conglomerates, and that's what I'm telling you. That doesn't mean that I'm not willing to deal with you, but I'm tired of you guys chasing me, one after another. You have my word as a free trader that, if I want to sell, there's nothing stopping me. Since you've made your bid, you'll have to leave me to consider it according to custom."

The plani's face melted into a snarl. "Is this what you said to the others who approached you?"

"To the plani. Different people need to be treated differently. By the way, how many of the plani conglomerates have the ships to mount an intercept like the one you tried here?"

"That is information, Captain. I should charge you for it, but since it is trivial, I will present it in exchange for goodwill. There are eighteen such conglomerates, including our own."

"So that's . . . six down and twelve to go," Captain Pierce sighed. "I don't suppose you would be willing to spread the word to the others in exchange for . . . ," she looked at her first officer, who promptly whispered a couple of words she repeated, ". . . preferred consideration."

"I am afraid not, captain. Information about you – any information including the details of our exchange – will be highly valuable. I will attempt to sell it through intermediaries. But before we conclude, the offer to protect you was not a proper offer."

"No problem. It's been the same way every time. You had

something more concrete?"

"For the specific information about the hyperspace drive including relevant equations, four billion credits. For any additional finds occurring during exploration of ruins you guide us to, a ten percent share of the profit. This is what we are prepared to offer. May I ask how it compares to the other offers you have received?"

Captain Pierce grinned broadly and wagged her finger in admonishment. "That information will cost you."

The signal delay gave Fletcher time to consider four billion credits. It was enough to buy a brand new ship and keep it running for years. But the information was priceless. Was it a fair deal? If Pierce was really interested in selling the secret, she should just gather all potential buyers and have an auction.

Fletcher also had trouble getting over how cooperative and respectful the plani captain suddenly sounded. Was that normal?

The plani continued. "We will leave you on your way for now, but expect to hear from us after we have given you due time to consider the proposal. At that time, if you remain obstinate and have not accepted the offer of any party, we will press the issue with all our power."

The video link winked out and the forward view returned to the default exterior image. To Fletcher's surprise, it was a full-on view of the sunny side of Mars. Without pausing to muse at the splendor of the red planet, the captain stood, motioned for her first officer to take command, and made her way out of the bridge. At the sliding door, she cleared her throat to get Fletcher's attention and indicated with her head that he should follow her out.

Disappointed that he would miss the chance to survey the red planet up close, but interested in what the captain had to say, he followed and waited for a chance to ask questions. For now, just keeping up with her was enough to take the wind out of him and prevent him from talking. Down the corridor from the bridge, they started passing the crew quarters, and Fletcher realized that the captain must be trying to decide where to stow him. But the crew quarters were all doubles – for privacy, you had to be a paying passenger. Fletcher had never shared a room with anyone before.

Seeing the expression on his face, the captain stopped and

said, "you're lucky I decided not to leave you in that container till we got to Plani. You'll be bunking with an old friend of mine. He's the ship's technical advisor. His name's Ethan and unless you want to talk to him, he won't bother you."

Desperate to seize the opportunity to get a question in, Fletcher's mouth popped open with the most useless one imaginable. "What are the plani going to do with the puppies?"

Captain Pierce stared at Fletcher with incredulous eyes, then laughed. "Out of all the things you must want to know, you pick the puppies? You really are interesting."

Struggling to keep from blushing in embarrassment, Fletcher pressed on. "Well? Why do they want them?"

Pierce shrugged. "The vampires like them."

"The vampires . . . ," Fletcher didn't know how to react. "The vampires . . . like puppies."

"Yeah. They call themselves dribrora, and they don't go around biting necks or anything. Except for a bunch I met on . . . but that's still classified top secret. I guess you weren't taught about them. A bit of the plani population has a disease that used to force them to drink blood, but they have synthetics now. They're more like us than regular plani, really – like the part about keeping pets. A bit more color to their faces, too. Oh, and they don't like being called 'vampires' anymore. I got used to calling them that before they found out how humans looked at vampires, and it's gotten to be a bad habit. Don't do it."

"Don't . . . do it," Fletcher repeated. Captain Pierce clearly had dribrora on her mind, and Fletcher couldn't shake the feeling that there was more to this than a pack of puppies.

They continued on their way to the room Ethan and Fletcher would share. Even though the rest of the crew was at their stations, Ethan was in the room sitting on the floor. Around him in a semicircle were sheets of e-paper, some flashing with schematics and others static with complex sequences of equations. Ethan manipulated the figures on the paper in his hand with a stylus shaped like an ancient fountain pen. Some of the other sheets seemed to change in response. The smell of coffee filled the air.

Ethan's eyes were quick to look up as they entered, as if tired of staring at math and desperate for a change in scenery. He stood up gingerly, briefly looking as if he had blacked out, then shook out numb legs. He was about average height, standing around five inches taller than Fletcher. Since he probably spent most of his life planetside, it was a surprise to see that he had roughly the same weak build as Fletcher, who had spent so many years on Newport Station.

"Ethan, this is Fletcher Wilson," the captain introduced. "Fletcher, I'm going to let Ethan do all the explaining. He knows what's going on and it looks like he could use a break. I have other important captain-type things to take care of. See you two later."

With that, Fletcher was left in the care of a young man who barely seemed able to take care of himself. Ethan's unkempt jet-black hair shadowed eyes that spoke of many sleepless nights. He tried without hope of success to straighten out the maze of creases in his khakis, gave up, and finally extended his hand to Fletcher.

"Nice to meet you. I suppose you want to know how we knew you had snuck on board, why we didn't just leave you back on the station, why we'd be carrying the secret of hyperspace travel with us, and what we're really planning to do on this trip. I've sort of covered the floor with my papers, so if you could . . . sort of tiptoe around them and sit on the bed, that'd be great. This is going to take a while."

2

ETHAN

Tired as he looked, Ethan spoke as if he had been denied anyone to talk to for days once he got revved up. Fletcher, who had never been in a regular classroom, imagined Ethan to be the type of student in comedies whose hand always shot up when the teacher asked a question. By contrast, Fletcher pictured Captain Pierce as the student in the back of the room with her friends looking cool and punkish sending humorous doodles on their handhelds while Ethan had the teacher's attention.

"Okay, let me get through it all before you ask any questions," Ethan said. "First, we knew you were here because that security loophole in the camera system was left there by Commander Raiz. There really isn't any loophole – it's just bait to see who will bite. He knows everything that happens on Newport Station thanks to little tricks like that."

"Not everything," Fletcher murmured darkly.

Ethan smirked. "Even that. When you say not everything, you mean the way your father, Captain Wilson, treated you, don't you?"

Fletcher's mouth dropped open. There was no way they could know about that. He should have figured out about the camera thing – Raiz was a well-known computer genius, after all. It had been silly to believe that he had left a flaw in his security that even a teen with the barest skills could exploit. But this? Had the station commander bugged the Wilson apartment?

"Well . . . there was someone on the station who you liked talking to wasn't there? The station has an antique shop that specializes in books . . . ."

"Yeah, but I never told him about . . . anything like that. I didn't think he . . . I didn't think he would do anything about it." The confusion burned inside him.

"But there were plenty of hints from the way you talked about your father and the bruises on your arms and face. Since Raiz is the only real legal authority on the station, the shopkeeper told him about you. There wasn't any proof, though, and Captain Wilson controls the largest human fleet outside Earth Forces and has a lot of friends in the Council. Charging him with anything is a tricky business. When the laws for the station were written, they only considered commercial and safety issues. They never imagined that kids would be living there full-time. Raiz needed a pretext to look into your situation without your father's political friends putting pressure to squash the investigation."

Fletcher lit up. "So when I decided to sneak aboard the ship, I sort of solved the problem. Now he has to look into my running away, which should mean he can look at . . . ." Look at what? Fletcher's heart sank back down. "Will there really be enough evidence?"

"I don't know. When you're ready, the Captain would like you to write a full statement – everything you remember. Commander Raiz says your statement and whatever he can dig up should be enough to give him negotiating power. He'll try to get your father to agree to leave you in the station's wardship. In exchange, the details of the case won't be leaked out. That's all I know. I don't even know what your father really did to you . . . except it must have been bad."

"How . . . how long will we be away?"

"Maybe months," Ethan smiled. "We're doing a bit of exploring. If your father wants us back earlier, he'll have to cover our losses out of his own pocket, and he won't be able to do that. Since we don't know what we're going to find, Captain Pierce can estimate the potential loss as high as she likes. And that's all assuming that your father figures out which ship you're on."

Fletcher took a deep breath. It made sense, and the results were better than he could have dreamt. Well, that wasn't exactly true. He had dreamt about a vague superhero stepping in and adopting him as a sidekick. Still, this was a close second. Could it be that he finally had some people on his side?

Thinking back, hadn't he mentioned his interest in hacking to Isaac, the shopkeeper? And it had been Isaac who had mentioned how old and vulnerable some of the systems on the station were. He had even dropped the hint about the dockside cameras. Looking back now, he realized it was an odd thing for the shopkeeper to say, but Fletcher had been so taken by the idea that he had ignored the strangeness of it. Raiz himself must have been behind that little conversation, and behind Fletcher's entire escape plan in the first place. The thought turned Fletcher's cool relief into chills.

Ethan went on. "That's all the stuff you want to know. Now I have to tell you what you need to know. Emily . . . the captain, I mean . . . thinks there must be some other reason Raiz is interested in you, but I don't know why."

"Maybe . . . sort of a hacker brotherhood thing?" Fletcher ventured.

Ethan shrugged. "Raiz and the captain are in the middle of something very complicated. The captain's a bit obsessed with trying to outguess Raiz."

"This is about the hyperdrive?"

"Right. Raiz and the Council want to keep the secret quiet so Earth can become Eldrand's only competition in the shipbuilding business. The captain wants to publicize it because the way the hyperdrive works isn't really . . . good. Raiz convinced the captain not to release the information yet."

"Wh-why? I mean, why would she want to give away the secret?"

"Not the whole secret. More like . . . what fuel to use. It's not the whole picture by a long shot. The rest of the secret is this," he gestured to the sheets of equations and diagrams on the floor, "and the captain agrees with Raiz that the other worlds'll have to discover all this on their own."

Fletcher frowned. "The fuel. Is it really that bad? I mean, do they burn puppies or something?"

Ethan started to answer, but then decided, "I think it'll be easier if we went into engineering. I know the captain goes there when she's thinking about it, and I think it helps put everything into focus."

Ethan led Fletcher down the corridor. Fletcher was already exhausted by the conversation – this had been the most interaction he'd have with a stranger in . . . maybe in years. And there was so much to digest. So when Ethan asked, "you know about magic, right? You know, the type the eldrandii and asparii think they do – not the magic trick kind," on the way to engineering, Fletcher's mind couldn't even register what Ethan was talking about for a few seconds.

"Only what my father told me," Fletcher finally said, his intonation conveying that on all matters unrelated to captaining a ship, he didn't put much faith in his father's words. "He said it's just something we don't understand yet. He said that once we figure it out, it'll be science instead of magic."

Head tilting from side to side as he weighed that point of view, Ethan decided, "that's actually true. I wonder if some of what we know leaked to Captain Wilson. Anyway, the explanation is exactly what I've been working on – all those equations and everything."

"I thought you were working on the hyper . . . oh."

"Yeah. The physics of the hyperdrive is the magic of the hyperdrive until we organize what we discovered on into a real theory. There're plenty of big-time physicists working on it in secret on Earth, of course, but Emily . . . the captain wanted me to give it a try, too. I haven't really been very useful to her so far, so I thought I owed her this much." He blushed.

Fletcher couldn't help himself. "What have you figured out so far?"

Ethan sighed. "What the Eldrandii call magic uses the observer effect on a quantum mechanical field that distinguishes parallel universes from one another. Some of that we call consciousness is a quantum-level interaction with this field. Each universe has a unique wavefunction, but mages can use consciousness to collapse . . . to convince a bit of space that it belongs to a different universe. Even if you could do it, there's a hopelessly tiny chance that you'll get a safe universe at random. So the people who first figured this out must have used physics to map out a lot of parallel universes – a lot of the cosmic landscape – so that they wouldn't end up in any unpleasant places when doing their magic."

Fletcher's mouth opened and closed mutely. Well, what had he expected?

"Yeah, I didn't think you'd get it. It was nice to get a chance to say it anyway. It's totally basic to what I'm doing, but I don't have anyone to talk to about it. Emily and Kaz are really interested, but even though Kaz is good at math and Emily can do magic, I don't seem to get anywhere. Their eyes glaze over a minute in. I'm not much of a teacher."

Latching onto the first important information in the last few minutes that he could understand, Fletcher repeated, "the captain . . . can do magic?" First vampires, and now this.

With a tight grimace, realizing that he had probably said too much, Ethan amended, "not that much. I mean, you'd be more impressed by some card tricks than the sort of things she can do. She wouldn't even count on Eldrand – as a magic user, I mean. On Earth, though, yeah. One of my old teachers would have said she's got a bit more aptitude in that direction than the rest of us. Please don't tell her I told you. That wasn't on the list of things she wanted me to tell you."

"How did she ...."

"I think I've said too much about it already. Anyway, we're here." The corridor ended at an archway opening onto a narrow room with a bank of computers on either side, with scattered seats for those monitoring the read-outs. The smell of coffee was so thick that just breathing a couple of times gave Fletcher a boost. All but two of the engineers were paying rapt attention to critical systems like the antimatter rockets, life support, and hull integrity. The remaining two at the end were minding the hyperdrive. Fletcher supposed that they must not know much about what those readings signified, and simply pressed predetermined buttons at the right times. It must be rather boring and unsatisfying to be a hyperdrive engineer when the eldrandii prevented anyone from knowing how it all actually worked. Did it even require training?

As Fletcher neared the bulkhead at the far side of the room, at what must have been close to the tail of the ship, the two faces he saw were grim and jaded. They glanced with contempt at Ethan – the young man who claimed to know what it was all about, but didn't know how to explain it to them.

The bulkhead itself was featureless and bizarre in its absolute lack of imperfection. Fletcher felt that the engineering crew could have at least put up a dartboard. The wall's mysterious aura left no doubt that the infamous hyperdrive was hidden behind it. The eldrandii made it clear to anyone buying one of their ships that any attempt to probe beyond the wall would trigger a self-destruct sequence. There was too much at risk to test the threat, and every reason to believe it.

Ethan appeared hesitant to start talking with all the engineers staring at him, so Fletcher prompted, "So, now that we're here, what's so important about the fuel?"

With a dozen eyes stabbing his back, Ethan mumbled. "It's not really a fuel. That . . . was just an analogy. It kinda needs a kind of fuel – we used to think it was a fossil fuel because it was a mixture of specific carbon-based molecules, but now we know it was a nutrient supply. I . . . I guess the only way is to say it right out. The hyperdrive is basically a person behind this wall. It's an eldrandii mage who uses his or her mind to change the reality signature of the space around the ship. The engineers are mostly monitoring the mage's vital signs, though we don't really know what's what. Some of the dials could be dummy gauges to throw us off. The mage must need very little nutrition, since we haven't had to restock that as long as I've been here. We'd have to take the ship to Eldrand for that. I think the mage gets the nutrients intravenously. . . ."

"Hold it, hold it," Fletcher begged. "You mean there's a person back there? When you push the hyperdrive button, that person does some . . . something, and we get into or out of hyperspace."

"Exactly. That's the main point. Oh, and we think the mage

might also be doing the artificial gravity, but that could just be some other technology we can't figure out yet."

On reflection, Fletcher came to a definite conclusion. "That's insane. How does he do anything in there? Or she. It's like we have a slave in prison in there. Our space ships run on . . . torture."

While seeming sympathetic to Fletcher's reaction, Ethan tried to apply reason in the face of the emotional words. "They volunteer for this. The mages, I mean. We're applying our own cultural standards to the eldrandii. They think about it differently. It's considered a great honor."

"Bullshit. They're probably told that all the way from when they're kids, so they think it's normal. When I was a kid, I thought what my father did to me was normal, too, because it was all I knew. I only figured out how . . . that I was . . . I only knew because I figured how to sneak out while he was away on trips. Then I saw how everyone was and realized. I cracked the protections on our computers at home so I could watch any video I wanted, and that's how I figured it out. The person behind here just didn't know any different. If you showed them how we lived . . . . Why do they have to be trapped in like this?"

"To keep the secret, of course."

The light flicked on in Fletcher's mind. "So that's why the captain wants to tell everyone. If everyone knew about what was behind here, there wouldn't be any secret and the mage could be free."

"A regular part of the crew," Ethan nodded. "That's definitely the idea. The captain's also worried that, once we figure the magic out, we might try to seal our own people in like this when we sell ships to other species. You might think that no humans would go for it . . . but then, I guess you already know it could happen."

"That's evil."

"Well, at least you understand where the captain's coming from."

"But why don't we just tell everybody now? Why wait?"

Ethan stooped slightly so that his eyes could meet Fletcher's. Behind him, Fletcher could see that the conversation had made the engineers uneasy. They were all paying attention to the exchange, and Fletcher suddenly felt embarrassed by his lack of re-straint and reddened.

"Fletcher," Ethan said, voice level and quiet, "I think you're right. The captain thinks you're right. We've gone over it for two years. Why don't we do it? Because the eldrandii won't go along with it. We can't get through this bulkhead because the eldrandii rigged the whole ship to explode if we tried. I don't know if the mage will do it or if there's a separate anti-tampering device in there, but we aren't going to try to find out. So, even if we spilled the beans, the galaxy would know the secret, but no one could do anything about it. The mages would still stay trapped, and we wouldn't suddenly stop using the ships to get into hyperspace. Even worse, the eldrandii might take revenge against Earth and order their mages not to cooperate with us. Then we'd be stranded until we can develop our own hyperdrive. I'm hoping that we can figure out how to use a computer instead of people, but that's still a long way off."

"And that's what you're working on."

Ethan stood up straight again. "Right. I know it's . . . frustrat-ing. But for now, this is all we can do. Leaking the secret won't change anything. At least our mission's clear. We need to look for other clues about the hyperdrive so we can produce our own auto-mated replacement – no humans or eldrandii involved."

Fletcher nodded. At least they weren't settling for the excuse Ethan had given first – that the imprisoned eldrandii felt privi-leged and honored, not oppressed. He knew the type of person who would have turned a blind eye, and was glad he wasn't in that kind of company on this ship.

"Come on," Ethan said, "I think we've disturbed the engineers enough. Let's get back to our room."

On the way back, Fletcher asked, "why did you even tell me about the mage behind the wall? I know the captain wants to tell people, but Commander Raiz still wants to keep it a secret . . . ."

"Emily told me to, but I don't know why. You'll have to ask her. Anyway, like I said before, the important part is the theory behind what the mages do. Without that, no one can come up with a non-eldrandii hyperdrive."

After Fletcher danced his way around the e-paper to get to the bed and Ethan got back to the middle of his mess, an awkward silence hung in the air as they both tried to think of what to say next. After a minute, Ethan spoke up. "I just wish all these other ships would stop chasing us. Things are going to be hard enough without them."

"But the captain didn't have trouble with that plani ship, and it sounded like she had done the same thing with a bunch of them."

For the first time, Ethan looked at Fletcher as if the latter was a child and spoke with a touch of deserved condescension. "Do you really think they backed down? They had no chance to catch us in space anyway. It was all just show so they could catch us off our guard on Plani – their home turf. You just wait. We're going to catch all sorts of hell once we land."

3

PLANI

Increasing tension among the crew as the ship exited hyperspace and approached Plani confirmed that everyone shared Ethan's fears. Except for the four members of the hyperspace crew, everyone else had slept through the hours in transit. They were all fresh and fully alert to the grim possibilities that might be awaiting them.

Fletcher had never felt more out of place. Captain Pierce allowed him full freedom to wander around the ship as long as he didn't bother anyone or touch anything sensitive, but this liberty turned out to be pointless. No one was in the mood to deal with a kid hanging around, and eating in the recreation room was the most exciting activity he managed. Curious though he was about everything, he retreated to his room.

Ethan was tense, but at least he was less intimidating company. He was also willing to talk, but did so in the morose tone of someone complaining about life to a bartender after a few drinks.

"I'm basically going to be trapped on this ship until all this is over, you know," he said suddenly. He had been looking through rough translations of the texts recovered from Selparis, occasionally throwing out a comment that Fletcher couldn't understand. Fletcher was lazing on the top bunk and using his handheld to access the ship's public records. Those open files were the only source he had to satisfy his desire to learn about his temporary home.

Since Fletcher was between topics, he decided to ask Ethan,

"why?"

"I know too much, right?"

"Yeah, but they don't know who you are. They can't recognize you."

"Oh yes they can. Found that out the hard way . . . don't want to talk about that. They've had years to check out who's who on our crew. The captain's fired two crew members who turned out to be spies. They were each on board for less than a week and we have rules about what we can say when a new crew member is brought on. The captain told me what she wanted you to know, but the rest of the crew won't talk to you about any of this – probably not until you're with us a couple of months. So far, nothing really important has leaked out. All of us – every member of the crew – has been contacted by people wanting us to give them information. I got a couple early on, but haven't in a while. The money they offered was . . . enough to make me think about it. Since I don't get any more offers, I'm pretty sure they know I'm the guy. I'm the one Emily trusts."

Fletcher reminded himself to ask the captain *why* she had wanted him to know anything at all. For now, he just expressed sympathy with Ethan. "That . . . sucks."

"Thanks. Well, you're lucky. I don't think anyone will be looking for you, and you don't know the critical details anyway. The captain won't want you to wander around, but the spaceport itself should be safe. And it's practically a city. You'll get to see all the other species doing their things. I . . . I never really appreciated it until now."

That was an idea. The prospect of seeing the great variety of the galaxy passing through the port would be fascinating. Cheered up and anticipating the activity waiting for him planetside, Fletcher turned his information gathering towards the other ISC species and the port cities of Plani, daydreaming about what it would be like.

The main spaceport at Dael was nothing like Newport Station. It was on the planet rather than in space, for one thing. The volume of trade coming through Plani made the mass use of small shuttles too dangerous because it would be impossible to get them all clearance. Instead, everything was packed tightly into larger dropships. The *Azar* would pay a surtax to get its own cargo shuttle landing clearance. That and the cost of the fuel to get it down and back up again was a burden, but the ability to take off at a moment's notice and make a quick escape was priceless.

Much of the port's activity actually occurred within the dropships, managed by the various cargo crews. As long as everything was properly handled, hundreds of conveyor belts promptly carried all the passengers and cargo out within an Earth hour of touchdown. Each belt clearly indicated which terminal or train it would connect to.

"I don't think you'll like it out there," Captain Pierce said when Fletcher begged for the third time to be allowed onto the shuttle. "The port is actually pretty dangerous with all that stuff moving around, and it's huge and confusing. A whole city, really."

Fletcher cleared his throat. He didn't have much of an argument ready, but basic pleading had so far failed, so he went with honesty. "I've been trapped on a space station my entire life. Ethan told me that once we get back to Newport Station, I'll probably be under Newport Station . . . ."

"Custody?"

"Right. So I want to see as much of everything as I can before that. I didn't escape just to be stuck on this ship for a few months. I was ready to be stuck in a box for a day and . . . I guess be delivered to a bunch of vampires . . . ."

Captain Pierce stroked her chin. "Hmm. That might not be a bad idea."

Eyebrows up a notch, Fletcher said, "Fine, I'll get back in the box."

"No, no. I was thinking of having you deliver those puppies. It was a special order, and the buyer will be coming to the port to pick them up."

Fletcher jumped at this. "That's great! So . . . what do I do? I mean, am I really going to handle it myself? That would be so cool." Then he paused as his mind translated "buyer" into "vampire." His mouth went dry and his confidence melted away.

"I'll have someone with you on this one. These sorts of things are a bit . . . sensitive. Just look at it as a chance to stretch your legs and to get to know the place. Kaz, my first officer, was planning to take care of it himself. I think it'll be good if he has some company. You'll have to do what he tells you to." Her face then turned grim. "I'm betting that no one will think we told you anything important since you're a kid and not really part of the crew, and really we haven't told you anything that anyone can capitalize on. They might go after Kaz, though. He knows the drill, but I want you to be on your guard. If you see anything suspicious, tell Kaz right away, even if you think it might not be important. He'll be looking, too, but you'll be seeing everything for the first time, so you might catch things he would just pass over. Got it?"

Fletcher nodded firmly. Excitement bubbled in him, and he practically bounced with energy behind the captain as she led him to his chaperone. If Ethan had been right about the vampires – the dribrora, Fletcher corrected himself – they were nothing to be afraid of. They just had a disease. They probably deserved pity instead of fear, if that.

Kaz was in the captain's seat on the bridge, but promptly vacated as usual once the captain entered. Now that Fletcher had a better look at Kaz, he recognized him from somewhere, but couldn't place the memory. Maybe Kaz had just been roaming around Newport Station and they had seen each other on the sidewalk.

Instead of taking her seat, Captain Pierce introduced Kaz to Fletcher and informed the first officer of her plan. The disbelief on Kaz's face made Fletcher's heart sink.

"Captain, could we have a word about this?"

Pierce nodded as if this was entirely expected, and led them to her tiny office just outside the bridge. The captain sat behind her desk, but there were no chairs for the other two.

"Captain," Kaz continued, "this is going to be tough enough without making it more complicated than it has to be. He doesn't have any idea what to do or what it's like out there, and I don't have time to teach him the basics.

Fletcher now realized that he had heard that voice before. Kaz had been an officer serving under his father a few years ago. Trying to place the memory, Fletcher decided that it had been at least seven years ago, since his mother had still been alive then.

"I'm not asking you to teach him anything," Pierce said. "Fletcher just needs to get out a bit. How long has it been since you've been on solid ground, Fletcher?"

"Seven years," Fletcher mumbled. Kaz's voice had brought back a whole host of memories, including that one.

"Have you ever spent that long without setting foot on some real land, Kaz?"

"Not more than a year. But captain . . . ."

"I know it's going to be tough and I'd be surprised if the kid doesn't get into some trouble, but I know it'll turn out all right."

"When you say you know . . . ."

"I mean what I always mean, Kaz."

For a flash, Fletcher got the strong sense that the relationship between Pierce and Kaz went beyond the normal one between a captain and first officer. If Fletcher had not been in the room, the words exchanged would have probably been more personal in tone. Since the captain had to be the primary owner of this ship to be considered a free trader, there was nothing keeping her from having her boyfriend be first officer.

Kaz sighed. "So something's going to happen, isn't it?"

Captain Pierce leaned back. "Yup. I don't know exactly how it'll go down, but it'll be clever. The plani are always clever."

"And I'll have to settle for arguing with you about it later, as usual."

The captain shrugged and said, "if you like."

Kaz nodded and walked out. Not sure he should, Fletcher followed Kaz. The captain didn't call him back.

"So . . . ," Fletcher started, trying to break the ice, "this isn't really about some puppies, is it?"

Fletcher looked up at Kaz's face, hoping to gauge the first officer's mood. It was a thin, long face, well-suited to the frown Fletcher saw there. No other hints of Kaz's thoughts showed.

"Why do you say that?"

"I mean, if it's so dangerous to go out of the ship, we'd just get the buyer to come on board the ship, right? And most of the cargo's being delivered automatically. I know they're puppies, but . . . ."

Kaz wasn't biting. He showed no intention of offering any information.

Fletcher cleared his throat. "So . . . what should I call you? The captain called you 'Kaz', but I don't know if I should call you that. What's your full name?"

"Kazuhiro Kamiki. I've been called Mr. Kamiki, but it's been a long time. I've gotten used to Kaz on this ship, so you might as well call me that."

"They called you Mr. Kamiki on my father's ship, right?"

Kaz stopped in his tracks and turned to look at Fletcher directly for the first time. The eyes were cold, tired, and . . . something else. Maybe afraid.

"You remembered me? You couldn't have been more than eight the last time I saw you." Fletcher didn't know how to respond. Left to consider the young man in silence, Kaz said, "you have your father's memory. He never forgot a face or a voice."

It was a test, and Fletcher knew it. His impulse was to deny the comparison and to say something sharp about his father, but he bit his lip. Kaz had to know the situation, and had thrown the comment out to gauge his temperament and self-control.

"I can't do faces."

Kaz let a few beats pass before he said, "Yes, it is about more than just puppies. The man we are meeting had been gathering information for us. His daughter is an animal . . . enthusiast, and even though she's about your age, she runs a small pet shop for those on Plani who like them."

"Just the vampires, right?"

"Dribrora. Yes. Commander Raiz thought of using a puppy delivery as a pretext for the meeting."

And to give me the perfect container to hide in, Fletcher thought. "But why don't they just come into the shuttle? Would it get too much attention or something?"

As they talked, Kaz was loosening up. Fletcher was managing to ask the right questions – the ones Kaz himself would have asked. "It would get attention if it was even an option. The dribrora are an oppressed minority on Plani. They are not allowed on the landing apron except as passengers – and that's only if they're outbound. It was meant to keep them from working in interstellar trade."

"Why did we pick one to get information for us, then? There must be a lot of places he can't get into, people he can't talk to, things he can't see, and all that, right?"

"That's definitely a problem. The upside is that regular plani see the dribrora as less devious and less intelligent. They also pretend that they don't notice them. They have trouble believing that a dribrora could do what our friend has done."

They reached the cargo bay, and the container Fletcher was most familiar with now sat in the back of the shuttle along with a few others. He soon joined it, strapping into one of the jump seats next to it. Kaz was with the pilot at the front of the shuttle.

The trip down was loud and uncomfortable, but uneventful. Fletcher didn't have anyone to talk to, so he just tried to keep the straps from digging into him too hard as the atmosphere of Plani slammed into the shuttle and jostled it this way and that.

Accustomed to the silence of Newport Station, Fletcher was deafened first by the noise of Plani entry, then even more so by the din at the port of Dael itself. Workers were constantly shouting to be heard over the pads and the activity outside – especially the flow of cargo and people out of the nearby dropship. Annoyed, Fletcher wondered why they couldn't simply use headsets.

Kaz handed a pair of earplugs to Fletcher, and then put on his own pair. Something about the port outside must preclude the use of headsets, Fletcher reasoned. Maybe interference? Anyway, there wouldn't be any conversation on their way to meet the informant. That was all right, because Fletcher was completely preoccupied by what he saw. The sheer size of everything was overwhelming. Could the dropship be a mile wide? How could they possibly get a ship that size back into space?

Kaz quickly arranged to rent a hovercar and maneuvered it to the back of the shuttle, loading the container with the puppies onto it. The pilot was left to take care of the remaining cargo pallets as Kaz and Fletcher went to sit in the front of the hovercar.

They floated out into the dull grey light produced when the system's intense sun was obscured by the constant haze hanging over Dael. Eyes wide, but still unable to process a fraction of what he saw, Fletcher's attention was drawn to the largest and fastest moving figures. The true gargantua were the four gol hired to act as living cranes. Natives of Delaur, the gol were rarely seen off their own world since few ships could accommodate passengers of their size. These four each stood more than twenty-four feet tall, and spent their time picking up containers and placing them on higher belts. Seeing them move as quickly as they did was a wonder, but Fletcher couldn't make out their finer features. They were extraordinarily thin and smooth, though. Whizzing around the gol and a rich variety of other species were the speed devils of the place – the hovercars. Fletcher appreciated Kaz's phenomenal driving skills as they weaved around obstacles without slowing, sometimes an inch away from an unconcerned trader or worker.

Fletcher was in a daze broken only by the heart-stopping moments when they narrowly missed a crash. The problem was that deal-making started right when the cargo saw the light of day, leading to an atmosphere opposite to the serene silence of Newport Station's dockside. The port of Dael was the hyperage equivalent of a bazaar. Fletcher realized that the entire city-sized area had to be cleared whenever the dropship took off and landed. How long did the transition take? He couldn't quite picture what the tide of people in and out would look like.

Kaz stopped the car in front of one of the port's main buildings, miles from the dropship landing zone. After taking a minute to get a new cargo pad under the container, they headed into the building with the merchandise. The atmosphere indoors was more sedate and organized, allowing Fletcher to blink and rest his synapses. Kaz took out his earplugs and Fletcher followed suit.

Within minutes, they were approached by two dribrora – an adult male and an adolescent female. The male had a beige hue to his skin in addition to the normal plani grey. There was no way he could be mistakened for a human, though. His arms and legs were no more than sticks. Standing more than a foot taller than Fletcher, he must have weighed around ten kilograms less.

The girl was something else entirely, and drew Fletcher's rapt attention. While pale, her skin was a color associated with living humans rather than dead ones. Her clothes, meant for a plani's morbid straight lines, were tugged and stretched along slight but noticeable curves. The way she moved was also less rigid – less economical – than everyone else. It seemed to Fletcher that she was in no way ashamed of the way she was different, and was eager to use that difference to her advantage. She could have passed for human – a dangerously underweight human, but still . . . .

She sensed the attention from Fletcher, looked back at him with curiosity, but retained an impassive face. A portrait of intensity, she scrutinized everything in sight. She paid minimal attention to the container with the puppies she was supposed to be infatuated with. Without a doubt, she knew the ulterior motive of the meeting.

Her father was the picture of cordiality. He put on a mild, non-menacing smile and shook Kaz's hand without any apprehension. Fletcher was not wearing a translator headset, so he didn't understand the dribrora's words, but did catch the introductions. The man was called Drakrit, and the girl Sensha.

After they were through with the basics, Kaz opened the contianer so Drakrit could check the goods. Since he knew nothing about the animals and was wary of approaching them incorrectly, he motioned for Sensha to look them over. She snapped into her role and began enthusiastically playing with a puppy. Any onlookers would be too distracted by this public show of affection – completely alien to plani sensibilities – to pay attention to the boring business transaction conducted between Kaz and Drakrit.

The exchange was subtle, and except for one detail looked like a normal payment for delivery. Each side took out his pad, the buyer entered his account and asked for the *Azar* account number. Kaz gave it to Drakrit on a card, which he connected to the pad. Once the payment was made, Kaz checked that the credits had been received, then took back the card. As soon as Fletcher realized that the card now contained not only the account number, but also the secret information this meeting was really about, he turned away and became interested in the daughter with her new puppy. That wasn't hard. Her face was now bright with delight and positively adorable.

With a final exchange of bows between Kaz and the dribrora informant, it looked like everyone would be leaving satisfied. The plani pair took possession of the container, with Sensha reluctantly returning the puppy to it. The *Azar* team headed for the exit out to the apron. Just as the sliding doors opened for them, a scream rang out from no more than a dozen yards behind them. Its source was unmistakable. Kaz and Fletcher both snapped around and stared frozen at the scene, understanding exactly what the sharp cry meant. Drakrit and Sensha were surrounded by five armed plani. At the scream, the puppies started yelping, but they were the only ones to react. As was customary for businessmen everywhere, others in the port pretended not to notice what was going on while delighting in the exciting drama. They'd have a story to tell over their drinks this evening.

Fletcher's legs started moving of their own volition and he tried to catch up to his physical instincts by coming up with a plan. In the few seconds he had, he decided the best bet was to grab the girl's hand and make a dash to the car outside. Hopefully, Kaz would catch on and they'd get her back to the safety of the ship.

Fletcher was counting on surprise, and only started sprinting at the last moment. Running with force, he could easily knock down one of the sapling thin plani, creating the gap needed to get the girl out.

With only an arm's length between them, his target abruptly stepped aside. Fletcher stumbled a bit, but avoided falling flat on his face. For just a second, he was aware that he was in the middle of the circle now and in just as much danger as the person he was trying to rescue. Then a thud rang in his skull followed by a dull pain. His vision blurred and he had enough time to turn to the girl with an apology on his lips before another blow landed and he lost consciousness.

4

Sensha

Fletcher woke to a splash of cold water on his face. His head still throbbed. The room he was in was so dark that he at first worried he had gone blind. The light from a doorway dispelled this fear, replacing it with his real peril as a dark figure approached.

It was nothing more than a shadow until Fletcher's eyes adjusted. Then he saw it was the sneering plani captain who had tried to chase them over Mars. Fletcher wasn't able to tell the face apart from that of other plani men, but the elaborate clothing was a giveaway. He hadn't noticed it back when he had seen this captain on the *Azar*'s viewscreen, but his experience at the spaceport told him that plani typically wore drab clothing and that this one was a bit of a peacock.

But the plani captain wasn't holding a bucket. That meant someone else in the room had splashed Fletcher with water. Guards were without doubt waiting in the dark, ready to pounce if anything went wrong.

"Well, well," the plani captain said, "finally our young human has decided to wake up. I thought your people was more resilient physically."

Fletcher didn't answer, taking stock for a moment. He didn't have a translator on, and neither did the plani. On the ship, transmissions had been automatically translated by the ship's computer, but they weren't communicating through a computer here.

"You can speak English?"

Delight and self-satisfaction filled the plani's face. "Yes, and rather well, I think. I have made it a point to study Earth and human psychology. Your people is prone to be . . . sentimental. I was hoping one of you would make the mistake of trying to rescue the criminals."

"Criminals?" Fletcher spat. "Like you're not a criminal, kidnapping me like this."

The plani clapped once, and with the echo of the sound still in Fletcher's ear, he said, "No, I am not. You see, I captured a criminal and that criminal is now in official custody. By law, anyone who attempts to interfere with a law enforcement action by assault or threatening assault can be detained until compensation can be negotiated."

"You don't look like the police."

"All law enforcement on Plani is handled by private security forces."

"And you're going to try to get the hyperdrive as ransom," Fletcher said gloomily, only now realizing what an idiot he had been. He should have been more careful. Now he had betrayed Captain Pierce's trust in him, putting her in an impossible situation. If he got back to the *Azar*, she would never let him out of the ship again. Assuming she didn't arrange for him to be returned to Newport Station.

The plani tilted his head to the left, to the right, and back again in what served as the equivalent of a shrug. "We will hope for that, but it is a . . . a long shot. We calculated a win-win situation in all circumstances since we would at least get the reward for capturing the spy, and the ransom for his daughter. I am surprised no reward was offered for her – by my estimation she is far more dangerous than her father. No matter. Before you ask, she is hiding in that corner over there. She does not speak English, you see, so she cannot know what we are talking about. She is also a creature of night and more comfortable in shadows. Be careful around her, human. She might seem like one of yours, but her kind is prone to irrational passions. They do not think logically."

Fletcher sniffed sarcastically. As if he had thought logically before getting himself in the middle of this mess. He was thrown off by the plani captain's manner. Sharp and cold when discussing business with Captain Pierce, he seemed so much more normal in person – less like the caricature he had been on the *Azar*'s viewscreen. Which was the act, though? If he had such a good grip on English, maybe he knew psychology as well as he claimed, too. Was Fletcher being played?

While the plani was in an obliging mood, Fletcher decided to ask another question. "Couldn't you have just captured me and . . . ," he paused and decided not to give Kaz's name, "my friend from the *Azar* right there? You could have accused us of dealing with criminals." Fletcher phrased the question carefully to avoid admitting that the *Azar* had been buying secret files, just in case the plani lacked evidence on that.

The smile on the plani turned patronizing. "You are not as clever as I thought you were. Even if that plan was possible, it would hardly serve our purpose. By the wisdom of the Council of Conglomerates, it is only illegal to sell corporate secrets – it is legal to buy them. It is legal to buy anything. By custom, we waited until the transaction was complete and your party was a distance away. We were lucky you were the one to try to interfere. If it had been one of the *Azar*'s crew, Captain Pierce could have made a counterclaim against us for losses incurred because of delay. She would also have to be concerned that we would pry some information out while the suit was contested. Capturing you reduces the level of conflict. Pierce cannot sue us and we will not interrogate you. Your government would take a dim view of such treatment of a child, anyway."

In the middle of the plani's explanation, Fletcher remembered that Captain Pierce had expected something would happen, but that it would turn out all right. Hadn't she known that he would be the perfect hostage? He swallowed. Maybe she had been counting on him to do like he was supposed to and not react insanely at the first sign of trouble.

"In any case, young human," the plani captain said, relaxed, "you will eventually be returned to your captain, so feel at ease while you are here. We have no interest in keeping you, since the cost of feeding you will promise less and less return and allowing you to die of starvation will mean compensating your family. So, since you will definitely be returned to the Azar, you may introduce me to Pierce. She did not ask my name in our last conversation. I am Kaeden Rivel, and I will pursue the knowledge she has without rest."

"If she gives it to you in exchange for me, then . . . ," Fletcher blinked, "but you don't expect she will."

"Of course not. Pierce will overprice you because of sentimentality, but you overestimate yourself if you seriously think she will weigh the hyperdrive in balance against you. As I said, this was a long shot. I already have far better plans in motion. I wouldn't have discussed this one with you at such length otherwise. But enough of that. This room may be dark, but it is clean and warm. The only thing you have to be concerned about now is your company. If she moves out of her corner, make a threatening move and she should shrink back to it. They usually react best to animal intimidation."

With that, Captain Rivel left, followed by three guards who had stood behind Fletcher during the talk. The door clanged shut behind them, but the guards opened a square foot of window in it to allow light into the prison. It was enough so that Fletcher could gauge the size of the place and see the outline of its only other occupant.

She was stone-faced and still. Did she realize that he had tried to save her? What did she think of him now? He couldn't tell if she saw him as a fool or as somewhat courageous. He had been disgusted by the way Rivel had talked about her, but since she didn't move to communicate at all, Fletcher was left with that impression in his ears. He tried to remember her cuddling the puppy, but that image was irreconcilable with her forbidding aspect now. When he thought back, though, she had given him a cold shoulder from the start, as if he wasn't worthy of notice. She had the same attitude now.

Well, at least, he had a sense of what she thought of him, even though it hurt his pride and caused a bit of pain in his chest. Or was that his stomach? He was acutely conscious that it was empty. Since his kidnapper had contemplated the consequences of leaving him to starve versus the cost of the food, Fletcher supposed the meals would be sparse and infrequent.

With nothing better to do, he moved to his own corner and sat with his knees up in the hope that his legs would muffle the sound of his stomach growling. He shivered, still soaked from the cold water used to wake him up. Deciding to take off his damp jacket, he felt his trusty computer in the inner pocket. He was surprised that they had let him keep it, but then realized that it wasn't much of a security threat since it wouldn't connect to the planet-wide network anyway. Nothing was given away for free here. On the bright side, the plani had a strong sense of property – they had to properly cheat you out of it, not snatch it from you when you were sleeping.

He started playing the most time-consuming strategy game he had. His battery would last a few days, so as long as he could keep his mind off his stomach and his eyes didn't get strained staring at the screen in the dark, captivity might not be so bad. He had been through worse.

Out of the corner of his eye, he saw Sensha was now looking at him. Actually, if he was honest, she was staring at his computer. As he got more absorbed in the game, he stopped paying attention to her. He had decided to play the game without earphones since there wasn't anything in the room he could disturb. At least, that was what he told himself. He hoped that the sound would get a response from Sensha, even if she just motioned for him to turn it down. Maybe she would just plug her ears.

Just when he had given up on her, she started moving towards him. She was so quiet that he didn't notice when she stood up and slid across the room. By the time he finally sensed her presence, she was only six feet from him. He jerked away from her on instinct, pushing himself against the wall. How could he have been so oblivious in the company of a vampire? Even if what Rivel had said was untrue, it would have been better to stay alert. Now he was cornered.

Appreciating his apprehension, she said, "Asparis 2064."

It was the name of the game. She must have recognized the sounds from it. Earth games had grown more popular around the

ISC, and this was one of the more successful ones. Still, Fletcher was a bit surprised that she would know about it. Not really a pet shop owner's sort of game. Then again, what did he know about the tastes of a plani vampire?

"Yeah," was all he could say in response, and it was an open question whether she could understand even that.

She moved closer and looked over his shoulder. "Jardan." Her voice was soft, but had depth. It could have been alluring if she had wanted it to be. For now, it was merely curious.

Fletcher was playing as Lord Jardan in the game. Sensha knew this was unusual. Casual players liked to play Kentak or Tylin for a relatively easy win. Hardcore types played as Shint Bellar, who would eventually get Earth's help in 2100, but was pretty much constantly under siege until then.

"Yeah. If you play Shint, then you can really only use your army since no one will negotiate with you. If you play one of the big powers, you really don't need to do much diplomacy. This way, I get to use all the tools like spies and treaties and . . . ." He tailed off, remembering that she couldn't understand a word he was saying. Looking at her face, though, it seemed like she grasped his meaning anyway.

Just as they were establishing a rapport, a guard came in with some food. Fletcher didn't recognize anything on the plates, but it all looked inoffensive enough – sort of a fruit and cereal mix. Nothing wriggling. He waited for the guard to come to his corner with the plate, but Sensha was more proactive. She stood up and walked toward the guard. At first, the guard took a step back, but then stood his ground with his eyes fixed on hers. Sensha moved in a peculiar way. Fletcher wasn't sure it could be called sexy by human standards, but it grabbed the attention and was a touch hypnotic. The guard set the food plates on the ground without breaking the connection between their eyes, then moved to her. To Fletcher's disgust, they kissed and started making out. He would have thrown up, given something in his stomach to do it with.

Fletcher was sure the girl – maybe more of a woman than he had been led to believe – was seducing the guard to win an escape. But how could it be so easy for her? Regular plani were proud of their lack of passion, so what was with this guard breaking down in the blink of an eye? He was as pale as the rest of them, even in the middle of the blood-rushing scene.

As his incredulity reached its peak, Fletcher's nose caught hint of a sharp acidic scent just on the edge of his sensibility. Immediately putting two and two together, he pinched his nose shut. Sensha must have sprayed the stuff directly at the guard, so that it was only now wafting back to Fletcher.

Then it happened, just like in every vid involving a vampiress Fletcher had ever seen. The girl dug her teeth into the guard's neck. He struggled for a second, kept twitching for the minute it took her to finish, then collapsed to the ground. The whole sequence was virtually soundless except for the last thud, but that was enough to draw the attention of another guard standing outside the door. Before he even had time to be alarmed at his comrade sprawled on the floor, Sensha planted a kick to his face with enough force to snap his neck. He dropped a body length away from the first victim. Sensha landed from the flying kick with a grace that would have won high marks in a martial arts competition.

The vampire then turned to Fletcher, and his back was flat against the wall again. She motioned for him to follow her, but he shook his head violently, still pinching his nose shut. His mind was blank with fear. He had never seen a person die before, and though such grotesque ways had occurred to his imagination and his vid screen, the sight of them really happening paralyzed him. In the room's dim light, the blood on Sensha's lips glinted like a mad lipstick.

Impatient, she rushed to him, grabbed his left hand, and pulled it to the limp body of the first victim. She forced the hand down onto the plani's chest and held it there, waiting. Even though it was a few inches lower than it would have been on a human, the steady throb of a heart could easily be felt. The guard was still alive, just unconscious.

Fletcher wasn't certain how reassured he should be by this, but he nodded to Sensha to show he would follow her. Before standing, he crawled over to the plani who Sensha had kicked and checked for a pulse. There was none. Sensha had snapped the guard's neck with the blow.

Out of their cell, Fletcher squinted at the sudden sharp lighting and it took a while before he could open his eyes more than what was required to keep Sensha in sight. They dashed together down the hallway and made some quick turns through a series of narrower corridors. Sensha seemed to know where she was going. That unsettled Fletcher, as it dawned on him that Drakrit must have known the capture would take place, and which building his daughter would be taken to. Knowing that, and given her already proven talents, all she needed was a thorough knowledge of the building's layout, and she had a fair chance of escape.

When they stopped in front of a door and she started hacking the keypad that locked it, Fletcher knew he was missing a huge part of the picture. On the other side of the door was a small room, not an exit. Before he could even ask what this was all about, they were inside and Sensha had kicked the room's only occupant in the stomach, then the head. No alarm was raised.

Fletcher collapsed back to the floor, completely winded from the run, as Sensha went to work. In a minute, she was done with the first computer and onto the second. The two consoles were really all there was to the room – its entire reason for being. She was putting the retrieved information onto a datacard. Where she had pulled that out of, Fletcher couldn't guess. Rivel had been right – Sensha was as much an agent as Drakrit was. They had planned for her to get captured and to gain access to this room. But who was pulling the strings here? Fletcher doubted that Captain Pierce had the first idea about it.

Acutely conscious that every second they spent in the computer room reduced their chances of escaping, Fletcher fixed anxious eyes on Sensha. Already, the adrenaline that had carried him this far might be waning and the next effort to run could have him stumbling. Before his nervousness turned to panic, she yanked the card out of the computer, and they were on the go again. He didn't know how he managed to get himself up and keep moving.

They were spotted within seconds and a chorus of shouts rose behind them. The way forward was miraculously clear, and no one seemed ready with weapons. This wasn't a proper prison, after all, but a regular business building that just happened to have a prison room – or maybe it was just an unused storage space - for the occasional private law enforcement action. The building was probably the headquarters of whatever company Rivel represented.

Passing through a more crowded portion of the floor, employees obligingly got out of their way, too concerned for their own safety to try and stop the escapees. Sensha and Fletcher flew up a pair of escalators and reached the ground floor of the building – an atrium so busy that unless an alarm was raised, no one would notice as they slipped out. Hundreds of plani were rushing this way and that, mostly heading out of the elevators and exiting the place. The workday was over, and except for the basement levels, the building was emptying.

An announcement started up just as Fletcher and Sensha were about to exit the place. They managed to get out to the street before guards moved to block the doors. Sensha quickened their pace, putting as much distance between them and the building as possible before being forced to stop to let Fletcher catch his breath. Once again hampered by his years in zero-g, he drew the scorn of the dribrora girl, who had no idea why he should struggle to match her pace. Even worse, he was having trouble controlling his desperate intake of air in the thin atmosphere. It was like breathing at high altitude.

Before he had really recovered, they heard shouting from the building's entrance and started sprinting again. Muscles protesting, Fletcher didn't think he would get much farther before collapsing even if he could avoid passing out. Sensha was starting to feel the strain, too. The road was climbing up a steep hill, and fit though she might be, she had to slow down to a brisk jog. Neither of them dared turn to see how far away their pursuers were, but there was nothing in front of them that gave any hope of refuge.

The slope taxed Fletcher's legs to their limit, and a stumble had him on the ground, panting. He squirmed around so that he was sitting properly on the cold pavement. Sensha was to his right, out of breath but still standing. They saw a team of seven plani rushing to them, but still at the bottom of the hill about two hundred yards away. The plani had weapons, but weren't trying to use them. It didn't matter – within a minute, the two escapees would be captives again, except this time they would face far more hostility, and possibly criminal charges.

The sound of his hearbeat filled Fletcher's ears as arteries strained to carry blood around his numb body, otherwise he would have heard the hum of thrusters sooner. The other pedestrians and hover cars on the street were more aware, and cleared the descent area. Finally registering what was going on, Fletcher looked up and saw the cargo shuttle coming in to land, its length fitting snugly in the breadth of the street. The seven pursuing plani were forced to stop on the other side of the shuttle or risk getting blown away.

Seconds after touchdown, the shuttle's rear hatch opened, nearly scraping the glass windows of nearby buildings. Out stepped Kaz, who urged them on board with absolute anguish on his face. There was no question that the whole escapade had at least caught him by surprise. Seeing that Fletcher wasn't moving quickly enough, Kaz called for the pilot to help him carry the boy in. Before the plani pursuers snapped out of their surprise and worked up the courage to intervene, the shuttle's doors were shut and its engines flared to lift-off power.

5

CAPTAIN PIERCE

Fletcher and seven others packed themselves into the *Azar*'s miniscule conference room, waiting for Captain Pierce to speak. The shuttle had rejoined the *Azar* in orbit around Plani, and they were now waiting for clearance to jump. Even though everything seemed to have turned out all right, the captain was a bundle of barely-contained fury. She was staying silent until sure that her voice would be level, but no one was fooled about her state of mind. She was simply being careful not to direct her anger at the wrong individuals. After all, the ones really responsible for the chaos on Plani weren't in the room.

Of those present, though, Fletcher was worried he might catch more flak than the captain's earlier easygoing attitude had led him to imagine. He couldn't tell who was more likely to get blasted once the captain decided to speak – himself or Sensha. The way the captain looked at them was hard to read, but the two of them got almost all her attention. Her eyes alternated between them, probing for something – Fletcher couldn't fathom what. For his part, Fletcher wanted to apologize to her, but was reluctant to break the silence. Besides, he didn't even know whether his mad attempt at rescue had really displeased Captain Pierce.

Sensha sat stiffly and ignored the look Pierce was giving her. Their eyes occasionally met, with Sensha throwing all the cold haughtiness of a queen at the captain. They had given her a translator set, but she had so far put it to no use.

Kaz gave the captain an I-told-you-so look at every opportunity, which always sent her eyes back to Fletcher. The first officer had given Fletcher a thoroughly taxing lecture as soon as the teenager had gotten his breath back in the shuttle. Fletcher didn't want Kaz to start this conversation off and, looking for someone to act as an alternative, he gave Ethan a hopeful nod.

Ethan got the message. "Em . . . uh, Captain, I was wondering how we knew when and where to rescue these two. That place was a hundred miles outside of Dael, and your timing was perfect."

Captain Pierce drummed her fingers on the table a few times, then let out a sharp exhale. This wasn't really what was on her mind, but it was a safer place to start things off. "Actually, we were late as far as the plan went. Not our plan – their plan." She pointed an accusatory finger at Sensha. "We were supposed to be waiting there for them. It was all in the front of the file Sensha's father gave us. Right when we opened it to see if the information was there, we got wind of this whole . . . extra bit. On the bright side, their plan gave us a chance to save you," she turned her fierce finger to Fletcher. "What did you think you were doing?"

Fletcher's face flushed. There was no point hiding the truth, though he was loathe to admit it in front of the strangers in the room. "I thought I was saving her." He didn't need to specify who he was talking about. The statement drew some chuckles, but not from Pierce, Kaz, Sensha, or Ethan.

The captain sniffed. "Great work there." A bit of levity in her sarcastic voice gave Fletcher hope. "And you," she turned to Sensha, "I still don't know what this was all about, and I'm not happy about having an extra passenger on this trip. Can you explain?"

The translator headset's computerized voice took most of the condescension out of Sensha's voice, but some still managed to leak through. "We – our organization – has an agent in Rivel's conglomerate. We found out about their interest in you, and that they were looking for a way to get you to negotiate. Our agent saw an opportunity, gave us the layout of the building and its security, and gave them the details of our meeting with you. Drakrit is not really my father - he took that role for our purposes. He sacrificed himself so that we could get this," she held up the datacard.

"Of course, the group will find a way to get him out. I am glad you followed the instructions we gave you – it would have turned out badly otherwise."

Pierce's drumming fingers increased their pace and she murmured, "gave them the details . . . glad we followed instructions." Then in her full voice, she asked, "so what's on that card?"

Sensha hid the square-inch card in her fist and said, "first, tell me where the dogs are."

The captain blinked. "What?"

"Tell-me-where-the-dogs-are."

Captain Pierce looked at a confused Kaz, who answered, "they . . . well, you paid for them, so we had them sent to your pet shop."

"Good. I promised Sivkrina. She is Drakrit's daughter – the one who actually likes these animals. She was very upset when we told her what her father was going to do. I hope the animals will comfort her until we can reunite them. I cannot stand the creatures myself."

Fletcher felt his jaw drop and quickly forced it shut before Sensha could notice. He wasn't the only one dumbfounded.

"Who the hell are you?" said Captain Pierce, fist thudding into the table as a final punctuation to her drumming. "And why is it that whenever Raiz arranges something for us, it always turns out like this – ten times more complicated than it was supposed to be."

"Our organization is working to gain rights for dribrora. I may be young, but am related to the leaders, and am trusted by them for missions like this. On Plani, wealth is power, and dribrora are prevented from gaining wealth. Our only choice is to threaten the existing corporations. The information I retrieved are corporate secrets. Each conglomerate uses espionage to discover the secrets of all the others, using those secrets as leverage in negotiations. On this card, I have the results of one conglomerate's espionage – enough to undermine most of the top companies on Plani."

The captain shook her head in disbelief. "Are you telling me it was that easy to get information like this? I mean, the plani are the plani – you guys don't leave stuff like that lying around."

For the first time, Sensha looked less than triumphant. "The files are all encoded, so we cannot read them. They also do not include the secrets of the company we stole them from. They are absolutely paranoid about their own secrets."

"So that's . . . totally useless," the captain slumped. Fletcher almost smiled at her reactions. The revelations were like a rollercoaster ride, putting strain on the captain's face at every turn.

"We can bluff them into thinking we can decode them," one of the other officers in the room suggested.

Sensha shook her head. "There is no need to bluff. Commander Raiz's ability to build and tear down technological defenses is legendary. The idea that these files have already been transmitted to Raiz is the only thing keeping us safe from attack right now. It should also make the conglomerates hesitate before they try anything else against you, Captain."

Her voice ended on a note of firm conclusion, as if all was settled to her satisfaction. Captain Pierce was not so sanguine. Neither was Fletcher, who couldn't help making the obvious objection. "But Captain Rivel – the guy who captured us – could still try something since we don't have any of his company's secrets."

The captain answered, "we don't have to worry yet. Rivel's company planned for us to escape with these secrets. Information is information, and if a plani lets you get your hands on some, you have to wonder whether they're feeding you the stuff deliberately."

Kaz's eyes widened. "So you're saying that this Rivel let us get the secrets to clear the field. Now his company is the only one that can come after us because he's the only one with nothing to lose."

"Exactly. 'Cause what we've got is worth more than an edge in negotiations. They'll wait until we're safely away from here before they make their move." The smugness in Captain Pierce's voice at unraveling the whole messy business was mixed with concern about what might be waiting ahead.

Sensha was furious. The muscles in her face were so taut to the point of snapping, and her brow was tilted at a severe angle. "Why are you making up this story, as if to say we could not get these secrets unless the conglomerate handed it to us? There is no evidence for what you say." She made a grandiose sweep of her arms through the air to show how empty their words had been. "It seems you do not believe the dribrora are capable of getting the better of the majority. We are not the imbeciles that they claim we are. I refuse to believe that our planning and sacrifices were all anticipated."

"Anticipated, but not for nothing," the captain said with as much conciliation in her voice as she could manage. "There has to be real information about the other conglomerates in that data, and it will still be useful for your cause – it just doesn't help us out. By the way, why don't you just hand that card over and let us send the files over to Raiz? They're no good to you while they're still encoded."

"I will deliver it to him personally. And in exchange, I want to know about the hyper –"

"Forget about it," Captain Pierce said without a blink.

The firmness in the captain's voice gave Sensha pause. She had badly overplayed her hand. Shifting to Plan B, she said, "then accept me as a member of your crew. I have unique skills that would be valuable to you. I will be loyal. I cannot go back to Plani since every mercenary on the planet would be paid to hunt me down, and Earth is the only world sympathetic to dribrora. The rest of the ISC believes the lies the *sedso* – the majority – tell about us."

"So you can get the information you want by hanging around us long enough? You already tipped your hand. And you're trained as a spy. We don't need that. We're looking for knowledge that's been lost, so there isn't a place for us to send a spy into, but we have the biggest secrets this side of the galactic center, so we have a lot to lose by letting you stay."

The young dribrora was silent and downcast. Fletcher almost felt sympathetic to her, but her attitude had left him with a sour taste, making him wonder why he had ever been driven to save her.

After a minute's pause, Sensha answered. "I was not trained as a spy, and those were not the skills I was offering. I was trained in survival tactics and reconnaissance. In the past few years, you

have landed on one untamed planet after another. You must have
lost many crew members on such difficult missions. You are not a
normal free trader. I do not have much experience on record, and
I do not know how I compare to the people you already have, but
I am prepared to –"

"How were you trained?" Kaz asked, looking at Sensha with
earnest interest.

Sensha lifted her chin an inch. "The best way possible. The
asofi training regime. You use it to train special forces on Earth,
except your trainees begin as adults. I began when I was six years
old – my years, I do not know how many Earth years. I would
have trouble matching an asofi, since they begin after their first
year, but I am confident of my abilities."

There was no doubting her confidence, but to Fletcher's surprise, everyone seemed impressed by her claim to asofi training.
The eyes of the captain met in silent conference with those of her
first officer. Kaz's eyebrows went up in expectation and the captain sighed in resignation and nodded.

"It so happens," Kaz said, "that we are headed to a planet
that's . . . sort of a question mark. You know that because Drakrit
got us the best information we have about it – the discoveries of
the ISC survey team sent there. We lost one of our specialists a
couple of months back and haven't been able to find a . . . reliable
replacement."

"Of course, that rules you out, too, doesn't it?" Captain Pierce
piped in suddenly.

Sensha stiffened again. "I am reliable. If there's an oath you
would like me to take . . . ."

"Things don't work like that around here. You'll prove yourself on Kentak. Until then, you'll be confined to the passenger
side, and the crew will be told not to discuss anything with you."

With everything seemingly settled, the captain gave the dismissal. But when Fletcher got up to leave, she pointed at him,
then at the seat. Kaz stayed as well. Ethan took the job of escort-
ing Sensha to her room.

"Do . . . do you think it's a good idea to have Ethan take her?"
Fletcher said hurriedly, squirming in his seat. "I mean, he really

likes talking about the hyperdrive."

"Don't try to change the subject. Or are you hoping I'd let you escort the girl you bravely tried to rescue?" The captain's tone was taunting, not menacing, but her smile was strained. "I knew you'd get into some kind of trouble, but I'm not happy about the way you got into it. I let you go with Kaz because I thought you had a good head on your shoulders, then you go and rush into a situation like that without thinking."

Before Fletcher could respond, Kaz jumped in, "Captain, I think after this incident, we should be clear that Fletcher is not to leave the ship. After all, we are responsible for his welfare until he gets back to Newport."

Captain Pierce leaned back. "You mean you didn't take a few steps toward Drakrit and Sensha, thinking about how to save them, Kaz? I know you did. Anyway, I knew you'd say that, but the two of us have different ideas about what "welfare" means. Keeping safe is one thing, and doing what's best for him's another." Before Kaz could object, she added, "but I think you're right that he should stay on the ship while we get a sense of the situation on Kentak."

"So . . . you don't have any sense about how it will turn out?" Kaz asked Pierce, then looked at Fletcher, realizing belatedly that this might not be the company in which to bring up the topic.

The captain sighed. "It's alright, Kaz. I think Fletcher deserves that explanation anyway. This stays between the three of us, all right?" Her eyes fixed on Fletcher, who nodded. "I developed a little gift after I spent some time around an asparii mage. Didn't really believe in the magic thing until then. I started getting images of possible futures. It used to be that I'd only get them in my dreams, but I've figured out how to get them when I'm awake. They're just snapshots – they don't tell the whole story at all – but they're accurate. Before I let you go with Kaz at Dael, I had seen you being rescued by the shuttle and you . . . well, you didn't look too beat-up, anyway." Fletcher gave the captain a you-should-have-told-me look, and she grinned apologetically.

"And about Kentak, Captain?" Kaz urged.

"Nothing." She turned instantly grim. "And I've tried. It's

like there's some sort of wall. That can happen when there're too many possibilities, but this feels like something different. I don't know." She passed frustrated fingers through her hair. "And considering our casualty list even when I do get a sense of what's coming, I can't say I'm happy with the idea of sending anyone down to this mystery planet. We don't have anywhere else to go to find what we need, though."

"Oh," Kaz managed to say, his face a shade paler. "In that case . . . ."

"In that case, I'm going to go down with the team myself, Selparis-style. You'll be staying on the ship this time Kaz. I hope you don't mind."

"Oh . . . no. No, I don't mind, but Captain . . . ." Kaz couldn't find the words for what he wanted to say.

While Kaz was trying to convey his thoughts to the captain without speaking, Fletcher took advantage of the silence to express contrition and get some questions answered. "I'm sorry I got into that mess and made you worry," he started, eyes focused on the table in front of him. "I've been feeling horrible . . . I hate myself for letting you down."

"Because you knew we wouldn't let you set foot outside of this ship again," Kaz said. "You have no idea how frantically we tried to figure out a way to save you until we saw the message from Drakrit. Rushing into something like that without a plan was . . . stupidity."

Fletcher, compelled to defend himself, was about to explain that he had come up with a plan, but the captain held up her hand to stop both of them. "I learned not to rush into things when I was ten years older than you, Fletcher. Kaz isn't being fair. Half of the crew would have done something like what you did. That's why we get into so much trouble, but also why we are where we are. I wouldn't even be captain of this ship if I hadn't taken a really stupid risk. But I think you were about to say something else, Fletcher?"

He had been. He was curious about the captain's magic, being firmly in the camp that said magic had to have a physical explanation. As far as he was concerned, using the word "magic" was just a sign of ignorance. He wasn't going to press the captain on that issue, though.

"It's just that . . . if you can see what's going to happen, and Commander Raiz planned everything out, why am I here? You . . . I don't think you just took pity on me, right? If that was all it was, you wouldn't have had Ethan tell me about the hyperdrive. Why did you have him tell me about the mage behind the wall? I know you want to tell everyone, but Raiz doesn't want you to. I don't even have Sensha's training, so I can't get how I'm going to be useful."

"I can't speak for Raiz and what he had in mind, of course. But it's not really true that you haven't had training. Your father's been drilling you on everything he knows about captaining a ship and running his company, hasn't he?"

Fletcher swallowed. "Drilling's a pretty nice word for it. He wanted to turn me into his clone, yeah. But that's . . . I'm not . . . well, you're the captain anyway, so what's the point?"

"The point is that you know a lot more than you let on," the captain said. She was grappling with something – trying to avoid the real answer.

A spark lit behind Kaz's eyes, and he said, "it's magic, isn't it? I mean, what else could it be?"

Captain Pierce nodded. "I didn't want to say anything until it was clearer to you, Fletcher, but I guess now's the time. You're the first person – the first human, anyway – I've seen in the past two years who has a stronger than average magical field. Much stronger. I can actually feel your potential . . . tug at me. Ethan would explain it better. I don't know if Raiz knew it or not, but you're the first human I've met who might eventually learn how to take a ship like this into hyperspace."

6

MAGIC

Thoughts of magic occupied Fletcher's mind through most of the hyperspace trip between Plani and Kentak. He couldn't believe the captain's claims – especially the ones about him – and frankly thought that she was misinterpreting something coincidental as magic. Dreams that mirror what really end up happening misinterpreted as visions. Well, no one was perfect.

Still, the topic grabbed at Fletcher's curiosity. Tickled by the chance that he could learn to do something amazing, he was not yet so old and jaded that he had pushed aside all his childhood dreams.

Ethan was suddenly ecstatic about having Fletcher as a roommate. Fletcher suspected it was the same sort of excitement a researcher felt on receiving a fresh batch of lab rats. Conversations between them were mutually frustrating, since both of them wanted information and neither had satisfying answers. Worse, Ethan kept staring at Fletcher as if the latter was going to suddenly throw sparks or make rabbits appear. As Fletcher grew more annoyed, though, Ethan compromised and stopped asking questions, conceding that between the two of them, he was the one with the information advantage.

"Listen, it doesn't matter whether you believe in magic or not. Maybe you should just stop thinking of it as magic. I've seen it work, and if I thought I could do it, I wouldn't waste any time," Ethan said impatiently.

"I'm not wasting time. I want to know everything. Just don't expect me to do stuff. I don't want anyone to think that I can take the ship into hyperspace or anything."

"Of course not. It could take years . . . ."

"Not even after years," Fletcher said firmly, picturing imprisonment in the tail of a spaceship. Before Ethan could reply, he added, "could Commander Raiz have thought that I had this . . . whatever? He can't do magic, can he?"

"No, no he can't. Emily said so. The way Raiz acts sometimes, it makes you wonder. But Raiz would definitely have a word with any mage that passed through the station, and if any of them saw you on the street, that'd be enough. It's tough to say, though."

"Why can't the captain take the ship into hyperspace herself, then?"

Ethan shook his head. "Doesn't work like that. It's all about fields. I guess . . . the only field you'd know about is the magnetic field, so we'll go with that. You can take a bit of metal and . . . magnetize it, but there's a limit to how strong a magnet can be based on how many particles you've got. Basically, you're a bigger lump of metal than the captain, but you're not magnetized. The captain is a tiny magnet. Now, two lumps of non-polarized metal don't interact, right? I mean, if you put them together, it doesn't take any extra force to pull them apart. But if one lump is a magnet, then there's a force you have to overcome to pull them apart. If both are magnets, then you get . . . well, don't stand between them. Of course, when two mages are in the same room, they don't get glued together or anything. That's . . . that's where the analogy breaks down."

"Huh." Fletcher cocked his head and his eyes lit up. "You know, I think I get it. That actually made sense."

Surprised by this favorable reception of a hastily constructed comparison, Ethan said, "th-thank you."

Sticking to magnetism as a way to convey the ideas, Ethan worked out some of the key points of the theory. Most of it still failed to leave an impression on Fletcher's mind.

"There are basically two pictures that can explain it, and they might both be right. The easy one would use the observer effect

– the fact that any quantum field is changed by observation. The problem is that no matter how I look at it, there's no way that can totally explain the kind of control mages have over the field. There might be a clever way of getting around that, but I can't think of it. Saying that, it's still true that the way the hyperdrive works definitely involves collapsing a wavefunction. The way I look at it – the second picture – takes a few hints from string theory. You can look at different fields as sitting on additional dimensions – electromagnetism adds one, the weak nuclear force adds two, the strong nuclear force adds three, and gravity works in the three dimensions of regular space, giving nine dimensions of space total. So, what if our field sits on another dimension or bunch of dimensions? Imagine if one pole of the magnet was stuck in regular space – say the positive pole – but the negative pole was stuck in some other dimension. Then, what happens in that other dimension could have real effects on the physical world. Now imagine our minds are the exact same way – part in normal space, and part in this other dimension – so that our thoughts knocks the charges around and changes the field. I think that's the best picture to explain what's going on."

"More dimensions . . . wouldn't we have already figured out they were there?"

"That's . . . complicated. If they were spatial dimensions of any kind, we should have seen them in the equations of the physical theories we already have. There are ways we could still sneak them in, but figuring out how to do that without breaking other parts of the theories would be . . . well, too much for me, anyway. It could be that we're not talking about dimensions of space and time at all, but something different. That would be even worse, because we don't have any equations to describe it or any easy way to start building them."

"All right," Fletcher said, putting his hands up to stop Ethan, "that's enough for now. I need to get something to eat and maybe some coffee before I hear any more of this. Let me grab something from the rec room, and I'll be right back."

Fletcher hopped off the top bunk and headed out across to the leisure side of the ship. Though tired, hungry, and confused, he still remembered that Sensha had been confined to this side of the ship, and vaguely hoped that he would run into her. Since she was going to join the captain on Kentak, she should be sleeping through hyperspace, but she didn't seem the type who did what was normally expected.

Stepping into the recreation room, he saw that his guess was right. Sensha stood at the windows, looking out at what the external cameras captured of the complex patterns of hyperspace. Her ears were poised, ready to catch every word spoken in the room, but the few members of the crew present were scrupulously silent. Sensha nevertheless continued waiting like a stone gargoyle, fooling no one with her statuesque stillness.

To Fletcher's surprise, Captain Pierce sat at one of the tables, staring at the wall with unfocused eyes. For a captain, sleeping during the hyperspace phase wasn't optional, so Pierce must be having trouble sleeping. Fletcher was no expert in psychology, but she looked like she needed someone to talk to, and he decided to take the other seat at the table after grabbing a snack pack.

The captain registered his presence and a tiny smile appeared at the corners of her mouth, but she seemed to lack the energy to complete the expression, much less start the conversation. With Sensha in hearing distance, Fletcher wasn't sure what kinds of topics the captain would find acceptable – certainly not the ones he was most anxious to discuss. He went with the most obvious question in the hope that she would at least handle the steering.

"So . . . Captain, I didn't think you'd be awake."

"Mmm."

No luck there. "Are you worried about something?"

The captain let out a breath and nodded slowly, but then shook her head. "No. More like I'm not worried about anything, and that worries me."

"You're worried because you're not worried? I think that's a . . . what was it . . . ."

"Paradox. No, it's not a paradox. I'm very used to worrying about things before a mission. The point is that I know what to worry about, and that gives me something to prepare for, and I satisfy my need to worry. This time, I don't know what's coming, so my worry just sits there. It's sort of like the feeling you get when you've just left a place, and you think you've forgotten something. The information Drakrit got for us didn't reveal anything that would keep us from getting to where we need to go once we get to the planet. The plani who conducted the survey said they found the locals completely cooperative. My . . . other sources don't seem to be working."

"Well, if you need something to worry about, you could take me along," Fletcher grinned.

The captain finally managed to smile. She leaned back and stretched her arms. "Nice to see you don't give up, but that's not going to help."

Fletcher understood what the captain was leaving unsaid. She had been trying to have some of her visions, and was at a loss. He wondered whether a person could become too dependent on a gift of the sort the captain claimed to have. Or, more to the point, was the captain too dependent on it? That was tough to say, since he had only been on board for a few days. On the one hand, she had tried to get additional information about Kentak from Drakrit, so she wasn't totally dependent on clairvoyance. Then again, here she was, set to plunge in even though she wasn't satisfied with the information she had.

Fletcher tried to choose his next words carefully, more conscious than ever of Sensha's nearby ears. "Is there some sort of interference around the planet that keeps your other sources from . . . contacting you."

Captain Pierce suddenly snapped to alert and scrutinized Fletcher's expression to check that they were on the same page. Fletcher decided to give a quick glance to Sensha to indicate that he was talking in code.

The captain nodded. "Yeah. It's something like that, but I'm trying to figure out how they could possibly do it. Does it mean they know we're coming, or is it just an accident – some sort of natural interference? If it's someone doing it deliberately, it's safe to say that person's going to make life hard for us, and is powerful enough to cause real trouble."

Fletcher tried to fathom it. The captain believed she could

catch glimpses of the future. Assuming her ability was real, there might be someone on Kentak with sufficient power to prevent her from seeing what would happen there. And the motive to do so. Looking at the light-years that still separated them from Kentak, it would seem to be an impossible reach for any power. But if the captain could probe into things from the same distance and through time . . . maybe Ethan's picture was exactly right. If everything happened in another set of dimensions, distances in space-time would not have as much meaning. Still, Fletcher felt the possibility of deliberate interference was slim.

"Maybe Kentak just has a really big magnet sitting around somewhere that messes up the field," Fletcher mumbled without checking himself.

Captain Pierce barely heard him, but repeated, "a really big . . . magnet. Yeah, that would do it. Put like that, it might not be anything to worry about. Which . . . still leaves me with my problem," she slumped dramatically.

Sensha watched the captain and the boy by their reflection in the panoramic rec room windows. The room was kept dimly lit, but enough of a glare still appeared on the glass for Sensha to make out facial expressions. She had special disdain for the behavior of the captain, who Sensha judged to be too transparent about emotions. How could someone so guileless have survived this long? There was something about the captain that didn't add up.

What about the child? He was something of an enigma. There was nothing wrong with having a young man on board a ship, of course, but he did not seem to have a proper place on the crew. Sensha had examined the crew listing – part of a bundle of carefully selected information allowed on the passenger room computers – but found nothing about him. At the same time, there were no passengers except herself. Who was he? He had accompanied the first officer on Dael, and now the captain was confiding her thoughts to him. It was too much to think it was all down to the captain's confused whims.

It was a shame Sensha's English was too rudimentary to understand the conversation between the captain and the boy. Her ears could pick up every word, but even if she had been allowed the use of a translator headset, the device would not have been able to pry the words out from the background noise. Could the discussion contain anything of interest? Sensha wondered. If the boy was privy to any sensitive information, it would have been prudent to keep him on board the ship, and out of the question to put him in danger on Dael. Then again, he and the captain were acting as if they did not want to be overheard, and there was no doubt whose presence they were concerned about.

If she had been in the mood, that observation would have brought a malicious smile to her face. After all, she had been completely transparent about not knowing their language, yet they were still paranoid enough about her to overestimate her abilities. That was fear. She loved the taste of it, and would have delighted in it except for the fact that she was not in a position to take advantage.

On Kentak, though, there would be opportunities. Sensha imagined the critical point when the captain would inevitably show fatal indecisiveness. At that moment, Sensha would be ready to step in and take charge, thereby gaining the trust of the crew in the most compelling way possible – by saving their lives. That done, learning the answers to all her questions would be child's play. Confidence was key. Confidence combined with ability could overcome any difficulty, while lacking one or the other inevitably led to failure. Sensha tried to make sure she was never short of either one.

As much as she tried to stick to that principle and to face adversity with a defiant jaw, she could not shake off the sense that she was hopelessly out of her depth. The scenarios produced by her imagination were fortifying, but were also belied by the flow of reality. She had lived her entire life on Plani, and adjusting to the confinement of a spaceship tested her. She longed to reach Kentak, if only for the chance to stretch her legs and breathe the open air. But what kind of air would it be? If it was not safe, they would be forced to wear suits on the surface, rendering her sharpest skills useless.

Seeing uncertainty in Captain Pierce gave her both hope and

dread. Being honest with herself, she knew that she was as nervous as the captain, even if she managed to keep it off of her face. If the captain led them into a disaster on Kentak, it could very well be a pit that none of them would climb out of.

Fletcher returned to his bunk still thinking about the captain, and repeated the rec room conversation to Ethan.

"Don't worry about it." Ethan, unperturbed by the news, shook his head and waved his hand to indicate that there were more important things to discuss. "She gets like that every now and then. Broody. Especially right before we have to do a bit of exploring. It's sort of like stage fright. Once she gets down on the planet, she'll be all business – though that doesn't mean everyone will come back safe, just that she'll know what she's doing. If you ask me, we'll be in more danger up here than she will be down there. That's not saying that Kaz doesn't know what he's doing – he's the best – just that you never know when someone will chase us down and make trouble."

"But she really seemed down, like not being able to see into the future was unusual."

"It's not. It's no different from anything else you do with your mind – at least that's what I think from watching Emily. If you're stressed, sometimes you can't concentrate right or do simple things you'd be able to do otherwise. And looking into the future's not simple. Even at the best of times, she only catches glimpses here and there and has to guess what they mean. Worse than an oracle. That doesn't mean that she might not be having extra trouble this time, but there are plenty of possible reasons for that. First of all, it's a place we have very little information about, so it's hard for her to aim her mind at it – there's really nothing to focus on. There are other reasons, but do we really have to go through them?"

"No, I guess not," said Fletcher, not entirely satisfied. "What about the idea of interference blocking her view? Is that possible?"

"Well . . . it's not impossible, but there are plenty of things that are possible with a very, very small probability. I don't think there's even the slightest chance that there's a person standing on Kentak doing it, but we've come across artifacts and devices that seem to affect the field. That's why I think there might be a way to build a hyperdrive without using a person at all. If there's a device on Kentak making this kind of interference, then we've got to find it, 'cause it might be the key to the whole thing. Put that way, and this might be a worthwhile trip, after all. Anyway, since we're on it, let me explain how we can measure the strength of a person's field by its effects on real space, and why I don't think a single person can cause the interference you're talking about."

As Ethan lapsed into increasingly technical terms, fatigue caught up with Fletcher and he drifted off to sleep.

7

Kentak

The best Sensha could say for the planet Kentak was that the air was breathable – barely. While that allowed the landing party to move freely without wearing suits, the thickness of the air was uncomfortable, as if syrup flowed through their lungs. It wasn't just the composition of the atmosphere, but also the impurities in the air even miles away from major settlements. On top of that, the briefing had warned of background radiation levels between fifty and one hundred times normal. That would not be a problem unless they decided to settle on the planet for over a year, at which point their cancer risk would start increasing exponentially, but it did mean that the food was probably unsafe. They had testing equipment with them in the hope that something would be edible, but also three weeks' worth of compact food and a water purifier. Beyond that, the radiation did not bode well for the inhabitants they might encounter, and Sensha tried not to think about what kind of beings lived their entire lives in this kind of environment.

It was lucky that, of all the ships she could have stumbled onto for her first journey through space, she had ended up on the *Azar*. It was the only ship likely to carry a supply of synthetic blood specifically for dribrora passengers. Captain Pierce was well-known as a friend to the dribrora community and one of only a handful of captains who allowed dribrora on their ships. Thanks to that, Sensha was also carrying two liters of blood in her backpack – a few weeks' supply if she stretched it – so that she wouldn't have to risk the tainted blood of the locals or beg a drink from fellow members of the landing party. Human equipment and fatigues also fit her better than regular plani wear.

Instead of worrying about radiation exposure, the captain seemed to be more interested in what was causing the emissions. As long as it was natural to the planet, that wasn't a problem. If, on the other hand, it emanated from the lost technology they were searching for, the level of radiation close to the source would make it inaccessible and their journey pointless. A preliminary scan of the planet showed no major sources of radiation, though – it all seemed spread evenly.

The trick now was making the right inquiries that would lead them to what they were looking for. The plani survey team that had made the initial investigation of Kentak discovered plenty of important information about the government, culture, and economics of the planet, but they had not been on the lookout for long-lost technology. After all, Kentak was a backward planet, having only recently made its first journey to another star system, and wasn't expected to offer anything by way of high tech. That meant the Pierce team would have to start mostly from scratch – by approaching those in charge and getting in touch with experts who might have seen the right signs.

The pilot stayed with the shuttle pod along with another member of the team as backup. Alongside the captain and Sensha were three others. Sean Brown from repairs was the most approachable. He introduced Sensha to the rest on the way down from space, then spent the rest of the time proposing crazy scenarios for how this mission could go horribly wrong. In Sensha's opinion, the man spoke far too much, but he didn't have the listlessness of someone normally given to that fault. Instead, he was carefully observant of the reactions of the others as he spoke. The other two – Julius Marquez from the cargo crew and Jaidee Chao from engineering – were stoically silent throughout the journey to the surface. It did not take long for Sensha to decide that none of the three was formally trained in survival, and that while they were each substantially stronger than she was, her skills would give her the edge over any of them in one-on-one combat.

On the trek across the wasteland surrounding the reported

capital of the largest civilization on the planet, Sean brought up the subject to kill time. "So you're a survival expert, huh? Well, I didn't get any fancy training, but if you count being good at staying alive after being in the worst possible situations, then I think the three of us are the best on the *Azar*, which is as much as saying the best on all trading ships, since none of them get into nearly as much trouble as we do."

Sensha chose not to take interest in the words, since Sean was either fishing for information on her skills or eager to prove the superiority of his practical experience. Such talk would be useless to her, though the trip into the city was tedious enough to make any conversation tempting. Except for the towers in front of them, the landscape was barren to the point of lifelessness. It was enough to make them wonder whether the city would even be inhabited, or if it was the remains of a nation crushed by an environmental catastrophe. If not for the fact that they had already made contact with the local government to warn of their arrival, Sensha would have been worried that the information she had brought was a pack of lies.

"Captain, why did we have to land this far out this time?" Sean asked, keeping his voice free of complaint. "I mean, they know we're coming. We could have just landed in their airport or something."

"If they had an airport inside the city. They build their cities tight to avoid wasting energy and they don't do air travel. This country's only space facility is about as far away from here as Cape Canaveral was from Washington D.C."

"And they couldn't send a cab over to pick us up?"

"They'll meet us at the city limits. It's not more than an hour's walk, and I wanted to get a feel for the place before we plunged in."

Sean looked around and said, "What's there to get a feel for? It might as well be the Sahara. I couldn't tell the difference."

Captain Pierce frowned. "Mmm. I was expecting there would be a little more to look at. Anyway, it's better to make the shuttle a little bit difficult to find. It's a pretty valuable prize. But yeah, looking around, the place doesn't give you much hope."

Just then, a truck carrying half a dozen locals rolled by at the best pace possible on the rough ground. Its speed was unfortunately not fast enough to blur the forms of the kentaki, which were both grotesque and varied. It was usual to have difficulty telling members of an unfamiliar species apart, but there was none of that trouble here. Each Kentaki had its own unique malformations, from the shape of the limbs to the color of different parts of the body.

The sight was enough to give reality to the dismayed recordings of the plani surveyors.

After the dust kicked up by the vehicle had settled and it was safe to breathe again, Sean said, "Geez, they really are as disgusting as the plani said. I just thought the plani said that about everybody. I don't think I'll be able to look them straight in the face. If it's the radiation, how the hell do they stay fertile? I mean they're so different from each other, I'd believe it if you told be they were different species. Say, you don't really think we'd turn like that if we stay here long, do you? Or will our kids turn out like that, if we survive long enough to have kids, I mean."

"Shut up, Sean," the captain said. "I warned you. I don't want anyone making faces at them. We need their help, and there's no telling how they look at us. Don't even think about asking them about fertility or any other touchy subject while we're here. What if most of them are sterile, and it's a serious problem, huh? This could be a diplomatic minefield." She shook her head, knowing keeping relations smooth was largely on her shoulders. After all, she had to do all the talking.

"Better than Selparis, though. At least the folks here have cars," Marquez offered.

"No hovercars," Sensha pointed out. She considered hovercars a pitifully simple technology, and was surprised to see any spacefaring species still lumbering along on wheels.

"Marquez is right," Sean said. "From what I heard about Selparis, the captain had to ride in carriages drawn by animals. That's real ancient."

Pierce grinned at the memory. "Worse. We actually had to ride on the back of animals, if you can imagine that, Sensha."

Sensha sniffed in dismissal.

The city was soon at hand, starting with some stray hovels on the outskirts and rapidly growing into the jungle of buildings, complete with bridges between buildings overhead like vines between trees. The kentaki gave the travelers cautious looks and optimistic smiles – or at least what Sensha assumed were smiles on those lopsided faces – as they passed. There was no fear, though. To Sensha, the expressions pointed to one of two possible realities. Either these people were innocent fools and completely guileless, or their lives were so difficult and tortuous that they felt the outsiders could not possibly do anything to make matters worse. It was impossible to tell which described the kentaki, but Sensha sincerely hoped it was the first.

There was no mistaking the government officials tasked to meet them. As the explorers approached the city limits, they saw a group of six Kentaki standing at attention shoulder to shoulder, with backs ramrod straight. They stood a head taller than any of the citizens roaming around on daily business. More striking, they were dressed from head-to-toe in black and silver uniforms. Most of the locals wore only what was necessary for this planet's version of modesty, displaying the patchwork colors of their skin. The key to the uniforms worn by the officials, though, were the masks. These were made of the same sort of flexible material that make-up artists used to turn humans into aliens in sci-fi movies, while still giving the actors the ability to convey emotion. The masks were broadly similar to each other, but had distinct touches to distinguish individuals. To Sensha, they looked like the puppies from the crate back at Dael, except their skin was smooth instead of hairy and their snouts were stubbier.

Sean had a similar idea. "Wolves," he murmured to Marquez, "and ugly ones at that, if you're only judging between wolves and not looking at the rest of the company around here."

"Sean!" the captain snapped a warning before turning her attention to the officials, who were hopefully still out of translator distance. From what the kentaki government told them in the communication on the *Azar*, these six would be equipped with translators supplied by the plani surveyors, and would have Kentak language upgrades ready for the headsets carried by the landing party. That would help. Sensha guessed that the captain also felt more comfortable speaking to faces humans vaguely recognized, and wondered whether the kentaki had chosen their masks with that effect in mind.

Sensha was not comforted. The uniforms gave the officials a look of martial regimentation. Their posture spoke of discipline. Their anatomy was such a mystery to her that she would be too disgusted to try charming them, even if it would work. That left very little she could use to maneuver her way out of difficulties with the kentaki except actual combat. They stood two heads above her, towering over the humans as well, so the probabilities in an actual fight were up in the air. Hopefully, the radiation exposure had weakened their bodies, but Sensha knew that those conditioned to survive in difficult environments often came out stronger.

"Captain Pierce," the kentaki official greeted in a computerized voice that completely obscured his natural tones. "Welcome to our planet. We hope this will begin a long history of beneficial interactions between our species."

The captain blinked, surprised by how well the translators conveyed the kentaki's words. It usually took many years for the subtleties of languages to be worked into the programming. The quirks of how the translator dealt with English became so ingrained that diplomats in the early phase of Earth's ascendance into space took courses on ISC-safe English. That the kentaki language could already be so well-rendered was suspicious.

Captain Pierce overcame her initial confusion and proceeded with the formalities. "It is an honor to be received by you and, for our part, there is nothing we would like more than to foster a mutually beneficial relationship between Earth and Kentak."

"Excellent, excellent. If you would please follow us, we will bring you to the government house. We will speak further there after you are rested."

Again, Pierce couldn't avoid being hesitant. Normally, in this sort of first contact situation, the initial pleasantries took much longer. There was an attempt by both sides to get a feel for each other and to learn as much as possible before higher-level meetings took place. Was there any good reason for cutting that phase short? Maybe these officials were not trusted to feel out the situation with sensitivity, but in that case, why give them this task?

The journey to the center of kentaki power was a bumpy one, as the wheels of the vehicles transferred all the unevenness of the roads directly to the spines of the passengers. Sensha could not tell from the interior what kind of engine powered the cars, but they ran silently except for the rumble of the ground beneath them. Without any conversation to fill the monotonous silence, the ride seemed to stretch for hours.

The government house was a tower indistinguishable from any other building in the city. In fact, Sensha had not realized that they had reached their destination until the vehicle stopped and the doors opened. There was simply nothing to mark the place out. Captain Pierce's body language was now so obviously tense that even the kentaki could not fail to notice it.

"Captain, there is nothing to be concerned about. The government house is not the capital building, but a hotel for visiting dignitaries. It has a conference room suitable for our purposes, and rooms available for your stay. The plani provided us with files on all the ISC peoples, so we have been able to accommodate your rooms to human standards. We trust you will be comfortable."

"Oh, right," the captain said, embarrassed about how clear her apprehension was. "Thank you very much for your consideration."

"We will lead you to your rooms first, where you can rest for some time. Our leaders will be here to meet with you at dawn tomorrow. This is customary. "

Sensha didn't like the delay. Pierce also seemed dismayed, but had no basis on which to argue. They headed up to the rooms and found the accommodations were as advertised – beds with proper bedding and even side tables with lamps – leading Sean to step into one room and immediately backpedal out of it in shock. "Hell, I think they looked at the picture and got it down exactly. You don't suppose they actually put a Bible in the bedside tables, do you? I'm too afraid to check." The captain sighed. "I might be overreacting, but this feels creepy somehow. Sensha, do you mind roaming around a bit and checking things out?" Sensha nodded. She had intended to do so anyway, but it was a pleasant revelation that the captain was planning to use her skills properly instead of simply having her tag along.

"Sean, you go, too. You have energy to burn."

The recon team found no obstacles to their search, but nothing to report, either. "And that's real fishy," Sean pointed out. "Even in a normal place, you'd think we'd find something interesting to tell you. The best I've got is that the kentaki are brilliant at customizing rooms. I saw a storage room full of furniture shaped every way you can imagine. I guess you have to have stuff like that if everyone's . . . you know . . . shaped differently."

"Nothing from you, Sensha?" the captain asked.

Sensha shook her head. She was of the same mind as Sean – the place was too clean for comfort. Without any hints about what to expect, though, all they could do was wait for their hosts to act. With that in mind, she said, "I will keep watch over night."

Pierce's eyebrows went up. "You didn't sleep last night. Don't you need to catch up on rest?"

Sensha shook her head. "Even normal plani have more night in them than you humans, and I can stay awake for five or six standard days without any deficiency in my faculties."

"Deficiency in your faculties, huh? All right, sounds good. The rest of us need to get sleep."

Marquez stepped forward to object, but the captain put a palm up to halt him. "Don't tell me you're too nervous to sleep or you'll feel better if you keep watch. My guess is that we won't be bothered tonight." Marquez shook his head and rolled his eyes toward Sensha. The captain pursed her lips, but didn't say anything more, letting the order stand.

To Sensha's annoyance, Pierce was right and the night passed without incident, leaving her with more time to contemplate than she normally liked. Even in the eerie quiet of the hotel corridor, her blood rushed and her awareness stayed sharp. It tired her more than expected, and also burned a lot of her blood. With every heartbeat, some of her blood broke down, needing to be replaced by mechanisms her body lacked, but her digestive system had adapted to compensate for. Part of her survival training included the cultivation of stillness in the face of danger, but she had never managed the same self-control when confronting the unknown. In the dribrora resistance, she answered to superiors who had her confidence. Now, she was alone, and as much as she liked to think that her training gave her the ability to function independently, she had never put them to the test in a genuinely alien environment.

These doubts eventually led her to wonder what she was doing here. Being rescued by Pierce had been part of the plan, but there was really no chance that she would secure the secrets of the hyperdrive. And even if she did, would it be comprehensible? Her organization had too many files to decipher as it was. They had treasure chests worth of material sitting useless because the dribrora resistance lacked an expert cracker – the one thing practically every other revolutionary group in history seemed to have an abundance of. How much more difficult would it be to find a theoretical physicist?

For now, Sensha's sensible half was in favor of following Captain Pierce's plans, such as they were. This was no time to risk working at cross-purposes against the only ally she had on this forsaken planet. The thought of gaining some kind of advantage over Pierce excited her, though, and the part of her that enjoyed challenges was fixated on a vision of the defeated captain forced to hand over the precious secrets. It would be a profound vindication of Sensha's abilities if she could outthink or outdo the infamous Earth captain – in a way the most wanted person in the galaxy. Through mission after mission in the resistance, nothing had really changed, but maybe she could find the catalyst here on Kentak, even though right now she felt smaller than ever.

As dawn broke, she could not honestly say that she was fresh for the new day, whatever her claims last night. A night with her thoughts had taken the spirit out of her in a way a fair fight never could. If anything, Captain Pierce looked even worse. Despite a night's sleep without disturbance, she was pale and fidgety. She still spoke with her regular commanding tone, but it was quite possible that she would do so even on her deathbed. The rest of the party noticed the captain's state as well. They gave her worried glances, but even Sean was reluctant to bring it up.

They didn't have time to talk anyway. The kentaki were evidently early risers – already calling for their guests to come down to the hotel atrium with the planet's sun only a crack above the horizon, and not even visible within the density of the city.

"Seem to be rushing a bit, aren't they?" Sean commented, checking his sidearm as the team was led down to meet with the local dignitaries. Sensha decided that she preferred seeing the kentaki rushed. Yesterday, they had been too calm and self-assured. But that left the obvious question – if Captain Pierce and her team had failed to throw them into a fluster, what had them rattled now?

Led just outside of the doors of the government house, Pierce's team found the answer.

"Captain Pierce! How good it is to finally meet you face-to-face," Captain Rivel said, all malicious grin.

Pierce stood blankly for a moment, then said, "oh, it's you. I guess plani trade custom's out the window, then."

The reaction was so low key that Sensha wondered whether the captain had already guessed at Rivel's involvement. Sensha could hardly believe that, but on seeing Rivel, she no longer knew what to believe. She had been sure that her mission against Rivel's company had ended in a decisive success, and bristled now, giving the other plani a malevolent glare that only fed into his prejudices of dribrora.

After throwing triumphant eyes at Sensha to stoke her flames, Rivel said, "no, no, Captain Pierce. You misunderstand. Setting aside the little manner of you aiding corporate espionage, I came all this way to warn you."

"Warn me?"

"Yes," he said, painting concern onto his face unsuccessfully, the delight in his eyes and lips getting in the way. "You see, we deliberately left out a vital piece of information from our files about Kentak – the files which your dribrora agent stole from us."

"I deny the accusation."

Rivel waved the issue away. "Surely you must have known that previous survey teams sent to Kentak did not return, and that it was only after many attempts that there was a success. Didn't you wonder why?"

Pierce cleared her throat. "It's normal for survey teams to get into trouble on an unfamiliar planet. As far as I know, there are no reports of hazards on Kentak except for the high level of background radiation."

"On the surface, that is correct, but in space," Rivel pointed up, and Pierce's eyes looked awake for the first time this morning, suddenly catching on. "The key piece of information left out of the files was that the ship of the successful team only stayed in orbit long enough to allow the landing shuttles to exit their bays. They left the system and returned only when a relay message from the team requested retrieval. This was an overabundance of caution, though. We were able to secure flight records from one of the failed missions which had the disaster occurring after a little over half a day in orbit."

Captain Pierce activated her comm link through the shuttle to the *Azar* and shouted, "Captain to *Azar*, come in," but it was too late. Just above the top of one of the buildings, there was a tiny flare in the sky, and static was the only response from the comm. Almost a minute of silence later, a mild shockwave passed with a dull thud, and Captain Pierce dropped to her knees as her legs failed her.

8

SURVIVAL

The *Azar*'s corridors were lit in red, just like in the movies, but in place of a generic alarm or siren, there was a computerized voice repeating, "Hyperspace core critical. Abandon ship."

No one had started the alarm – it was built into the ship's systems – and in the list of things that could go wrong on a spaceship, nothing could get a crew rushing for escape pods faster than something to do with the hyperdrive. How much power was actually packed into it? How far away would you have to get to survive a failure in it? No one, not even Ethan, knew for sure.

Fletcher dashed back to his room from the rec room. From his training, he knew that the hatch to the escape pods was underneath the beds in each room. He even knew how to get a pod safely to the ground, though it was mostly controlled by program. As he ran, his main worry was whether he and Ethan, the two scrawniest lightweights on board, could manage to move the bunk at all.

As it turned out, the bunk bed had wheels – he had never noticed it before, but thanked whoever chose to put those on for the foresight. Four electronic latches kept it bolted down, and Ethan had already freed those when Fletcher arrived. Too panicked to exchange words, they pushed the bed aside and opened the hatch to the pod. Ethan urged Fletcher in first, grabbed what sheets of work he could, then dropped in after. As soon as Ethan was in, Fletcher closed and sealed the hatch. Once they left the ship, the hatch would not open again unless there was a safe pressure outside. Unless they got to the surface, they would be able to count the hours remaining in their lives by looking at the air content gauges on the panel in front of them. Assuming whatever was about to happen to the *Azar* didn't kill them first, of course.

"This isn't some sort of sadistic drill, is it?" Fletcher said, wanting to check before doing something difficult to reverse.

Ethan shook his head firmly.

"All right, then. Strap in. Here we go." Fletcher tapped the confirmation on the screen in front of them, starting the escape sequence. Explosive bolts blew, and pent-up pressure pushed them away from the ship. The computer automatically oriented the craft and fired a burst of its thrusters. Released from the *Azar*'s artificial gravity, Fletcher felt waves of relief sweep his limbs as they returned to their more familiar weightless state. He had ignored the strain in them for days.

The escape pod was built for two people, emergency backpacks, and pretty much nothing else. The hatch was above them, computers in front of them, air tanks behind them, the thrusters were side-mounted, and the landing gear was currently hidden by formidable thermal shielding below them. Ethan and Fletcher were each half the volume of an average marine, so they had room to spare. Ethan didn't move a muscle, though. He just clutched his work and watched as Fletcher brought navigation on line.

Just as Fletcher was about to zoom in on the likely landing region, the *Azar* disintegrated. The escape pod was enveloped in light, then knocked by a shockwave throwing both passengers against the forward console. The harnesses kept them from serious harm, but the pain from the straps left no doubt about future bruises. The computer was ready, and quickly reoriented the escape pod to ride the waves. The shape of the craft was ideally suited to this.

As the severity of the concussions diminished, Fletcher asked, "What the hell happened?"

Ethan looked at Fletcher, tried to come up with something, and then shook his head. "Don't know."

For reasons he couldn't explain, Fletcher felt a burst of rage at the answer. "What was all your studying for, then?"

"Just because an engineer knows all the equations that describes how an engine works doesn't mean he automatically knows what's wrong with a particular engine – not without some information like the kind you get from a black box. The computer said it went critical, though . . . what could that mean if you're talking about a person? Don't tell me it just caught the flu."

Fletcher pondered the question, too, as he looked over the projected landing region based on their new trajectory and tried to find a soft spot close to signs of settlement.

"What if . . . could some mage have thrown a bolt of magic and overloaded our hyperdrive?" He thought the idea ludicrous as soon as he said it, and blamed it on being distracted and distraught.

Ethan thought it over. "I don't think so, since it would dissipate over the distance. Aiming at our ship isn't like creating interference. What I don't understand is why the ship had to blow just because the hyperdrive had an issue. Was that because of the protective stuff the Eldrandii put in, or did the hyperdrive just lose control? Thing is, when a mage loses control, an explosion's sort of the simplest thing that could happen. You could get the ship accidentally flung into a different reality. Or maybe have it collapse into a black hole. A hundred different things. Why an explosion?"

Fletcher wasn't entirely sure there was an explosion. There had been light, and he would be sore for days from being slammed forward, but they didn't actually see an explosion. Many other things could cause the combination of light and shockwaves, though he couldn't put his finger on one now.

Frustrated at himself for bothering with theories at a time like this, he turned to practical concerns. On the plus side, the two of them had made it out safely, and the rest of the crew probably had as well. Since the captain had not been on board, there was no going-down-with-the-ship nonsense to worry about, not that Captain Pierce would have been that stupid, anyway.

They really couldn't have picked a better planet to bail around as far as landing was concerned. Kentak was a patchwork of landmasses. Water was abundant, but there were no oceans on the scale of Earth's Atlantic or Pacific. With sufficient time to adjust reentry trajectory, it was always possible to find some solid ground to set down on. Even better, since planetary conditions weren't conducive to large photosynthetic growths – forests, given a very broad definition of tree – the soil was mostly free from obstructions that could make a landing tricky.

Fletcher found a safe area close to what looked like a town, though close at this scale could mean several days' walk. He locked it in well before reentry, giving the computer the chance to make final adjustments before the planet's atmosphere rendered the tiny maneuvering rockets next to useless.

Once the vector adjustments had finished, Fletcher checked the fuel screen and shook his head. "Hope the computer got the drag calculation right, 'cuz there's no fixing it now. We need every bit of juice we've got left to slow down enough to deploy the parachutes."

The capsule started hitting the atmosphere and the intense turbulence had both passengers on edge. Despite the computer's best efforts to compensate, they gripped what they could, gritted their teeth, and hoped fervently that none of the jolts would be fatal. Each knock felt like it could rip their pathetic little vessel with ease, but somehow it held together. Even with flames outside and g-forces that had Ethan and Fletcher blacking out, the capsule held together on reentry. Slowed by the unusually thick outer atmosphere, their trip through the stratosphere was smoother, and Fletcher changed one of the screens to the external view camera. Unfortunately, the view was of Kentak, which was uninteresting to look at for the exact same reasons it was ideal for an emergency landing.

"The computer did a great job. We're exactly where we need to be on speed," Fletcher said, real relief in his voice. He trusted computers and relied on them as much as anyone, but still liked to have a sense of control when his life was on the line. He couldn't help being nervous when putting his fate in the hands of a machine – even one a billion times more capable at this particular function that he was. Ultimately, the computer handled the parachute deployment with near-human artistry, leaving Fletcher wondering what he had trained for.

It was a miraculously soft landing considering the dry barrenness of the soil, which left nothing but the escape pod's landing skids to cushion it. They didn't even hop before settling down.

Ethan swallowed and took a deep breath. "We made it. I can't believe . . . I still can't wrap my head around what just happened . . . the ship gone . . . ." It sounded like he was reflecting on the loss of his home.

Fletcher tried to be consoling. "Don't think about it now. We've got a lot to deal with. We have to wait until the outside of this thing cools down – it must be flaming hot right now – but we should look through the backpacks and see what we've got." He grabbed the one behind his seat. "There's only four days worth of food here, maybe more if we stretch it, but only two days worth of water, so we need to get somewhere fast. The compass . . . seems to be working here, and according to the map on the screen . . . looks like we go northeast to that town. I still have trouble carrying my own weight around in normal gravity, and Kentak's has a bit more gravity than Earth, so I'll be feeling the strain fast, but it . . . doesn't look like . . . there's much in here we can leave behind to lighten the load. I've got a translator headset, infrared goggles, a radio, and I guess this vacuum packed thing is supposed to work as a bed, but it doesn't look like more than a sheet. How about you?"

Ethan blinked, dumbfounded. He grabbed his own pack and sifted through. "I think I've got the heavier bag. Got a translator, bioscanner to check what might be edible . . . which seems to also have a Geiger counter which should be handy, first aid stuff, the bed or sheet or whatever, and this." He lifted a tiny blaster out and held it business-end pointed up in a comic pose, face serious and eyes shifting from left to right as if looking for enemies. Fletcher snorted with a laugh in spite of his mood. "I don't think this thing could kill anything bigger than a cat, but I might be wrong. I guess we should take it along just in case anyway. I've also got a cup-sized water purifier and this cooker thingy. I'll take the purifier, but I don't suppose I could get you to carry this instead."

It was a small device, but dense with metal and surprisingly heavy. Fletcher shook his head.

"I didn't think so. Do we really need it? I mean, am I going to

. . . ." Ethan pointed his gun at an imagined local animal, mock fired it, pulled the invisible carcass to the cooker, and pretended to sauté the meat. "And even there I forgot to skin it, drain the blood, and all that."

Fletcher sighed. "You're right. I don't think either one of us is up for that kind of stuff without losing our appetite. Leave it behind. If it turns out we need it, we'll just have to come back."

After a bit of sitting around, the computer gave them the all-clear, and Fletcher threw open the hatch. Ethan handed him the bioscanner, and he took a radiation reading. It was more than ex-pected – at the high end of what was considered safe for a nuclear reactor worker – but some of that was due to the escape pod it-self and the residue of reentry. Giving the scanner back to Ethan, Fletcher tossed his pack out, hoped that the thunk it made on the outside soil didn't signal damage to anything important, then scrambled after it. The capsule's surface was still hot to the touch, and Fletcher's palms refused to keep contact with the handholds. He tumbled down to the soil next to his pack. Ethan's dismount was a bit more graceful, except that he said "ouch" with every grasp.

Reality hit both of them hard as they surveyed the surround-ing landscape. It was open and nonthreatening, but frightening in its endlessness. Neither Ethan nor Fletcher had much experience outside ships, stations, and cities, so the sense of freedom was disorienting. Desperate to put something between himself and the horizon, Fletcher put on the goggles and zoomed in on dis-tant objects. After a few moments, he had their destination – the settlement he had seen on the map – in sight. He could see little more than blocks, and gauging the distance without landmarks or a sense of scale was impossible.

"This is crazy," he heard Ethan say behind him.

"You're telling me!" Fletcher shot back. "When I snuck onto your ship, I sure didn't expect it to blow up."

"Yeah . . . I wonder if Emily knows. She's going to be so mad. Or maybe it'll be like the five stages of grieving, so it'd be denial then anger. Knowing Emily, she'll probably just stop at anger."

Fletcher took off the goggles and looked back at Ethan. "And what about you? It was sort of like your home, right?"

"Sort of. I don't know. I can't really sort out how I feel about it right now."

Fletcher wondered about his own reaction. He couldn't say that he was sad about the loss of the ship. Shaken? Yes, but more . . . excited. His adrenaline was still pumping, as it had all the way down in the escape pod. If his whole goal had been to get away from his father and Newport Station, there was no more definite way of accomplishing that than being stranded in the middle of nowhere on a barely discovered planet. A planet with a safe atmosphere and possibly-friendly inhabitants. He couldn't help but feel that he would rather be stranded here than back on Newport Station.

Snapping him out of his moment of reflection, Ethan asked, "what does it look like through those goggles? Could you see signs of civilization?"

"Yeah, but it's hard to tell how far away it is."

"And . . . what are the chances the Kentaki will be friendly?"

Fletcher shrugged. "Your guess is as good as mine." He wanted to sigh. Why did it seem like he was the adult, and Ethan was the kid who needed reassurance? It was a good thing he was optimistic rather than scared, or Ethan would be no help calming him down.

Without another word, he started walking, and an apprehensive Ethan followed.

After an hour's walk, it was clear that the town was closer than Fletcher would have guessed. "We might get there tomorrow. That's good, 'cause I'm already running out of steam." Awareness of his difficulty moving in Earth-like gravity had steadily returned. "It's going to be a rough night, and I don't want to be out in the middle of nowhere for longer than we have to be."

"You and me both," Ethan said, yawning. The lack of features on the desert-like barrenness made travel across it especially wearisome. Even the weather was depressingly mild. It was neither blisteringly hot nor did the wind assault their eyes with dryness. Other than the wind, there was only eerie silence all around, giving no hint of life.

Fletcher decided that Mars must be a lot like this, except that life outside the domes required biosuits. In his mind, he had always romanticized life on Mars, imagining that the struggle to survive gave people both a definite purpose and the drive to keep going. Here on Kentak, staying alive promised to be an exercise in unending tedium.

"What were we supposed to be doing here?" he asked suddenly. The pain in his legs was growing faster than the system's sun was setting and he needed a distracting conversation. "I mean Captain Pierce and the landing party. What were they trying to do?"

Ethan straightened his back. The thought gave his stride a bit of extra energy. "That's right. That's right. If we could find it, then maybe we would meet up with the Captain. Maybe the rest of the crew will try for it, too. Hey, wait a minute, wasn't there some sort of radio in your pack?"

Fletcher slapped his head. How could he not have thought of it before? He brought it out, and turned it on. There was nothing. "What do I do now?"

"It should already be on the *Azar*'s normal frequency."

"Without the *Azar* up there, I guess the range of this thing must be pretty short." Fletcher shook his head. "And it's probably even worse with the radiation around here causing interference."

"Take a good look at the preset frequency and fiddle around with it. Try to pick up a signal."

No amount of tuning seemed to help, and Fletcher eventually decided to leave it on at the original frequency in the hope that someone would eventually send a message.

After a few minutes of walking, he remembered his original question. "The reason why we're here. What was it?"

Ethan switched to his professorial tone, explaining, "on Selparis, we found an underground city which had the secrets of the hyperdrive. It was actually a long buried colony ship designed to support its population for the trip, but they had to leave it and survive the hard way once they touched down. There were originally lots of these ships, and the ones inside were refugees. We found out where the rest of the ships were going, and one of them was supposed to come here – to Kentak."

"So somewhere on this planet there's some sort of under-ground city – a buried ship? "

"Could be above ground. And we're looking to see if, this time, there's stuff that can close the gaps in what we know. You see, the colony ship on Selparis was from a different wave than the one we expected to find here – it was a much later one and there was evidence that they didn't have the kind of experts that were on board the early colonization missions like the one to Kentak. Maybe, I'm hoping at least, there's information on a mechanical hyperdrive that can be used in place of the biological one we already know about. The thing is, there hadn't been any successful expeditions to Kentak, so it was at the bottom of our list, and we tried other planets first. Then the plani survey team had their success, and we had sources on Plani that could secure us the details, so that's why we're here now."

Looking up at the sky, Fletcher sighed. "I think they must have left out a few details. Was it easy to find the city on Selparis?"

Ethan snorted. "Hell, no. That was almost total luck, and it was mainly because the locals found it first but didn't know what they had. There aren't any reports like that from here, and the plani didn't find anyone who looked like they came from another planet. Everybody they reported on looked like evolution had gone chaotic and was trying some nasty experiments on them. You heard all about what they look like already."

"Yeah." Fletcher didn't relish the thought of meeting kentaki. Unless the plani team had deliberately put the worst possible face on them in the report, the sight would likely make him sick to his stomach. His impulse was to feel sorry for them, as he did for anyone born with some difficulty, but he doubted that was the right approach here. After all, on a planet where everyone faced the same oddity, was it really considered a problem?

Fletcher and Ethan decided to stop for the night with the sun still a palm's width above the horizon. The thick atmosphere scattered the sunlight in stunning gradients, giving some character to the landscape.

They had no fuel to start a fire, but with nutrition bars as their dinner, they saw little need to. As the night wind picked up, though, they inflated their bedrolls and tucked in for warmth. With the sun out of sight, the wind came alive with an unexpected ferocity, at times whispering to them, but mostly shouting. It packed such unpredictable strength that Fletcher doubted he'd be able to stand against it for more than a few seconds without being thrown down by a gust.

As expected, sleep was intermittent for both of them, and they woke drowsy and in more pain than when they slept. Luring themselves awake with the hope of better accommodations the coming night, they forced themselves into action with a duet of groans and yawns. At least they had a definite goal – to reach the town on the horizon before sunset.

The rough wind proved to be a phenomenon of the night, and the morning air was back to deceptive stillness. Fletcher almost asked Ethan why the wind would act this way, but thought better of it. Fletcher didn't feel awake enough to listen politely to the answer. It was pretty far from Ethan's knowledge base anyway.

They stopped frequently for rest, but made steady progress. The soil beneath them grew darker every step, so that their shoes now made prints and left a trail of marks behind them. The layer of soft soil was thin, though, so it didn't hinder them by making every step a struggle. Patches of blue photosynthetic growths started to appear, making use of the scant moisture and nutrients available. Ethan tested their leaves for edibility and found them completely useless – containing nothing that the human body could digest. That got him worrying.

"If these plants are at the base of the food chain here, I don't see how the more complicated stuff is going to work for us, either. Radiation might not be the big problem."

"How was the radiation in that leaf?"

"Safe." Ethan shrugged. "I guess it's got ways to keep from absorbing it."

"The plani said they had meals here, so there has to be something we can eat. But that was a different continent . . . ." The kentaki had air and sea travel, but not in great volume. Presumably, it was enough to globalize important food species, but were those food species fit only for kentaki, or also for eldrandii-type metabolizing species like the plani and humans? How rare and specially selected had the food supplied to the plani survey team been?

With nothing better to do during the walk than worry about starvation, Fletcher was happy that, by high noon, they had made more progress than expected. Or, more precisely, the buildings ahead turned out to be shorter than he thought when he first gauged the town's distance. According to the reports, the kentaki habitations were supposed to be packed together and built tall, with even settlements of a few hundred preferring to be in a few towers rather than individual households. Fletcher had made the same assumption about the town up ahead, but on closer inspection, it didn't hold true. The buildings were mostly two stories and not apartment complexes. There were a few scattered towers, but nothing like the towns described in the reports.

"Maybe they just couldn't find the materials to build anything tall," Ethan pointed out. "There's a limit to how tall you can make a building of mudbricks."

The land around the town was bare of any activity, so Fletcher guessed that whatever the kentaki grew for food was on the other side of town. Or was planting even how they produced food?

The edge of town was a sheer front – a line of houses arrayed as if against a wall. From this side, at least, the town seemed like a solid square, simultaneously speaking to some sort of planning and warning against intrusion. One of the gaps between buildings was wider than the others and roughly through the center of town, so the traveling pair aimed for it, hoping it was the main avenue. As they drew closer, though, the sight on the street made them hesitate.

"Seems like there's a lot going on," Ethan said, looking through the goggles after Fletcher had passed them to him. "Could just be some kind of market day. Anyway, it's not like we want to sneak in, right?"

"Do you see the guy on the platform?"

"No, I could barely . . . oh yeah, now I see him. Looks like he's making some kind of speech. Looks like he's got two arms and legs, too. That's a good sign. I say he, but it might be a she."

"The way he's waving his arms around, though," Fletcher paused, "I don't know. It's probably wrong to use Earth stuff to judge the kentaki."

Ethan thought about it, still looking through the goggles, then said, "yeah, but I think in this situation, we need to go with what we know. I don't want to tangle with anyone who talks with his arms waving like that, but it's the people watching him that make the difference. I can't see the expressions on their faces. If they're smiling, he might just be a comedian or one of those crazy people who rant about stuff in the park. If they're serious, then maybe he's a fiery preacher telling them to repent. If they're shouting and cheering, then maybe it's a political rally, and I never liked the kind of politics that had someone on stage shouting like that."

Fletcher nodded. "I think we should try to find another street. I don't think we're going to get the help we need from that bunch, and we might end up walking into the middle of something. Now that we're here, though, I don't really know what we're supposed to do. Our translators don't do Kentaki, do they?"

"Shit, I forgot about that," Ethan said, the rare curse sounding unnatural coming from him. "I guess we need to find someone very, very patient."

"Or maybe someone who knows one of the languages that our translator can handle," Fletcher said, suddenly hit by inspiration. "Look on the top of the buildings for a hyperspace relay receiver. The planet's radiation wouldn't interfere with that, and you don't need anything special to receive the messages, just to send them."

Ethan's brows furrowed. "But you still need to know how to build one. And who would send messages here?"

"Wasn't it you who said that the kentaki had been trying to make contact with the ISC for ages, and only managed it by sending a ship to Plani the long way – through normal space on a really long trip? They knew exactly where to go, so the plani had to have been sending information here the whole time, trying to make contact with the kentaki. I don't know how they sent the plans for the hyperspace relay in the first place. Maybe one of the early survey teams brought it. But once they did . . . ."

". . . then any place with one on top of it will probably have someone who can translate Plani. Okay, but finding one in a place like this is a long shot. This doesn't look like a capital or anything."

"But it looks like it was laid out from some plan, and you wouldn't have to put something like that in a capital or major city anyway. You could put it out in the middle of nowhere, like a semi-secret research center."

Shaking his head at the leaps Fletcher seemed willing to make with scant evidence in hand, Ethan scrutinized the town through the goggles in detail, walking in a zig-zag as he focused in on different features. "I don't believe it. There's one right there on the tallest building in that neighborhood. It's as plain as day." Lowering the goggles and taking in Fletcher's smug look, he said, "You knew it was there all along, didn't you?"

Fletcher shrugged. "Saw it earlier but didn't realize what it was until just now." A guilty grin crossed his face.

They aimed for the tower in question, which was around half a mile to the right of the crowded main street and close to the edge of town. Just in case, they had the translator headsets on as they took their first steps into town. The path of their choice was deserted, and barely qualified as an alleyway - it was wide enough for no more than two people to walk abreast. Ramps above them bridged the flat roofs of the houses, and half their attention was directed up at them, just in case someone walking across spotted them. No one was in sight. It seemed like everyone was either on main street or staying indoors, at least in this neighborhood.

They didn't have to go too deep into town before reaching the building with the relay on top. Approaching the door with uncertain curiosity, they were taken aback when it didn't simply slide open to admit them.

"I didn't think it'd be a private building," Ethan said, "why would it be locked?"

"I don't see a comm. I guess we'll have to knock." He did so, and they waited. There was no point being impatient, since they had nowhere else to go. After a minute, a head peered out from a second floor window, looking down at them at first with obvious panic, then with delight. It shouted something that they could not understand, but didn't wait for a response, retracting into the interior.

In a second, the local opened the door and gazed at them in wonderment. His expressions were so exaggerated that there was no mistaking their meaning. His skin was brown and patchy, ranging from cream to darkest black, and each of his features seemed completely malleable. His eyes could widen to twice their minimal area and his mouth, first pursed to nothingness when he had gazed down at them from the second floor, now stretched clear across his face in delight. As if that wasn't enough, his arms, lengthy in proportion to a short, stout body, were spread wide in welcome. After mere moments, his face contracted and hands pulled in to massage his forehead, and they took that to mean that he was struggling to figure out what to do next.

"I am Kordon," he said in a hurried but pristine Plani that the translators had no trouble dealing with, "You must come in quickly. It is dangerous. It is good that you came here."

9

IMPASSE

Pierce's shock overwhelmed everyone present, and for minutes after her failed attempt to contact the *Azar*, everyone was silent. Sean eventually stepped up to get answers, but he did so with frequent glances at his superior. He didn't want to overstep himself at this critical point. He also had no confidence that he could speak to Rivel without at some point taking a swing at the plani's smug face, so he questioned the kentaki instead, hoping at least one of them was important enough to give some answers.

"Why didn't you warn us?" Sean asked. "I'm guessing here that you didn't actually blow our ship up, but just by not warning us this could happen, the government of Earth . . . ." He wanted to say that Earth would consider it an act of war, but that really was going too far. "Well, you can forget about starting relations with Earth on a good note."

The kentaki all looked toward one of their number – only distinguishable from the others by gold inlayed features on its mask – and he responded, "We are sorry. There was no way . . . ."

Marquez stepped up and growled, "No bullshit answers."

Whether it translated properly or not, the kentaki seemed to catch his meaning. "I apologize. The plani, especially Captain Rivel's group, have been very generous to us. They have brought gifts that will change our world. Whatever they asked of us, we felt bound to do. Withholding this warning from you after they sacrificed so many ships in their attempts to come here seemed . . . fair. In our communication with you, you did not offer anything.

Our government has to act in the best interest of our people."

"So if we gave you some fresh technology, you might have warned us?" Sean asked through clenched teeth.

"We would have had to weigh the value of alliance with you against potentially angering our existing friends the plani. I think the plani would understand, though, if the economic value of your gifts were substantial," the kentaki official looked to Rivel for confirmation, and the plani nodded.

Sean couldn't stop himself from mumbling, "you guys got too much color in your face to be thinking like a plani." Fortunately, that was the moment that the magnitude of her indignation gave Pierce the energy to stand. She strode forward so that she was uncomfortably close to the gold-masked kentaki. None of the other kentaki moved with alarm, though.

"What happened to my ship?" she asked, voice strained.

The kentaki shook his head. "We do not know why it happens, only that it happens. It only affects hyperspace ships. The spaceships we build are not affected because they lack a hyperdrive."

Pierce turned her attention to Rivel. "Well? Do you know?"

"Pierce, as the one who presumably has the secret of the hyperdrive, I would think that you were the one who would most likely be able to come up with an answer. Without the knowledge you have, our people are at a loss as well. All we can do is order our ships to maintain a safe distance."

Rivel was being absolutely level and Pierce knew it. Sensha knew it, too. She had spent the entire time as if part of the audience to a movie scene, and only now remembered that she was supposed to have stepped in and to ask the questions Sean had in Pierce's moment of weakness. She could console herself by thinking that Rivel's appearance had thrown her off, but the truth was that she was as shocked by the destruction of the *Azar* as the Captain. Did the loss of the ship mean that she was now stranded on Kentak, with Rivel the only one able to bring her back to Plani? The very thought made her pale. This time, they would definitely throw her into the deepest, darkest pit they could find.

Sensha put her question to Rivel bluntly. "Why are you here? Just to gloat? What are you going to do with us?"

Rivel sniffed. "You brought this one along with you, Pierce? I can't approve of your choice."

"Just answer her question," Pierce snarled.

Sighing, Rivel said, "Why else would someone like me come all this way? To make a deal, Pierce, to make a deal."

Pierce's weary eyes lit up. "Let me guess. You want the only bargaining chip we've got, and you'll give us a ship in exchange."

"Under the circumstances, it is not a bad exchange. My company will even be willing to have one refit to human preferences."

Pierce had a sharp response ready, but didn't deliver it. She really didn't have many options left to her, assuming she didn't want to rot on this planet, and she couldn't be too forceful while playing a weak hand. She had to leave options open. Still, she didn't have the stomach to give into Rivel here, so she equivocated. "What if I told you that the secret was destroyed with the ship? Didn't have a reason to risk bringing it down here."

"Then that is unfortunate," Rivel said, "but I do not think that is the case. You must have a copy of the files on your personal computer, just to keep your bargaining chip . . . how do they say it? Handy."

And Rivel wouldn't just take it from her because that would be theft on a level that would spark a serious incident with Earth. A fair trade would leave Earth's leadership angry, and would probably keep Pierce from ever docking at Newport Station again, but it would be irreproachable as far as the politics were concerned. Pierce had the information by right of discovery, and could make whatever trades she liked with it.

At the moment, though, she didn't look at all ready to make a decision. The muscles of her face sagged and she constantly shifted her weight and shook herself to get the blood flowing. Anyone with an inkling about human physiology knew that she must be somehow sick beyond even the stress of the situation.

Appreciating her own state, she said, "I'll have to consider it."

"Of course, of course. However, there is a little issue," Rivel said, leaning a bit forward as if in confidentiality. "You are somewhat inconveniencing me by forcing me to stay here while you decide. There is also the matter of our kentaki friends who are a bit nervous about what you – or more precisely your people – might do to them if you were to leave here on unfriendly terms. Kentak is no match for Earth. So, I am afraid they will have to keep you here until you decide."

"Imprisoned here," Sensha said.

"Like hell," was Marquez's response. His hand drifted to his sidearm. Sean and Jaidee changed posture, readying themselves to back him. The odds were bad, though. They were surrounded by dozens of Kentaki and a spare handful of plani. While their weapons were not out in the open, they stood with all the confidence of people who were prepared.

"If you do not accept my offer, I will leave. The rest is up to the kentaki. From their point of view, it is much better that you get reported as another failed mission to their world."

Head down and hand on her forehead, Pierce said, "Nicely played. I'm still going to have to take my time, though." Her companions gazed at her in surprise, having expected a sharp remark about the illegality of imprisonment without charge and how it might affect Kentak's standing in the ISC, and not just with Earth. It was important to give the kentaki every reason to reconsider, but none of the others dared to step forward to make that case – not even Sensha, who knew that her credibility in making the threat could be shot down by Rivel easily anyway. Sean and Jaidee looked to Marquez, who pointedly crossed his arms. The captain didn't want a fight, so they would have to play along.

"As you wish," Rivel said. Turning to the lead kentaki, he said, "It looks as if we are done here. You may take them to the special rooms. Only, make sure that this one," he pointed to Sensha, "is in one by herself and far away from the others. We would not want a repeat of her previous escape."

The kentaki stiffened. "We lack your technology, but our security . . . ."

"Is formidable, I am sure. But this one has a demon's luck, and escaping is her one verifiable skill. She will find a way somehow. I just want to ensure she does not bring any of the others with her."

Sensha was so stunned by this backhanded recognition of her

abilities – well, one ability anyway – that her mind momentarily blanked.

Their weapons and gear were confiscated and they were led to their prison rooms – each still furnished in human style, but with heavy locks on the outside of the doors. Sensha immediately started trying to think of ways to prove Rivel right, but it seemed impossible. She was used to standing out on Plani, where her physical features were different from not only the regular plani but also the dribrora, but that was nothing compared to how obvious she would be in a crowd of kentaki. And the government house was full of Kentaki around every corner, all aware of the unusual guests. They would have no preconceptions about dribrora and none of the disdain that made regular plani likely to ignore one. When they reached her room, the mere sight of the lock filled her with despair. Electronic locks were often made too flimsily and could be forced apart. This one – a series of heavy bolts on a reinforced door – gave no such hope.

Sensha would have preferred the honesty of a dusty bunk and half-functional toilet over the elegant bedspread, dresser, and artwork on the walls. You could get a bit too comfortable in a prison like this. No windows, though. As the door slammed behind her and the bolts slid into place smoothly, defying her final prayer that they were aged and corroded, she turned off the lights and sat on the floor in the dark.

What was wrong with Pierce? Much as Sensha wanted to come up with a plan, her thoughts kept turning to the odd behavior she had seen. Her instincts nagged at her, insisting that it was important, but without more facts, she couldn't even begin putting the picture together. And, she told her rebellious mind, there was no way to get those facts from inside this room, so escape was the first priority.

The kentaki would have to open the door to give her meals, so if she just convinced one to take off their mask, she could slip them some poison with a kiss. Assuming that her poisons even worked on kentaki. Among the masked and cloaked class, there wasn't even a bit of bare skin she could sink her teeth into, so her best shot would be if an uncloaked commoner was sent in. Under the circumstances, she would have to set her tastes and concerns about radiation aside.

Pierce's team had not been given dinner last night – a forgivable bit of neglect since everyone had eaten before the trip down. Even Sensha's stomach now growled for breakfast, though, and the humans must be positively starving. They had rations in their packs, but those had been confiscated along with the rest of their equipment. So, assuming that the kentaki were at least as hospitable as the plani, there would be a meal delivery soon. Her fate would be decided by how that encounter went, so she sat still in the darkness, waiting to put her full energy into the critical moment.

It didn't take long before she heard a conversation outside and the sliding of the locks. A mask-cloak Kentaki entered with a tray filled with enough reheated Plani rations to make two or three meals. Sensha took a careful look at the corridor outside while she could, and saw the other guard leave. For some reason, the meal-bringer must have relieved the other guard, but why would the kentaki leave only one body to guard her after Rivel had warned them about her talent for escape? Did they think the plani captain had been joking? More likely, Rivel was finally planning to get rid of her, and wanted to use the kentaki to keep his own hands clean.

Her alertness went critical when the meal-bringer closed the door behind him. To Sensha's mind, there was only one reason he would do that, and she didn't wait to find out whether she was right. She leapt at him, throwing him to the ground and pinning him there with as much weight as she could push into his chest. Time slowed to the crawl as she moved with unnatural speed, taking her target completely by surprise. Before the meal tray crashed to the ground and spilled its contents, she already had his mask off and found herself gazing not at a kentaki face, but a plani.

"Don't," he gasped, but she was beyond accepting pleas for mercy. There was now no doubt in her mind, and she sank her fangs deep into his neck with every intention of drinking him dry. Rage, especially at her recent weakness, broke through her carefully cultivated self-control. At her first taste of the vital liquid, though, her fury melted instantly and her visceral instincts were thrown into confusion. It wasn't the blood of a normal plani, but the bitter unsatisfying taste of dribrora blood – the same as her own when she licked her wounds during training. Her intended victim was of her kind, but one capable of passing as a regular plani. Sensha pulled away from his neck, but stayed on top of him, wondering whether he was a traitor to his people who sought to attack her out of some sort of personal vendetta, or if he was compatriot.

Whatever he was, Sensha could feel his racing heart through her knee. His ribcage strained to expand enough to contain the deep breaths he was taking. He did not have the cool calm that she would expect from an assassin, but perhaps he had just been over-confident. By the time he steadied himself enough to speak, the wounds on his neck clotted shut – the accelerated breakdown of blood in dribrora had that beneficial side-effect at least. It didn't seem as if the clang of the tray or his absence outside the door had drawn any attention, but Sensha hoped that he would speak quickly – the window of opportunity for her escape would not remain open for long.

The pinned dribrora seemed to understand this and, once he got his wind, he spoke with rehearsed speed. "I'm not part of the resistance. I passed as a pale one to get a job on the survey team. I had always dreamt of leaving Plani, and since I didn't have enough money to go as a passenger, qualifying for the survey team to Kentak was the only way. I was part of the first team, so I didn't know what would happen. We were stranded here, so our commanders used our technology to get influence. Now, about a fifth of the ruling class – those that wear the black – are actually plani. Because of the costumes, most kentaki don't know this. If they were told, though, most would not do anything. Since we came, the technology we brought has made the quality of life much better. Still, knowing the pale ones, it will take no more than a day for them to go from benevolence to exploitation, so I have quietly found friends among the kentaki to tell about this. You must go to them." He handed Sensha a card with the contact information on it. "Tell them about the humans. The humans could counterbalance the pale ones and give the kentaki options – keep them free. Take the mask and cloak. That way you will not be stopped by anyone until you are safely away."

He started unclasping his collar and Sensha decided that it was safe to release him from the pin.

"I'm too short . . . ."

He smiled. "With all the shapes the kentaki come in, nobody will notice as long as you stand straight. None of the ruling class is allowed to have a bend spine. Other than that, the kentaki see the dark clothing and nothing more."

Sensha donned the mask, wrapped the cloak around herself, and finally raised the hood into its place to cover her hair.

"Why did you free me instead of one of the humans?"

"The plani would be more likely to hunt for one of them. They won't blink at the loss of a dribrora. Didn't Captain Rivel say he expected you to escape anyway?"

"But what about you?" she asked.

"I'll tell them the truth – that you overpowered me. Don't worry – I wouldn't have gotten this far if I wasn't a good actor. Now go!"

Sensha obeyed, closing and locking the door behind her and adopting a hurried business-like stride as soon as she hit the hall. To her relief, there were no other kentaki around. The humans were no doubt being held on a different floor. Heading down to the ground floor in an elevator, Sensha reflected that she had not even asked her savior's name, and vowed that she would soon return – in force – to make good his efforts. There was still a possibility that she was being set up, that Rivel simply wanted to use her attempted escape as an excuse to kill her, but she didn't think so. She had faith in her ability to read fellow dribrora. The only question was whether Rivel had also anticipated this method of escape. After being outmaneuvered by the plani captain so completely, Sensha had to take the possibility seriously.

Emerging from the elevator, her eyes scanned the room ahead for obstacles to her getaway. No one seemed to give her a glance, but as she started for the exits, a plani – one of Rivel's underlings – moved to intercept her. She didn't change anything about her pace or direction, pretending not to notice.

"Wait!" the plani said. Sensha fought against her instinct to dash out. The voice had sounded urgent, but not hostile, so she turned to it with apparent curiosity instead of apprehension. It was risky, but if she wasn't forced to act desperately now, she would have all the time she needed to escape.

Rivel's underling had a package in his hand, and without any preamble he handed it to her and said, "Give this to Corcoris personally. No one else, you hear?"

Sensha nodded firmly and, cradling the package to show that she took the errand seriously, she continued on her way. For the next few heartbeats, she wondered if she was headed in the right direction to reach this Corcoris. If not, a shout from behind her would demand to know what she thought she was doing, and she would be left with no choice but to bolt. But no uproar came from behind and no one else accosted her as she left the government house.

The card given to her displayed a map from the government house to her savior's friends. She was sure it had other information programmed into it, since its previous owner was clearly a man of patience and planning who would anticipate her needs. She didn't shift it away from the map yet, though, not knowing if she would be able to navigate the interface to return to it. Having both a clear escape and something concrete to do on this alien world, she went forth with renewed confidence and determination, but cast occasional backward glances just to be sure.

10

Lost in Translation

Kordon had prepared for this moment his entire life, and told them so repeatedly in the midst of as complete an account of the local situation as they could have hoped for. While their arrival at his doorstep had been a surprise, the presence of humans on his planet was not. He had been monitoring the communication between the *Azar* and the kentaki central government, and apologized for not being able to warn them about the danger to their ship.

"This station, like all the others of its kind, is only able to receive messages," he explained. As soon as the kentaki had shown sufficient technological development, the plani sent probes to the kentaki surface with instructions on how to build the relays. This was standard practice once the ISC took a planet off the protected list, and it was followed by an information stream with lessons on Plani and the complete ISC core database. According to Kordon, there were scholars in every city on Kentak huddling around the relays, still translating the database after years of work. "The probes came thirty years ago – our years, that is – and we finally had enough people fluent in Plani about five years ago. We have all the basics translated, but the historical records they sent us . . . they dwarf all the writing ever produced by us kentaki, I'm sure."

Before Fletcher could even ask the questions on his mind, Kordon was well into answering them. The kentaki seemed to have an extraordinarily organized mind, and a gift for putting his thoughts into Plani that justified his position as head translator at this facility.

"It has been my dream to someday talk to offworlders instead of just receiving their messages. I made sure I would be able to speak fluently. And look, here I am." He clapped his hands. "This is so exciting. I had been jealous of the central government officials who were able to speak with the plani and with your ship. Well . . . I call them the central government, but they are really . . . not. They are simply the most powerful government on Kentak, but there are many independent nations here. We all agreed long ago that the Grikorat – what I called the central government – should take the lead in interstellar affairs, but that agreement is breaking down. The Grikorat does not share information as freely as it once did, and that has led to heighted suspicion. There is a very charismatic politician in this city holding a rally about that issue right now, and that is why I said it was dangerous. You see, they all think the Grikorat is engaged in a conspiracy with aliens to undermine the other nations on Kentak. Some have even threatened us here at the institute because we would have to be in collusion as well. Luckily, most of them are sensible enough to know that we are only starry-eyed maniacs." His face split into a disconcertingly broad smile. "Of course, if any of those outside were to see you two, I think their attitude would become hostile very quickly. You must not blame them. There has been much frustration building, and it was certain that somebody wanting power would find a target to focus the crowds on. We have been having trouble, you see."

"Trouble?"

"The crops do not survive, and we have no idea why. Also, strange creatures attack those outside the town at night. We have felt more and more isolated, more and more under siege. Even I am unhappy about the situation, and I rarely leave this building, much less the city. However, I do enjoy eating, and the rations are growing increasingly thin."

Fletcher's stomach chose that time to growl. Fortunately, Kordan didn't seem to know enough human anatomy to understand what that meant, and chose to ignore the sound in case bringing it up would embarrass his guest. While thankful for this lack of response, Fletcher sympathized with his stomach. He had hoped that reaching civilization would mean something edible other than emergency rations. Now, even if the kentaki knew of food that humans could eat, it was going to be difficult to get any. And with Kordan the only kentaki they could trust – aside from any assistants he had tucked away somewhere in the building – the two humans were cornered without any safe options. Unless . . . .

"Well . . . ," Fletcher started with a doubtful glance at Ethan, "I guess we could help figure out why you're having this trouble. I mean, we've got some equipment and maybe we know a few things you don't. You never know . . . ." Fletcher's voice faded in worries that he sounded arrogant – implying that two humans were so much more advanced that they could solve problems that thousands of kentaki were having trouble with – and waited for Ethan to tell him so.

Ethan was about to oblige, but Kordon cut him off. "I was really, really hoping you would say that," the kentaki said, eyes beaming. "I am convinced there is a straightforward explanation to our problems, and that an outside perspective is just the thing we need. Unfortunately, our leaders are either focused on avoiding blame or too eager to take advantage – none of them have made the slightest move to investigate or to get help. If only I could inspire people to take action, but I have only two assistants and I struggle to get them out of bed by midday. If I tried to get them to go out at night to look for a murderous creature, they would just lodge a complaint against me and go back to bed."

Panic in his eyes, Ethan said, "listen, we don't have a clue about these sorts of things. I'm barely a theoretical physicist and Fletcher here . . . well, his father tried to make him into starship captain material, but I don't think that really helps us here."

Kordon looked puzzled. "If you are worried that I think you will work some magic and solve this overnight, I assure you that we kentaki lack any of the . . . optimism that I have seen in the records of other species."

"I'm worried that we're going to get ourselves in the middle of trouble we don't know anything about."

"We're already there," Fletcher pointed out.

"Indeed," Kordon said, "and you are going to need help to

contact or find your comrades. You can hardly do it while trapped here. If you can be part of the solution, I think the townspeople will offer you whatever help you need."

"Great. And what do we do in the meantime when they have a shoot-aliens-on-sight policy going?" Ethan shot back.

Kordan couldn't answer, and he sat in thought pondering the problem. Fletcher was disappointed in Ethan. Sure, there was no way anyone who surrounded himself with theories and equations all day would ever try to escape a space station in a crate full of puppies, but there was no point being reluctant when there was no choice.

To convince Ethan that there really wasn't any other option, he decided to get a few questions answered. "How far away is the nearest town from here? Will they have the same issue with us as the people here do?"

Kordon scratched his head. "We know they have been having trouble – different symptoms than we have, but the same result. You would have to expect that they would not be happy about outsiders wandering in, but I am not certain. It would be two days' walk for you – we have no vehicles at this station since this is purely sedentary work. There is no facility like this there, so you will be taking an extra risk as there will be no one who can communicate with you. When you think about it, it is lucky that you came to this town."

"Lucky," Ethan repeated with a sniff.

Fed up with Ethan's attitude, Fletcher snapped at him. "I think we can at least try. I don't see why we can't try. And I do think we were lucky to find someone like Kordon, especially when other people in the city might have treated us worse."

"You're assuming he's telling us the truth," Ethan said, immediately regretting the words, knowing full well that Kordon couldn't have been lying. Ethan had never met any creature whose thoughts were more plainly displayed on its face. He couldn't even look at Kordon right now, because the hurt expression he saw out of the corner of his eye was heartbreaking enough. Kordon had all the guile of a puppy.

"Yeah, I am," Fletcher replied, giving an encouraging smile to the kentaki. "Anyway, just think about it. What could be killing the crops?"

"How am I supposed to know? I'm not an ecologist or soil expert or anything like that."

"Okay, but pretend you are for a sec and tell me what kind of test you'd do to figure this out."

Never having met a direct question he didn't try to answer, Ethan said with more hesitation than he normally showed, "test the soil, of course."

Fletcher turned to the kentaki. "Kordon, I guess you have soil scientists and already did that kind of test, right?"

"Yes. Agriculture is vital here. Most people in this town would normally work in the fields, if not for the trouble. Their spare time now makes them easy to agitate. But yes, there are soil specialists, and they did tests at the first sign of decay. They did not find anything."

Fletcher snapped his fingers with a flourish. "So the question is, what might the kentaki have missed in the soil that we would have found."

"Nothing."

"Oh, come on."

Finally, Fletcher could see the gears in Ethan's mind whirring up. "Well, something small, I guess. The kentaki in this town might use a regular microscope to check the soil, but I don't think they'd have anything high-powered. They probably expected to find a larger parasite, but not something on the nano scale."

"Do we have anything that could see that small?"

Ethan shrugged. "Depends on what you mean by 'see'. The biotics analyzer can go right down to the atomic level to check if something's safe to eat, but it doesn't actually let us take a look, and I have no idea what it'll come up with if we just hand it dirt."

"But we have something to try, right?" Fletcher said, pleasantly surprised. Stabbing blindly with questions, he had expected a dead end.

With a heavy sigh, Ethan replied, "yeah, but it's a long shot."

A delighted Kordan clapped his hands. "Excellent, excellent. Now, we only have to find a way to get you out there. Or . . . or maybe we can bring the samples you need here. Yes, that would be better. We would not want our first human visitors to get eaten, would we? I think it is about time I get my assistants out here and put them to some use."

Kordon pressed what must have been an intercom button, because his voice then blazed throughout the building. "All assistants report to the ground floor immediately. This is an emergency." He disengaged the intercom with a smirk. "That should get them down in a hurry. They have been worried for days that protesters would storm the building and do unpleasant things to us – or at least destroy the relay. Ah, there they are."

A thoroughly mismatched pair bounded down a staircase on the far side of the office. The shallow stairs were exactly what Kordon's ponderous rotund frame required, but suited neither of the assistants. The first, who Kordon introduced as Toran, was a tall graceful figure – almost eldrandii-like in shapely elegance. Unfortunately, Toran's legs had trouble adjusting to the lack of depth on the staircase, so that she made a jarring thunk with every step down. The scowl on her face reminded Fletcher of Kaz, but it was somehow worse. She had an arrogant air, and clearly considered the staircase a personal affront. Refusing to adjust to it, she made every step a protest in the hope that it would eventually be replaced with one that suited her. Fletcher had no doubt that she had friends in high places who would ensure her rise through the ranks so that she could eventually punish the architect of this building.

The other assistant, Shestori, was short due to legs only half the length that would be proportionate to his upper body. His knees seemed to have an on-mode, off-mode, and nothing in between, so that he had to be careful, pausing at each step to make sure he didn't unbalance himself. A ramp would have suited him better, but to his credit, he seemed to take the staircase as a challenge. His face was intense, but Fletcher couldn't read anymore into it.

There was a quick discussion between Kordon and his assistants in the local language. Toran was obviously unhappy about being disturbed for anything less than a life-threatening situation, and certainly didn't think much of the first non-kentaki she had ever seen. Shestori, on the other hand, kept a safe distance from the aliens as if they were as much of a danger as a raging mob would have been. Not that he could have gotten very far running away, Fletcher thought with a dismayed shake of his head. At first glance, neither of Kordon's assistants gave much sign of intelligence – no curiosity.

That impression faded somewhat once the assistants started talking in Plani instead of their native tongue. They were slower in forming their sentences than Kordon, but once they gave voice to the words, the translators had no problems. It was all textbook Plani. Fletcher only knew English, so he had to give grudging respect to anyone who could pick up another language to the point of fluency.

Toran was all too eager to have her thoughts heard. "When you call us down for an emergency, I expect more than this." She threw a contemptuous nod at the two humans, as if they were some new pets Kordon had brought home.

"But Toran, communicating with them is our whole purpose here. That is why I insisted that you learn to speak Plani. And look, they understand you perfectly. Is it not wonderful?"

"They would understand better if we spoke their language. Are we not supposed to be talking to plani? What good is it, talking with these?"

Kordon slumped, then he straightened with his arms stretched wide as if in an attempt to wrap around the bountiful package the humans represented. "There is no limit, Toran, no limit. The plani have been as they are for hundreds of generations – stagnant at their pinnacle. The humans – in just two or three of their generations they rose from being where we are now to challenging the plani for supremacy. What could they teach us, eh? They know more about what it takes to rise up than the plani do, since the plani have had it all handed to them from the past."

Toran took a second look at the humans, appraising them. In the end, she still shook her head, unimpressed.

"Kordon . . . ," Shestori said with a musical quaver in his voice, "if these aliens are here . . . the people that have been causing all the noise recently . . . you do not plans to keep these . . .

these humans here, do you? Associating with them . . . will not be safe. No, very dangerous, I am sure." He took another step back away from the humans as if worried his life would be in peril if even a particle of alien material was found on him.

Kordon shook his head, his face imploring his guests to forgive Toran and Shestori. Rather than reply to Shestori, he explained to Ethan and Fletcher, "as you can tell for yourself, my assistants are very good at what our duties require. However, I worry sometimes that they do not understand why they do it. They simply go through the motions and receive their paycheck. They never seem interested in what they are translating." He finally turned to Shestori and said sharply, "where else are our guests supposed to turn? Who else can understand what they have to say? I am sorry if you thought this was a comfortable job where you could sleep past midday and never be inconvenienced. Get ready, because this is where our work truly becomes interesting."

"Perhaps more quickly than you realize, Kordon," Toran said dryly. "I hear a crowd growing outside. Maybe you should take a look through that window of yours."

Fletcher couldn't hear anything, but though Toran's ears looked normal, there was no reason to believe she was exaggerating. Kordon certainly didn't waste time second-guessing her, taking to the stairs in a heartbeat. Fletcher and Ethan barely had time to give each other ominous looks before Kordon was back down again, face pale.

"I am afraid you must have been noticed when you entered the city. They already have the building surrounded. They are very quiet, even solemn. I do not know what to make of it except . . . I am truly sorry."

Ethan turned to Fletcher and, voice soft and cracking in fear, asked, "what do we do now?"

Rebels

For Sensha, it was almost as if she was home. The desperation, far-fetched plans, and unyielding suspicion of outsiders filling the air in the room were all as familiar to her as her own sweat. Certainly, she had never seen a group of rebels come in so many shapes and sizes, but they were unified in purpose, and that was what counted.

So, when they tied her to the chair and started interrogating her, she didn't take it personally. She also didn't lie, knowing that these people would be hair-trigger paranoid and looking for the slightest inconsistency in her words. The only worry in her mind was that the kentaki-enabled translator headset she had been allowed to keep might make mistakes in rendering her words.

These kentaki were not a bunch of anti-alien fanatics, and they were not opposing the government because of some irrational conspiracy theory, so they were open to embracing help from unexpected quarters. Once Sensha gave them a complete picture of what had happened to bring her to them, she could feel their excitement growing. It was unfortunate that her savior had not given his name, but the card that had led her here seemed to do more to convince the rebels of her veracity than any name-dropping might have. That card had been her ticket through the door in the first place. Without it, they would have pretended to be some sort of legitimate business.

Even after they decided to untie her and give her something to eat, not one of them introduced him or herself. For now, at least in this small ill-lit room, names were off-limits. That was all right, because Sensha found it easier to keep track of everyone using their physical characteristics anyway. The interrogator had been slightly hunchbacked with green patches on his skin that made him look like he was molding. Whenever he was unsure of how to proceed, his eyes turned to a tall, slim figure with dark brown skin and only a stub for a left arm. Sensha supposed the slim one was either their leader or put in charge of speaking to outsiders. She wasn't sure whether his left arm was an abnormality at birth, or if he had lost it in some accident or fight. Other than that, he was the most conventionally shaped kentaki Sensha had seen.

When it came time for them to give her information as a gesture of goodwill, the slim one did the talking. With each of his words, Sensha became ever more convinced that a kind fate had carried her to this planet. In a way, her people and these kentaki were fighting the same enemy.

"Until a few decades ago, life on this planet was all that was known to us," the one-armed Kentaki started. "For some of us, the changes are in living memory. Before the plani sent their probes and their information, life was beyond difficult. Most pregnancies failed and most live births died in their first year. For those that survived their first year, life expectancy was about twenty-five years – our years, of course. All the nations of Kentak pooled their resources into the Grikorat to build a single space program in the hope that we could leave this cursed planet and colonize another. We are convinced, you see, that something about this world causes our difficulties. Our biologists say that the problem is not with the processes of life, but with the exposure to radiation and other influences in the womb. Even before we knew about life elsewhere, we were convinced of this. Or, at least, we were willing to try anything with even the slightest chance of success.

"We had just sent out our first interstellar mission when the plani probes came, as if they had been waiting for us. Everything started to change quickly from there. The technological transmissions they sent us included medical information and devices that allowed us to cut the infant mortality rate to a quarter of what it once was, and to extend our life expectancy by fifteen years."

Sensha could see where this was heading, but wanted to speed things along. So far, the one-armed kentaki had kept his words sterile, as if reading an academic report on the issues. Sensha wanted to see if the kentaki were capable of the kind of passion that real opposition required. To push him into it, she said, "it sounds like you have a lot to thank the plani for, and things are better than they were before. Why would you want to change anything? My own people are oppressed – we actually have a reason to fight."

That put a blaze behind the slim one's eyes, but his voice kept its cool. "We know about your people's troubles from the one who you spoke with to get that card. The fact that you are clearly one of his kind and not a regular plani is the only reason why we considered trusting you. I do not doubt that your circumstances are more difficult than ours, but we accepted the technology as a sign of friendship and compassion, not as a precursor to domination. Before the plani came, we were not surrendering to our problems, but had joined together to find solutions. Even though it may have taken longer, we could have dealt with it on our own. When we accepted plani help, we did not expect to become their slaves."

Sensha snorted. "You are far from being slaves. In fact, there cannot be more than a hundred plani on this planet."

"And every one of them is now a part of our government, masquerading as our own officials. Everyone has chosen to be blind to it because of what the plani can do for us. And you should know, the plani have no limits to how much they can exploit those they consider not of their own kind. In the end, if we do not push back, we will be building our own cages and forging our own chains."

Sensha nodded and leaned forward. That was the kind of thinking she liked to hear. When the threat of complacency was highest, there were always a few precious voices who could see the truth behind the good times. But one thing now worried her. "What do the plani want, though? This is not a rich planet. Unless . . . the estimates were lies."

"No, it is not a rich planet, and we have asked ourselves that question as well. The entire planet has been eager to find something that other species would want to trade with us for, and we looked carefully through the plani transmission to find hints of what might be valuable. We have nothing. But tell me, what was the human captain coming here for?"

"I do not know," Sensha said, implying by her tone that she really wished she did. She had plenty of guesses, but she hated airing speculations. Theorizing was a game to be played when nothing was at stake. With lives on the line, you either offered hard information or kept your mouth shut.

Her host, though, was desperate for some hints. "There must be something you can tell us. I will tell you this: I do not think the plani expected to find anything useful here at first. The first survey team came here simply to prevent other species from seizing the opportunity first. Our informant within their ranks has said as much. I think something has been found, though, otherwise neither the human captain nor your nemesis would have come here now."

Sensha had to give a lopsided smile at the words "your nemesis." Rivel was definitely becoming that, but she doubted the plani captain thought so highly of her, otherwise he would have found some way to permanently dispose of her. She admitted to herself that she was probably no more than an itch to Captain Rivel's mind right now. Given time, though, who knows?

"I am sure you are right," she said, "but I had not earned the trust of the humans yet, so they did not tell me why they were here. If you want a guess, it either has to do with the hyperspace drive or the source of the radiation on this planet, unless there is something else they did not tell me."

"And there is nothing you might want to hold back from me?"

Sensha took a deep breath before answering. "Not about this. I want these answers as much as you do. But if you think I have nothing more to offer, you would be wrong. I also know that you have a lot more you could tell me. Actually . . . ," aiming her eyes directly at his, she decided to push her luck, "I think you have your own idea about what the Earth captain wanted. Am I right?"

The slim kentaki made a non-committal sound. They had reached the point at which he should either accept her as an ally or dispose of her. By indicating her continued usefulness, she signaled her willingness to help. She had been as forthcoming as only a true sympathizer could be, and the organization was too weak to turn her away. Sensha had known that from the start. The only question left was whether the kentaki realized it, and from the slim one's hesitation, she knew he did.

Deciding to start with the basics, he said, "my name is Orekantal, though everyone calls me Orek. I am the leader of this group, though we are hardly the only group in the city that opposes the plani usurpation. I do think that we are the only ones who do not accept alien fear-mongering, which is how we attracted the dribrora who helped you."

"Well, Orek," Sensha said, shifting her posture from open and earnest to her usual demure and confident, "what do you think Captain Pierce might have wanted?"

Orek shifted his weight and extended his right arm. "Follow me."

The other kentaki in the room looked uneasy, but didn't object. As Orek led Sensha out, they followed in a combination of suspicion and curiosity. They took a short walk down a grimy corridor to a double-locked steel door. Sensha reflected that the kentaki seemed to prefer having two different locks on the doors they wanted to secure rather than a single supposedly unbreakable one. She wondered what that said about their psychology. Sensibly, two different kentaki had the keys – Orek had one, and Sensha's interrogator, who she now mentally promoted to second-in-command, had the other.

Everyone – six bodies altogether – packed into a room barely larger than a walk-in closet. Originally built as a storage room, it now only held one item – a cylinder sitting on a table at the room's center. Sensha instinctively tried her best to keep some distance between herself and the other kentaki, still unsettled by their bizarre appearance, but the room offered little breathing room. She decided to stick close to Orek, who at least did not look diseased.

"We wonder . . . ," Orek started, "we wonder whether this is what they are all after. Or, maybe, it is merely a hint of what there is to be found here."

Sensha looked at the cylinder, which was about two of her

fingers in width and about a foot in height. It was half full with a grey metallic liquid which shined even in the dim light. The liquid had an eerie stillness to it, and Sensha knew enough to guess that it didn't always stay so placid.

"What is it?" she asked.

"We were hoping you would tell us."

She had been afraid of that, but there was no choice except to give them something. They had shown her one of their secrets, and now they wanted to see if she could deliver on the promise of information. Wracking her brain for what a grey liquid could signify, she was hesitant to ask questions which might reveal too much of her ignorance. Instead, she went on the offensive. "It could be any number of things, so you will have to give me some details about . . . about how it behaves in reaction to things . . . if you want me to narrow the possibilities down."

Orek's lips were drawn in something between a smile and frown, and for a moment, Sensha thought he had seen through her. In fact, he was trying to find a way to deliver his words less bluntly. He failed. "I can tell you it reacts to flesh by eating right through it." He lifted the stub of his left arm to avoid giving voice to that part of the explanation. "And it is no acid. It has all the malevolence of a predator." He put his right arm close to the glass cylinder and, shocking even Sensha, the grey liquid pounced to the side facing the arm with animal eagerness, almost toppling the cylinder. Rather than being a still puddle, it now seemed to squirm, testing the glass for weakness by pounding against it, rocking the cylinder.

Orek pulled his arm away and the liquid returned to its former placidity. "Is that enough information for you?"

No, it wasn't, but Sensha knew that it was all she was going to get, at least until she offered something in return. She was no analyst, and her knowledge of biology was . . . extremely specific. Considering what the liquid had done to Orek's arm, though, she would definitely have to add it to her knowledge base. But what was it? It looked like an organic slime – a silicon organic of the kind that could be found in the Altair system. But then it wouldn't be anything special, and she needed a more compelling answer if she wanted to impress the kentaki.

So, she needed the predatory liquid to be something that looked organic, but wasn't. That thought finally snapped her neurons into place and her eyes lit up triumphantly.

"Nanobots," she said firmly, as if knowing the answer the whole time.

Orek looked to the others, but none of them offered any sign that they had understood, so he asked Sensha, "what are nanobots?"

"Tiny robots – molecule-sized machines that work together to do things that normal machines cannot. They are sometimes part organic, and they can be made to self-replicate."

"Machines . . . that make more machines. And they are the size of . . . germs," Orek said, digesting a far more horrific picture than Sensha had intended.

"Yes, but self-replicating nanobots are banned in the ISC. You never really see them, since they are usually used inside other machines for repairs or in medicines to fight diseases. These," she gestured to the cylinder, "are either not capable of replicating or they violate our rules. Since they seem to be programmed to attack organic material, that probably breaks ISC law, too." Sensha's breath quickened at the prospect. What if this was plani work? What if the lost survey teams were just a cover to get engineers onto this planet while discouraging other worlds from sending their own trade missions? Kentak had just enough local industry to supply a plani nanobot lab while the kentaki were decades away from the technology themselves. If Sensha could get evidence of an illegal lab like that, it could give her people the serious leverage they could use to gain their rights. The realization that the plani had violated a core ISC agreement would almost certainly lead to demands that the ISC capital be moved to another world like Earth – a massive loss of revenue to all businesses on Plani.

Orek seemed satisfied with her answer as well, convinced that the nanobots were valuable enough for two species to send ships for the sake of them. She could see that he, too, was busy thinking of the possibilities.

The second-in-command, though, had latched onto Orek's ominous way of describing the nanobots, and asked in the stereotypical executive officer concerned-about-impending-doom tone, "Orek, is it likely that it can replicate? You are the only one that has ever seen what it can do outside of that cylinder. What do you think?"

Orek thought it over. "I saw no growth in it, even after it . . . fed. It has been its current volume since I first saw it. But that does not rule out replication, since it might require a specific chemical. We have to be careful with it."

The worried lines on the second-in-command's face softened, glad to see his chief advocating caution. "But why, why would someone want to create machines that devour living matter like this? It is worse than any plague."

Orek crouched so that his eyes were level with the grey goo. Staring at it as if at his own nemesis, he said, "is it not obvious? This is a weapon."

1 2

SUETON

The scene was so surreal that Fletcher wondered whether he was dreaming - dumped by his imagination into the middle of a medieval witch trial. Except that the mob looked like the type that would eschew the drowning test in favor of going straight to burning at the stake. They had rammed the door of the institute in, and Fletcher had chosen not to run since there weren't many places to hide anyway, and he didn't want to give the appearance of guilt. He wondered about that choice now, but supposed it would have caused even more trouble for Kordon and his assistants. As it was, only Fletcher and Ethan were hauled out to confront the stern stares of the crowd, with Kordon following behind in case a translator was needed.

The crowd's intention was impossible to read. The tension in the air had the taste of hostility, but the faces of the kentaki had none of Kordon's transparency. Their expressions also seemed inconsistent by human standards, with different parts of any individual's face giving conflicting messages. Kordon didn't try to explain the side comments being passed back and forth that might have given Fletcher a heads-up. Fletcher understood why Kordon held back – he didn't want to feed the mob's suspicions of a conspiracy by looking as if he was priming the aliens with lies to deal with their captors. Kordon would have to stick to translating with permission from the other kentaki to avoid pushing events in the wrong direction.

Without even looking at him, Fletcher could feel Ethan's nervousness grow by the second, as if his elder companion's trembling disturbed the air and sent shock waves between them. While it would have been nice to have an experienced and trustworthy adult he could depend on to save them, Fletcher was hardly used to relying on anyone else like that, and was resigned to doing most of the talking. Maybe all of the talking. There was really only one chance – he had to highlight the distinctions between humans and plani, the fact that he himself had actually been held as a prisoner of the plani, and that humans stood ready to help the kentaki with whatever problems they faced. He thought the words out in his mind, but had trouble focusing. The situation, combined with the lack of a recent meal, left him weak and in a daze.

The institute didn't have anything like a platform or stage in front of it, so they were moved to a nearby building that had been built on a slight hill, so that it had a broad flight of stairs leading to its door. The humans, with Kordon alongside, were positioned on the top step with a dozen guards surrounding them. They waited for a few minutes wondering what was going to happen. Then the crowd began to part to allow a single kentaki through. Fletcher was sure this was the wildly-gesticulating politician they had seen, even though that figure had only been a blur in his goggles. Given the way the crowd let the politician through, Fletcher knew that he would have to be cautious and respectful. On the other hand, they would probably receive the complete opposite in return, as the kentaki leader tried to score political points.

Able to see how the scene could play out even before his interrogator was in clear view, Fletcher could not have anticipated how the powerful kentaki would actually look. Rubbing his eyes in disbelief after getting his first clear view, Fletcher couldn't keep himself from saying, "he's . . . he's so smooth!"

Ethan nodded, unable to give voice to his thoughts. The figure was clearly kentaki, especially with the uneven blue-green patches in his skin, but he was hairless and practically without pores. His skin looked plastic in its sheen, as if manufactured. Even in a throng with so many odd shapes and colors, he stood out. Fletcher wondered whether that was a quality that kentaki looked for in their leaders.

The plastic one walked up to Kordon and greeted him as if they were old friends. Kordon couldn't hide the distaste from his face, but took the opportunity to say as much as he could. At one point, he was clearly indicating that he wanted to act as translator, and the politician reluctantly assented to this, though he had not given Fletcher and Ethan a glance. With the permission given, Kordon drew closer to the humans and the plastic one began speaking to the crowd.

His voice was projected through the open air so effortlessly that the translator headset initially had trouble picking up the mumbles of Kordon's rendition.

". . . and we have here some of the very aliens whose presence we know is disrupting our world. And when they entered our city, did they present themselves to the elders or our local leaders? No. They went to the one building we know has had contact with them – has been colluding with them this whole time."

Bursting with indignation, Fletcher almost shouted that it had been the sight of the plastic politician's incendiary rally that had stop him from entering the city on the main street. Instead, he said in a more muted voice, "I can explain that," but his voice was too thin to carry more than a few yards and the politician ignored him.

"Of course, I do not know why they do what they do. I do, however, intend to find out." Turning to the dozen guards, he said "arrest them and Kordon as well. Bring them to headquarters."

Looking to Ethan and Kordon, Fletcher saw relief all around. They were apparently not going to be lynched but that left the motives of the plastic one a mystery. Before Fletcher could turn his mind toward figuring the politician out, a shout came out of the crowd.

"You are not the authority here. How dare you arrest them!"

The crowd moved aside, revealing the speaker to those on the steps. A heavily wrinkled grey kentaki stepped forward. Comparing the voice to that of Toran's, Fletcher decided that the speaker must be a kentaki woman, but the face that now confronted the plastic one had the aspect of a bulldog. Fletcher stood in wonder that the two of them were representatives of the same species.

"Council leader Yarun," the plastic one said with a taunting tone, "I did not expect to see you out here today. You have never bothered to hear what I have to say before. I got the feeling that the council would rather that I did not exist. Perhaps . . . ," he gave a meaningful look at the humans, "you had some visitors you wished to greet instead."

"Insinuation!" Yarun said, pointing an accusing finger. "Of course I do not come to hear you, Sueton. I would not have my ears so filled. I came here just as you came, hearing from those who like to speak that a pair of aliens had walked into the city, heading for the relay. Since you arrived so much sooner than me – soon enough to arrest them, as you said – I wonder how you came by your information. Besides that, you are only seeking election to the council. How does that give you a right to arrest people who wander into our city?"

Stance still firm and projecting confidence, Sueton said, "a poor choice of words. I meant protective detainment, of course. After all, we would not want our guests to get hurt, would we?" That brought some unpleasant sounds from the crowd. "And even in our fine city, there might be those who would take advantage of them."

"And I wonder who that might be," Yarun grumbled. "But no matter. They have done nothing wrong, and they are to be allowed their freedom."

"Of course they have their freedom." Sueton turned to Ethan and asked, "would you mind accompanying my men to my office? I assure you that you will not be harmed. If you do not come with me, I cannot make any guarantees."

With the crowd standing ready to back it up, the threat was hardly veiled. Ethan had to answer, but looked for help from Fletcher and Kordan, both of whom were at a loss. Curious as to what Ethan's answer would be, Yarun kept silent. Without any promise of protection from the council leader, Ethan felt that he had no choice. "We'll go with your men."

A slight tilt of the head from Sueton seemed to be his way of saying *of course you will*. He turned back to Yarun. "You see. There are no reasons for you to be troubled, council leader." Then, to satisfy the crowd Sueton added, "and while they are my guests,

I am sure we will have the time to talk about what they are doing here, what they know about the blight that has struck our land, and who they have been in contact with." He threw challenging glares at Kordon and Yarun.

Yarun could only turn away, but as a parting shot with her back to Sueton, she said, "we will take your assurance that they will not be harmed as a legal guarantee. Be sure to hold to it, or we will see who gets arrested." Her words were directed as much to the mob as to Sueton.

With a wave of Sueton's hand, his men encircled Kordon, Fletcher, and Ethan, walking them down the steps. Ethan, still stiff and shaky, moved too slowly for the guard behind him. The guard gave him a rough push on the shoulder and Ethan, never the firmest on his feet to begin with, stumbled down three steps before regaining his balance. For the first time, Sueton gave an angry look – his smooth face suddenly had sharp edges to it. The guard at the receiving end bowed to Sueton as an apology, but didn't direct any regard to the human he had pushed. Sueton may have taken Yarun's threat of legal action seriously, but the people around Sueton were all too ready to treat aliens as non-sentient animals – in Earth terms, to dehumanize them. The thought that Sueton was the only thing standing between them and brutality wasn't heartening.

With all that he was trying to process keeping his mind busy, it seemed to Fletcher that they reached Sueton's headquarters in an instant. The office was nothing special, giving a sense of both bustling activity and solid organization so that visitors would have confidence in the man in charge. Fletcher wondered how the dozen young staffers all managed to look busy when they were presumably only dealing with a population of less than ten thousand citizens. No one could doubt that Sueton's ambitions and reach extended beyond this town's stark borders.

The three semi-captives sat around a desk, waiting as everyone in the office took turns eyeing them with a rich mix of curiosity, foreboding, anger, and concern. At least, Fletcher thought he saw those emotions, but it was tough to tell. When Sueton arrived, he wasted no time and immediately took the last seat at the desk, confirming the thought that had been brewing in Fletcher's mind: Sueton had no idea what to do with them, was worried that mishandling them could derail his ambitions, and needed to figure things out quickly before the narrative was taken out of his hands. He had "arrested" them out of fear that the crowd he had riled up would actually attack the humans, and that he would be blamed for Kentak's first interstellar scandal. It had been safe to play the scapegoat game when the targets of blame were out of reach. Now that they were here, Sueton had a problem on his hands.

Exhausted from the rally, he didn't mince words, and Kordon relayed everything he said with all its terseness. "When they told me aliens were seen in town, I was expecting plani. But what would they know about the difference between one alien and another? Humans . . . well, this can go one of two ways for you – either very well or very badly. It will end well for me no matter what. I can tell the people out there that you are our salvation and try to explain who you are, who the plani are, and . . . that is a lot of trouble for me, and it risks splitting my following into factions. If I am going to do that, I need you to give me a good reason. Otherwise, I will give you to Yarun whether the hag wants you or not, tell the crowd that the council leader took custody of her alien friends, and then stand back and watch. I told everyone the answers I wanted from you, so start with those. Talk."

Even though Sueton directed his words at Ethan, Fletcher decided to respond. Ethan might have been older and more relaxed now that he wasn't facing hundreds of kentaki, but Fletcher was better prepared. He started with the competition between Pierce and Rivel, leaving out anything to do with the hyperdrive, making it the main reason for the human presence on Kentak. Putting special emphasis on his own captivity on Plani, he went through everything up to the destruction of the *Azar*, framing it all as an Earth-versus-Plani economic struggle.

"For me and Ethan here, though, all we want to do right now is find the rest of the crew. We talked about trying to figure out what happened to the ship, too. You don't suppose it has anything to do with your problems here, do you?" Fletcher asked the question innocently. It was a long shot, but he hoped Sueton had some more information they could work with.

As it turned out, Sueton liked to ramble when he was tired. "I think it has *everything* to do with our problems. I do not lie to the people. I do believe you aliens, starting with the plani, caused this disaster. Ever since the first plani ship came, things have gone from bad to chaotic. It is as if there was a sleeping demon on this world, and it awoke to suck the energy from that first ship. Every other ship that has come along has only made it stronger, letting it unleash these plagues on our already hellish world. Now, with your ship exploding, the demon now has another burst of energy, and I wonder whether it will finally destroy us for good. Mind you, the Grikorat and those in the core cities will survive thanks to their new technology and will not give a care when we who struggle to survive have given our last breath."

Out of nowhere, Ethan said in a dreamy voice, "that . . . could be it. Not a demon, but . . . yeah. Something very, very unstable acting like a huge sink in the field like a black hole does for gravity. Except it lets a lot more radiation escape. I wonder if it would draw energy from other sources, and not just the hyperdrives."

Sueton snapped. "What are you talking about?"

Ethan looked into the kentaki's eyes with sudden confidence and a smile on his face. "I think you were right about the energy sucking demon, except it's more like a hole than a demon. It might explain why hyperdrive ships have trouble around this planet and . . . ," he thought about the failure of Pierce's clairvoyance when trying to probe Kentak, "and other things. I can't exactly be sure why it would suddenly affect your crops, but it might explain the radiation on this planet. If I'm right, the radiation levels here have gone up – maybe only slightly – every time a hyperdrive ship exploded in orbit. It might be only a bit, but it would be more extra radiation than you would expect even if the ships were using nuclear fuel."

Eyes wide with surprise, Sueton said, "You are right. There was a slight rise in radiation each time. That is why I pointed at the plani ships as the cause of the problem in the first place. But the rise should not have affected our food – not with the background radiation already so high." As an afterthought, Sueton admitted, "I only learned that after I pointed to the plani ships as the cause of the crop failure." Then, more defensively, "but the plani are not innocent, are they?"

"No, they aren't," Fletcher mumbled in a tone calculated to remind Sueton of his captivity under the plani. Sure, it was for less than a day, but he was going to play the card as often as he could. He could see that Ethan had unintentionally pulled Sueton to their side, and that Sueton favored the idea of using the humans for his advantage. It was time to remind the kentaki that, though stranded, his human guests were not helpless – even though they really were.

"You wanted a reason to call us saviors. What if we could figure out the cause of your crop problems for you? I mean, really find out exactly what is going on."

"I am listening."

"If we could find the rest of the *Azar*'s crew, you'd have an expert team that's had to deal with all sorts of problems on a dozen worlds. It would be easy . . . ."

"Not a chance. I cannot trust that you will keep your word after we help you."

Of course not, Fletcher thought, what politician would be that stupid? But Sueton had acknowledged that the rest of the human force on this planet would be enough to get Fletcher and Ethan to safety. As long as the kentaki was willing to accept that, Fletcher was comfortable with making his real offer. If there was one practical skill Fletcher had, it was negotiation.

With a sigh of pretended frustration, he said, "all right. We were just talking with Kordon about getting a soil sample from the affected area. I don't know if we'll be able to do anything with it, but if we can . . . . Maybe you could get some of the soil here and we could take a look?"

Sueton leaned back, thought it over, and then pointed a finger at an aide who had been listening in. The aide took a few steps forward, Sueton pointed at the door, and the aide went out on the implied errand. Straightening up, Sueton said, "let us find out if you have any hero in you. Anything we can sell to the masses. Otherwise, there are thousands of people out there ready to take you as villains."

"Great," Fletcher said, "but do you think we could get some food first?"

13

CORCORIS

Sensha had forgotten about the package handed to her at the door of the government house, so when one of the rebels burst into Orek's room and asked him to come look at its contents, she was instantly apprehensive. What had she accidentally brought with her? It probably wasn't a bomb, but if it was anything electronic, they might need Orek's expertise to decide whether it was a bug or some other tracking device. She had been speaking with Orek about practical techniques for resistance she had learned on Plani when the interruption threw liquid nitrogen all over the warm atmosphere. If she had unwittingly undermined the rebels in any way, the shame would plague her memories for years.

Seeing what the box contained for herself after a panicked jog down the corridor, Sensha started breathing again. The counterpoint to her relief was Orek's anger at the messenger.

"You idiot! You come to my room looking like you saw the monster of the wastes and make me think that the Grikorat planted something on Sensha. My heart is pounding like mad. What is this, though? Looks like a collection of maps."

"That is what they are," the second-in-command said, stepping forward out of the shadows. "Sorry about sending the kid down to get you. He gets too excited about everything. I think you will find these interesting, though – both of you." He nodded to Sensha.

Unable to read what the symbols on the maps meant, Sensha waited for Orek to explain what they were. Instead of getting to the point, though, he simply examined the maps silently in increasing agitation. Finally, he asked her, "Who did you say these were to be delivered to?"

Sensha searched her memory for the name. "Corcoris," she answered with little delay. When the two lead rebels gave each other a startled look, she said, "what?"

"Corcoris is one of the most powerful men in the government. He heads the department that was once in charge of our space program until the plani probes came and funding went to analyzing the information we were receiving. He is still in charge of the satellites we launch and all energy projects. We should have thought of him – he is the one person in the government who might detest the plani interference. Instead of being the latest in a line of heroes who brought us further into space, he has been marginalized."

Interesting as that was, Sensha had reached the end of her patience. "What are the maps? What do they show?"

Orek went sheet by sheet. "This is the standard background radiation reading across Kentak. As you can see, it is fairly uniform. Even when we zoom in," he touched a slider on the edge of the map and the image on the sheet went to a more local view, "you can see the variation is within ten percent. This next sheet is the reading within a five minute interval this morning."

"When the human ship was destroyed?"

Orek nodded. "As you can see, there are waves of radiation emanating from a very definite source, but not from the ship's location, which is marked here. The rings expanded quickly, since they were already this far in less than five minutes after the disaster. This next map shows the radiation levels an hour later, and we already see some equilibrium setting in. I think once they see this, every scientist on this planet will want to know what is at that source point, since it does not seem to be intrinsically radioactive, but only responded to the human ship's destruction.

"This last map has the tracked debris from your ship that landed on the surface. Since the event occurred outside the atmosphere, most normal debris would have burned in the atmosphere, except . . . ."

"Except for the escape pods," Sensha said hurriedly. "So some of the crew survived. The map shows where they landed?"

With a tilt of the head, Orek hedged. "Not exactly. Some of this might be other debris that survived the atmosphere. Though . . . there are fourteen points indicating a heavy mass. I would expect a starship to have at least that many escape pods."

Sensha and Orek looked at each other and shared the thought of having an Earth crew oppose the whims of the plani, giving room for the kentaki to secure freedom by playing the two against each other. Assuming the Earth ships were about the same size as the plani ships, the humans would have between a quarter and a third of the number of plani, but the Grikorat would have to adopt an apologetic posture toward them when they demanded the release of their captain. With Sensha acting as their way of gaining the trust of the humans, Orek could finally have a way to oppose the plani domination of the Grikorat.

But the maps brought more hope than just the humans could offer. Orek continued, "It looks like Corcoris might be interested in where the humans are. He could be collecting the information for the plani . . . ."

Sensha shook her head. "The plani have satellites around Kentak and their own equipment. They could have done the tracking themselves. Besides, the person who handed me the box definitely did not want anyone but Corcoris to see the information."

"Which leads to what I think has happened. I think the person who handed you this box recognized your cloak and mask somehow, thought that you were our dribrora contact, and that is why he entrusted you with this. Our contact must also be working with Corcoris. The space minister and his circle do not want the plani to know that they have the whereabouts of the humans. It might be that Corcoris wants to secure the humans before the plani get their hands on them, and for the same reason we do."

"But we have the information now. It would be better if we get to the humans before a government official did. Then we would have the leverage." Sensha wondered whether she was pushing the "we" too much, but stuck with the assumption that Orek had accepted her.

"The problem is distance. All these locations are within the same region of our planet, but the area is on a different continent and has very little transportation. It is isolated. I do not think we could get there at all with our resources. Even Corcoris' men will probably take a week to get to the first few sites, and a few days more to cover the rest. Corcoris will have other trouble, since the people of that continent have grown hostile toward the Grikorat and the core cities."

Hope fading, Sensha grasped the only plan of action available. "So your group here cannot get to the humans and this Corcoris has a chance to?"

"That is correct."

Sensha nodded. "Then we need to check Corcoris out. We need to move quickly to get the maps to him or he will have another copy sent, and we will lose our excuse for seeing him. Have you made copies of the maps?"

"No," the second-in-command said, "but that will take no time at all."

"Then do it. I will use the cloak and mask to take the box to Corcoris, and see what we can do with him."

"Wait! Why you?" the second-in-command said, drawing a scowl from Orek.

Sensha smiled. There was no question in the universe she enjoyed answering more. "First of all, they must have realized by now that I escaped by taking the cloak and mask from your agent, which means the one who gave me the box also knows it was given to the wrong person. If he and Corcoris are working with the plani, then I will be walking into a trap, but it will not expose the rest of your group, and you would not only have copies of the maps to use, but also knowledge of Corcoris' allegiance. If you sent one of your own people, you would risk exposing your group and also reveal that I am with you. Besides all that, I believe I am the only one here with formal infiltration training, and probably the only one with experience walking into the headquarters of an enemy without breaking a sweat."

Orek looked to his second-in-command, who gave no further sign of objection, then said, "Many kentaki have underdeveloped sweat glands, including many in my team, but we accept your point. As we will have copies of the maps, we have nothing to lose and potentially another ally in the government to gain. In case you try to betray us, or you are followed back here, we will move operations to an alternate location. One of our men will wait here, watching for you. If you are not followed, he will lead you to our alternate base. If Corcoris is willing, you are to get some indication from him to bring back to us – some token or something in writing. Nothing that would implicate him if you are captured after meeting with him. Do you understand?"

Sensha nodded. She itched to get back into action, but tried not to give any hint of her impatience. After a bit more talk about the possible security around the space department headquarters, Orek was satisfied that sending Sensha was the right decision, and that he had the countermeasures in place to survive her failure.

"The only problem now is that I do not know the way to Corcoris," Sensha pointed out.

"The card!" the second-in-command suddenly burst out. "She still has the card!"

Sensha pulled out the card that had shown her the way to the rebels, almost handing it over to Orek before realizing that it was exactly what she needed. She tried to navigate the menu to see if Corcoris' location was programmed into it, but with everything in Kentaki, she was lost.

"Do you think this might have Corcoris' location in it since your contact might have been working with him?"

"It might even if they only met because of their government duties," Orek said. "Let me take a look."

The second-in-command was beside himself with anxiety. "Are you going to allow her to take that with her? Seriously?"

Exasperated, Orek said, "Not before you download everything on it and wipe out the sensitive information. Has everyone around me turned into a fresh recruit? I understand the child getting excited, but you? We cannot have our newest agent roam around in the city lost because we could not give her a map."

Orek found Corcoris in the data card, handed the card over to his second to deal with the cleaning, and soon enough, Sensha was ready to go. Box in hand, cloak and mask concealing her identity, she went back out into the streets.

Making her way to Corcoris' offices proved no trouble. The real test would be whether there would be substantial security at the entrance. Unless they were expecting her to come, Orek felt it unlikely that they would stop a member of the Grikorat. It was not the capitol building, but rather a separate ministerial office occupied solely by the Department of Space and Advanced Radiation Affairs. Since the space department had no competition on Kentak and enjoyed practically universal popular support in its mission, its security was nonexistent compared to similar agencies on Earth or Plani.

A crowd near the entrance forced Sensha to check her approach, but it dissipated. Either a meeting had just ended or, with the sun once again low in the sky, perhaps working hours were ending. None of those in the crowd had been wearing the cloak and mask, making Sensha feeling more confident in the exclusive privilege her costume would bring.

She walked into the building with the lofty stride she had seen other Grikorat officials adopt and, checking the card, saw that it was now showing a detailed view of the building's interior and how to get to Corcoris' office. Taking a few steps into the building, a female kentaki to her right accosted her. The kentaki had been standing by the door and, considering how stiff and awkward her walk was, she might have been waiting there for hours. She got Sensha's attention with a tentative "excuse me, your honor," but closed the distance between them before continuing.

"Are you here to see Minister Corcoris?"

"Yes," Sensha said, realizing that it was all right to speak through the translator since all the masked plani must do so as well.

"Come with me."

Sensha doubted that this was just normal treatment for Grikorat officials. Corcoris was expecting someone in official garb to appear with a box – with *the* box. Sensha had no idea whether it meant things were going well or badly, and feared that she would only find out when face-to-face with Rivel's malevolent grin. With every step she took away from the entrance, her apprehension grew, and she looked around every corner expecting signs that the dreaded captain was preparing to spring his trap.

This time Rivel did not appear, and Sensha was soon in Corcoris' office, which was surprisingly on the ground floor rather than the top of the building. The space minister remained in cloak-and-mask until the two of them were alone, then took off the mask but left the hood up. Sensha held her breath as he did so, remembering the last time a Grikorat official had been unmasked in her presence, but this time there was a genuine kentaki underneath. In fact, he looked similar to his snout-faced mask, though not as ideal in shape. His nose and mouth extended forward in a shape Sensha associated with carnivores. Since he was also more than a head taller than her, her instincts turned defensive even though everything had gone according to plan and the minister was a potential ally.

Corcoris was unsurprised by the reaction. "Relax. I believe we are on the same side, yes?"

Sensha nodded slowly, then said, "maybe," but kept her muscles tense. She wondered how he guessed her stance with the clothing so effectively masking it.

Amused, Corcoris rolled his shoulders to show that he, at least, was unconcerned. "So, my young dribrora friend found another of his kind, is that right?"

Shocked, Sensha took off her own mask to confirm Corcoris' words. "How . . . how did you know?"

"He contacted me, of course. My friend is a master at lying low and not getting himself into trouble. He says your people value this skill. I am much the same type. I have retained my position by keeping out of trouble, waiting for an opportunity to present itself. And here you are, you and your human friends."

Skeptical, Sensha said, "You are trusting me very quickly."

"And that trust is never given frivolously. You brought that box back here because you want to find the rest of the human crew. So do I. If my people approached them, they would not be trusted. The humans might think we attacked their ship, after all. With you there alongside my people, though, we will have less difficulty. I must say, I caught sight of the humans as they entered the government house yesterday, and you look more like them than like the plani. Perhaps that is why they trusted you enough to bring you on this mission?"

Sensha let that point pass as a more pressing thought came to mind. "You could have warned the humans about the danger to their ship. Do not make any excuse. You could have."

Corcoris shifted and his snout, held high before, now pointed down. "Perhaps. But would the humans have been as willing to get involved in our domestic situation with the plani? They had other reasons for being here and, with their ship intact, they would leave after finding what they wanted. Meanwhile, I would incur the wrath of the plani and no longer be in a position to help anyone. The loss of a ship weighed against the benefits . . . I did not need to think twice. I knew from the destruction of the plani ships that the crew would be able to escape. Considering the harsh realities we face on Kentak, I only feel the slightest sympathy toward those who come to exploit what we have."

Sensha relaxed. She knew all too well that scruples often had to be set aside in struggles against superior powers. Corcoris had given thought to the lives of the humans, so Sensha couldn't find fault in his decision. In fact, it was a brilliant move. In her eyes, the mark of the enemy was a disregard for life. Captain Rivel would rue the loss of the billion-dollar ship more than the death of the crew, since the former a difficult-to-replace asset while the latter was not.

Just the thought of her nemesis galvanized her into action. "Let us say that I would be willing to help you. When can we leave?"

"As soon as I have those maps, I think."

"About the maps . . . there was one that measured radiation right after the human ship exploded. It showed that the radiation came from a specific source that does not normally emit more than the background." Just as she said the words, it hit her. "I wonder . . . if you let the human ship explode just so that you could make these measurements." Shocking herself with the idea, she hoped the suggestion would not anger the minister.

Corcoris was silent for a moment, and then said, "Not just so I could make the measurements, but the ability to collect the data was a consideration."

Appreciating the honesty, Sensha said, "I think the humans would be interested in that place as well. It might be what they are looking for."

"That had occurred to me. If they are willing to help me, I will extend to them what help I can."

"There is something else." Sensha hesitated. They had spoken all this time as if Sensha was an independent agent, avoiding her association with Orek's group. She could continue leaving Orek out of it, but she felt she owed his people a part. There was no telling what resources Corcoris could bring to bear against the plani, but surely a few more willing bodies couldn't hurt with the enemy only numbering a few dozens. "I received help understanding the maps – help from a group in the city that also opposes the plani. The dribrora who saved me knew about them, but they did not realize you . . . ."

"Of course not. I know about them, though. What about them?"

"If I do not report back to them and show them that you are on their side, they will assume you betrayed me and that you are working with the plani."

"Which is exactly what I want everyone to think until I have my resources in place. Prove that I am on their side? You must be joking. What would I have to gain from that? I am afraid that, in their eyes, you will have been recaptured and I will be more of a villain that they thought I was."

The reproach in his tone stung so much that Sensha wondered how she could have brought up the topic in the first place. Then again, her strong sense of loyalty to friends led her to try one last time on Orek's behalf. As if explaining the reason behind her mention of Orek's group, she said, "They have something important. Maybe you already know what I am talking about? They made a sort of . . . discovery."

Corcoris' eyes narrowed. "Discovery. I was not told about any such thing."

Sensha almost smiled. The dribrora were brilliant at keeping secrets, and her savior had betrayed neither of his allies. Neither would she.

"I can only say that I was shocked when I saw it and immediately thought that it could give us a way to bring down the plani without even a fight if they are responsible for it. It is . . . evidence."

Corcoris suddenly had trouble standing still, but his movements were too erratic – too choppy – to be called pacing. Sensha would have been concerned about the sanity of any plani who acted this way – flipping from calm confidence to agitation in the course of a sentence – but she made allowance for the fact that Corcoris belonged to a radically different, and perhaps inherently troubled, species. She was glad that he didn't doubt her word, though.

Stilling himself, Corcoris decided, "No, we will have to leave that for later. If I reach out to them now, it will be too risky. Reaching the humans before the plani is the priority. Do you agree?"

Sensha nodded. She opened the box, took out the maps, and handed them to Corcoris.

"Another copy of these is on its way, of course, but I appreciate the gesture. I assume this means you will work with my people?"

That was what she came here for, so why did she feel so reluctant? Sensha sighed and nodded again.

"Good. Let us get to work. You have some long journeys ahead of you and not much time in which to undertake them."

14

Hypotheses

Instead of returning with a soil sample, Sueton's aide came back with Yarun, the council leader, to the visible shock of everyone in the headquarters.

The wait had been long – so long that Sueton rested in a back room, the humans had their first taste of local food – which somehow proved safe and even nutritious – and they still had time to wait in mind-numbing boredom.

Sueton said "what is taking so long?" right before the arrival of the aide with Yarun. His apprehension at the sight of the council leader caused the tint of his skin to darken. That soon cleared and he regained his composure, switching from private mode to public. Fletcher guessed that Sueton would either demote or fire the aide as soon as Yarun left.

"Why Yarun," Sueton greeted with a plastered smile, "I honestly never thought I would see you in here. I am not even sure what the protocol is."

"As if you were ever one for protocol. I never expected to have to come here, either. Your assistant here was very . . . persistent in his desire to bring some dirt to you – a request no one had expected to receive. When the receptionist at the Agriculture Institute could not agree to provide it, he asked the scientists working on the project. When they said they did not have the authority, he went to the institute administrator. When he could not allow it, your assistant had the temerity to put the request before the city council. And that is why I am here. I am . . . curious about why you have made this request. You never seemed bothered about evidence before, so why start now?"

Yarun must have had a fierce sense of her own invulnerability to speak this way in Sueton's office. The various staffers, near fanatics in their belief that the council and all government officials were in league with aliens, were all turning unpleasant shades as if barely restraining the impulse to rip Yarun apart.

Sueton was too accustomed to the bitter jabs for them to bother him. "Curious, council leader? If it was just that, I would have expected you to send a letter rejecting permission and asking for a reason. You are here because you know why I asked for the soil sample – I wonder if these humans may be able to tell us something about the problem. But why did this have to come to you? It is only a bit of dirt, as you said. I would expect the scientists would be willing to share some. It is not as if it is difficult to find."

"Find, no. Handle, yes. The soil may be contaminated with something harmful – something we do not want spreading on this side of the river."

"May be? I do not remember hearing you ever say that, Yarun. You must mean it *is* contaminated and it *is* dangerous."

Yarun was nonplussed. "Normally, I would not tell you anything, Sueton, but I am interested in the opinions of the humans. If I try to take them away from you, stories will be concocted that would undermine this city more surely than anything in the soil, so I had to come here. However, what I have to say is not for the gossip mongers to spread around and distort," she looked around the room at the staff, "so perhaps we could speak more privately?"

Sueton was tempted to reject the request in a show of solidarity with his people, but there was concern in Yarun's voice that warned him against pushing his populist image too far. Yarun had already made a concession by coming down here in person to share the information she had. Nodding to the council leader, Sueton led her, the humans, and Kordon to a side room.

As was her habit, Yarun skipped over all prologue and went straight to the trouble. "Our researchers were careful throughout the collection and examination of the soil except at one point. The only time one of them came in physical contact with the soil was when he accidentally flipped the tray he was examining and some of the soil dropped on his left hand. It was no more than a pinch of soil, but it ate through his skin and to the bone before he could wash it out. The water supply for the lab is contained, so please do not go starting rumors about the water. Anyway, the hand is healing slowly, but the researcher is otherwise in good health."

Sueton shrugged. "This sounds like some strong acid in the soil."

"The acidity of the soil is normal. The worst of it is that the soil does not stay still at night, but shifts like sand in the wind, even in the lab. It was also at night that our researcher was injured. He swears that he did not flip the tray, but that the soil made a sudden shift that toppled it."

"So what are we talking about? Ghosts? I hope your scientists have better answers."

Before Yarun could answer, Fletcher said, "I don't get it. When we walked from our crash site to the city, we spent a night out in the open. It was miserable, but our skin's fine."

Kordon translated, then immediately replied in both Kentaki and Plani. "Whatever it is has not come across the river. The town and wastelands are on one side of the river. Our croplands are in the watershed, on the other side. Which means . . . ." He looked to Yarun to continue.

"Which means we must be careful not to let those soil samples loose. Luckily, it cannot be transported by air, otherwise everyone in this city would be pock-marked with wounds. The malignancy in the soil clearly has a reaction to water, though only if in contact with it for a long time. Our researcher took many minutes before he was sure his wound was not becoming worse. The croplands are irrigated and moist, so it cannot be that the malignancy is easily washed away, or it would not have caused trouble in the first place. We were planning to try controlled flooding of the plains, but now the stories of monsters on the other side of the river have taken hold and our workers are unwilling to cross the river. Even though it is said that the monsters only attack at night, our workers will not risk themselves during the day. They do not trust that they are being given the whole truth, you see, and in this case I cannot blame them."

"Monsters," Ethan murmured in deep thought. "I guess . . . that the monster is really the flesh-eating soil, right? How sure are we that it is only active at night?"

"We have had people on the other side of the river during the daytime with no ill effects, but none have returned if they were on the other side at night. Whether the soil took them, there is no way to be sure, but it is likely. The malignancy in the soil is enough to deal with. We do not need a new predator to make matters worse, and I cannot see why the predator would not also be harmed by the soil."

Ethan was now in full swing. "At night . . . there were some serious winds at night. Any idea why the wind is like that?"

Sueton and Yarun began answering, but Kordon beat them to it. "The Furintal Howl, it is called. We know from our satellites that a region of high pressure builds up over the day in the mountains north of here. Why it happens, we do not know. It is difficult to send anyone there to investigate, and the area is heavily wooded so that it is impossible to see anything from the air. Legend is that the wind is the forest breathing out."

"Mountains? Forest?" Fletcher repeated. "I didn't think there was much of that on Kentak."

Kordon was starting to see where the questions were going, and his voice grew excited. "Now that you mention it, it is the only such formation on the planet, and lies about a twenty day walk north of here. And I think I know what Ethan will ask next – you want to know if the winds have increased in strength since the plani came. The answer is yes."

"Is there any way to tell if the slight radiation increase Sueton mentioned also comes from there?" Ethan asked.

Kordon looked to Yarun for the answer, but the council leader remained silent. When Kordon failed to grasp what the silence meant, she said, "I do not know. The Grikorat has the resources to look into it, but we do not, and they have trouble sharing information. To some degree, radiation always follows the air patterns."

The thread of the conversation escaping his grasp, Sueton said, "What are you saying? What is this all about?"

"This is just an idea," Ethan said, "but what if the wind carries something that activates whatever is in the soil? Maybe some chemical from the forest. That would explain why it's only active at night."

"Perhaps," Yarun said, "but so might a great many things. We could . . . build a greenhouse around a portion of a field, filter the air getting in, and see if the plants will grow. Do you have any other reason to believe there is a connection?"

Ethan shook his head. "Just a hypothesis. I have another thing I'm wondering about, though. I tested all the food we ate to see if it was safe for us, and it was, but all of the plants I scanned on the way in were useless. Could I get a sample of each of the plants the food was made from?"

"What does that have to do with anything?" Sueton asked.

Ethan didn't hear the frustration in Sueton's voice. "I don't know. But this is all about what is happening to your plants, right? I just have a hunch that getting a better read on them might give me some ideas."

Yarun's wrinkles seemed to smooth and, as she turned from Ethan to Sueton, she looked a decade younger. "Well, Sueton, they are your guests, so I suppose you have to send that persistent lackey of yours to the fermentors to get what he wants."

"Now wait . . . ."

"Fermentors?" Ethan shouted in a high pitch.

Yarun smiled softly. "Yes. We use the word generally to describe a large number of chemical changes we make to our food. Long ago, we were able to eat our food raw or by normal cooking, but it was extremely unhealthy. The nutrition was so low, we had to work a great deal of land to feed only a meager population. We have various ways to process our food to improve its suitability and nutrition – some millennia old, others only centuries. Over that time, our bodies have grown accustomed to the processed food and we can no longer digest any of our staple crops raw. Neither can you, I suppose. Because processing can take months and even years, we have a store of food even though our crops have failed. Now Sueton, stop looking so sour and get the samples as the humans have asked. Here is a release form for the soil sample as well. One of our ecologists will have to bring it to make sure it is handled properly. I do not know if we will get the answers we are looking for, but after hearing these humans, I am willing to give them what they need to try. Our own people are so accustomed to things like the Furintal Howl that they would never see the connection between them and the nighttime activity in the soil."

Trying to hide his inability to follow the ideas, Sueton grabbed the release form with a flourish, peered out the door to his aide, and explained the new errand. When he returned to his seat, his lips were tight.

While they waited, Yarun took to asking questions about Earth, keeping everyone except the restless Sueton interested. To Fletcher, only minutes passed before the aide returned with the goods and the uncertain scientist in tow. Instead of leaving the room after making his delivery, though, the assistant whispered something into Sueton's ear.

"What?" Sueton said, alarmed. The aide took it to mean that he had spoken too softly and leaned forward to repeat his words, but Sueton pushed him away.

Straightening himself out, the politician said to the room, "it seems as if my people are a bit worried about our talking with the council leader here. Word of our meeting has already reached the street. I need to go calm them down. I will . . . have my assistant here listen in on whatever you discover and report it to me."

Fletcher was surprised that Sueton was giving this aide such responsibility. It looked as if the politician's office had some gossips, so that Sueton could only trust this one assistant. Certainly, as the aide sat down at the table, he pulled out a notepad and was ready to earnestly perform his new assignment.

Yarun had nothing but apprehension on her face as Sueton departed. Fletcher deduced that she was worried about Sueton's ability to control the monster he had created. With just a hint of all these feelings leaking into her voice, she said, "go on, humans, show us what you can do."

Eyes already fixed on the plants brought in, Ethan passed the bioscanner over them and made careful mental notes. He thought about the results for a few moments, but couldn't hide his excitement.

"They're almost edible – better than the plants we saw coming in – but they wouldn't be nutritious at all for us. Their metabolic system is just different enough to make them useless. According to this, they wouldn't suit any of the plani-like ISC species, including humans, eldrandii, asofi . . . you get the idea. Whatever you do to ferment them must take the useless chemicals and make them worth eating," Ethan concluded. "Now, about the soil."

The ecologist cleared her throat. She spoke as if unused to communicating verbally, and her halting words forced Kordon to pause in the middle of his translation. "I . . . the sun has set . . . if you notice . . . ," she pointed to the soil in the sealed dish, and it was shifting very slowly.

"Well, look at that," Ethan said amused. "What direction do you think it's moving in, Fletcher?"

Having followed Ethan's thinking better than Sueton, Fletcher said, "probably to the south. Either totally away from those mountains, or towards them."

Ethan nodded. "As if they could feel that Furintal Howl even in here, which means a greenhouse probably wouldn't work. I think we can still use the bioscanner if we keep the soil in its container." He passed the device over the dirt, and read the result aloud. "By mass, it's mostly dense metal. I'm not sure what soil around here is normally, but there are biochemicals in this soil, so the . . . the malignancy, like the council leader calls it, doesn't break everything down. I wonder what it attacks."

"Could this dense metal *be* the malignancy that is responsible?" Yarun asked.

"I think so. I really do think so. We've got to try my other idea. Is there any way we can put a bit of the plants and a bit of the food we ate into the dish on top of the soil?"

The ecologist pulled back from the soil sample as if wanting nothing to do with it. "It is dangerous . . . if it is not contained . . . cannot know what will happen."

Yarun looked ready to pound the table, but held back considering the precarious position of the dish. "Listen you," the council leader said, "I had you come here so you could handle the sample properly. Do your job, or we will find someone else and your failure will be noted." Then, to Sueton's aide, she said, "get us a scrap of any food made from the plants here."

When the aide seemed to ignore her order – in fact, ignore her entirely – Yarun barked, "I am still council leader in this city and I demand the respect of my station, even here in the headquarters of the great Sueton. Now go do as I say, or may all your ancestors frown down on you. I guarantee that nothing of moment will occur until you return."

Bristling, the aide shot up and left the room. In his absence, Yarun remarked, "it is getting more and more difficult every day. When I have to threaten them with eternal damnation to get them to fetch water, I will have to retire." Kordon translated, punctuating every other word with giggles.

When the aide returned with the required crumbs, his attitude was markedly different. He closed the door in a hurry and leaned against it for a few seconds, as if afraid of what might try to come through after him. He did not sit down, as if wondering whether sitting at the table, or even staying in the room, was safe.

That brought Yarun to her feet. "How bad is it out there?"

"Candidate Sueton knows his people," the aide intoned with rehearsed confidence.

Yarun groaned. "That bad, eh? Hurry, human. Your arrival has thrown off a delicate balance."

But it was the ecologist who had to hurry, and she was so hesitant that nothing could make her move any faster. When the first plant sample introduced into the dish quickly melted away into the surging soil, she once again leaped back from it, afraid that the dirt would next take aim at the hand that fed it. It did not. In the ecologist's place, Ethan quickly rushed in with a bioscanner to get a reading. He ultimately shook his head.

"Nothing worth mentioning. Keep going."

The ecologist looked at Ethan with oppressed eyes, but did as was demanded. With nothing new regardless of which plant was added, Ethan decided to alternate the plant bits and food crumbs. From the very first crumb, everyone understood why Ethan had wanted to do the experiment. Even Sueton's aide failed to maintain his impassiveness.

"The soil is not destroying the food."

Ethan looked around triumphantly. "So this fermentation process of yours inoculates the food from the attack. Maybe the malignancy is a hyperactive form of whatever ferments your food, though my scan doesn't pick up any edible products being produced, so maybe that idea's . . . wrong. Anyway, if you didn't realize the fermentation process does this already, council leader, then this is a major breakthrough!"

"No, we did not realize it," Yarun said, initial delight at the experiment's success melting away. "Now, if only we could ferment our population and pre-ferment our crops, we would all be safe."

"I'm guessing that won't work," Fletcher said.

"No."

The ecologist sealed the volatile soil sample back in its container just as Sueton burst into the room, eyes wild.

"I tried to tell them," Sueton said, shaking his head. He closed the door behind him, but there was commotion outside. "But they did not want to listen. So . . . so I told them what they wanted to hear." If not for his skin's lack of pores, Sueton would have been sweating. He seemed to be overheating.

"What do you mean, what they wanted to hear?" Yarun said, eyes warning everyone in the room.

Sueton kept shaking his head as if trying to get something out of his skull. "You know how it is, Yarun. I just felt the words, and they came out. The crowd cheered, so I went on." Then, latching onto a definite thought, he stilled himself. "I told them," he pointed to the humans to show that he was no longer talking about the mob, "I told them that it could go well or badly for them, but that I would be fine either way. Well, it is bad. I . . . I had no idea . . . people had grown this desperate." He swallowed. "But it is done."

Just having tasted the thrill of success with Ethan's experiment moments ago, Fletcher found it hard to grasp this new turn. "So . . . what does this mean? I mean, what's happening?"

"It means," Kordon said, "that there is a mob outside that wants to kill us."

"Oh, hell. Not again."

15

Expedition

Sensha soon realized that Corcoris had ears all over the capital. Treating her like his most valuable asset, he kept her close by as he conducted his regular business, though she had to stay silent and under the mask and cloak throughout. Since his official work – to bring the kentaki to the stars – had been undermined by the arrival of the plani and declining political interest, he spent most of his time and resources trying to neutralize the plani influence. From what Sensha saw, the minister was trying to do this in two ways. First, he fomented distrust between the kentaki Grikorat members and the plani members behind the scenes – entirely at the personal level. It went so far that the plani had come to rely on his people for information on who to trust with key assignments. The second way was to try to break the communication barrier created by the peculiarities of the planet Kentak, which prevented the planet from sending messages via hyperspace relay rather than just receiving them. For that, he was interested in finally discovering the source of the problem.

The arrival of the Earth ship had been a boon to all his efforts. Among the kentaki in the government, two factions formed as soon as the Earth ship announced its arrival in orbit. Those who took a status quo approach supported the plani recommendations for how to handle the humans – essentially, to hand the newcomers over to the plani. The other side wanted to treat the humans with more caution, and to avoid putting Kentak in the middle of any dispute between two greater powers. The latter view required a lot more political finesse, though, and the pro-plani way won out. Members of both sides sent messages through Corcoris' people because they saw him as neutral and discrete. They didn't dare speak openly on the capitol grounds with the plani there to listen.

The space ministry's unique combination of low profile and high regard was the key to Corcoris' success. He did his best to make his department look as inconsequential as the plani wanted it to be, while maintaining the noble heritage it represented. As a result, the plani treated him like an obsolete hanger-on – a bureaucrat simply interested in securing regular paychecks for his people, running something akin to a museum or monument. They never visited, and rarely interfered.

Corcoris hand-selected his staff, weeding out those unlikely to share his vision of patient opposition, over a period of years. Standing beside the minister opened Sensha's eyes to the kinds of games that could be played by a political survivalist. One report, though, surprised even Corcoris.

"We have word from the government house," an analyst said, reading from a summary of various end-of-day messages, spy accounts, and general staff observations. "Earth Captain Pierce is not well. She is responsive during the daytime, but increasingly unsettled at night, seeming delirious. Her activity at night is making her weary in the morning so that she spends much of the day sleeping."

Not sure how to digest the information, Corcoris asked, "how are the Grikorat taking this?"

The analyst flipped a few pages. "There is more nervousness about detaining the human captain. Even among the pro-plani contingent, they are quieting their support for the current arrangement. Those who support treating the humans with equal respect are becoming vocal even in mixed company. They insist that it is not too late to apologize and to salvage our relations with Earth."

"Any observations about how the plani are taking it?"

"Only a few, but they seem to be in general agreement that the plani are growing nervous as well. Speculation is that they detained Pierce in the hope that she would agree to an exchange with them, but in her current condition, she cannot agree to anything."

"Exchange. That means she has something of value except for her ship. That should be pointed out to our Grikorat members. It means she can easily secure a return to Earth and our treatment of her will become known to her people. Continue."

"The plani were hoping she would give in quickly since she has no choice, but now that is dubious. Worse, they are afraid that the illness might be life-threatening – certainly our own people are deeply worried about that – and no one wants the death of the human captain on their hands. The old bluster that Earth will simply ignore it as another failed Kentak mission has disappeared."

Corcoris thought for a moment. "How to make use of this . . . ," he mumbled. He looked at Sensha and said, "maybe we can get more support." To his analyst, he ordered, "have our people whisper in some ears, suggesting that the human captain should be placed in official medical care. Tell them that the official line should be that the Grikorat had her in medical care from the start. As a gesture of goodwill to her three companions – to encourage them to go along with this story, I mean – they should be given their freedom. The plani business is with the captain herself, after all, and there is neither anywhere for the humans to go, nor any way they can contact their world for help. We want to make it clear that her three companions present no threat to anyone, and can be used to demonstrate the goodwill of the Grikorat without any risk."

"Will they not simply stay with their captain?" the analyst asked.

"Without any other options, yes. And you should make that clear to our politicians. Do you understand what you need to do?"

The analyst stopped looking through his notes and, snapping to attention, said, "Yes, minister."

"Good. Dismissed."

Once alone with Corcoris, Sensha asked, "Do you really think we can get those three to join us? They are very loyal to the captain, and I cannot see them leaving her."

"But they will want to find the survivors from the ship. They will know that their captain would want them to help the rest of the crew. I expect one will stay with the captain while the others will join us. We will have to delay your departure until they come in. I wanted you to leave before dawn, but perhaps it will be tomorrow night."

"Will the Grikorat make the decision that quickly?"

"I think so. Even the plani should support changing the story to medical care, and they will not be able to see how two or three humans could substantially destabilize the situation. Not without help. It is not as if they will have the ability to go find the rest of the human crew, will they? They do not have the necessary information." Corcoris pointed suggestively to the maps.

Sensha was not as confident. "I cannot rid myself of the feeling that Captain Rivel noticed your ability to collect the information on those maps, and will try to stop us. Or worse, try to use us."

"Good. I like a healthy dose of paranoia in those working with me. Let me worry about throwing Rivel off. We need to convince the humans to trust us, but I do not want to send you to the government house. Losing you would undermine my effort entirely, while not having the humans will simply make it more difficult. Any ideas how I might convey that my people are trustworthy?"

If she was honest about it, Sensha realized that she had not gained the trust of the humans at all. Still, they would know that she was a dedicated enemy of Rivel, and maybe that was enough. But how would she convey that she was with Corcoris voluntarily? The landing party knew very little about her – really only what they had seen of her in the landing shuttle and on the way into the city – so there was a very limited spectrum of shared knowledge between them and her. Thinking about that time, a memory startled her.

"Oh! The pilot! The shuttle pilot stayed behind. He should still be there."

"Excellent. But he will be unwilling to leave the shuttle without Captain Pierce's orders. We might fetch him on the way out. On the matter of . . . ."

"I know. I am thinking." She continued to look back. "There are a few things. It has been on my mind lately, but I could use a drink."

"Certainly. I can get a . . . ."

"No. Blood. You can tell them that they need to bring their friend's supplies because she needs a drink, or something like that."

"Ah, I see." He didn't look comfortable with the topic, so he moved on. "What else? That might be too obvious, since Captain Rivel would also know of your need."

"Tell . . . tell Sean that the place might look like the Sahara, but there was plenty to get a feel for before we should have met with the kentaki officials. It is about something he said as we were on our way into the city."

"Good. Specific. Anything else?"

"Sean did most of the talking . . . tell him that the kentaki might look disgusting, but they are more like you than you think."

Not sure whether to be offended or amused, Corcoris went on, "if there is nothing better than those, it will do. I guess you do not have any tokens on you that the humans would recognize?"

"No." The only things she carried with her were not for show or sharing.

"Very well. Get some rest, then. You can have the resting room adjacent to this office through that door. I will sleep in here. I often fall asleep in my chair, anyway."

Honored by the offer of the minister's own accommodation, Sensha thanked him and wasted no time. Unless her instincts were failing her, she would be safe for the night, and there was no telling when her next chance for sleep would be.

The next morning was calm but expectant at the space ministry. No one walking in could suspect anything, but the staff knew that they were putting together something big. There was suddenly more work than they usually saw in a week. Most of it was requisition and information gathering, but some of Corcoris' orders were so obscure, Sensha couldn't understand the reason for them, and was not at liberty to ask. The government was not the only power broker in the city, and the other players – businesses, gangs, and social groups among others – all had a part to play in the way Corcoris ran his shadow government.

The only real asset the space ministry had, apart from the space program itself, was three aircraft. In fact, the space ministry was in charge of the only government aircraft available to Grikorat officials. The Grikorat only had legal control of a small, though populous, area of Kentak. It was the most powerful nation on the planet, but its representatives had no problem visiting their constituents using land vehicles. The space ministry was the only department of the Grikorat that received funding from all the countries on Kentak, and therefore required the means to visit its disparate benefactors and to carry back parts manufactured in distant locations.

Everything else for the *Azar* crew recovery effort had to be procured from outside the ministry – preferably under the rest of the government's radar. That meant a host of black market deals and secret negotiations for everything from food, radio devices, weapons, and survival kits. Corcoris' people each had a piece of the puzzle, but no idea about the full picture. Nevertheless, they went about their work with dedication and got the mission together by noon. By the time the final readiness reports were in, Sensha was sure this would be the best prepared mission she had ever been on.

"We have contacted the landing shuttle pilot," Corcoris said to Sensha after reading the memo handed to him. "We explained the situation to him and what we are trying to do about it. He was so grateful for the update on the captain's situation that he did not seem to doubt our word. I decided it would be best if he stayed out of the picture, acting as a wildcard – a means of quick escape if we need him. We gave him a local radio and the frequency we use. He agreed on the condition that we bring a member of the *Azar* crew out to him to confirm our story within two days. Otherwise, he will make his own decisions about when to intervene."

Corcoris just finished the explanation when the final piece of the puzzle requested entrance. The minister's main political agent was a dark character with eyes barely open and the expression of a janitor hard at work. Entering to report on the machinations within the Grikorat, the agent said in a raspy voice, "We had the votes with plenty to spare, minister. We did not have to stick our necks out, so no one knows the push came from us. The three humans except for Captain Pierce will be allowed liberty so long as they remain in the capital city."

Corcoris waved away the limitation. "No problem there. I suppose someone clever pointed out that allowing them to leave the country might put their technology in the hands of another nation?"

"That was the argument, sir. As expected, the humans have so far chosen to remain in the government house. I imagine you have different plans for them."

"Now, now," Corcoris wagged a finger, "you are far too dangerous already. I cannot have you using your imagination. That would be too much."

Without a muscle on his face moving, the agent said, "of course not, sir. I could not contain myself. This is the most excitement we have had in a long time."

Corcoris dismissed him and arranged to get the humans from the government house.

"What about the dribrora who allowed me to escape?" Sensha asked after the room was clear. "Should we have him along as well?" She desperately wanted to see him again and to thank him properly for him efforts. Instinctively, she also felt that the two dribrora on this planet, so far from home, should stick together.

"No. Nice as that would be, he is being watched after the incident with you. Captain Rivel probably guesses his secret already. Contacting him would draw too much attention."

"Rivel must plan on following the humans wherever they go . . . ."

". . . which is why we have arranged for kentaki with human facemasks and replicas of human clothes to act as doubles along the way, multiple decoy vehicles, and we are doing everything we can to make it seem like the Defense Ministry is responsible for the whole affair. The defense minister has angered the plani by insisting they allow his people access to the humans. Of course, he wants to see if the humans have information on weapons technology that he can use and he is oblivious to the fact that the plani find the idea . . . counter to their own interests. The defense minister is uniquely apolitical in both neutrality and acumen, and the plani will be all too ready to believe that he is responsible for the removal of the humans from the government house. I doubt any others in the Grikorat will defend him – he has done many unpleasant things to get what he wants. We have taken other precautions as well, but I hope that much is enough to convince you we have been diligent in our preparations."

Sensha nodded, stung once again by the rebuke in Corcoris' voice. No one had been able to tell her off before – not to any effect, anyway. She didn't like his ability to influence her, but wondered whether it was simply the mark of a great leader – people valued his respect and feared his condemnation.

Sooner than she could have imagined, Sean and Jaidee entered Corcoris' office. They looked neither happy nor willing, so Sensha guessed that Captain Pierce, during her daytime lucidity, had ordered them to take this chance. Their expressions grew more complicated when the door closed behind them and Sensha was able to reveal her face. Unable to decide whether to be startled, wary, or relieved, Sean managed to show all three emotions on his face. Jaidee was almost as stone-faced as Corcoris' political agent, except with a malevolent stare instead of barely open eyes.

As usual, Sean did the talking. "Well, they gave us every reason to think you were working with 'em. I don't know . . . wasn't sure . . . why're you wearing that?"

Sensha explained the particulars of her own escape, how she got Corcoris' maps, and the conversation that led her to work with the minister. She left out Orek's organization without hiding the fact that she was omitting details.

Sean ignored the gaps in her narrative. "Okay, so here we are. I've gotta hand it to the people here – I've never seen so much misdirection in one day. I mean, they took us into the sewers – can you believe that? Found out the hard way that they actually have sewers. And being strip-searched was fun. Boy, did their eyes bug out when they saw how . . . how well put together us humans are. So, are we really trying to find the rest of the crew?"

"That is the plan," Corcoris said. Sensha nodded in support.

Sean turned his back to Corcoris and faced Sensha directly. His eyes aimed straight at hers, he asked, "do we want these people to find the crew? Do you know what type of people we'll be putting our men and women in the hands of?"

At first, Sensha couldn't answer. Did she really trust Corcoris? She had accepted the minister's line with little question, maybe because his goals matched hers, but what would he do with a contingent of humans? It would have to be for his own political benefit, so the question was whether his goals were compatible with those of the *Azar*'s crew. She didn't know.

Putting things another way, she said, "If we do not go with Corcoris to rescue them, the plani will. Rivel must also have tracked the escape pods and he is probably already sending teams for your crewmates. They could use any humans they capture to convince Captain Pierce to agree to what they want. Or . . . or maybe one of the crew will be able to give the plani what they want even if Pierce does not agree, and torturing the captives might get the information out of them."

"Torture's not the plani way," Sean said, less than confidently.

Sensha sniffed, wordlessly reminding Sean that she had far more experience with what the plani were capable of. He took her meaning and said to Corcoris, "All right. I guess you have the info and the resources, so we'll go along with you. Any hint of something I don't like, though . . . ."

"As I said to your dribrora friend here, I appreciate and expect healthy paranoia among those I work with."

"Good, 'cause you're going to get a whole lot of it from the two of us."

In an effort to soothe tensions as well as out of genuine curiosity, Sensha asked, "How is Captain Pierce? Do you know what is wrong with her?"

Sean shifted with unease, but the question did calm the fire in his voice. "I don't think any of us knows much more than first aid, and we're definitely not psychiatrists. Anyway . . . you don't need to spend much time with the captain to figure out that she doesn't think like everyone else. She's always had trouble sleeping and comes up with some of her best ideas at night. It's almost as if that's gone haywire – like her brain is getting overloaded. She sleeps off the strain during the day."

Sensha had never heard of anything like that. She had expected something like night terrors or trauma echoes, but Sean would certainly recognize those if he had seen them.

Detecting a break in the conversation, Corcoris took the chance to move things along. "If there are no objections, then, let us do what Captain Pierce would no doubt want us to do. If you will follow me, the expedition to reunite your crew is ready to launch."

16

Across the River

This time, the crowd was firm in its plan for Ethan, Fletcher, and Kordon.

The night was cloudy and the sky had a purplish hue, giving the atmosphere a less claustrophobic feel than the events about to unfold warranted. The people of the town, accustomed to the harsh winds after sunset, were fully dressed in protective cloaks and the like, while the humans and their only kentaki friend were left to shiver, barely able to speak. Of course, they didn't have to say a word and the crowd would not listen to a defense anyway. With hundreds of flashlights pointed at them and the path ahead, the mob marched them to the edge of town – the wrong edge.

The procession stopped at the iron bridge spanning the river between the town and its plagued croplands. The dim light made it impossible to tell whether the movement across the river was due to the heavy wind pushing the soil, or if the soil rippled with a purpose of its own. No one had any illusions, though – the croplands held death.

"Unless . . . ," Ethan managed to muse, "Unless we had steel boots, or maybe plastic, since the stuff wouldn't eat through the inorganic stuff. The soil sample was on glass, so that would work, too. I think the soles of my shoes are real rubber, though, but maybe it'll be like the processed food. If there's just a layer of something synthetic, that would be safer. What about yours, Fletcher?"

"Rubber . . . probably," Fletcher said through chattering teeth. He really had no idea what his shoes were made out of.

"Kordon?"

But Kordon couldn't hear over the angry murmurs of the crowd, which confused the translator headset. Fletcher had seen little to no sign of plastic on Kentak, at least in this small town, so he doubted the kentaki had gotten down to making shoes of synthetic material. Still, if their material processing had the same effect as their food processing, their shoes might be soil-safe. The possibility that his shoes might shield him from the soil malignancy gave Fletcher some hope. They didn't know what the soil actually ate through. As long as they kept their bare skin away from the soil, there was a chance they would survive.

Then he remembered the ferocious predator rumored to be on the other side of the river, and the hope faded.

With everyone gathered at the riverside, a kentaki unknown to Fletcher and remarkable only in height – he looked about seven feet tall – began to speak. Kordon was unable to translate, being either paralyzed from fright or simply unwilling to give voice to the vicious words. Neither Ethan nor Fletcher needed the translation. They were going to be sent across the bridge and, if they didn't get killed by the horrors infesting the croplands, that would only prove that they were the cause of the problem. Fletcher now saw the kentaki pull out weapons – half the crowd was suddenly armed – and he realized that there would be no possibility of survival, no matter what their shoes were made of.

Would there be a chance to run away? Some of the weapons looked like guns, but nothing sophisticated. Attempting escape was the best chance they had once on the other side of the river. Fletcher tried to convey the plan to Ethan silently, but Ethan's eyes were transfixed on the river, bridge, and croplands ahead of them.

As they took their first steps onto the bridge, Kordon started to struggle and plead. At one point, he stood firm and made a speech in his defense before a member of the mob started firing pellets at his feet. Steps away from the deceptively innocuous dirt, Kordon dropped to his knees and begged.

Fletcher felt horrible at not being able to support the only kentaki who they had been able to trust. He longed to say that Kordon was simply a translator and not part of any plot – that the humans would accept their fate, but the kentaki should spare their own man. But there was no chance, especially since Kordon himself would need to translate the words, undermining what little effect they could have had.

A pair of huge kentaki with the same stature as the mob leader picked up Kordon, threw him onto the poisoned ground, then drew back a safe distance. Kordon was on the ground flat on his belly with bare skin on his arms and legs in contact with the dirt.

At first, nothing happened. Just as Fletcher began wondering if the soil was actually safe and the sample brought in by the ecologist was a fluke, Kordon leapt up from the ground as if bitten by something. He started scratching and clawing himself frantically. Fletcher could see what looked like burn marks on Kordon's arms and, remembering the story of the researcher's hand, he shouted, "Throw yourself into the river! Whatever it is doesn't like water!"

But the way Kordon was clutching himself, it was clear the malignancy had already burrowed deep into him and was eating him from the inside out. The kentaki's panic prevented him from hearing any advice. His naturally expressive face was contorted in anguish, with muscles bulging and twisting and eyes flowing with tears. Fletcher wanted to turn away, but couldn't.

Then, with Kordon starting to cough blood, the convulsions stopped and he collapsed to his knees. A grey liquid started to drip out of his arms – out of the burn marks – making an inches-wide puddle on the ground in front of him. Kordon was still alive and conscious, but in visible shock. No one watching believed that the end of the spasms meant that the malignancy had spared him, and the mob waited in silent fascination for the finishing blow.

In his churning stomach, Fletcher knew it was time for the beast to appear, but the form it took caught everyone – mob and humans alike – by surprise. The darkness made it difficult to see what was happening at first, as the ripples in the soil focused in on the puddle and more grey liquid accumulated. The malignancy was coming together like the full force of an ant hive converging on a bounty. The puddle grew into an iridescent metallic mound, then took shape. The indistinct grey goo morphed into a body with four legs and a head.

"It . . . it looks almost like a wolf," Fletcher said aghast. "Why would it . . . ."

"Nanobots! Of course!" Ethan shouted with so much inappropriate enthusiasm that it put the kentaki closest to him on guard. As usual, he didn't notice. "Why didn't I think of it before? We might be able to fix this!"

"I . . . I don't think we're going to get the chance," Fletcher said.

The nanobot wolf closed in on its target and, as Ethan pointlessly tried to plead with the kentaki who couldn't understand a word he was trying to say, Kordon was ripped to shreds in seconds by teeth stronger than steel. Kordon's scream was cut short when the beast snapped his neck. Before Fletcher could catch his breath, all that was left of Kordon was a pile of bones in water. The wolf melted back into the soil and, in its diffuse form, digested the disintegrated pieces of its prey.

Finally realizing that trying to convince the kentaki was futile, Ethan turned to see the last moments of the scene. He shook his head in disbelief, then said, "why . . . why didn't it just cross the bridge as a wolf? Why doesn't it just attack us right now?"

Fletcher didn't hear him. Any hope that the crowd would be so horrified by what had happened that it would spare the humans was dashed when the kentaki launched into a vicious cheer. The whole thing had turned into blood-sport – entertainment fit for the coliseum. And luckily enough, the audience already had more wolf-fodder lined up.

Forming a haphazard plan, Fletcher decided to take the chance that his shoes would protect him, and to walk onto the soil voluntarily. If he survived, he would make a dash for it, hoping the darkness would give him enough cover and keep him from getting shot in the back.

But before he could take his first step, he felt a pair of sturdy arms lift him a foot above the bridge and, just like Kordon, he was thrown to the bot-infested soil. A second later, Ethan was beside him. The rough dirt scraped their hands and face as they slid across it and, feeling the wounds, Fletcher knew it must be too late to save himself from infection. There was still a chance he could get to the river in time. He couldn't swim, but maybe dunking the infected areas close to the bank would be enough. Of course, if he survived, the kentaki would promptly shoot him, but he could only deal with one threat at a time.

Once again, his reaction time was too slow, and as he propped himself up on his hands to get up off the ground, he felt a stabbing pinprick in his palm. He yelled with pain, looked at his palm fearing the worst, but instead of the burn marks he had seen on Kordon, he saw only the scrapes from the slide and a tiny point of blood. Thoughts of the river forgotten, Fletcher could only wonder what would happen now, remembering Kordon's convulsions. He held his breath, waiting for the attack from within.

It didn't come. Instead, the grey goo leaked out from his palms and fell to the ground. The liquid also oozed out of a cut on his chin, tickled him as it snaked down his skin, then exited out from the bottom of his pants and over his shoes. He saw it do the same with Ethan.

Wasting no time in thought, he grabbed Ethan's wrist, pulled his companion up, and started running away from the bridge as fast as his legs could carry him. One of the armed Kentaki fired at them wildly as they bolted away, not landing a shot within five feet of them. The rest of the crowd was too stunned, not really expecting the humans to survive after Kordon's gruesome death, and before the mob leader could rally them, Fletcher and Ethan covered enough distance to blend into the night.

The human pair kept running, not knowing that the kentaki weapons were generally cheap since there was no local opportunity to hunt, and that no one had an infrared scope or any night vision. Ethan was soon the one pulling Fletcher, as the latter's muscles tightened from the strain. The cramping in his legs eventually brought him tumbling to the ground, and if he had not been so used to the feeling, he would have sworn that the nanobots had attacked him, after all.

Still worried that the kentaki would find some way to kill them, Fletcher used the goggles perched on his forehead to get a look at what the crowd was doing. They were only about three hundred meters away, so he kept himself low, trying not to think about the nanobots. Ethan followed Fletcher's lead, his lack of breath mercifully keeping him from talking.

The kentaki had quickly given up trying to shoot at the humans, and were now circling around the mob leader, who was probably focusing their anger on new targets. Fletcher thought that the tall kentaki was taking over Sueton's role – getting the crowd angry at some distant adversary so that they would back his ambitions – but then Sueton himself was invited to speak. There was no mistaking the plastic complexion, even through the artificial magnification of the goggles. Showing no regret at the death of a potential ally or embarrassment at the escape of two others, the politician was his normal rabble-rousing self. He had stayed in the shadows as Kordon, Fletcher, and Ethan were tossed across the bridge, hoping that would be enough to keep his hands clean of the events. Now, he was back to his normal tricks, pursuing his rise to power.

He whispered to Ethan, "let's stay low to the ground and back away. We'll talk once we're a safe distance from them."

They made slow progress and Fletcher kept an eye on the kentaki every step of the way. After half a mile, they decided it was safe to stand, and started to take stock of the situation while walking.

"Why didn't we get attacked?" Fletcher asked.

Ethan shrugged. "Can't say. Must have something to do with our chemistry. Somehow, we must be more similar to the processed food than the kentaki are. The nanobots aren't programmed to attack us."

"Why would they attack the kentaki or the crops? What's with the wolf?"

"If we knew who programmed them, we'd know all that. What I want to know is why the wolf didn't attack everyone on the bridge."

Fletcher thought about it. "Maybe it couldn't really see everyone on the bridge. It might need to be in physical contact or something. Must also take a lot of energy to put all the nanobots together like that, so it doesn't stay as a wolf for long. It could also be that whoever programmed them just wanted them to work on this side of the river."

"Hmm." Ethan weighed the ideas, but then the memory of what had happened caught up with him. "Kordon . . . ."

"I . . . ," Fletcher swallowed, "I don't want to talk about it." Fletcher's mind kept revisiting the fate of their kentaki friend despite his best efforts to divert it, and there was no end to his anger. He silently cursed everyone present, including himself and Ethan, for not being able to save such a gentle soul – someone as harmless as Kordon. If only Fletcher had known that he was immune to the nanobots, he could have taken Kordon's place as the first to go, and perhaps thrown the kentaki into the same confusion that had allowed Ethan and him to escape. Maybe then the mob would have forgotten about Kordon. Or . . . maybe they would have killed Kordon to make up for the loss of their intended quarry.

Fletcher shook the thoughts out of his head. They were far from comfort and safety, without any allies, and in the midst of a hostile landscape. This wasn't the time for him to think about Kordon.

"Except for my goggles and . . . it looks like you managed to hang onto the bioscanner all this time . . . we really don't have anything. They took our packs away. We don't have any food, water, or anything." Fletcher didn't want to make the situation sound hopeless, but he needed Ethan to join him in facing their new reality.

"I didn't even notice I still had this thing with me," Ethan said, checking that the bioscanner still worked. "But I wonder if we'll even need it. Everything on this side of the river has sort of been filtered out by the nanobots. I wonder if that means it's all safe to eat?"

"I wonder if that means we're the only living things on this side of the river," Fletcher pointed out gloomily.

Ethan opened his mouth, but then closed it. He looked into the distance and, though there was higher land to the north, the land was flat enough to leave an almost perfect hemisphere for the starry sky. The wind bit at them, reminding them of the legendary mountains to the north, but those wouldn't be in sight even in the clarity of daylight – not without the goggles, anyway. For all they knew, Fletcher could be right that the nanobots had turned it all into a wasteland. There was certainly nothing to stop them.

"At least we know where we're headed." Ethan pointed north. "Those mysterious mountains where the wind comes from. The answer to the mystery has got to be there."

"You've got to be joking. How far did Kordon say they were? Without any food or water, we'll probably die in a couple of days. We need to find somewhere to cross the river – to get back to land that might have food. Kordon said there was another town a few days away. We might be able to hold out until we get there."

"You're assuming there's no food on this side of the river."

"Yeah, I am."

Ethan didn't like the idea of turning away from the answers they were looking for and decided, "let's sleep on it. We've had a long day, and maybe in the morning we'll get a better view of what's out there."

"Sleep . . . ." There was only bare ground and nothing to shield them. Then again, they wouldn't get anywhere trying to walk against the wind. Fletcher was already at his limit both mentally and physically. "All right, but I think it's more like we're waiting for morning. I don't know about you, but I don't think I'm going to get any sleep at all tonight."

"Yeah, I know." Ethan took to the ground without another word, placed his translator headset next to the bioanalyzer within arm's reach, and closed his eyes. Fletcher was more reluctant, unnerved by the prospect of spending the night among the creepy homicidal nanobots with their inscrutable motives, like sleeping with the most hellish bedbugs imaginable.

"I'm really starting to hate this planet," he mumbled, setting himself down gingerly and taking off his own translator. Letting his hair touch the dry, dusty soil, he stared at the stars. "North. South. Where I really want to go is up."

1 7

Nightlights

Images flashed past Fletcher and swam around him, with no scene staying distinct long enough for him to recognize it. His dreams normally involved concrete imagery pulled out of his memory. Most of what he saw now was unfamiliar and he felt such a sense of bewilderment that he was sure, even if he was able to get a closer look at some of it, it would remain unfathomable.

He was also far more aware than he normally was when dreaming. He knew he was asleep. He could feel his body lying down and his eyes closed, so that it was almost like the eerie state between sleeping and wakefulness. Almost. The problem was that the sights dazzling his closed eyes were not products of his mind – nothing that could have come out of his imagination.

Unable to register any of what he saw, he nevertheless experienced sharp emotions at each flash, ranging from blissful comfort to dire panic. He could tell which scenes were safe and which were not. Most of them were dangerous. The tension conveyed to his mind, perhaps by an as-yet untapped instinct, kept building until he couldn't take it anymore. He snapped open his eyes and gazed at the sky.

Night still covered this part of Kentak, but Fletcher felt unexpectedly fresh, so he guessed it was close to morning. The sky looked different – far more alien than he remembered. A shimmering purple fog covered everything, hiding both the stars and the naturally colored clouds of water vapor. The haze flowed like a river and pulsed slightly. If it had been isolated in ribbons,

Fletcher would have called it an aurora, but it was instead diffuse, spreading out across the landscape.

Fletcher's eyes were transfixed on the phenomenon as he wondered what it could mean when a face suddenly materialized above him. He jumped up, blacked out, and sat back down to get his eyes back into focus. The face was the most beautiful he had ever seen, at least in real life. The most beautiful *human* face. From a slender smoothly sloping nose to a soft smile, it was angelic in every detail and somehow bright in the pre-dawn gloom, haloed by the eerie purple in the sky. Wondering if she was a dream, Fletcher turned his head away, blinked and turned back.

Sure enough, she was still there. She had taken a few steps back, so that he now saw her exquisite figure framed by the bleak landscape. Physically, her body's understated curves had much in common with Sensha's – so much so that Fletcher still suspected that she was a figment of his imagination. The face was different, though. Sensha's had been sharp and severe – beautiful in a dark, mysterious way. The girl in front of Fletcher, dressed in appropriate flowing white fabric, looked more like a fairy.

Not sure what to do and certainly not wanting to frighten her away, Fletcher said in his most disarming tone, "for a second, seeing you there, I thought I had died and gone to heaven. The pain in my legs, though . . . who are you?"

It was only after she gave a puzzled look that he realized that his translator headset was still sitting on the ground. Looking at her, it seemed so natural to think that she would understand him, but even on Earth the chances that a random human could speak English was fifty-fifty at best. He put the translator back on and wondered whether the angelic woman would understand any language it could render.

"Who are you?" Fletcher tried again. Not knowing what language to use, the translator started with the last one used – Plani. When Fletcher repeated the question, the headset started cycling through all its programmed languages, pausing between each to wait for a reply that would confirm the calibration.

To Fletcher's relief, one language finally clicked and the woman answered, "my name is Avelyn."

Fletcher didn't recognize the language, but being able to communicate with her was all he wanted. Knowing her name gave her a sense of reality, as did the way the wind tossed her hair and dress, but he wondered how she could wear so little in the chill and yet keep from shivering.

"My name's Fletcher. I'm from Newport Station . . . it orbits Earth," he pointed up at a likely looking star. "Where are you from?"

She pointed to the north, but didn't say anything, almost as if she wasn't sure of the answer herself.

"Were . . . were you born on Kentak?" Fletcher wondered whether the question would be considered rude.

"Kentak?"

"This planet. Were you born on this planet?"

She took a minute to answer the question, leading Fletcher to suspect that the translator was making errors or its standardized dialect differed from hers. Eventually, she decided, "yes, I was."

Fletcher shifted uneasily. Why wasn't she asking him any questions? Surely he was as mysterious to her as she to him, so why did she seem uninterested in him? He should have been used to it – it wasn't as if he was accustomed to girls lavishing attention on him – but they were one Ethan away from being the only people around. It wasn't as if there was something else to draw her fascination.

With a sigh, Fletcher shook his anxieties off and gave Avelyn his best winning grin. She gave a bright smile back and the tightness in his chest intensified. Did she glow? It was almost as if an intrinsic light gave her features clarity in the darkness.

"What are you doing here?" he asked, belatedly realizing that his tone was rude. He hoped the translator would pick most suitable words.

She took some time to process the question, then answered, "I am looking for people."

Fletcher's eyes widened. "There aren't many people around, then? I didn't think there would be – not after . . . never mind. So you must be immune, too. Are you?"

This time, she clearly didn't know what he was talking about.

He needed to keep his questions short and clear to make sure she could understand.

"Are you alone?" He didn't know why he asked the question, but it was unusual for a girl – or a young woman – to be wandering in a desert on her own.

"Yes," she said. There was no hint of loneliness in her voice, but rather a sense that being alone was not a bad thing – as if it was a natural fact of her life.

Ethan stirred, rolled over so that his face hit the dirt, then woke up with a grunt. His eyes were unwilling to open on their own, so he cleaned his hands on the underside of his shirt, then used them to rub away the intransigence of his eyelids. He then scanned the landscape with a few blinks until his eyes hit the mysterious stranger. Then he just stared.

"Whoa . . . that's . . . unexpected." He rubbed his eyes again.

"So you can see her, too. That's good. I wondered if I was losing it."

"Doesn't prove anything. We could both be losing it. Can we talk to her?"

"Yeah. She understands one of our headset languages. Not Plani, though."

"No. I don't think anyone looking like that ever learned to speak Plani." Ethan put on his translator and exchanged words with Fletcher to calibrate it.

"Well, hello," Ethan greeted Avelyn. "My name's Ethan. I suppose Fletcher's already asked you all about yourself."

"N-no," Fletcher admitted. "Not really. Her name's Avelyn, she's alone, and she says she was born here. That's all I know."

"She says she was born here?" repeated Ethan. Avelyn gave no defense, and didn't react. Fletcher guessed that the nuance didn't come through in Avelyn's language, but he knew exactly what Ethan was thinking. Avelyn looked so perfectly human that no one on Earth could have mistaken her for anything else. So, either Earth had sent a secret mission to Kentak before the plani had, or something even more interesting was going on.

Ethan had enough sense not to pursue the issue, and instead asked, "is there anything to eat? If you're all the way out here,

Avelyn, you must know where to find food and water. Can you tell us? I'm sure that whatever you can eat, we'll be able to eat."

"There is a place. I can show you," said Avelyn. Then, without waiting, she started walking briskly. Fletcher and Ethan looked at each other, decided that they didn't have any choice, and followed.

For a girl with such a graceful figure, Avelyn walked stiffly – with military efficiency rather than a dancer's flow. Still trying to get themselves fully awake, Fletcher and Ethan proceeded with care, worried about shadowed rocks that could make them stumble. They stayed a fair distance behind while keeping Avelyn in sight, and took advantage of being out of earshot.

"What do you think?" whispered Fletcher.

"Honestly? We're either the luckiest guys on the planet or totally out of our minds."

"Yeah, but where do you think she's leading us?"

"To food."

"Really?"

"Either that or a pack of cannibals."

"You say that like it can't happen." So far, pessimism had proven a better predictor of events.

The memory of recent events squashed any cheerful confidence that Ethan might have offered. He instead reasoned, "if anyone in this wasteland was desperate for food, I think they would just go back across the river, especially if they're this close to it. I . . . I also don't think we were spared by the nanobots just so we could be eaten by something else. Not in the same day, anyway."

"You just want to get to those mountains."

"And you don't?"

Before sleeping, Fletcher would have firmly rejected the notion. Now . . . now the combination of his vision-dreams, the striking purple in the sky, and the stunning Avelyn made him want to brave the heavy wind to see what it was all about. Brave was the word, since unlike Ethan, he had no illusion that the journey would be smooth. He let his decision hinge on whether Avelyn was honest about the food, and stayed silent.

Avelyn stopped at the top of a small hill that was just high enough to obscure what lay beyond it. Fletcher looked on either side, and saw that the hill was part of a broad uplift in the land, so that an entire hostile army could be waiting in the dark on the other side. He pretended to favor his right leg, limping to slow their approach to the crest, ready to dash away from danger for the second time tonight. Ethan understood and stayed beside him.

Avelyn waited patiently and, when they finally reached her, she pointed to the valley ahead. "There is food."

A tiny stream flowed on the opposite side of the hill and small bands of vegetation were arranged in tight belts beside it. Ethan no longer waited for Fletcher and hurried down the hill with bio-analyzer in hand. Fletcher didn't blame him. The curiosity was one thing, but their stomachs also longed for something substantial. The meal Sueton had provided seemed a lifetime ago.

"Well, I hope you like berries," said Ethan when Fletcher and Avelyn joined him. "I don't recognize them, but these are definitely berry bushes. Are they safe . . . ?" he scrutinized the read-out. "Yes, yes they are. Definitely a thumbs-up on nutrition." He looked at Fletcher. "Looks like we're good to go."

Fletcher rolled his eyes. "I don't think we can carry enough with us. We don't even have backpacks. And is eating berries for that long really good enough?"

"Actually, the nutrition's mostly there. They've even got fiber. The people who make military rations would love to get their hands on these." He turned to Avelyn. "How far north does this stream go? Does it go all the way to the mountains?"

"Yes. It starts in the mountains."

Ethan threw a triumphant look at Fletcher, who sighed and asked, "and do these bushes go all the way, too?"

"Yes. There are different types of food in the north as well."

"Sounds damn convenient."

Ethan grinned. "Where do you think streams start? You gotta have snow. The berries . . . well, we haven't tasted them yet." He snatched one up and tossed it in his mouth. "Not bad. Sweet. A bit too acidic for me. Let's see if we can find something different." He started walking upstream, sampling different bushes.

"While you're at it, check if the water's safe to drink," Fletcher said. He thought he knew the answer, though. He couldn't shake the feeling that there was something wrong with this picture. Since when did Kentak become the land of plenty? "Do the kentaki know about this stream?" he asked Avelyn. "They could send boats up the stream during the day if it's connected to the river. It should be safe during the day."

"Kentaki?"

Fletcher blinked. Well, maybe that wasn't what she called them. "The people across the bridge that way – across the river in the city."

"They cannot come here," she said with a snap, as if offended that the kentaki existed. The edge to her voice suggested that she would personally ensure that they would not invade her haven.

"Hmm." The kentaki had been kept from this side of the river for less than a year. Fletcher was sure that they would have come up the stream if they had known about the food surviving around it. That meant this growth was probably less than a year old, or else the kentaki couldn't eat these berries. Was it possible for so much to grow in such a short time? Probably not naturally. How long had the stream itself been here? The questions increased his nervousness and he suspected that Avelyn would find them incomprehensible if he tried to ask her.

A hint of sunlight crept into the sky and the purple tint that still drew Fletcher's interest began to recede. The wind grew calmer by the minute and gradually reversed direction.

"I have to go," said Avelyn suddenly, turning away from Fletcher without further explanation.

"Wait . . . what?" He hurried to follow her. "Why do you need to go? We . . . we just met." *And I really want to see you in daylight*, a corner of his mind said.

"I sleep when the sun is up."

"Oh." He almost added "can I come with you?" He couldn't imagine why she would prefer a nocturnal life. Maybe the wind made it too hard to sleep at night? Searching for the right words, he said, "but . . . can't you help us a bit more? We're new to this world. We just escaped being killed by the people in that town. We . . . we really don't have any friends here."

"I will see you again before tomorrow's dawn."

"But we'll be miles away. I guess . . . I guess we'll be going north now. We'll be walking all day. How will you catch up with us? It's harder to walk at night, and the night's also shorter. Should we wait for you and travel at night instead?" He tried to hide his panic, but his voice cracked.

"You do not need to stay here. I will see you again before dawn tomorrow." Her face was set with firm conviction and, though he had no idea how she would be able to do it, he believed her.

Then, as the bloom of daylight started giving clarity to her features so that he could fully appreciate her gently rounded cheeks and the color of her eyes, she started melting away. Without any sign of discomfort, the beauty which only moments before had made Fletcher's heart race was now muddied, with colors blending together into a familiar sickly grey. Soon, all that was left of Avelyn was a puddle just like the one that had given rise to the nanobot wolf.

The scene made Fletcher's mind reel as the pounding in his chest turned into queasiness in his stomach. Within seconds, he doubled over, wracked by dry heaves. Dizzy, he almost fell, but Ethan came to his side and supported him. Fletcher looked at his older friend with blurry eyes and saw none of the shock that he felt. Ethan was actually grinning.

"You . . . you knew!" Fletcher choked. If he had been supporting his own weight, he would have taken a swing at Ethan.

Shrugging, Ethan said, "well, yeah. It was the only explanation that made sense. Plus she acted pretty mechanical. I've seen more emotion on robot receptionists."

"But . . . she killed . . . ." Fletcher felt his composure breaking down. The stress was finally getting to him.

"Relax. It's some kind of program, not a person. If you want to blame someone, it's got to be the programmer."

"Why didn't you tell me?"

Ethan's smile broadened. "You two looked like such a cute couple."

This time, Fletcher did break away and aim a punch at Ethan's stomach, but the latter anticipated the blow and jumped back.

Fletcher lost balance and stumbled, but Ethan caught him again before he could collapse.

"Hey, look on the bright side – we survived and we've got food. It's all pretty sweet, but there're at least four types of fruit – at least, they're sort of like fruit – and plenty of clean water. So . . . I guess we're going north, then?"

18

Upstream

"What do you mean you didn't see any purple sky?" asked Fletcher incredulously. "It was all around us. It started to fade away close to dawn."

They had been walking for a few hours along Avelyn's stream and, with a textbook blue sky overhead, Fletcher had trouble convincing Ethan of the alien cloak the sky had worn the night before.

"I didn't see anything. Just the usual night sky with some clouds. That's what you'd expect since this planet's atmosphere is pretty similar to Earth's."

"No way. It was really purple. And shimmering a bit – almost like an aurora."

Ethan didn't disbelieve Fletcher's observations, but was equally certain of his own. Trying to put the two contradictory perceptions together, he gave the assimilation his usual incisive thought. Fletcher gave him some time to mull it over until finally his older friend was ready with a proposal.

"Emily – Captain Pierce, I mean – said she saw something like an aura around people and things with a concentrated magical field. None of the stuff I read explained what caused that. I've come up with some ideas. I think she can see it because she also emits a field with her own signature – at a frequency she recognizes. When her field interacts with other fields, there's interference, and that registers in her mind. It's sort of like radar, except she doesn't actually see the aura with her eyes. It gets processed as visual input in her mind because that's how her brain's wired to deal with it, but her eyes aren't part of the equation. Emily said you've got a magical potential and you've been absorbing energy from a field nearby. There's probably a massive source somewhere close – to the north, I bet – and it's so powerful that it looks to you like it's surrounding us."

Fletcher blinked. "So . . . I'm becoming . . . more magical?"

Ethan gave him a pat on the back. "Make sure you tell me everything you can about it," he said in a fond voice, eyes gleaming.

Fletcher squirmed away from the contact. Once again, Ethan was making him feel like a lab rat. He wondered if Ethan's explanation was just wishful thinking – what Ethan wanted to be true to suit his research needs. Then again, Fletcher couldn't come up with a better explanation on his own – except for hallucination.

Their walk was smooth compared to the flow of their thoughts. As their conversation danced around all their questions and fears without coming to any sort of resolution, Ethan's explanation of the purple sky was the closest they could come to an answer on anything.

The only sense of certainty they had was Ethan's firm desire to head north, and Fletcher was now resigned to it. Having a goal eased both their minds.

"What do you think we're going to find? You seem excited about it. I didn't think you were the type."

With genuine curiosity, Ethan asked, "what type are you talking about?"

"You know, the adventure type." Fletcher considered himself the adventure type, though this was the first adventure he had ever been on and, after last night, he was having second thoughts. To him, Ethan was the kind of person who reacted to life passively.

"I'm not," Ethan confirmed. "Emily wouldn't have been able to keep me on board the ship, hiding me from the rest of the galaxy, if I was some sort of thrill-seeker. I would've liked to stretch my legs a bit every now and then, but I didn't complain. Much. Anyway, adventures are messy." He waved his hands, gesturing to the situation they were in. "But I think that, with what happened to the *Azar* and with the nanobots, this is exactly the place Emily was looking for the past two years. I think the rest of what we need to know about the hyperdrive is here, and I want to find it. I've been messing around with all the equations for so long . . . I can't help being excited that maybe I'll have some of the missing pieces if I just head north. It might seem like a long walk to you, but it's nothing compared to the time I've spent trying to figure it all out."

"So . . . somewhere in the middle of the mountains there'll be a book lying on the ground with all the answers you wanted?"

"No. If it's anything like what we saw on Selparis, you won't regret walking a week or two . . . or three . . . to see it, but I can't tell you exactly what we'll see. Anyway, don't you think that the rest of the crew'll head for the same place? They're probably on this continent. As long as they get the information we did, or figure it out some other way, they'll make their way to the mountains just like us."

"What if they try to walk through the town back there?" Fletcher asked gloomily.

Ethan ignored the thought. "Since she's looking for it, Emily will definitely figure it out. She has a nose for anomalies. I'm sure the kentaki government will want to help her to show that they're not responsible for what happened to the *Azar*. Going by air, she might already be there. Although . . . ."

"What?"

"Just wondering what the magical field you saw at night might do to her. Depending on where she is, she could get overloaded or . . . or emptied out. If there's a strong field localized here, then maybe further away there's sort of a deficit. Sort of like a wave or . . . or a tide. If it's high tide here, it'll be low tide somewhere else on the planet. Maybe . . . ," Ethan's eyes widened and he looked meaningfully at Fletcher, "maybe the planet's field sapped energy right out of the *Azar*'s hyperdrive and the sudden loss of power meant a loss of control. Maybe that made the mage panic and do . . . what he or she did."

Fletcher scowled. "Too many maybes. You're using the thing you know the most about to explain everything. Don't you think that's a bit too easy?"

Ethan gave Fletcher an appraising look, then nodded. "You're right. I'm probably getting carried away. What do you think? Do you have any ideas?"

"There's . . . some advanced technology – at least, something way ahead of where the kentaki are at. Someone had to bring it here. Those nanobots . . . I know we have stuff like that on Earth and Mars, but nothing . . . nothing so . . . ."

"Nothing so sophisticated. Definitely."

"I mean, the way it made that wolf-like thing . . . and Avelyn . . . ."

"Stylish."

Fletcher sniffed. "I think that the source of the nanobots might have had some way to disrupt the *Azar*'s hyperdrive. I mean, it looks like they're here to colonize, and to attack anything that interferes."

"Except for us. What do you think about that?"

The least pleasant possible conclusion occurred to both of them. Fletcher gave it voice with appropriate hesitation. "I think it probably means that a human programmed the nanobots – that they were sent here to colonize the place for us. But since when did we colonize this far out? We have enough trouble with the Moon and Mars."

"The World Council has trouble with the Moon and Mars. A corporation, though? You can find the same companies operating everywhere without any problem. What if one of them sent a probe, found some rare resource in the mountains, and decided to send a force of nanobots to take control of it?"

Fletcher shook his head. "So first you suggest something that humans couldn't have done at all, and now this puts all the blame on us?"

"Hey! This one was your theory."

"That's why I hate theories. Now we have two totally opposite ideas about what happened that might both be true."

"Well . . . they're really hypotheses. And once you have hypotheses, you can come up with experiments to test them. For instance, if it's really a human colonization scheme, then we won't find any sentient life except humans here."

Fletcher made an exaggerated look around and said, "check."

"Hold on. We only know the kentaki can't come here. We would have to try out a plani at least."

"Great experiment. I guess you know where we could get a hold of one? And once they're dead, how many other species will we have to test? Will we have to let the nanobots kill one member of every species?"

Ethan shrugged. "It'd certainly be conclusive." Then, struck by the flames in Fletcher's eyes, he cleared his throat and added, "but these nanobots could just be programmed to kill the kentaki, or maybe just avoid killing ISC species. The kentaki only recently joined the ISC and there isn't good information on their biology. I don't think any programmer would have had DNA samples for the kentaki, or anything like that. We humans aren't the only ones who might try to occupy rare resources and, no matter who it is, the programmers would want to keep the nanobots from killing ISC species. They would want to avoid the wrong kind of attention."

"But they're all right with killing kentaki?" Fletcher fumed. Thinking back to his conversation with Avelyn, though, he had to admit that it fit her attitude. She hadn't recognized "kentaki" – as if her programmer had failed to add the species to her database. That omission alone could have been responsible for the way the nanobots attacked the kentaki. It would be a mistake due to limited information instead of a deliberate attempt at genocide. "If the nanobots were sent here before anyone knew about the kentaki, and they took this long to do what they were supposed to . . . I don't know how long this sort of thing would take, but decades is a lot, isn't it?"

"Way too long. And they should have checked if there was someone here first. I don't think we can pretend this was an accident. I mean . . . wait . . . ," he squinted his eyes and aimed them at a distant point. "Could you put those goggles on and tell me what you see there? I see a dot there that looks like it's moving. Could be just the light, but . . . ."

Fletcher didn't need any more prompting. "It's tough to . . . oh, there it is. Yeah . . . that's . . . a person." He handed the goggles over. "Two arms, two legs, and a head. I can't tell anything else.

Maybe you can do better."

Ethan gave it a try. "Nope. It's practically noon and there's a lot of glare coming off it. I have no idea. Something about it, though . . . looks familiar. Can't put my finger on it."

Whatever it was, more than two miles still separated them from it. "I guess we either go toward it or avoid it."

"We don't have any weapons and it might. Actually, it probably does. I think it had a pretty heavy pack on its back. Either that or it's a hunchback."

"If it was a kentaki . . . but I guess we're pretty sure . . . it isn't because of the nanobots?"

Ethan stopped in his tracks. "What are you thinking?"

"That the nanobots could just be on the other edge," Fletcher drew a circle in the air with his index fingers. "Then once they clear an area, they move on."

"But Avelyn promised to meet us tonight. Doesn't that mean they have to be all over the place?"

"Just along this stream, otherwise the kentaki could come up the stream, right? If you test the soil this close to the stream, you'll probably still find nanobots. Maybe further away . . . ."

Ethan nodded. "Yeah, you're probably right if the nanobots don't reproduce. And they're not supposed to. It'd be a colossal disaster if they did, and no good for anyone. So, if there's a limited amount of them, it'd be like you say. They'd also have a limit to the perimeter they could control, which is good news for the kentaki. But how would a kentaki find himself in the middle of the cleared area?"

"Don't know. By air? Maybe a plane crash? They do have planes, I thought." Fletcher paused, then shook his head. "You're a bad influence on me. You've got me on theories again. We're not dealing with the problem – should we go towards it or away from it?"

Ethan was unsure. He liked his mysteries . . . inert. Not walking around. "If it really is a kentaki, it could be . . . hostile."

Fletcher took the goggles back from Ethan. "How about we stay close to the stream and see if whatever it is comes towards us." The nanobots wouldn't be much protection if the speck had a better gun than the townspeople had – one that could shoot at them from outside the nanobot coverage area. Still, the stream with its surrounding plant-life provided the best cover in easy reach.

They went with the plan and, for a while, there was no clear sign which way the speck would go. After ten minutes, Fletcher was finally certain. "Hell, it's coming towards us, all right. Straight for us."

"Not much of a surprise. It's not like there's anything else interesting around here. Let's just hope that we'll be able to identify it with the goggles before it can see us through a weapon scope."

The stranger walked with a regular stride characteristic of a human, plani, or a very lucky kentaki. It couldn't be a member of any other of the ISC races. The hump on its back was clearly a pack rather than a physical feature, and that probably ruled out the chance that it was another figment of nanobot programming.

"I think it's got a mask on its face," Fletcher said. "I should be able to make out which species it is by now, but that mask makes it hard to tell."

Ethan frowned. "I was starting to think it might be one of the crew from the way you were describing it. But why would one of them wear a mask here? The air isn't perfect, what with the radiation, but it's safe enough."

Fletcher didn't like the sound of "radiation" and "safe enough" in the same sentence, but let it pass. "Wait . . . I think it's . . . it's taking off the mask!" Fletcher held his breath. "It's . . . oh my god it's Kaz!"

"What?"

"Come on." He started running and Ethan, trusting that Fletcher was sure, caught up with a light jog. They closed the distance to the first officer in minutes. Fletcher arrived winded and unable to speak, leaving Ethan to do the talking.

Ethan wanted to hug Kaz in relief, but one look at the stern eyes of the first officer put him off. Kaz remained his stoic, composed self, taking their rush to greet him with passive equanimity. He had a couple of days' worth of stubble on his face, but otherwise looked no different than he would have at the best of times.

There was, however, a hint of reproach in his brows, and before Ethan could start talking, Kaz asked, "where are your supplies? Your water and food?"

At first, Ethan swallowed, feeling like a child waiting for a lecture after being caught out. The snapback to adulthood came a few seconds later, and he said indignantly, "we didn't just leave them behind, if that's what you're trying to say. We got into some trouble."

"Trouble?" Kaz said, eyebrows arched. Kaz's eyes moved from the translator headsets to the nightvision goggles to the bioanalyzer, and then fixed back onto Ethan's face.

"Yeah, trouble. And how about hello, how are you doing? You know Kaz, you were never much of a . . . ." Ethan broke off. Venting frustration at Kaz was always counterproductive. The first officer only gave sarcastic glares in response.

Fletcher got his air intake normalized and broke in. "We've got a lot to talk about. I think we should sit down for a bit. If your escape pod landed on this side of the river, you probably don't know much about what's going on here. And there's a lot. This planet's . . . way too complicated."

Kaz was stone-faced. "Really? It's been a boring walk for me the past two days."

19

Fishing

Boredom was winning over Sensha's best attempts to fend it off. The first hour of the flight to the continent where most of the crew had landed wiped out the idea that the mission to recover the *Azar*'s crew would be exciting. That left another hour and a half for her to reflect on the tedium of the day's events compared to yesterday. Corcoris' planning had turned the whole thing into a bureaucratic exercise, sucking out all hope of action out. Sensha felt more like luggage than a vital member of a rescue team.

Never much of a team player, she preferred to be in charge when forced to work with others, but Corcoris had naturally put his own trusted underling in command. She dismissed all thoughts of somehow taking control as pointless, since the mission preparation made a crisis unlikely. Part of her still wanted something catastrophic to happen just to get her blood flowing, but not over the ocean. She couldn't swim her way back to shore from this distance.

Did they even need her here? Originally, her role had been to convince the *Azar* crew to trust Corcoris' men, but with Sean and Jaidee sitting opposite her in the plane, she was redundant. Jaidee didn't do much talking, but Sean's chatter more than made up for it, and he would have no trouble bringing the rest of the crew on board.

Jaidee unnerved Sensha. Staying silent, the engineer was a stone-faced enigma, giving no hint of temperament, ability, or weakness. Sensha suspected that Jaidee was formidable. Or else, she was a brilliant actor, fooling everyone with an air of cool confidence unsettling to any enemy and steadying to any friend. Sensha's problem was that she couldn't see herself as Jaidee's friend.

The mission commander, Gorenal, had logically decided to start with the escape pods landing in the dry region of the continent between the soaked coast and the badly charted interior. The area hadn't experienced any disruptive weather the past few days and the winds were calm, so the trails of the humans wandering away from their escape pods would be clear. Trying to keep the mission profile as low as possible, Corcoris had given Gorenal use of only one of the space ministry's aircraft. Fortunately, it was a vertical takeoff and landing cargo hauler with easily enough space for everything they could pack in, and no need for a runway. Once they reached the first escape pod, they landed right beside it.

The sight of a pair of unmistakable boot trails leading away from the pod dashed Sensha's hope that her tracking abilities would turn out useful. She, Jaidee, Sean, Gorenal, and a driver packed into a truck brought across the ocean in the hauler, and followed the trail in that. Less than two bumpy hours later, they reached the two crew members. Sean did the talking, but there was really no struggle – the two weary walkers were all too ready to accept rescue. They had been wandering without any sign of civilization in reach, growing increasingly concerned about their survival.

Catching Sensha's eyes as they returned to the truck, Sean dusted his hands off and said, "as easy as that." She wondered if her face was betraying her thoughts, or if Sean was simply good at reading people.

They retrieved the next two pairs of the *Azar*'s crew in much the same way, but then the expedition was out of easy locations. They had a choice between the fertile, weather-ravaged coast and the obscure badlands for the next leg of their search. Sensha knew that the radiation spike coinciding with the *Azar*'s destruction occurred deep in the continent, and wondered whether investigating it might prove a better – or at least more interesting – mission. She knew, though, that Gorenal was planning to sweep the coast first. Corcoris had given orders to play the odds, and there was a better chance of retrieval near the coast where the space ministry had contacts willing to help. Corcoris wanted numbers. It would do no one any good if the rescue team spent twenty days trying to find two humans in the windswept desert while Captain Rivel picked up all the rest.

Before they started the coastal leg, Sean made a token objection that those who had landed in the more remote areas would be in more immediate need of help, but Gorenal squashed the notion. When Gorenal mentioned the need to outpace Rivel, Sean mused, "I wonder why he didn't already pick up these guys," gesturing to the newest passengers of the cargo hauler. "I mean, it was pretty easy to find them. Six is pretty good for day one."

Sensha was also worried about Rivel's apparent absence. To her, it meant that they were missing something. He had to be lurking somewhere, waiting to undermine their efforts. Could it be that he had figured out a way to make the humans irrelevant? That wasn't hard to believe, since the idea that two dozen or so stranded humans could march into the capital and present themselves as a power to be reckoned with was far-fetched at best.

The trip to their first coastal town was brief, but enlivened by the sight of a beautiful sunset giving character to the landscape. The scenery suddenly had an uplifting feel to it, instilling a cautious hope in everyone. The day had also gone very well, so there was plenty of reason for optimism. Sensha never trusted such sentiments, but saw that the kentaki relied on rays of hope to keep them going through their natural obstacles. They certainly kept their faces pressed to the windows to take in as much of the heart-easing sight as they could.

The fishing commune itself was not as inspiring. Even at altitude, they could see that the place was impoverished and the buildings in disrepair. Gorenal scowled every time he looked out the window at their destination, and even more when they touched down and stepped outside. The air was putrid with the smell of fish mixed in with the stench of bad sanitation. No one, not even among the kentaki, failed to pinch their nose, breath reluctantly through their mouth, and pine for a gas mask.

"You've got to have thought of bringing gas masks on this

mission," Sean said, voice punctuated by coughs of disgust. "Bring them out or I'll get real unpleasant."

Gorenal was reluctant to distribute the masks, considering the impression it would give to locals, but decided that the cringing expression on everyone's face would be even worse and relented.

The cargo hauler had landed in what, in better times, might have been a park. Within minutes, curious townspeople began to appear, keeping a safe distance and often staying in the shadows cast by nearby buildings. Sensha grew apprehensive. The crowd formed a bit too quickly to be entirely natural. At least some of those gathered, and possibly all of them, had anticipated the landing and planned to come see it. That could be a good thing – meaning that the locals were ready to help the space ministry in the promise of some reward. Or, it could be a bad thing – like parking a top-line hovercar in a place where the residents wouldn't be able to afford the fuel for it.

Then the contact arrived. For Sensha, it was distrust at first sight. Maybe it was prejudice. Of course it was prejudice, but she couldn't help judging a person by first impressions, and this time the indications were . . . severe. The contact was of average height and had an unbalanced walk due to a false right leg that was a bit too short. Sensha was cautious about concluding anything from the leg after her experience with Orek, but guessed that this time it was a deformity from birth and not a nanobot attack. Scars, scabs, and warts covered the kentaki, making his face and limbs more rugged than the relief map of a mountain range. He wore only enough to satisfy what passed for modesty and Sensha would have gladly paid for more clothing to save herself from seeing so much of his body. She would have offered him the Grikorat mask and cloak, if only to save her eyes from his blemishes. Through it all, he wore a smile, and to Sensha the smile was the worst. There was no honesty in it. His loincloth was cleaner.

The contact, beaming, walked right up to Gorenal and confidently offered a disfigured hand. His grin broadened as Gorenal shook it, as if delighted that he could force the mission commander to touch his skin.

Sensha could feel Sean shifting uneasily beside her, struggling to restrain himself from commenting on the scene. She didn't blame him. The question was whether Gorenal also had second thoughts. Would a fellow kentaki be as dismayed by the physical persona of the contact, or would it be within normal business to deal with people who were so . . . incredible? Sensha would never have been able to touch that hand herself, not knowing which wounds might be the mark of a contagion, so Gorenal had already showed a greater-than-expected level of tolerance.

While Gorenal made introductions and described what the contact had already done for the space ministry to assuage doubts, Sensha scrutinized every bit of the surrounding area to plot her best route of escape. She began subtly tensing her muscles, warming them up for action. She also took an inventory of nearby weapons, especially those scattered among the visible parts of the crowd. There weren't many in the hands of the kentaki – far fewer than were stored in the cargo hauler – but there was no way to gauge the hidden firepower.

Sensha missed the contact's name and resumé, but since she had no intention of dealing with him, the information was worthless. Her instincts were on fire and she trusted hers more than Gorenal's. The only questions left in her mind were when to get away and who to get away with. She didn't want to wait until the locals made the first move, but everything depended on what kind of trap they would spring. This close to the hauler in the middle of the park, the aircraft was the only place to hide, but there was nowhere to go except up. For exactly the same reason, there was no way the locals would spring the trap here – they would want the cargo hauler intact, and might not even be able to shoot it down. There was an opportunity to escape if she could convince Gorenal of the danger, but seeing him pretend confidence in the contact, she doubted that she had enough words.

Her best chance would be to separate from the group as they were being led away from the park. The streets between the buildings were narrow and winding, so the opportunity would be there. That left the questions of whether she should take any of the humans with her. She had no stake in the rescue mission except for a desire to do damage to Rivel's ambitions. Without Rivel competing to secure the humans, she felt this whole enterprise was a distraction. The real game on this planet had to be the nanobots or the radiation source, or maybe they were both parts of the same secret. It might be dangerous to get close to the source, since any non-plani ship entering orbit could trigger another burst, irradiating anything nearby. It was a risk worth taking, though. There was a power there that, if harnessed, could give any faction the edge on Kentak.

Would the humans see that potential and be willing to give up on their comrades to seize victory? She doubted it. They were too sentimental. If she saved one or two of them from the locals, they would only want to turn around and save the rest no matter how futile the odds. Then, if they happened to succeed, they would continue wandering the continent in search of the rest of the crew. They would walk in circles when she wanted to go in a straight line.

A procession was moving away from the cargo hauler. The crew of the hauler stayed behind, but all the humans and Gorenal's team followed the contact. Sensha had missed where they were being taken, but didn't care. Gorenal should have refused to leave the hauler, even if there was only the slightest chance of trouble. Clearly incompetent, he had spent too much time in the comfort of the capital and had no idea about the mindset of people struggling to survive. Now the locals had the precious aircraft surrounded, outnumbering the crew by at least twenty-to-one. Of course, Gorenal would have reasoned that the locals were just curious about the huge aircraft, dismissing it as a quaint fascination, and that snobbery was exactly the problem. He probably believed there was no threat since the locals wouldn't know how to operate the hauler, and Sensha would have set him straight if he had said so aloud. The locals didn't intend to use the aircraft for its intended purpose, but to rip it apart and sell all the equipment. Sensha was not at all sympathetic to naïveté, and felt that a person had to be disabused of it the hard way.

She resolved to go it alone and, if the humans were competent, they would find their own way out of this mess. She broke her thoughts to get a better read on the town. The crowd was pushing them down a street that was once paved, but now had so many cracks and puddles in it that loose dirt would have served better. On closer inspection, the buildings had more than the marks of natural decay. There had been a deliberate salvaging of materials from the top-down, so that they looked horrible from above, but largely intact at street level. That hinted at some sort of organization underlying the activities of this fishing commune. But why salvage building materials? Certainly it wasn't to sell them – the price they fetched wouldn't be worth the effort. If you wanted to build something new and suddenly found yourself short of what you needed, maybe . . . . Sensha was getting the sense that this unremarkable community had aspirations. Perhaps the contact had really done significant work for the space ministry, but how had he done it, and why? Surely it wasn't for the sake of a government across the ocean – a technically foreign government at that – but to serve a local cause at the same time.

Winding down her appreciation of the carefully dilapidated buildings, Sensha suddenly realized that Jaidee was no longer walking with the pack. She looked around, and the unnervingly stoic engineer was nowhere to be seen. Not only that, but no one had noticed the absence. Except . . . except Sean looked a touch more confident now. Sensing her eyes on him, he turned a smug expression towards her. So he knew, but nobody else had paid it any attention. Sensha cursed herself. How could she not have noticed? She was letting her mind wander too freely.

She opened out her senses, trying to catch Jaidee following the procession from the sidelines on the guess that the engineer would want to be in position if there was a chance to extricate the other humans before anything malicious took place. At the edge of Sensha's hearing, she caught the echo of a choke – the kind that kept a person from shouting.

Sensha initiated her own inconspicuous escape, first getting into the middle of the seven humans – all taller than her by a head – then ducking out at a bend in the street when she no longer felt anyone watching. She got to a dark corner of her own, wrapped herself in it, and then used the shadows of dusk to stalk her way back to the alley where the choke had come from.

Jaidee had seen the move and waited for her, a strangled ken-taki lying on the ground a few steps away. The kentaki was still clutching a knife – more like a crude sword – in its left hand. The alley was a dead-end, so either the sturdy human had entered so quickly that she caught the intently watching kentaki by surprise or . . . came down from above.

Jaidee started moving with soundless footfalls and remarkable speed. Sensha could match the human, but had trouble keeping the amazement from her face. Where did a human get this kind of training? And Jaidee was supposed to be an engineer. Sensha's image of engineers did not include them climbing up buildings with dance-like grace and landing a two-story jump without star-tling a target.

There was no way the two of them would foil any plot the local kentaki might perpetrate – not without having a clear idea of the shape it would take. Jaidee continued to take down every armed local they came across, but it wouldn't be enough. They could only wait for an opening – a chance to insert themselves at a moment the kentaki were weak.

When the locals pounced, the execution was flawless and, more importantly, bloodless. They surrounded Gorenal, the space ministry people, and the humans with an unimpressive but still deadly array of weapons and promptly seized anything that looked like a communication device. While watching the proces-sion from the wings, the locals had made note of any technol-ogy they would need to confiscate, and immediately went for the items before the owners could breathe. Jaidee and Sensha could only watch, tensed. It looked like the locals would keep the cap-tives alive and, except for a token struggle, the humans were too shocked to contemplate any real resistance. That was lucky, since a wrong move could easily start a bloodbath.

Jaidee moved them to a deeper position – further away from the action. There were suddenly a lot of alert enemies out in the open, and it wasn't safe to stay close to the throng. Crouching with a more pensive expression than Sensha had seen from her so far, Jaidee finally turned appraising eyes to her companion.

In a deep, though still smooth, feminine voice, Jaidee said, "we can use your help. Are you with us?"

Her awe of Jaidee preventing her from responding any other way, Sensha nodded.

Kaz massaged his forehead, then ran his hand through his tangled hair. "Sounds like a mess."

"Told you so," Fletcher said emphatically. After a brief sit-down talk where Fletcher and Ethan gave Kaz an overview of what had happened, they had spent the rest of the day walking north while Kaz came up with questions analyzing every aspect of their experiences. The answers came easily, since Fletcher and Ethan had thought through all the same angles already. After hours of back-and-forth, they were finally settling down for the night. Dinner was a healthier mix of the streamside fruits and Kaz's rations. Since Kaz had taken the captain's escape pod alone, he had double the normal share of rations with him and shared freely. In his last moments on the *Azar*, he had also summoned the presence of mind to grab one of the translator headsets with Kentaki installed. He now used his headset to update theirs.

"Not like there're any kentaki around to talk to now," Fletcher mumbled. If they had been able to communicate in Kentaki in the first place, Kordon would still be alive. The thought made Fletcher's whole body sag, but he held back any other show of emotion.

Kaz was a steadying influence – an adult who was actually willing to take charge and who gave a sense that he knew what he was doing. Fletcher couldn't bring himself to trust the first officer, though. It wasn't just that Kaz had served under his father, but that was part of it. Fletcher simply had a gut reaction to anyone who might try to tell him what to do. Captain Pierce had been a more hands-off leader, making Fletcher feel comfortable under her wing because she seemed willing to give him a sense of liberty. The price of Kaz's competence was that he expected others to follow him without question because there was no way they could know what to do better than he did.

Fletcher would have been cuttingly abrasive toward the first officer if not for the fact that Kaz had continued leading them north even before hearing their explanation. If he had unreasonably insisted that they follow him on his southwardly course, Fletcher would have turned joined Ethan in turning rebel. Luckily, after their goal was clear to him, Kaz reassured them that he agreed with their plan.

"It makes sense," he said, nodding. "And considering the food along this stream . . . there's someone willing to help us along our way. I suppose sometime in the middle of the night we'll be visited by . . . what was its name again?"

"Avelyn," Fletcher answered in a heartbeat.

"Avelyn. Interesting name. I wonder where she got it from. I wonder how she managed to look like a convincing human female with only you two to look at."

Ethan cleared his throat. "She did have DNA. She took a sample from each of us."

"Figure out our DNA that quickly? Not to reconstruct a body. Why would it pick a female instead of a male? How did it know what you two would consider beautiful? Someone with a good grounding in human psychology had to have programmed it. It knew you were human males from your DNA and selected the human female program to interact with you, knowing that you would be most willing to trust it that way. I think Fletcher's right, too – it doesn't recognize the kentaki, and that's why it attacks them."

Both Fletcher and Ethan felt relieved to have the first officer on the same page as them, but Fletcher was still suspicious of Kaz's intentions. Did he agree with them so quickly to gain their confidence in him as a leader and to ensure their support later on? Kaz seemed like the type who would read books on leadership and pick up that kind of tip – the same ideas drilled into Fletcher's young psyche by a father who should have read books on parenting instead. After getting a solid dinner into his stomach, Fletcher decided to relent, and to avoid comparing Kaz to his own father. At least Kaz hadn't tried to pull rank – insisting on obedience based on his post on a ship that no longer existed.

They decided to sleep close to the bushes in the hope that the plants would shield them from the wind. The rustling was a bit annoying to Fletcher, who was used to sleeping in silence, but it also had a calming effect. Though moist, the ground they picked was not damp to the point that it would muddy their already grimy clothes. They already looked like nineteenth century vagabonds, so it was really a matter of discomfort. Fletcher had never been in clothes so filthy, and the smell of them in particular bothered him. The stench of the other two was intensely unfamiliar, forcing him to keep a few feet of distance to keep his face from crinkling.

The ground was yielding, and much more like a mattress than the solid clay they had slept on during the previous nights. With food to eat, no real enemies nearby, and Kaz added to their number, Fletcher felt that he had a good chance for sleep. But then the competing thoughts of Avelyn and recent traumas came to mind. Would it be a bad thing to sleep right through Avelyn's visit? In a way, she was the cause of the horrors he had witnessed. The thought of her both sickened him and tantalized him just as her programmer had intended.

With memories of the mangled faces of the kentaki mob made uglier by irrational hate mixed with the altogether different aspect of Avelyn in the forefront of his mind, he still managed to fall asleep soon after he laid down. He had the expected nightmares, waking up twice during the night with no clear sense of what time it might be. Each time, the sky had more of the purple he had seen last night, and that was all he noticed before falling asleep again. After his second stirring, his mind was yanked back to the stage of indecipherable images.

The pictures were no more comprehensible to him now than last night. He might have seen buildings, mountains, and galaxies colliding, but everything moved too fast for him to be sure. If Ethan was right and the purple in the sky was some sort of "magical" field, then it might be causing this bizarre new twist to his sleep. Rather than give him spectacular powers, though, all this magic seemed to do was make him feel lost with no sense of agency or control, imprisoned in his own mind. Wasn't that the opposite of what magic was supposed to do?

Fletcher had left out any mention of these dreams or the purple sky in the conversations with Kaz. Ethan also mercifully avoided talking about Fletcher's supposed "magical potential." What would Kaz think about it? It was hard to believe that a concrete thinker like the first officer would give in easily to the idea, but back at the staff meeting aboard the *Azar*, he seemed to accept the captain's abilities and her judgments based on them.

The array of different worlds and the deep emotions each elicited soon overwhelmed Fletcher's ability to think. When his mind couldn't take the flood anymore, his eyes snapped open and he gazed at the deep purple aurora now fully vivid. It was perfect déjà vu, except that his back wasn't sore and the shrill wind produced a regular rhythm as it tested the strength of the bushes. He turned his head and, sure enough, Avelyn was sitting close by watching over all three humans. Actually, Fletcher noticed with a tinge of jealousy that she was mostly observing Kaz.

Fletcher kept himself at minimal alertness, watching Avelyn with hazy curiosity. Why should he be jealous, anyway? He was like a nerd falling for a computer speaking in a feminine voice. Was he really that starved? Well, yes. Contact with girls his age had been rare on Newport Station. Maybe the right question was whether Avelyn had sufficient artificial intelligence to reciprocate his feelings, and the answer to that was probably no. If she could, though, being the boyfriend of a robot might not be so bad. At least while he was stuck on this planet. He would have to keep her creator from interfering or some hacker from changing her program, though.

That was an idea. He almost sat upright at the thought. Avelyn said she had come from the north. If they went north and found a computer with her program, there was a chance that they could stop her from attacking the kentaki. All they would have to do would be to add a kentaki entry into its do-not-kill database, and then add the crops the kentaki needed for food so Avelyn would leave those standing, too. Having no kentaki DNA as a sample was a bit of a problem. They would have the damnedest time trying to get a hold of some. Avelyn herself must have sampled plenty of kentaki including, Fletcher reminded himself with twist of his stomach, Kordon. So, with any luck, all it would take would be to switch the kentaki profile already stored on the computer from "kill on sight" to "do not harm" or even "protect."

It was too much to hope for that this would be easy, especially if the nanobots were sent to clear the kentaki out. And the programming language would probably be incomprehensible. Still, he now had his own reason for going north and wouldn't have to hope for ancient ruins or an underground city or whatever Ethan was trying to find. All he wanted to find was a single computer.

Kaz sat up before Fletcher decided to reveal that he was awake. There was no stiffness or stretching from the first officer, so either he was the ultimate morning person – not that it was morning yet – or he, too, had been watching Avelyn. Fletcher conjured up the image of Kaz and Avelyn staring at each other like two cats sizing each other up. Since Kaz was the one to flinch, Avelyn must have won the battle. This was her territory, after all, and . . . Fletcher shook his head. There was such a thing as taking a comparison too far.

Fletcher couldn't hide the fact that he was awake from Kaz. When the first officer gave him a questioning look, he shifted to a sitting position, finally gaining Avelyn's attention. With both of them glaring at him – at least, Fletcher felt as if their eyes had unusual intensity – he shifted uncomfortably and tried not to look directly at them.

With Fletcher too nervous to speak, Kaz gave Avelyn a try himself. His steely eyes drawing back her fabricated blues, he asked, "what are you?"

She blinked. "I am an Atlantian."

Kaz puffed. "Clever, but not true. Interesting that you didn't say human. You are not a person, so do you mean you were manufactured by Atlantians?"

Avelyn stayed silent. Fletcher explained, "she has trouble

when you ask her too many questions or complicated questions."

Kaz shook his head. "No, I didn't think I'd get an answer on that one."

"What . . . what does she mean . . . Atlantian? Do you know?"

With a sigh, Kaz said, "yes, unfortunately. I was hoping Ethan would have already covered that part with you. He likes talking about it more than I do. You know about Earth's war with Asparis around sixty years ago."

It wasn't a question, but Fletcher nodded in confirmation to urge Kaz on. That war was the most important event in Earth's history in the past century, bringing humans into contact with the rest of the ISC for the first time. It provided the source material for Fletcher's favorite game.

"Well, the excuse the asparians gave for attacking us was that they had colonized Earth before the last Ice Age, and wanted to reestablish control. They pointed out how similar we were to them genetically. The World Council shot back at the idea from the start and adopted the space seed theory as the official line."

"Space seed theory?"

"The idea that the same building blocks of life were spread throughout this region of space, which explains why all the ISC species have DNA instead of some other way to code genetics. Anyway, since we couldn't pronounce the name of the colony the asparians claimed to have built on Earth, it became popular to call the colony "Atlantis." The name stuck because it fit, and when Avelyn says the asparian name for the colony, it gets turned into Atlantis by our headsets."

"But if the colony wasn't real, how can Avelyn say that she's Atlantian? Does it mean that asparians made her?"

Kaz's eyes widened. "I didn't say the colony wasn't real. I said the Council denied it and the asparians used it as an excuse. One thing we – the *Azar* crew, I mean – found on Selparis was that it really did exist. Selparis had been an asparian refugee colony. When Atlantis fell, some of the survivors fled to Selparis, and we found their remains and some of their descendants. They're closer to humans than asparians are, but our species was already around when Atlantis was built. Some anthropologists think that maybe the Atlantians enslaved the Neanderthals and early humans, but there isn't much evidence except for the genetics."

"But then wouldn't there be ruins or something left of the Atlantians on Earth? They didn't find anything like that, did they?"

Kaz looked at Avelyn when he said, "that depends on how Atlantis was destroyed, doesn't it?"

At first, thoughts of nuclear weapons popped into Fletcher's mind, but that would have wiped out all species on Earth except for some insects and bacteria. Taking in Kaz's turn towards Avelyn, the answer struck Fletcher like a hammer to his ribs. "You mean . . . nanobots. Just like what's happening here?"

Kaz nodded. "Back then – we're talking more than fifteen thousand years ago – the asparians were the most advanced species in the ISC. They had nanotechnology and, from what we found on Selparis, it looks like someone used nanobots to wipe out the colony so that no trace of it was left."

Fletcher swallowed. "Not . . . her . . . ."

With an unnatural chuckle, Kaz said, "no. She would have been sent here before that if we believe what she says about being Atlantian. You could say, though, that it would have been one of her relatives. She would have to be more than fifteen thousand years old and . . . I just don't know how you keep something like this running for that long. I also don't understand why it would only start to attack the kentaki now – just in the past year from what you told me."

"But . . . who'd program the nanobots to do that? I mean to destroy Atlantis."

Holding back a caustic, jaded answer, Kaz cleared his throat and said, "there's no way to say."

"Oh yes there is," Ethan suddenly said. The darkness and loud bushes had hidden his awakening, and it was impossible to know how long he had been listening. "At least, I know what you think, Kaz. It's all about who benefits, right? Well, on the top of that list was us – humans. If early humans were enslaved, then maybe an extremely clever one – and it'd only take one who was trusted enough and clever enough to be allowed to work alongside the Atlantian technicians – decided to free his people by using Atlantis' own technology to wipe it out."

Kaz sniffed. "I thought you always said it was probably a civil war with someone on the losing side trying to get revenge?"

"Still do."

Fletcher noticed that Kaz didn't deny that he thought humans had used nanobots to destroy Atlantis, even though the idea was far-fetched and oddly romantic in contrast to the first officer's practical persona. To Fletcher, all the talk about fifteen thousand years ago was meaningless. Unless . . . it gave credence to the possibility that humans were also behind Avelyn and the use of nanobots on Kentak.

After staying silent through all of the discussion, Avelyn startled them, saying, "what do you mean?"

Kaz returned a perfectly level, "about what?"

"About Atlantis."

The hint of a genuine smile started to appear on Kaz's face. "I said that it had fallen fifteen thousand Earth years ago. It was completely destroyed. There was a civil war, but the records we found on Selparis didn't explain why all remnants of Atlantis were wiped out. The only reason that makes sense is that nanobot technology was used."

Avelyn straightened herself to her full height and said a touch indignantly, "that is not possible."

"Why not?"

"Atlantis cannot fall. Atlantis is the beacon. We are better than Asparis. Asparis is decadent. You . . . you are Atlantians, too. Why do you say these things?"

Ethan leaped up and shouted ecstatically, "what if she's the real thing, Kaz? Maybe the nanobots were dormant all this time but triggered by the plani survey ships. Think about it. The Atlantians could have sent her here to get the place ready for colonists and to keep the ships of other species away. They knew how the hyperdrive worked, so they could figure out a way to disrupt it. If she's the real thing, the chance that we'll find what we're looking for here is pretty much a hundred percent. I think these Atlantians might have developed a mechanical hyperdrive – a nanobot hyperdrive – which the Selparis refugees didn't have."

"And if she's not the real thing?" Kaz said halfheartedly. "How hard would it be for some corporation to program her to pretend to be an ancient relic? You didn't expect her to admit who really sent her, did you?"

Fletcher might have been imagining it, but it seemed to him that Avelyn was standing more stiffly than usual and, when she spoke, her tone was edged with growing anger. She repeated her question, "why do you say these things?"

"Because they are true," Kaz replied as if to a child. "And if you are confused by it, you are not alone. We're just as confused. If you will tell us what you know, we will tell you what we know, and maybe we can make some sense out of it. How many years have you been on this planet?"

"It is not true," Avelyn said petulantly, ignoring the question. "Atlantis cannot have fallen." Before Kaz could respond, she said, "I must go now. It is almost dawn."

Fletcher looked up, and indeed the violet tint to the sky had faded and the wind had all but died, but he still thought Avelyn was trying to run away from an uncomfortable conversation. Could a robot be uncomfortable?

If Avelyn's stubbornness surprised Kaz, he did a good job of hiding it. "Will you be back again?" he asked.

Avelyn seemed to think it over, but finally answered, "yes."

"Maybe I'll find a way to convince you that I'm telling you the truth by then."

Without making any sign about what she thought about this, Avelyn melted away.

Ethan shook his head. "That could have gone better. I don't think she was programmed to listen to reason, Kaz, so if you think she'll be able to change her electronic mind based on evidence, I think it's a lost cause."

Kaz stayed silent, casting caustic eyes at Ethan.

"But . . . you would have already thought of that," said Ethan.

Kaz sighed. "What I want to do is come up with a way to be sure what she is – something old or something new. The answer to that will tell us what we're heading into."

Fletcher didn't quite understand why Kaz thought it mattered, but he nodded. Either way, it was clear to him that Avelyn was a weapon, and probably one launched from Earth. He was more committed than ever to the idea that they should change her programming, so he supposed that if she was new rather than old, that would help. Cracking modern work would be tough enough – he doubted that he would even know where to start with a program written thousands of years ago.

Once again, he found himself with hopes opposite to those of his companions.

21

PIRATES!

"I don't believe this," Jaidee murmured, showing as much awe as she was capable of. Sensha was speechless.

The procession of townspeople and captives made a clear line down the beach, so Jaidee and Sensha didn't try to follow immediately – waiting in hiding until the town cleared before they went in the same direction. The locals had noticed Jaidee's handiwork and were conducting broad sweeps to find the two escapees.

After they were sure they could do so safely, Jaidee and Sensha made their own way down the beach and saw the very conspicuous destination outside of town. To call it a cave would imply a small, barely visible cutaway – this was a major geological feature – the mouth of an underground river no less than a hundred meters wide covered by a grand cathedral of rock. The huge scale of its entrance, though, meant that advantageous viewpoints surrounded it, so Jaidee had no trouble finding a concealed location from which they could examine the front of the hideout. But could they sneak in? Sensha was sure that their attempts to follow the kentaki and the hostages would have to end - she and Jaidee would have to scout out the area and try to find another less obvious way in. Perhaps the point where the river pushed its way underground was not too far away.

Jaidee thought otherwise and, with Sensha growing more apprehensive at every step, led them in through the front. There was very little activity in front of the gigantic cave, at least, but this approach seemed to Sensha to be testing their luck. As they pushed the limits of brazenness, she still resolved not to let Jaidee out of her sight.

Now, after scurrying their way up a shadowy rocky wall to a high ledge overlooking the scene, they gazed in wonder at the town's secret, hidden deep inside the enormous cavern. Sensha had no clear idea what it was, except that it was big and meant to be mobile. Peppered with engines above the waterline, it looked as if it was supposed to take to the air, but the size of it made the notion hardly believable.

"Too big," Sensha finally said with hardly any breath. The town had set out to build the biggest . . . something . . . that would still be able to get out of the cavern. The craft was an engineering patchwork – a mish-mash of parts scavenged or stolen from what must have been a wide region around the town. All Sensha could say definitely about it was that it was armed, and heavily. It had so many guns sticking out at all angles that a model of it would be dangerous to hold.

"With the cargo ship's engines, this thing could takeoff," Jaidee mumbled, making calculations behind her eyes. "Just off the ground, like a hovercraft. Spruce Goose in metal."

Sensha didn't understand the reference, but didn't need to. If the ship could get itself out of the water, it would have a speed advantage over anything else of comparable size, and would have to be the product of a profoundly eccentric genius. Plenty of planning clearly went into this as well. While the ship gave the appearance of severe improvisation, the cavern itself bore the marks of careful construction. Much of the interior was reinforced with materials from the buildings outside, answering Sensha's curiosity about the purpose behind the town's deliberate destruction. The kentaki also kept their hideout lit better than the town outside, with myriad arrays of small electric lights strung up all around, producing shadows of all shades and sizes.

"But why?" Sensha asked. An enormous amount of effort had gone into building a . . . a flying ship.

"Pirates," Jaidee said with a straight face but a mad gleam in her eyes.

There were such things as space pirates, so Sensha was familiar with the idea, but it mostly involved smuggling within systems. Pirates preferred inconspicuous ships that could outmaneuver authorities and had lots of fuel to burn. The ship in front of them was nothing of the kind. Centuries had passed since the plani ceased using ocean vessels to trade on their planet's seas, and Sensha lacked the imagination to grasp the workings of a civilization so much less developed than her own. Since the official histories ignored the existence of the dribrora, Sensha never spent any time on the subject. She thought about how large space warships were used – to enforce port blockades and launch surface invasions – and wondered if it was possible that these pirates could really be engaged in that level of hostility. Surely that sort of thing was left to governments?

The pirate ship, if that was what it was, sat deep in the river tethered and anchored by an array of ropes also used to board it. The perch from which they viewed the scene was forty feet above sea level and twenty feet above the upper deck of the ship, with most of the activity occurring on the well-lit shore beside the ship, where the bizarre contraption towered over its creators magnificently.

Sensha shook her head. How could Corcoris have so badly misunderstood this place? On a modern world, hiding this kind of construction would be impossible, but Kentak was truly every bit as backward as Sensha could have imagined. Any thought of forging an alliance between the dribrora and kentaki to the benefit of both against the plani was now far from her mind. The kentaki were not in a position to help her people in any way.

Jaidee didn't say much, but her face was suddenly full of energy. Her eyes darted this way and that, taking in every nuance. Did she see something completely different in this pirate operation?

Sensha focused on the shack on the opposite shore where the hostages were probably being kept. Sturdy, it was still much more vulnerable to attack than some of the other structures in the cave, and certainly easier to assault than the dreadnought at center stage. If the locals had forced the hostages onto the confusing hulk of metal instead, Sensha would have given up on the rescue without a second thought, leaving Jaidee to deal with the mess if the engineer was not willing to see reason. That shack, though, looked so unassuming and fragile that the steep odds against them looked almost manageable.

Jaidee seemed more interested in the comings and goings of the locals, all of which seemed random to Sensha – almost like watching folk in a plaza going about their daily business. The cavern had all the variety of a plaza scene – more so, since the kentaki themselves came in all shapes and sizes. But what was the point of wasting time watching them? They behaved so nonchalantly there was no way to tell what actions might be worth notice. Maybe the lack of chaos was fascinating Jaidee. How often did these people take hostages and commandeer cargo planes? It was almost as if the whole plot was just a natural part of their daily grind.

"The lights," Jaidee murmured. There, at least, Sensha understood what the human meant. With all the artificial light in the cavern, there was no chance to get close enough to the makeshift prison to do any good. In the dark, Sensha had an advantage with her exceptional night vision, and as far as she was concerned, turning off the lights was a prerequisite for any rescue attempt. Unfortunately, all wiring was beyond sight, keeping anyone from simply cutting off the juice the old-fashioned way. The only alternative was to find the generator – likely some sort of hydroelectric turbine harnessing the power of the river.

"Further in or outside," Jaidee mused, then added, "let's get out of here."

There was a better chance that the generators were further into the cavern, Sensha thought, but following the river deeper into the place would mean exposing themselves. Jaidee was finally willing to take the less dangerous route, hoping that the generator was located where the river surfaced, and Sensha felt a wave of relief as they exited the cavern. She didn't know why, but taking insane chances next to Jaidee was far more nerve-wracking than doing the same on her own.

From the surface above the cavern, there was no indication of the scope of what lay underground. Jaidee pointed to a column of smoke rising up from the top of the hill covering the secret base and, wondering what else might come out alongside it, they scrambled up the hill towards it. Hoping that the kentaki also sent the power lines out through the top, they instead found nothing more than the spout venting bad air from the base. Disappointed, Sensha sat ungracefully on the ground. She was growing impatient, but had no idea how to break through to Jaidee with any suggestion she might have – if she happened to come up with any. Jaidee was so much like her that it was frustrating.

Jaidee remained standing, surveying the surrounding landscape, taking advantage of the hilltop view. Weary of duplicating the engineer's efforts, Sensha rested her eyes for the critical moments when their powers would mean the difference between life and death. Rescuing the humans was Jaidee's mission, after all, not hers. She would play the supporting role until she felt it was time to turn back to her own purpose.

Brows furrowed, Jaidee suddenly said, "look there," pointing away from the sea and deep inland. Sensha was tempted to ignore the command, but curiosity won over petulance and she glanced in the direction of Jaidee's firmly extended arm. At first, she thought that Jaidee was gesturing at something on the ground, but then saw an unmistakable flare hovering just above the landscape.

"That's a shuttle – a landing craft strobe light," Sensha said, the worst of her premonitions coming to fruition. There were only two possible sources for that sort of lander – the humans or the plani – and she had no doubt that they were about to discover Captain Rivel's latest outrage.

The lander hovered just above the ground for a few moments, then departed. Had Rivel ordered it to just drop off his men because he knew about the pirate operation and was taking precautions? A heartening thought, since at least it meant he wasn't in control of the pirates.

"Let's go see what they're up to," Jaidee said, and started down the hill. Sensha followed eagerly, praying for a chance to foil whatever Rivel had planned. Tackling the plani party and interrogating them would be child's play, but neither Sensha nor Jaidee thought anything would come of it. Sensha was sure Rivel himself would not be with this group. If he had decided to come in person, he would have done so in full force. Information was a highly-prized commodity among the plani, with a monopoly on it securing a leader's position, so there was no way Rivel would trust his lackeys with anything except their orders. If any underling started to think that he had a better idea of what was going on and what should be done than his commander, a coup could be easily managed in any number of officially sanctioned ways.

So, Jaidee and Sensha scouted the scouts – dropping back into the sneaking mode and getting in close enough to hear the conversations of the plani team – four of the dullest plani Sensha had ever set eyes on or listened to. City life had clearly diminished their hearing and awareness, but they were clueless even beyond that explanation. Rivel must have chosen them specifically because they were unimaginative and expendable. One of them appeared to be a sort of sergeant by the way he held himself and led the pack, while little could be said about the other three except that they were well-armed.

While following the incurious four around was easy, it was also painfully boring because they never discussed, speculated, or argued. They didn't talk much at all, slowly killing all the excitement Jaidee and Sensha felt after spotting them. After fifteen minutes, Sensha was tempted to attack and interrogate them just to break the monotony.

The sergeant suddenly stopped in his tracks. Jaidee and Sensha had matched footfalls with him, careful not to take extra steps when he stopped, but they still tensed up wondering whether they had somehow alerted him. Instead of looking wary, he turned to his men and, forming his words slowly, warned them, "listen, these kentaki are touchy. The captain said we have had business with them before – some of it good, some of it bad. I have to tell you our orders now. We are to pay them to take Corcoris' team hostage, but we have to offer more than they think they can get for us. If we get taken by them, the captain has made it clear that he will not pay any ransom for us, so we have to be careful." Letting that grim point sink in, he continued, "but the captain has also set a maximum offer in exchange for the Corcoris team being taken, and if we can get the kentaki to take less, we get to split the difference between ourselves. Go in ready to get out in a hurry if the kentaki do not look like they will cooperate."

Without another word, the sergeant continued to move his troop forward toward the pirate cave. Sensha and Jaidee held back to discuss the new revelations.

"A bit behind, aren't they?" Jaidee noted once they were safely out of hearing range. Not only did the plani team not know that Corcoris' team was already captured, but they were ignorant of how ruthless and organized these pirates were. Sensha was sure Rivel's men would suffer the same fate as Corcoris' soon enough, but that wouldn't do Sean and the other humans any good. They needed a plan that would put the information gap to their advantage.

Jaidee's breath caught in her throat for a second, so that Sensha wondered if the engineer had swallowed something unpleasant, then she whispered, "we could tell them."

"Tell them what?"

"Warn Rivel's men about the pirates."

Sensha looked dismayed. "What good would that do?" She didn't like the idea of warning her enemies, and had already been looking forward to the joy of seeing them detained or, even better, killed while attempting some sort of ill-advised escape. In fact, the best plan that came to her mind used the plani escape attempt as a distraction to free the other hostages. It was risky, but as far as Sensha was concerned, they only had to try to rescue the humans, and if the humans happened to die in the course of the execution of the plan, she wouldn't be too troubled. She hoped to have Jaidee's talents at her side for her mission into the center of the continent, and perhaps Sean's as well, but she saw everyone else – especially Gorenal – as a burden. Without his cargo ship Gorenal was useless, but that would not stop him from trying to reassert himself as mission commander.

Knowing that her answer would anger Sensha, Jaidee allowed a few moments' pause before answering. "Because if we tell them everything, they will probably contact Rivel for further instructions. He'll figure that it's too much for them to handle and get involved. He'll do it. This way, he can say he was saving Corcoris' team, and he can come in like the cavalry."

"Why . . . ." Sensha tried to keep her voice in check. The shout that she felt like hurling at Jaidee would definitely carry to the plani team. "Why would we want to help him save them? It is better that your friends are in the hands of these pirates than with our enemy Rivel. We should just watch with a smile as these plani get slaughtered."

Jaidee shook her head. "Two days ago, I would have said the same. Now, I'm trying to think like Captain Pierce, and she'd have our enemies fighting each other in full force while she snuck out the back way. That means we'll also need to tell the pirates that Rivel is coming. Far as I can see, that's the real tricky part."

Sensha opened her mouth to say that it was a stupid idea with no chance of succeeding, but then closed it again. If they could actually set a trap for Rivel . . . the probability of success was low, but not impossible as long as they knew where the hostages were and Rivel didn't. And if they failed, as long as the two of them survived, there was no real loss as far as Sensha was concerned. She resolved to do exactly as the plani sergeant had suggested – bolt out of harm's way if everything started falling apart.

She took a deep breath and said, "so, we pin these four down and tell them what happened and what they are walking into?"

Jaidee nodded. "Let me do the talking. I don't think they'll accept it coming from you."

Sensha almost smiled at the idea of the laconic Jaidee, so good at staying silent, giving the explanations. Without exchanging another word, they started closing on their prey again, ready to pounce.

22

BATTLE

Tricky as it had been, tying up the plani team and getting them to listen was the straightforward part of the plan. Explaining what they wanted to the sergeant was the true ordeal. Hours after they started drilling it into his thick skull, the sergeant finally understood that Jaidee wanted her people rescued by Rivel, and that this happened to coincide with the plani captain's own. Jaidee and Sensha were all too glad to comply when, unbound, the sergeant insisted that they leave before he contacted his boss. They didn't go far, of course, and were able to overhear what he said to Rivel. He left out all mention of being tied up or Jaidee and Sensha's role in warning him, claiming that all the information came from his own observations and overhearing the locals. There was no way to hear Rivel's response to all this, but from the sergeant's relieved yet excited reaction, it was apparent that he had been told to sit tight and wait for reinforcements.

"It was probably Rivel's plan all along to come to the rescue anyway," Jaidee mumbled. "He's probably thrilled right now that he didn't have to part with credits or lose these men to set the situation up."

"Doubt he cares as much about the men as for the credits," Sensha spat.

Jaidee shook his head. "He doesn't have enough support on this planet to throw people away."

"He was going to."

"I wonder why. Anyway, time for me to turn myself in to the

pirates."

Sensha was sure that the translator had flubbed that sentence somehow. "What?"

Jaidee looked curiously at Sensha, betraying no humor on her face. "How else can we warn them that Rivel's coming? I have to tell them. We also have to make sure where the hostages are being kept."

"But . . . but that is insane."

"Think dropping them a note instead would work?"

"That's better than handing yourself to them."

"But they won't take it seriously. They'll think it's a trick, or they won't get the message at all. It'd be hard to make sure the right people get it. I go, and they'll see the truth in my eyes. I'll also be able to get our people ready to run."

"What makes you think they will not execute you on the spot?"

"I'll have to be clever about it – keep them interested long enough. Good timing will help. Come on."

Shaken by dismay, Sensha followed with less confidence, wondering what kind of person Jaidee was. For now, she suspended her disbelief and assumed that the engineer's plan made sense, leaving her only one question. "What will I be doing, then? I suppose I still have a part to play?"

"Unless you want to go your own way."

Wondering if she was somehow an open book to humans, Sensha took the message silently. Her help was not essential to the rescue Jaidee had planned and the engineer had no illusions about her loyalty. Fine.

They clambered their way back to the top of the hill over the pirate cave, which was still free of kentaki. If she had been the pirate leader, Sensha would surely have placed a sentry tower there, and even some heavy weapons to ward off threats to the base while the ship was prepared for launch. Clever as he was, why hadn't the pirate leader taken this simple step? Overconfidence?

Jaidee pointed out to sea. "Rivel's plane will have to come in from there. Once I catch sight of it, I'm going to turn myself in, but it's going to have to be believable. I'll get captured trying to save the prisoners. By the time the talking's over, Rivel will be right outside their door, but they'll be on alert because of what I tried and what I'll say. Hang back in the crevices of the cave wall and listen in. Don't get involved until the pirate ship gets launched, but after that move fast and take out anyone who gets in your way. Get the prisoners out. That's what I'll be doing, too. Look!"

Sensha followed Jaidee's finger to a tiny figure creeping up the beach, approaching the cave entrance – a member of the plani sergeant's team sent to check things out. He was being cautious, but there was no way he would escape detection. Of course, Sensha was amazed that she and Jaidee had, so maybe the kentaki were just naturally incompetent security officers. Then again, the plani grunt was trying so hard to avoid notice that he actually attracted attention. Would the pirates capture him or let him go and tail him? She watched eager to find out, hoping he would be captured, spill the details of Rivel's impending arrival, and save Jaidee from throwing herself in.

After the briefest glance into the cave, the sergeant's man quickly reemerged and scurried back to his commander. Sure enough, a nonchalant kentaki tailed him loosely. If they had that much guile, then how could they fail to place a tower on this hill? The question itched at her.

"Time to get our costumes," Jaidee said. "See those two kentaki there? They have our clothes. Come on."

The two kentaki in question looked to Sensha like priests or priestesses – their robes hid any sign of their gender. While they wore no masks, their hoods were so broad that even in light their faces remained shadowed, and the effect reminded Sensha of the Grikorat cloaks so much that she thought that one had to have been derived from the other. The priests, if that was what they were, walked somberly in the pre-dawn dimness, regularly kneeing at the tideline, cupping some water at the edge of the flow, and ritualistically drinking a sip before pouring the remainder on the dry soil. Sensha was no expert on religious beliefs, but it looked like some sort of water or sea cult to her, making total sense for a fishing town turned pirate haven depending on the favor of the sea.

Their noble purpose wouldn't save these two ritualists from a bit of humiliation tonight, though. Jaidee and Sensha crept up on them, prepared to knock them out– it didn't do to go around killing holy people in the midst of their prayers regardless of what planet you were from. Besides, the two targets were walking along an isolated part of the beach in the early morning with no other kentaki in sight – easy pickings.

Or so Sensha thought. A heartbeat from the pounce, their prey – both of them – turned in unison toward the approaching attackers and held their hands up in warding. In their split-second pivot, their hoods had dropped, revealing heads blacker than the night and shimmering as if filled with water of impossible depth. There was no way the effect could be natural, and Sensha was about to gasp "mages" when the priests let loose their strike, launching their bodies like serpents against Jaidee and Sensha.

Sensha and Jaidee managed to dodge the blow despite their surprise. Jaidee's attempt to catch hold of her opponent to use its momentum against it failed, as it somehow slipped from her grasp. The two priests regained their ground immediately and stood firmly without hint of a waver or lean that Sensha could take advantage of – the epitome of efficient movement. They hurled themselves again a second later like missiles without any thought except for taking their targets down. Prepared this time, Jaidee and Sensha dodged expertly, but neither could find a way to take advantage of the reckless move.

It was ridiculous. The priests were fighting like amateurs, just throwing themselves forward with full force, and yet they somehow avoided the punishment rightfully due to such mistakes in defiance of the laws of close combat. Sensha hated magic, and there was no doubt in her mind that it was at the bottom of this impasse – a stalemate that would benefit the kentaki pair as soon as other locals caught sight of what was happening. If the priests tired of the confrontation, all they had to do was shout for help, but for now they seemed confident that they would be able to dispatch the intruders themselves.

That self-assurance led them to try to break the situation in their favor by altering their attack, launching themselves at the flanks instead of head-on, striking Sensha from the left and Jaidee from the right. That creativity had a cost – one of the two would have to move slower to avoid colliding with the other as their momentums crossed. The slow one was Jaidee's, and the engineer took advantage of it by taking part of the intended blow to slow her foe down even more and throw it slightly off balance. The sacrifice left Jaidee flat on the ground and in no position to fight, but put Sensha, who had maneuvered successfully, right behind Jaidee's unbalanced priest. She leaped onto the figure instinctively and, wasting no time, used the only attack that had never failed her, sinking her teeth deep into the creature's neck and sucking with all her might. Her prey was limp in a matter of seconds and its blood flowed out from the corners of Sensha's mouth, too much for her to swallow. Breaking her grip from the body as its legs were about to fail, she let it drop to the ground beside her, not sure whether she had killed it or not, and not particularly caring.

Turning to the other priest who was standing its ground stunned, Sensha finally had a breath in which to taste the blood. So thin on her tongue that it was practically water, it did little to satisfy her hunger. With her feeding instincts activated, she held the other kentaki with eager eyes thinking, "I bet you thought you were the nastiest thing on the prowl tonight. Well, you were wrong."

No longer sure of what it was facing and taken aback by the bloodthirst in Sensha's eyes, the remaining priest took a tentative step back – an unconscious surrender to uncertainty rather than a preparation to flee. It was enough. There was no room for un-schooled movement in a fight, and this step left the priest's weight entirely on its front leg. Sensha didn't wait for it to correct its balance, tackling it to the ground then shifting to pin it down. It almost slid away from her again. Almost. She paused for a moment with it in her grasp, still tasting the unsatisfying blood of the first priest in her mouth. Well, at least the taste was inoffensive. She dropped her head down to her prey's neck for a second, more thorough, drink.

By the time she had finished, Jaidee had risen, dusted the sand off her fatigues, and was standing over her curiously. Sensha, embarrassed and defiant, waited for the expression of disgust she felt was sure to come.

"Not how I'd 've done it, but come on. That one's your size. Get into its robes."

They disguised themselves and tossed the priests into the sea. They were still alive, but just barely – with the thinnest of breaths passing through their nostrils – so it was up to the sea they worshipped whether they would stay that way.

Back up the hill in their new costumes, they spent an excruciating time staring out on the ocean waiting for sign of Rivel's approach. Sensha was about to drop out of full alertness back into waiting idle when Jaidee said, "there it is. I'm heading in," and started down into the cave. After leaving substantial space between them, Sensha followed, but moved much less openly. On reaching the base of the hill, Jaidee began mimicking the movements of the priests just in time to satisfy the brief glance cast at her by the first kentaki passer-bys.

Despite her disguise, Sensha kept herself well out of sight, but the cave entrance posed a problem for her. She didn't know by what magic or luck Jaidee had gotten them in undetected before, but she didn't feel confident that she could sneak in now. Outside of the cave, she wedged into a crevice and waited for some chaos to distract the kentaki enough to make her feel safe about creeping into their hideout. For the first few minutes, it looked increasingly difficult, with the sun peeking over the horizon and the flow of kentaki coming in from town starting to build. Then shouts from inside the cave signaled Jaidee's detection and those on the way in quickened their pace to see what had happened, giving Sensha just the confusion she needed to get herself in position high over the scene.

Jaidee was putting on a good show, struggling against the bonds on her wrists and the arms holding her back, snarling with contempt at the pirates in a way that drew their curiosity. Sensha's translator couldn't make out the words being exchanged with all the echoing in the chamber. The kentaki held Jaidee close enough to the prison shack for her furious shouts to carry to those inside – they had probably caught her trying to break into the shack. Hopefully, the hostages would be ready for action when the time came.

The kentaki were rattled, having only just detecting the plani intruder – the member of Rivel's team they were tailing – and wanted answers from this new menace wearing the garb of one of their priests and acting like an enraged demon. They wanted answers before they killed her for her sacrilege – or maybe an exorcism was more appropriate.

By the time Sensha settled herself in to watch for her chance to act, there was already further commotion brewing outside. The pirate leader had already ordered the ship readied and was working himself up to pass judgment on Jaidee when the dam burst and droves of kentaki dashed into the cave at top speed, pointing urgently outside the entrance. Jaidee's expression turned smug, but remained more menacing than any human had any right to be. Sensha shuddered and wondered, not for the first time, if the engineer was more than a touch insane – too quick to switch from emotionless passivity to crazed defiance.

With Jaidee's warning now corroborated visually, the pirate leader ordered his crew aboard the ship and for the launch to proceed. He tasked four kentaki to escort Jaidee to the prison shack, and she made a show of ineffectual struggling as they brought her to it. Aside from these four, around two dozen others remained off the ship conducting preparations on the shore around the cave. Everyone was busy – well-trained for what needed to happen if trouble materialized – reminding Sensha of professional mercenaries rather than pirates. Sensha continued to feel that they were too organized and heavily-armed to be pirates, no matter what Jaidee said. But if they were mercenaries, then who was their employer?

Events were unfolding too quickly for Sensha to give the idea much thought. The ship's engines revved up, generating a deafening roar on a whole range of pitches, echoing against the walls of the cave. At first unbalanced, the thrust of its various engines were adjusted so that it started uniformly tugging at its moorings – away from the cave entrance at first to counter the flow of river underneath.

The four kentaki guards had Jaidee at the door of the shack as the engines started. One of them had unlocked it and was about to throw her in when she sprang into action. She took him down with a vicious head-butt and then unleashed a sequence of dodges and flying kicks that dispatched the rest. Hands still bound behind her back, she bent to the ground and took the key of the shack in her mouth. Then, to even Sensha's surprise, she went into the prison and shut the unlocked door behind her.

The dozen kentaki who noticed the fall of Jaidee's handlers and her apparent escape would have rushed in to recapture her, but stopped in their tracks when they saw her close herself in. That gave them some time to reconsider, and Sensha was coming to realize that, backward though they were, these kentaki were far from stupid. They calculated that they might end up in a minor battle with the prisoners if they attempted to force their way into the shack, and the doorway was a natural choke point. At the same time, they would be abandoning their duties and potentially endangering the entire operation. If the prisoners escaped, they were still unarmed and at the mercy of the ship's guns – should it become necessary to take them down. Every pirate made the judgment in their minds, and every single one chose to continue with their duties to ready the ship for deployment.

Sensha wondered what they were doing, since from the sheer noise coming from the ship's engines, it sounded ready to go without any extra help. The moorings were loose, boarding planks and ropes were pulled in or dropped, and she would have sworn that all the ship had to do was power up to float out to sea. Then again, she knew precious little about how ships – whether in sea, air, or space – actually worked, having never been on one until her brief stint aboard the *Azar*.

Soon enough, floating out through the cave entrance was no longer an option. A new rumble joined the din, forcing Sensha to finally shove fingers in her ears, and it came from right outside the cave. She recognized the deep, almost profound waver, but scarcely believed it until she saw the blocky nose of the plani kandar-class enforcement ship through the cave entrance. The kandar was an in-system attack vessel used primarily in low-orbit or within the atmosphere, and was built to pulverize anything – natural or otherwise – that threatened Plani cities. Its single forward antimatter projectile cannon, now pointing directly into the cave, could disintegrate a small asteroid into harmless dust. Lacking any hyperspace capability, the kandar must have been transported here from Plani by a specialized carrier, which was why Sensha couldn't believe she was seeing one. Only two dozen kandar patrolled Plani at any given time and their deployment was tightly controlled by corporate consensus. Rivel's corporation would have had enough trouble getting their hands on one, and then an impossible bureaucratic mess to get the carrier to bring it here. They had to have done it early, using the loss of the first survey ship as an excuse, and then intimidating the kentaki with it. With a kandar present to demonstrate plani power, it was no wonder that the Grikorat had given in to plani domination – they had nothing that could stand up it or even scratch its hull.

The pirates were about to see their impressive ad-hoc ship torn apart unless they had more tricks up their sleeves. Still, as long as they stayed in the cave, Rivel would not dare to fire his cannon, since that would kill the only prize he cared for – the human crew and the secret of the hyperdrive. He couldn't even fire missles. He could potentially have smaller arms on board, and fire them from the cargo ramp, but would those be enough to rip up the pirate ship? Sensha wasn't sure, but she was definitely going to enjoy watching the result, the taste of blood once again on her lips.

Rivel knew the standard Kentak radio frequencies, and was surely communicating his demands to them and receiving . . . what response could the pirates give? Either be bold, delay, or surrender. She didn't see how the situation could change with delay, and the pirate leader was the type to spit in the face of his foe regardless of the odds, so surrender was out. The pirates would up the ante and taunt Rivel. It was lucky that the prison shack's position on the shore was safe from the narrow line of fire between the two ships.

The pirate ship fired the first volley while the kandar was still turning to around to its rear where the cargo ramp held the guns Sensha had expected to see. The pirates could only bring their forward weapons to bear, and these were light compared to the kandar's artillery. The kandar took some superficial damage, but nothing Rivel couldn't shrug off. The plani response was more significant, punching definite holes in the pirate ship and starting a small fire that was quickly extinguished internally.

There was a pause, so Sensha supposed that Rivel was repeating his demands a bit more forcefully this time, and the pirate leader's retort would have a bit of extra snarl. The kentaki still working on the cave shore seemed to have a different understanding of this lull, and frantically cleared the place, dashing deeper into the cavern. Had they decided that the situation was hopeless and that it was better to desert after only this first exchange of fire? Not after all this, surely. No, they were up to something, and Sensha suddenly felt exposed. There was no one else out in the open in the cave – Jaidee and the prisoners were still in the shack and the crew of the ship was safe in its interior. Everyone else had bolted away.

The entire cavern shuddered with a seismic shock that came from neither ship, but felt like it was bubbling up from the ground itself. A light rain of dust fell from the cave ceiling. Sensha instinctively looked up after swatting away a fine mist of rock and her eyes went wide. There were clear fissures in the ceiling – unnaturally straight ones – and she suddenly understood what the workers on the ground had been up to, and why no kentaki had been stationed on top of the hill.

A volcanic explosion followed, blowing the very top of the hill high into the air and clear away from the gap that it left. The thunder was followed by secondary charges around the opening that widened it enough for the ship to launch upward comfortably. As soon as the vent seemed to have stabilized, the pirate ship applied maximum downward thrust and, just as Jaidee said it would, rose up with some jerking and swaying, its natural instability kept under control by a master pilot.

The cavern was filling with toxic fumes, but before they clouded the place, Sensha saw the hostages led by Jaidee making their run for the entrance. They were running right for the kandar, hoping that it would be too distracted by the unexpected turn in the battle and rise of the pirate ship to pay them any attention.

Sensha made a series of leaps down to the cave floor and helped to lead all of them out. Jaidee had freed all of them from the ropes tying their wrists, so that they were able to cover their noses and mouths against the choking smoke – the only defense they had against it. Jaidee got out into the open last, making sure that the other hostages, short not only on breath but also food and sleep, did not succumb to dizziness. Sensha stayed closer to the front, intent on not being recaptured by Rivel and ready to abandon the humans and Corcoris' people at the first sign that the plani captain was moving to corral them.

Despite her worries, the pirates had Rivel's entire attention. Emerging from the hill, their ship fired on the exposed topside of the kandar, its zigzag drifting making it hard for the plani ship to fire a response. Mostly used to deal with objects entering from space, or at least objects moving in a regular trajectory, the kandar was ill-suited to a match against a completely erratic target. It might have been able to track regular aerobatic maneuvers, Sensha supposed, but the pirate ship was doing nothing of the kind – it wiggled because it was a nudge away from going out of control.

She and Jaidee had to keep the escapees running, since there was no telling what kind of debris could fly at them as long as they stayed close to the action. The *Azar* crew members were mostly fit, but Gorenal and his men were not quite as agile. They headed southwest – away from both the town and the pirate haven – over land moist enough to make every lift of a foot difficult and unpleasant. They managed to clear the battlezone with the combat still raging, and turned to look at the surreal scene.

While both ships used thrust to make up for severe aerodynamic inefficiency, the kandar had the pirate ship beat in terms of looks. In the actual battle, though, the pirates seemed to have the upper hand. They kept their ship either above or below the kandar, taking advantage of the fact that the kandar had to pitch in order to aim its guns up or down while their own guns swiveled in broad arcs. The pirate ship was not at all nimble, having much of the control characteristics of a hovercraft, but it had the advantage this close to the ground. The kandar was ungainly in heavy gravity, designed to confront threats in a fraction of the downward pull now exerted on it. Slower to gain altitude and maneuver at this level, it would have had the pirate ship beat if only it could gain a mile of height.

"How do they know to fight this way?" Sensha asked Jaidee as they looked on the scene together.

Jaidee just shrugged, but Sean overheard the comment and said, "smells a bit funny, doesn't it? And I'll tell you what else smells funny – look at that." A cargo plane, identical to the one that had brought them across the ocean, was coming in from the south, keeping discretely low and slow. "Should we run because it's Rivel, or stay out in the open to be picked up because it's Corcoris?"

"It is a space ministry plane," Gorenal said. "I . . . I will have a lot to answer for, I think."

There was no doubt in Gorenal's voice, so they waited for the plane to make a landing after spotting them and headed towards its rear door. The first two to exit it were kentaki guards, but they were followed by Corcoris himself, slumping a bit from fatigue but with a face filled with relief.

"You are safe then," he said, seeing everyone gathered behind Jaidee, Sean, and Sensha. "I did not dare hope for so much. Once I saw Rivel mobilizing, I knew something must have happened here and followed."

"Pretty quick," Sean mumbled.

"Rivel took time getting enough of his people together to feel safe about coming here. He more or less took every plani except for those in the Grikorat. Before he got off the ground, we found out where you must be, and also prepared another surprise. Quickly, come on board."

Unlike its twin, the interior of this plane was filled with seating and had no room for cargo. Aside from the kentaki, two humans turned around in their seats as the new passengers came in – Captain Pierce and Marquez.

Eyebrows raised, Sean mused, "wow, you *have* been busy."

23

Rebellion

The way Pierce looked the newcomers over, Sensha was sure she was looking for someone in particular. A disappointed expression passed over the captain's face, but she quickly replaced it with a smirk.

"Well, here I am."

Sean grinned. "You're looking a lot better."

She nodded. "Still weak, but the change of scenery's helped. Don't ask me why, but the air in the capital's definitely no good for me."

Looking from the captain to Corcoris and then back again, Sean asked, "Okay, so how did this happen?"

Corcoris answered. "We caught the plani in a manpower shortage. They left some local – kentaki – hirelings in charge of guarding the government house and Captain Pierce. It was easy enough to pay them more. We did it minutes after the plani cleared the building to get to their warship, leaving to intervene here. I think the plani captain smelled an opportunity here to get what he wanted from one of you and became less concerned about Captain Pierce, who seemed delirious and not at all . . . forthcoming."

The space minister must have noticed the way Pierce had looked at the resuced members of her crew, because he added, "I do not suppose we happen to have everyone of interest here already?" He was fishing, wanting to know if he held the more valuable cards in his hand so that he could place the right bets.

"Every member of my crew is 'of interest,' Minister," Pierce snapped.

"Of course," Corcoris sighed. "If you would all be seated, I will confer with Gorenal to see where you left off and we will continue the retrieval of your crew."

Almost too quickly, Pierce said, "Sensha, could you sit next to me. I want to have a word with you."

Puzzled that Pierce would want to speak to her instead of the *Azar* crew members, Sensha was slow to comply, but ultimately took the offered seat as the cargo plane's hatch closed and its engines increased thrust for takeoff.

Pierce made sure the engine noise kept her voice from reaching anyone but Sensha. "Tell me everything that happened from when you escaped the government house, all about Corcoris and this mission, and what happened here."

"Why not ask your own people about it?"

Pierce smiled weakly, still showing sign that she had not fully recovered from whatever had ailed her. "Except for Sean and Jaidee, they wouldn't know anything. Sean would say too much, Jaidee would say too little, and neither of them knows as much as you do. Please."

Sensha nodded and proceeded to give as full an account of the actual events as she could, leaving out all of her observations and opinions. Pierce leaned forward, tense throughout the account, then relaxed back in her seat with a satisfied but thoughtful expression on her face once it was over, digesting all the information. It had been quite a lot of activity to pack into a few days.

"Jaidee called them pirates, huh?" Pierce said. "But the way you say it, I guess you don't believe it. I don't either. Jaidee can be weirdly romantic sometimes. How did they know how to fight the plani ship? I'm sure Rivel was caught off guard by that, too. Someone had to have told them how to fight the plani, and that person must have set the whole thing up." She cast a pointed glance at Corcoris, seated two rows in front of them. "As if he didn't know who his contact was. I'm sure he didn't tell Gorenal, but I bet those so-called pirates were under his control the whole time."

That was . . . brilliant, Sensha had to admit. She had wondered how Corcoris could have been so blind as to mistaken a pirate leader for a trusted contact, when all along the whole thing had been a ploy to draw Rivel away from the capital.

"But what if Jaidee and I hadn't escaped and then found a way to free the hostages?"

Pierce sniffed. "You were allowed to escape and they magically didn't notice you creep into their hideout so that you could do your part. I don't think they expected you to tip off the plani squad as well – they must have had some way to handle it themselves." She shook her head, "it's all really complicated, and I'm sure there are plenty of details to work through, but I'm not up to untangling it all. It's enough to know that Corcoris was probably behind it, which tells us what kind of person we are dealing with."

Sensha saw problems with the explanation, but kept them to herself, certain that Pierce was right. It was natural and wise to be suspicious of someone as powerful as Corcoris.

Pierce continued. "This is a game of chessmasters, Sensha, and the only thing that let me keep up with them doesn't seem to be working anymore. I can figure it all out after the fact, but I can't see it ahead of time before falling into it. I . . . I still can't believe I've lost my ship."

The pain in the simple whispered words was palatable. At first, Sensha kept herself to a respectful silence, unable to comprehend what the sudden loss of such wealth and power could feel like, but after a minute, decided this was the right opportunity to stoke some flames. For the former captain's own sake, she needed to be driven to action, and there were few motives as potent as revenge.

"Rivel was the one who lured you in, who deliberately caused what happened to your ship. You . . . you are not going to let him get away with that, are you?"

"Easy thing to say, but I'm just a washed up trader now. What am I supposed to do against a plani corporation? The only thing I can do is keep my mouth shut, and get my people to keep their mouths shut."

"There is the source of the radiation – it only emits the radiation when space ships like yours . . . you know. It should be safe to approach. Then we can also find out what really did that to your ship. You came here looking for more information about the," her lips formed the word 'hyperdrive' silently, "and I am sure it has something to do with it. You have to keep Rivel from getting to it."

Pierce marveled for a moment at the impetuous dribrora. "I don't have the resources to stop him from doing anything."

"What about Corcoris? We could tell him, and he would definitely want to stop Rivel.

Pierce chuckled, then lowered her voice even further so that Sensha could only hear her words with difficulty. "Yeah, putting the two of them head-to-head sounds like a good idea, but I don't think you understand what Corcoris is all about. This whole pirate thing is just the tip of the iceberg. He's probably got a hundred little groups like this peppering the planet. Like he said – he's been at this thing for ages. When it comes time, all these little pieces will start raising trouble, all at the same time, and the Grikorat'll find itself surrounded. The space ministry will be the whole government, and Corcoris will be in charge."

The word "dictator" formed on Sensha's lips, but she didn't dare give voice to it. Pierce nodded and went on, "so I'm not sure if I want to hand him any advantages he doesn't already have."

Plani had always, as far as Sensha knew, been ruled by an oligarchy composed of the heads of the corporations. Dictatorship was the spectre – the vile alternative to the existing system that had to be avoided at all costs. To every sin of the oligarchy that made it to the press, spokespeople instantly responded whether reporters would prefer a dictator. Every plani understood that democracy always descended into dictatorship. Even Sensha, in her dribrora community, had been taught all this as a child, and now she looked at Corcoris with apprehension.

"So we need to split up from Corcoris and try to make our own way," Sensha suggested. That had been her intention in the first place, though adding the "we" and "our" took a bit of effort.

"That's sort of difficult, with him being our only transportation." Sensha detected amusement in the former captain's voice and was put off. In Pierce's eyes, was she simply a naïve young girl?

Turning the tables, Sensha replied, "I was hoping you could think of a way to do it. I think I have done a great deal for your people I did not have to. I stood by them even though I could have easily made my own way. It is not as if you can offer me a way off of Kentak."

Pierce turned serious. "Don't count me out just yet. You're right, and don't get me wrong, I'm thinking about it. Thank you for the support you've given, and I'll find some way to pay you back for it. For now, though, I want to stick with Corcoris as long as he's willing to continue hunting for my crew. If he starts to make political moves, though, I might want to be somewhere else."

"But finding your crew could take many days. It could take forever."

"There are some – at least two – who I absolutely need to find as soon as possible. You would want me to find them. At least, you wouldn't want Rivel to find them."

"Where will they go then, if they wanted to meet with you and the rest of the crew? They must know they are not on the same continent as the capital, and they do not know about the plani be- ing here, so they would guess that you are heading to the goal as well. To the source of the radiation."

"They would," Pierce conceded, "but they don't know where it is."

"There might be other signs on this continent, especially if they landed closer to the place."

Pierce sat silently, giving no indication of her thoughts.

Sensha took a different tact. "Suppose Rivel does not come after us or the rest of your crew, but goes to the source instead since he is already on this continent. He may also guess that your people would go there, or that we would go there. What then? He might not need you anymore."

Pierce sniffed. "You just want to engineer some sort of huge confrontation. His people 've been here for years. They probably know what's there and that it's not anything important," she said flippantly.

"But he also knows that your lost crew members might not

know that, and might go there anyway."

Pierce tapped a rhythm on the armrest with her fingertips, then cleared her throat. "Your opinion is noted. Let me sleep on it." She immediately sunk deeper in her seat and closed her eyes.

"But . . . ."

"I need to catch up on sleep – didn't get much while I was under the weather. Wake me when we're about to land again."

And that was that. Sensha Still, Sensha had gotten to say her piece, and could be satisfied with that. For now.

When they landed, it was on the outskirts of another coastal town, though this one looked to be in good repair. Because the pilot had transmitted news of the minister's arrival prior to the landing, they were met not by a contact, but the council of town elders, who came to pay their respects to the prestigious guest. When the minister explained to them the purpose of his visit, they all grew excited, taking a minute to compose themselves enough to report delightedly that they had detained four aliens exactly of the sort that stood behind the minister.

Sensha was cautious of another trap, but sensed none of the warning signs that had tipped her off in the fishing town. They were led through town to the prison, where the reunion of the four members took place as promised. Pierce gave no sign whether the four included the members she had been especially concerned about. With them, she now had more than half of her former crew.

Corcoris allowed the humans time to huddle together, and they seemed to make full use of it, speaking quickly with each other, bringing together all they could possibly know about the situation. Sensha wondered if it would be all right for her to join in on that discussion, but made no attempt to move herself into it. Something about the way they gathered put up a force field – a human-only zone that made it clear she wasn't welcome. She wondered why that should bother her, and supposed it was because Jaidee and Pierce had so recently treated her . . . not as an equal, but at least decently. It was . . . irritating to be reminded now that she really didn't belong with these people.

At the end of the conference, Pierce gave Sensha a nod. Sensha didn't know what that meant, but because she felt like it, sniffed and turned her back on the former captain in response. Pierce approached Corcoris, who stood up from his seat and motioned for his people to prepare for launch.

"Are you ready to continue, then?" the minister asked. "We had to spend some time here on formalities, but there is still enough daylight left to make one more flight."

"I think a change of plans might be appropriate," Pierce said. Then, to Sensha's surprise, she made exactly the case Sensha had about Rivel and the other crew members perhaps heading for the radiation source. "Would the plani have already investigated that place, do you think?"

"I was wondering when you would discuss this. No, I do not believe they have. They prefer to gain knowledge from afar and to deal with people they can manipulate, would you not say? They likely know where the disturbance is – a disturbance that led to the loss of their early ships, after all – but it is so deep in woodlands and in a sparsely populated part of our world. There has been no indication that they have investigated it, or wish to. They have regarded it as a natural phenomenon."

Pierce sighed. "Then maybe we should go for it, after all. At worst, we waste a day."

"That is not quite true. We cannot land anywhere near the location – not only does the forest make it difficult, but the winds in that region are known to be strong and unpredictable. The gusts would make landing and takeoff too much of a risk. Since we will have to land a distance from the location, we need transportation. Our plane is only carrying one land vehicle, and it may not be suited to the terrain, so we will have to land in the closest town, and hope we can organize some ground transportation from there. My point is that it will be a multiple day journey. It is difficult to say how long it will take."

Sucking at her bottom lip, Pierce said, "changes things, doesn't it? And I guess you don't think it's a good idea?"

"No, captain. Since we took you out of the capital and the plani ship has gotten into its trouble on this side of the ocean, the pace of events will no doubt quicken, and we need to take advantage before it is too late. I would like to have as large a group of humans as possible appear at the capitol building just as the Grikorat sees the plani warship limp back, damaged. It would likely lead to strife within the government, as many in the Grikorat will believe they have been duped into supporting the plani under false pretenses – they will suspect that your people are actually superior. Then . . . then things get interesting. If we travel deep into this continent to pursue this mystery, we take a risk not only in finding something that would be a danger to ourselves, but also risk missing an opportunity to right the wrong done to my people."

"So, if I want to do it – to chase the mystery – you would . . . oppose it?" Pierce let the taste of the last two words linger.

Corcoris, always careful in his words, paused to be more than judicious this time. "No, no, of course not. And my resources are at your disposal. I was merely suggesting since you asked. I do not doubt that you have information I lack – information about why this mystery might hold some value. Is that right?"

Pierce had to concede something to him, or she would have appeared dishonest. "Yes. We came to this planet for a reason, and the reason might be there. If Rivel's people didn't think to look into it before, they will now. In fact, they probably started going in that direction as soon as they found out I was interested in this planet. Rivel had to have put two and two together. You're right about the plani, though – they don't do well outside of cities. I'm hoping that it's delayed them enough so that we're not too far behind."

Corcoris nodded. "Very well, captain. If you feel it is necessary, we will take that chance. Two of your escape pods landed in that region, so perhaps we can rescue those humans as well. I have a contact in a town in the area who should be able to arrange things for us. It is too far to travel in the daylight we have left, so we should stay in this town tonight, and then make the flight first thing tomorrow."

24

Pathways

For Kaz and Ethan, the past few days had been utterly boring with the tedious walk punctuated by . . . by nothing, really. Though he didn't dare say anything, Fletcher experienced something completely different – something that was growing in intensity as they headed further north. Every now and again, he would ask to use the food analyzer, and check the Geiger counter reading on it, just in case he was somehow seeing radiation and getting affected by it. It was a silly idea, and the readings turned out to be normal – well, normal for Kentak background radiation, anyway – so he was left wondering.

He was coming to believe that he really was seeing the hyper-space field – he refused to call it the magical field. To him, the word 'magic' should be left for stuff that lacked physical reality, and this field clearly had physical reality. At least, it did for him.

He could see the purple in the sky during the day now, though it was nowhere near as vibrant as it was at night. Worse, his experiences at night were no longer brief flashes but more like – he hated to think of the word – visions. But he was actually registering things now, and some of them plagued his mind as he walked during the daytime. He had been on Newport Station with missiles slamming into the towers, slowly falling rubble cracking the pressurized tubes, and eventually doing enough damage to break the formidable material and suck people out into the vacuum of space. He had been pulled out of a hole, too, choking for air until the scene changed. Was it a vision of the future or an unfulfilled past? Or was it nothing more than the subconscious fear that his normal nightmares were built out of?

No – even though the Newport Station vision was the most vivid one, he saw plenty more that had less emotional impact because they were related to nothing he had experienced before. He had seen aliens unknown to him going about their daily business with almost human behaviors, and other aliens whose behavior he couldn't understand at all. Every now and again, he would find himself in strange voids – nowhere near any sign of life – sometimes able to breath, other times not. He was growing less and less worried during the breathless parts, since he knew he would be pulled back to safer ground, but there was no diminishing the instinctive panic built into his body when the lack of breath started to become critical. Fortunately, excursions into places not suited to his vital necessities were growing less frequent. More and more of what he saw involved humans specifically, as if an extremely broad search was narrowing down to a match. What would happen when the vision finally came to match his reality?

He kept everything to himself – not a problem, since all three of the travelers were lost in their own thoughts while walking. Ethan was the most talkative of them, but even he had trouble finding things to say, and ultimately brought out an e-paper with his notes on hyperspace theory and spent his time trying to resolve the gaps in it. Kaz occasionally gave Fletcher a curious look, but Fletcher always smiled back in a reassuring way.

That all changed when they reached the edge of the forest, and the plants – more tall-stemmed shrubs than actual trees – looked eerily familiar to Fletcher. It took a moment for him to remember, because they were still spread out instead of packed together, but he had seen them two nights before. He had seen . . . something crash into them, hadn't he? He had been standing in the midst of a thick grove of the plants, looking straight up at a streaking fireball making a quick and steep descent overhead. No, more than one, and some were not fireballs. He remembered what looked like a plane that was mostly intact – though it couldn't have stayed that way coming down at that angle. It couldn't have been the remnants of the *Azar* – there was just too much material for that. Was it something that would happen in the future?

Seeing the shrub-trees shook Fletcher, and he decided that he couldn't keep what he saw from the other two any longer. What if it meant other ships would soon enter orbit around Kentak and suffer the same fate as the *Azar*? Then their lives could be in jeopardy, going closer to the source of the disaster.

After asking them if it was all right to sit down and rest for a while, he summoned up the courage to tell them everything – from the start of the visions and seeing the purple sky to the increasing intensity of both. Ethan's growing excitement was annoyingly just as expected, but Kaz stayed unreadable throughout Fletcher's explanation. If anything, he seemed troubled and confused by what Fletcher said.

"I knew it!" Ethan shouted, barely able to wait for Fletcher to finish. "You're absorbing energy from the field. This is great! God, you could become like . . . I don't know. You probably have way more potential than Emily – she only ever has dreams, and they're all vague. You actually feel like you're standing there. That's impressive."

"It doesn't feel that impressive. I mean, I can't control it."

Kaz nodded. "Exactly. It sounds dangerous. Maybe if Emily was here, she would know more about it, but probably this is beyond even her. Until you can control it, it sounds like you're allergic to magic, and you're sneezing yourself into different worlds. Could be dangerous. I hope I'm overreacting."

"You are," Ethan said firmly. "I mean, nothing bad's happened to him except he's a bit rattled by it. He looks fine."

"Are you a doctor? Would you be able to tell if Fletcher had really spent part of the night in a vacuum? I don't suppose somewhere in those equations, they might have taught you something practical like that? Unfortunately, I don't know, either, but I do know that Fletcher was making choking sounds in his sleep the previous nights. I just thought it was something natural or bad dreams, but now I know different, and I'll be keeping a closer eye on him. I don't know, though, whether I can wake him up when he's in that state – whether it might do some permanent damage if I tried."

Ethan waved his hands. "Hey! You're going to scare the kid out of sleeping at all tonight if you go on like that!"

"Maybe that's for the best," Kaz murmured ominously.

"No. Geez, he can't stay awake forever. He's going to have to learn how to control it somehow."

Kaz pointed at Ethan. "That's the first sensible thing you've said."

"Well, of course. I mean, it's no good for anyone if you let it run wild, right?"

Kaz sighed. "Well, at least we're somewhat on the same page. Fletcher, you have to try to control it. Maybe . . . before going to sleep, try to think of a particular place. That's what Emily does, but she's only dealing with dreams. I don't know if it's enough to work for you. You have to try, though. Do you understand?"

Fletcher nodded. "I'll try, but I'm as sure about it as you are."

"Good. Be careful with this sort of thing. This field . . . I guess it's like any other physical field. Playing around with electricity or gravity can be just as dangerous. It takes a lot of knowledge to harness a field for useful purposes, and I don't think this field is any different. I'm worried that what's happening is . . . is as if you're being struck by lightning."

Fletcher nodded again, amazed at how sympathetic the cold-seeming Kaz could be. He wondered why Kaz reacted this way – why the first officer should care at all if he got struck by lightning or anything. Ethan was more like his father, trying to figure out how to put him to use. Fletcher didn't blame Ethan, who was on a mission to break one of the universe's greatest mysteries and was necessarily single-minded about it. Wasn't that also Kaz's mission? Maybe he was just going about it a different way – sort of a good cop, bad cop tactic.

That night, Fletcher did as Kaz had suggested. It was tough to think of a place that he actually wanted to be. He decided it shouldn't be somewhere he had actually been, since it would be hard to tell that apart from memory. Besides, he was a bit nervous about what might happen if he met himself, even intangibly. It shouldn't be possible, but he wasn't sure of the rules yet, so it was better to play it safe like Kaz had said.

Ultimately, he decided on Utopia-1 – the main dome on Utopia planitia on Mars. Its triple language signs in English, Chinese, and Japanese were distinctive in his mind, especially when they were lit up at night. It was the most Earth-like city on Mars, and a favorite vacation spot, though he had never been there to find out personally. Anyway, his mind was filled with the images of luxury unexpected on the Martian surface – bright lights everywhere, fountains, and all sorts of waste that the original colonists of the planet would have scorned.

At first, he dreamt of going there, bringing himself to sleep with thoughts of visiting the red planet. This time, without any interlude of other dreams, he slipped into a numbing fog, sightless, and finally found himself opening his eyes in Utopia-1 in the Martian night as planned. But not as planned. Unlike any other time he had experienced the scenes, he no longer felt his body lying down on the soil of Kentak. No, he felt entirely here, on Mars, smelling the scents that people threw into the air to test the limits of the air management systems.

The street was packed with people shopping – mostly tourists, with locals doing the selling – so he had drawn little notice. A few people had taken notice, but only two – an old man and an unrelated teen girl– were impolite enough to stare. The old man shouted something at him, but not in English, and Fletcher had taken off his translator before sleeping as usual. Without understanding the words, Fletcher guessed that the old man had just seen him wink into existence and was saying, "Where the hell did you come from?" Fletcher shrugged to indicate that he didn't understand and eventually the old man gave up, putting the whole experience down to a trick of the eyes, perhaps.

The teen was not so easy to shrug off. She didn't say anything, but as Fletcher moved away from the old man, he noticed her turning to follow him. This was not good. After days on the boring landscape of Kentak, all the lights and noise were disorienting to Fletcher, and the pounding in his skull was starting to give him a headache. He didn't know where he was going, and just tried to keep with the flow of pedestrians. That girl following him suspected something about him, and that left him feeling very exposed.

He had to gather his thoughts about what had just happened. Had he really just transported himself across light years to Mars? He pinched himself on his arm, said the obligatory "ow," and concluded from the redness in his skin that he wasn't completely dreaming. He was fully clothed, thankfully, but in the same soiled clothes he had on Kentak. What else? Well, if he could go from one planet to another at will . . . the pain in his head was starting to get in the way of his thoughts. Something was very wrong. If he had been absorbing the hyperdrive field on Kentak, he was now away from that source of power. How long before he would lose the chance to go back? Could he do it while he was awake?

He turned onto a less crowded street and, leaning himself against the concrete wall of a shop, he closed his eyes. His last thought before focusing with all his might on Kentak, Ethan, and Kaz was that he should find somewhere more concealed, but there was no time to worry about who was watching. Remembering an old trick, he changed his breathing to a sleeping pattern – a trick his father had taught him so that he could sleep in uncomfortable shuttle seats – and quickly drifted back to sleep. The tailing girl was standing right next to him when he winked out of Mars existence again.

Back in the fog, he tried to open his eyes, but couldn't. Maybe it was self-preservation again. Something in his consciousness seemed to be keeping him alive and safe from harm even as he had no clue what he was doing.

When he finally felt free to open his eyes, it was to the purple night sky of Kentak and a pain that was ripping apart his skull. He screamed from the pain. He screamed hoping that the sound would carry out the demon ripping his brain to shreds. Something was wrong, all right. Both of his hands grabbed at his hair, instinctively trying to get to the source of the pain, and to pull it out. His eyes watered and his voice quickly grew hoarse from its shrieking. That left his ears, which heard Kaz say loudly, "get the anesthetic from the medical kit! Quickly!"

"Do you think it'll work?"

"Now!"

A few seconds later, Fletcher felt relief coursing through his veins and, when it finally reached his head, he collapsed to the ground and fell into a sleep beyond dreams.

25

Headaches

When Fletcher woke, the sun was already high in the sky, and the tint produced by the hyperdrive field was at its weakest. A migraine still wracked his skull, but it was nowhere near as bad as it had been last night. He didn't even want to think about last night. If not for the hope of a pill to relieve the pain, he probably would have stayed horizontal until the afternoon. He didn't feel up to a day of walking at all.

Kaz had the pill and some water ready for him, and Fletcher downed them gratefully. Ethan was itching to ask him questions, but Kaz held him back with a caustic pair of warning eyes, for which Fletcher was also grateful.

Fletcher was having trouble putting thoughts together. His emotions were raw, and while moving around was simple enough, making sense of what he was doing was difficult. He knew that he was not his normal self, but couldn't think beyond having the barest sense of frustration. It was as if, mentally, his arms and legs had been cut off. He panicked, trying to use faculties that simply weren't there.

"Easy, easy," Kaz said, putting a comforting hand on his shoulder. Kaz tried to look calm, but Fletcher could feel the concern in his hand and behind his eyes. "Ethan thinks you'll recover just fine. He says it shouldn't take more than a day."

Fletcher was barely able to make sense of the words, as if they were in a language he was still learning. He looked to Ethan, who nodded.

"I'm pretty sure about it. The way mages interact with the field is through their mind, after all," Ethan tapped his head. "Parts of your brain functions are dependent on the field. You used all the field energy you had stored, but part of that's used for your higher brain functions. In fact . . . I wonder if you might have gone into negative territory, sort of creating a vacuum in your head. The way you screamed . . . I think that might have been what was happening, but I'm not sure that's even possible."

Fletcher understood precisely none of this, and managed to say, "don't get it."

Ethan went on as if this was expected. "Well, anyway, you're in luck. From what you said, this planet's full of field energy, we're probably going closer to the source of it, and you seem to be really efficient at absorbing it. I'd really like to know . . . when you've rested up a bit of course," he gave a nod to Kaz's warning stare, "what you actually did. Since you used up everything you had doing it, that'll tell me exactly how much potential energy you stored the past few days. I can actually calculate stuff like that using these equations."

Fletcher turned back to Kaz, who made more sense, "what happened?"

"All we know is that you disappeared and, a few minutes after we noticed you were gone and started looking around for you, we heard your scream and ran back here. I gave you something to kill the pain – probably a higher dose than was right for you, but I didn't know if even that would work for . . . for whatever it was that had you like that. The rest, you're going to have to tell us. For now, you just need to recover. I guess that means absorbing . . . ," Kaz shook his head, "I'm sorry, I'm still caught between not understanding it and not believing it myself."

Addled though his mind was, Fletcher was sure that not understanding was no longer a luxury he could afford. As soon as he could put his mind up to the task, he would try to understand all of this, and hope that understanding it would make believing irrelevant.

Mentally fatigued, the night's rest had still restored him physically, and after an hour of sitting around he insisted that he could walk and they continued to make their way north. It wasn't boring for him today, since he spent the time pushing at the clouds in his mind. By sunset, he felt the old pathways opening back up and was more confident in his recovery. Looking back on the day, it had been an ordeal – a trial that, even though it happened entirely inside of himself, he was powerless to affect the outcome of. As Ethan had said, the energy around him had filled the wound. All he could do was make sure it didn't happen again.

By dinner, he was ready to hear some answers, though it meant he would have to start things off by giving them first. They waited respectfully for him, but their desire to know had grown with every hour, and even Kaz would soon have trouble holding back his curiosity. With their campfire blazing and meals solidly in their stomachs, Fletcher decided it was time.

"I . . . I was on Mars. In Utopia-1. I was really there – like physically," he said, and then let the words sink in.

"That's impossible," Kaz said, "Even by hyperspace it's an overnight trip from here. You weren't gone that long."

Ethan shook his head. "Not impossible. Not if it wasn't our Mars."

"What?" Kaz snapped at him.

Ethan cleared his throat. "Well, it could have been a reality next door to ours." He had done a lot of figuring through the day, and had his explanations ready. He held his palms next to each other to illustrate. "Hyperspace itself is another reality, after all, and we can jump into and out of it pretty much instantly. We spend time in hyperspace to go from place to place in this reality, but there's nothing stopping him from going to a different Mars without going through hyperspace first. It should be easier, even."

Fletcher sighed. "Totally don't get it. Why . . . why do we have to go through hyperspace to go from place to place?"

"Ah, that's a tough one."

"Then forget it," Fletcher said quickly, ready with another question. He wasn't up to tough ones.

"No, no, I think I can explain it. It's all about causation. If you travel light years and back – and back being the important part – instantaneously, then that's the same as traveling back in time.

Trust me on that one, you don't want me to explain it. The universe doesn't let you go back in time, because that almost always leads to paradoxes and infinite energy loops and . . . basically the probabilities of you ending up going back in time are zero. Wormholes that would let you do it collapse as soon as anything – even a photon – goes in. The energy released by the collapse includes the energy of whatever went in, so nothing's lost."

"Okay, what about hyperspace?" Kaz asked, trying to get Ethan back on track.

"Right. Hyperspace is another reality where space didn't end up inflating to the size ours did. For some reason, all the spatial points in it are mapped to points in ours on a scale of about a light-minute to every light-year. That's the minimum travel time if you want to end up in the same reality, unless someone finds a better hyperspace. It's like our reality is the crust of a planet, and hyperspace is the core, except it only takes time to travel within the reality. While you're traveling in a particular reality, the speed of light's still the limit. It doesn't take any time to go from one reality to the other – to go from the crust to the core."

Fletcher wasn't sure about that. He remembered it taking time – remembered the void in which he could not open his eyes – but let the point pass.

Ethan continued. "The no-going-back-in-time thing only applies to the same reality. If you were never in a reality, then there's no way you could create a paradox by coming in at any time you wanted. Now that Fletcher's been to Mars in this other reality, he can't go to an earlier time in that reality, and if he went back without going through hyperspace first, he'd probably be limited to Sol system for the next few years."

"Wait. You mean there wasn't a me in this other reality?"

Ethan shrugged. "I guess not."

Fletcher pondered that for a moment. A reality without him in it. How did he get there? He had thought of a place he had never been to before – well, that had turned out totally right, hadn't it? He had focused in on Utopia-1, but it was the Utopia-1 from all the ads. He didn't know what the real Utopia-1 was like – it was probably completely different from the way the ads made it out to be. So, he had ended up in a different reality where Utopia-1 was like it was in the ads. Weird. Did that girl who had stalked him exist in this reality, then?

"This is incredible," Ethan said, standing up. "Do you know what this means, Kaz?"

"Don't get ahead of yourself, Ethan."

"But he's a full blown mage, isn't he? I mean, if he practiced a bit, he could just zoom off of this rock and back to Earth or wherever."

Kaz rolled his eyes. "If he wanted to stay in this reality, then according to you, he'd need to go through hyperspace and he isn't moving anywhere near light speed – it would still take him a lifetime to get back to Earth without a ship. And he'd have a bit of trouble breathing in hyperspace without a ship or space suit."

Ethan waved off the inability to breathe as a technicality. "I mean in principle. Give him a ship, and he's a walking hyperdrive."

Ethan was getting on Fletcher's nerves and at the last comment, Fletcher decided it was time to let off some steam. "I'm not a walking hyperdrive! Hell, I don't know what this is, but even if I could take us all back to Earth, I swear I'm leaving you behind just so I don't have to hear you talk about it! And I can't, you know. I guess I brought myself there, and I guess I managed my clothes, too, which was nice, but a ship is . . . ," he waved his arms around a broad sphere that was much smaller than he intended it to be, "it's big, all right? Anyway, and I want to make this totally clear, I'm not taking you with me anywhere! You got that?"

Slapped hard by the rant, Ethan sat dumbfounded. Kaz shook his head, but had a broad smile on his face – the most sincere amusement Fletcher had seen from the first officer. Fletcher even got an approving nod when the first officer turned to him. He let out a breath and relaxed a bit. There was plenty more frustration where that outburst came from, but he could put it to better use some other time, or cancel it out by figuring things out on his own. They were still in a tough situation on an alien world – there was no point pushing more onto the others once he had made his point.

"I wasn't . . . ," Ethan stammered, "I mean, I didn't mean . . .

I hope you didn't . . . ."

"It's enough," Kaz said. "The question now is what we need to do, or what Fletcher needs to do. I was completely wrong about the advice I gave you yesterday, Fletcher, I'm sorry."

Fletcher waved it off. "Not your fault. Sounded good to me, too, or I wouldn't have done it."

"So what do you think you need to do tonight? Just let yourself drift like you were before without controlling it?"

"That might be the best thing to do until I can talk to someone who knows a bit more about this stuff."

Ethan opened his mouth, but then closed it.

Fletcher continued. "I'm not too worried about tonight. I think I'm still recharging, and I probably won't even see the usual scene-flashing thing." Then, throwing Ethan a rope, he added, "what do you think, Ethan?"

"Yeah. Yeah, you're just getting back to normal human levels. Of course, you said the field gets more intense at night, so there's no telling how much you could get out of the late night boost. I don't suppose you can feel how much of the field energy you have?"

"Like some sort of fuel gauge? No. Not until it's gone, of course." On reflection, Fletcher amended, "except I think I have some sort of instinct telling me whether I can or can't do something. When I thought about Mars here, I sort of knew it was do-able. When I was on Mars, I knew I was pretty close to not being able to get back here at all."

Ethan sniffed. "I'm surprised you bothered to come back."

Fletcher had to think about that. Why wasn't he surprised that he came back? After all, he could have been free to do whatever he wanted in Utopia-1. Granted, whether he could survive on his own was a question, but he had taken that problem on from the moment he had decided to flee Newport Station. Was it just curiosity that brought him back? It wasn't Avelyn, that was for sure. Was it Kaz and Ethan? That was something. It would have been . . . wrong to leave them here, worrying about what had happened to him. Not when they had actually cared. But there was something more. He thought back to his feelings when he was on Mars.

"I . . . I didn't feel right there. I didn't belong. I don't think I could have stayed there very long even if I had wanted to and tried. But then, if I had stayed there any longer, maybe I wouldn't have been able to get back here. I don't know what would have happened. Maybe I would've adjusted, but maybe I would've gone insane."

"Do you think you would have been alright if you had traveled through hyperspace and had gotten to this reality's Mars?"

Fletcher frowned. "Don't we already do that in our ships? Of course I would've been alright. Or . . . are you asking me whether I would have been okay with leaving you two behind?"

"No, I wasn't . . . ."

"I hope, if I was in my right mind, I would have tried to get you guys help. I guess, since he helped me before, I would have tried to contact Commander Raiz and tell him what happened." He was edgy, but still had one question. "Ethan, what the hell is this field, anyway? I mean, I know gravity is the way mass and energy bend space-time, and I sort of get electricity, but what is this field?"

Ethan's eyes went wide. "It's the field in which the realities interact, of course. Realities sort of leak and exchange particles that keep them separate or pull them together. One reality can splinter into two, and two realities can merge. That sort of thing. It takes more than a cat in a box living or dying, though. I think it does, anyway. Otherwise, there'd be a mess of realities, wouldn't there be? If the other reality has different fundamental physics than ours, that would keep even you from going there. It so happens that even though there wasn't an inflationary period in the hyperspace reality, everything else is fine – our atoms don't fly apart or squash together or anything. I'm sure there're plenty of other hyperspaces where the ship would get crushed or would disintegrate as soon as it jumped in."

"A field in which realities interact," Fletcher repeated. "Okay, I think I can handle that. About how many realities are we talking about?"

"On the order of ten to the five hundred power. That's one with five hundred zeroes after it."

"I know what exponents are." Actually, whenever Fletcher heard 'ten to the,' he automatically translated it as 'too many.' "How many could we survive in?"

"Well, even in this universe you'd die pretty quickly in most of it, since so much of it's space. As far as the universes in which the basic particles are the same and act the same, so chemistry still works, it's probably around a googol – ten to a hundred. But these are all based on what older theories said. Once hyperspace theory is totally worked out, it could give different and better answers."

Fletcher ignored that. The point was that there were plenty of realities, and most of them were not hospitable. That was enough for now. "I'll ask you more questions tomorrow. I'm too tired now."

Kaz nodded. "I was just about to say that you should rest. I hope you're right about your sleep being smooth tonight."

Luckily, Fletcher's sleep was untroubled by anything – neither visions of other worlds nor nightmares. He woke up shortly before dawn to find Avelyn making her daily visit. She had become even less forthcoming with answers than before, and mostly stood silently watching them. More and more, he found her presence creepy. Uncommunicative, she was even more the bane of the kentaki and the beast that had killed Kordon.

He turned his eyes away from her and looked around. It struck him then that they were in the middle of the forest, with the shrub-trees thick around the clearing. He had completely forgotten about the vision he had told Kaz and Ethan about before the Utopia-1 incident. He had intended to bring up the issue again yesterday morning. Concern growing in him, he looked to see if he could talk to one of the others about it, but they were both still asleep. He looked to Avelyn, but that was pointless. How did you tell a robot about premonitions? Would she even know what a dream was?

Luckily, Kaz stirred, saving him from trying to find questions that Avelyn could answer. As always, Kaz was quickly alert once he woke up, and noticed Fletcher staring at him.

"What's wrong?"

Fletcher reminded Kaz about the ships crashing into what

seemed to be this very forest. "We're getting deeper into it. Don't you think we should . . . hold off a bit?"

"I thought about it, Fletcher. But not only do we not know whether it was something in the past or something in the future, but now we don't even know if it's our reality. Waiting around doesn't get us anywhere, and there's only one direction to go."

Not sure what to say to that, Fletcher looked up, stretching the tension out of his neck. He noticed then that the purple of the field was no longer as even as it had been. It was far more intense, far brighter, in one direction than the rest – northeast rather than flat north. That wouldn't carry them out of the forest, but it was different from the direction they were planning to travel in, pulling them away from the river that had fed them, and which presumably led to Avelyn's home.

Fletcher knew how the first officer would respond, but told him about the intensity in the northeast anyway. As expected, Kaz said, "I don't think we can do anything about that. We can't drift too far away from our food and water. I still have rations in my pack and can carry a few days' worth of local food and water with me, but I don't want to get us sidetracked for no reason."

"It's not for no reason. Maybe what affected your ship's hyperdrive isn't the same thing that controls Avelyn. The whole Atlantis thing could be in one place, but the reason why the *Azar* exploded in a different one."

Kaz sighed. "I understand, but between those two we're more interested in the technology that Avelyn represents than whatever might be at the center of this field. I also don't like the idea of bringing you any closer to it. I'm not sure what affect it will have on you. Remember, when this thing destroyed the *Azar*, it did it by affecting the hyperdrive, which really means it affected the person that we call the hyperdrive. I don't know what happened, but I definitely don't want it to happen to you."

"But it's practically doing the opposite to me. What if, going there, I can get some real answers about what's happening to me?"

Giving Fletcher a probing look, Kaz eventually said, "maybe. Think carefully about it, though. You're the only one who will face any risk, so I will let you make the decision. But I'm not willing to go more than a day out of our way. After a day heading in that direction, if we don't find anything, we have to come back to the river. Do you understand?"

Fletcher nodded.

"Take your time to think about it. Remember what making the wrong decision almost did to your mind."

"No!" came a sudden shout. It was Avelyn, suddenly stepping forward after hearing the discussion. She had learned some English since the first day, but not enough to converse with. She waited as Kaz and Fletcher put on their translator headsets before continuing with her objections. "You must not go there. It is a dangerous place. It is not a place of ours. It made everything wrong. You must not go there."

Kaz and Fletcher looked at each other.

"And here I thought that someone who understood human psychology programmed the thing," Kaz commented. "Tell a person that they absolutely shouldn't look down . . . ."

Fletcher sniggered. "Maybe it wants us to go. That'd be clever, right? Reverse psychology. Don't want to disappoint it, do we?"

26

Gateway

Expecting to see something fascinating in every clearing, Fletcher was tired and morose by noon. Even in the glare of the sun, he could see that the strength of the field was growing, so they were definitely going in the right direction. How much more powerful did it need to become? He could actually feel the energy flowing into him now, like a buzz on his skin tickling him and a hum in his mind more musical than mechanical. If he wasn't already, he was close to being able to jump again. The thought both thrilled and terrified him. Never having thought of himself as anything special, he found himself in possession of the sort of ability that, if it was really his to control, would have everyone in the galaxy after him.

He saw the possibilities with frightening clarity. Kaz and Ethan already knew about him and, if they got back to Earth, Commander Raiz and the World Council would also know. Even if Fletcher couldn't bring a ship into hyperspace, they would be . . . interested. If he chose to cooperate, he would lose his freedom. If he didn't cooperate and tried to escape, they would hunt him and he wouldn't have any peace as long as he was around other humans. If other species found out about him, it might be better to surrender himself to Raiz instead of having to watch his back everywhere in the galaxy.

Of course, if he was really able to take himself anywhere, maybe he could just take himself into a reality that suited him where no one knew where he was. He didn't like the idea, but if he could find the right one, it would be better than losing a freedom he had only experienced for . . . was it more than a week yet?

Even though they could be the cause of his future misfortunes, he couldn't bring himself to blame Kaz and Ethan, nor to ask for his share of the food and go his own way. After all, the thought of them had helped to bring him back to Kentak and they had taken care of him while he was out of his mind. He felt more of a connection to them than he had to anyone else in his life, except maybe his mother before she died. Ethan did have a habit of coming out with comments that annoyed him, though.

Shortly after lunch, Ethan checked the local radiation as he had been doing with ever-greater frequency the past few days.

"I have to tell you, the radiation levels are getting pretty high," he said after looking reluctant for a few minutes. "Nothing immediately life-threatening, but we're talking more than a millisievert a day here, closer to two, really. In two days, we're going to get the equivalent of a whole year's worth on Earth, or a month's worth on Newport Station. If we had the anti-radiation pills the repair crews use, it'd be no problem. But if it gets any worse as we get nearer to whatever this thing is . . . ." He looked apologetically at Fletcher, who was not in a forgiving mood and didn't want anything forcing them to turn back.

"It's higher than close to the river?" Kaz asked.

"Yeah, it was closer to the normal Kentak background there."

"Keep taking readings. It'll be too late if we wait until we start seeing the trees glowing."

Ethan nodded. The radiation climbed slowly but steadily, until it was at two millisieverts by the late afternoon, but the climb was shallow compared to the growing intensity of the hyperdrive field. Nearing sunset, Fletcher felt like a light bulb – just glowing without a care – and hope returned to him in full force. When Kaz suggested that they would have to stop for the night, gently suggesting that they had gone far enough, Fletcher objected, telling him that they would only need to go about an hour more. He said it with such conviction that Kaz didn't think to insist on stopping.

Fletcher led them ahead, and started to feel warm, as if wrapped in a snug blanket. The sensation was so enticing that he almost held back, not trusting it. Almost. He didn't really have a choice now, though. Turning away from the solution to Ethan's theories would have been easy, but doing the same when he was affected so deeply was to remain ignorant about himself. He wouldn't be able to live with himself, constantly revisiting the memory of this lost chance.

Before his hour was up, they all saw it. Framed in the night was a dagger of light piercing the sky, coming from a clearing ahead. Through the trees, they could see a flickering light there, like a movie screen.

"Okay," Kaz said. "How close are we to getting baked, Ethan?"

Ethan shook his head. "Holding steady around eighty-five microsieverts an hour. I think it's more of a broad spectrum light source than radioactive material, but I wouldn't actually touch whatever it is."

"No kidding. Alright, I guess we have to check it out. Tell me if we go past a hundred. Fletcher, you ready?"

Fletcher turned to Kaz with what even he knew to be a disturbingly manic grin, but he decided not to hide the fact that he was being seriously affected by . . . by whatever it was. He could have hid it, but alongside the excitement was a very real sense of danger, a realization that he was going to face the universe in a way that could easily overwhelm his mind's ability to deal with it, just like it had done at the end of every night. Except this time, he wouldn't be able to break off the way he had before, by waking up.

They walked forward together, Fletcher with eyes ahead, Ethan with his on the radiation reading, and Kaz keeping a close watch on Fletcher's reactions. The nature of the phenomenon soon revealed itself as a stone arch within which scenes changed within the blink of an eye, like a video on an extreme fast-forward. Fletcher was a bit underwhelmed – it was little more than what he had seen in his mind given physical reality – but he supposed it made sense. To his surprise, though, Kaz and Ethan seemed to relax.

"Oh, it's one of those," Ethan said. "Somehow, we totally forgot about the one we saw on Selparis, didn't we, Kaz?"

"Yes. Because its keeper, Makis, said all sorts of wild things and, by the end, we couldn't tell if it wasn't just the magical equivalent of a vid screen."

"Really stupid. We should have made the connection between it and the hyperdrive, shouldn't we have? I mean, if what it's showing is other worlds in our reality, that's impossible, right? I should have realized that it must be showing other realities, but by the time I got into studying the physics and the theory, I had totally forgotten about it."

Kaz shrugged. "Well, it looks like you're going to get another chance. Up close, too."

Fletcher was taken aback by the exchange. "You mean . . . you've seen one of these before?"

"Yeah," Ethan said, "close to where we found the ancient ruins on Selparis. Would have thought more about it, but we were being chased by some very dangerous people and were, as usual, interested in exactly what they were after. The gateway was weird, but we didn't know what to do with it except put it in the official report."

"So, it's not dangerous?"

Ethan cocked his head, looked up at the sky, and decided, "not to us, but you . . . I don't know. I think Kaz would still want you to be careful. For the two of us, though, I think the only trouble will be dealing with the gateway's caretaker, since he's bound to be an arrogant bastard and unpredictable."

"Is he . . . like me?" Fletcher asked.

Shaking his head, Kaz answered, "I don't think Makis was able to go between realities without the gate, otherwise it wouldn't have kept his attention. But Ethan, I didn't think the other one gave off radiation."

"No, it didn't. Not that I remember."

"And it definitely didn't destroy ships. It didn't seem to affect Emily, either. What do you suppose is up with this one?"

Ethan smiled. "Well, let's go see."

They entered the clearing and, sure enough, there was a single figure seated cross-legged in front of it.

"An asofi," Ethan said, "that's different."

To Fletcher, the meditating asofi looked like a forest sprite. Bony and wiry with prominent muscles, it looked ready to leap into action at any moment. Its skin was a green that matched the nearby foliage, and nearly all of that skin was visible except for the region between the legs covered with hide. So, there was no mystery about whether the asofi kept their private parts in the same place as humans did. Its mouth extended from its head like that of an alligator or a cormorant – somewhere in the middle ground between the avian and reptilian. Its eyes were set apart as they would be on a predator, so perhaps it was closer to the alligator. Still, the asofi were among the species in the ISC with two legs and two arms, and this one was able to sit with legs crossed easily.

The asofi took note of their approach, turning his head to appraise them. For a moment, he turned away again, as if deciding that they were nothing special, but after realizing what he had seen, he did a double-take and fixed on Fletcher, wide-eyed.

"You! Come no closer!"

But it was too late. A lightning-like bolt broke out of the gateway and, crackling through the air, landed on Fletcher's forehead. Instead of dissipating, the energy continued to flow from the gateway to Fletcher, tying him to it like a rope. When it finally broke, Fletcher was no longer on Kentak.

Knowing what was happening helped a little, but Fletcher still trembled in the sightless mist between worlds, more from the zap he had just received than nervousness. He had more than just the energy to get back. It was like his battery was plugged into an AC socket – there wasn't going to be any drain at all unless the power plant or the connection failed. Right now, even though the visible connection between him and the gate no longer held, he could feel it right behind him.

He was dropped at the back of a lecture hall, with everyone's attention on the lecturer at the front, who had all manner of experimental apparatus arrayed in front of him. With his immaculate hair, moustache, and most importantly the sparks from his machines, Fletcher had no trouble identifying the lecturer as Nikola Tesla. Fletcher had seen a picture of Tesla sitting in a room with lightning darting everywhere, and it had always stuck in his mind. Being hit by a sort of lightning himself must have brought back the image, bringing him here. Enthralled at being at this moment in history, but realizing that it couldn't be exactly *his* history, Fletcher simply stood and watched.

Tesla seemed to be wrapping up his lecture, saying in less of an accent than Fletcher would have expected, "with the power derived from it, with every form of energy obtained without effort, from the store forever inexhaustible, humanity will advance with giant strides. The mere contemplation of these magnificent possibilities expands our minds, strengthens our hopes and fills our hearts with supreme delight." The audience, a more impressive array of moustaches than Fletcher had ever seen assembled in one place before, applauded respectfully and, once that had died down, some rose to ask Tesla questions in person while others left. Those leaving passed Fletcher on the way out and each made a point to give him a disgusted look but made no comment. He was certainly no problem of theirs, though they would mention to college staff about letting children – especially children reeking as much as Fletcher was – into the hall.

Fletcher was suddenly extremely conscious about how filthy he was and how grimy his clothing had become, but he had no way to deal with that now. He wondered why the people in Utopia-1 had not given it as much attention as these men did. Uncomfortable, he still stayed standing as he was, waiting to see if he could meet Tesla. It wasn't that Tesla was one of his heroes, but the scientist was definitely a larger-than-life figure worth shaking hands with. He couldn't go back to Kentak, tell Ethan that he had been in the same room with Nikola Tesla, and then admit not even trying to approach the man.

Thankfully, it looked as though either this was a break before another speaker took the podium or Tesla was in a rush for some reason, because those speaking to him cleared out quickly, giving Fletcher a chance to move forward. Tesla was busy getting his materials packed away, so Fletcher said, "Mr. Tesla?" to get his attention.

Tesla instantly registered the fact that the voice was not one belonging to an engineer, but was the higher pitch of a teenage boy, and looked up in curiosity. His face quickly twisted in badly disguised revulsion – a far more intense loathing than any of the other men had shown.

"Please, come no closer!" Tesla said "My . . . your hands!"

Fletcher looked at his hands. He had rinsed them in the river yesterday, but without having a good source of water except their drinking supply for the past day, they had gotten a bit . . . well, he saw Tesla's point. There would definitely be no handshake.

"Who let you in here? Your clothes are . . . unacceptable." And then a suspicion rose in his eyes. "Who sent you? No, do not answer. I have no time. I must get to the pigeons and then back to the laboratory. One of the questions . . . might lead to a valuable experiment."

Fletcher, embarrassed, tried to find some way to turn things around. He thought at first about telling Tesla about the future – about how electricity would affect the world – but wondered how that would affect this reality. He also had a suspicion, from the ending of Tesla's lecture, that the scientist understood the future he would create even better than Fletcher did. Fletcher decided to be honest . . . sort of.

"I was somewhere far away just a minute ago. I was struck by lightning and found myself here," he blurted out.

That got Tesla's attention, but not in the way Fletcher wanted. "I knew it! It is Edison again, is it? Always telling the papers that the alternating current is dangerous. Did he pay you to spread this lie around?" Then Tesla paused and reconsidered. "But the idea that alternating current can be used to transport a person from one place to another . . . would not be considered detrimental. Unless it left the traveler in your state, it must be considered a benefit. A benefit that is impossible, though. While the alternating current can be harnessed to provide power for transportation, it cannot move a person from one place to another instantaneously."

"What about one reality to another?"

Tesla looked blank for a second, then sighed. "You are wasting my time. Is this metaphysics, then?"

"No. I . . . where I come from is another reality. A scientist friend I know explained it to me. We are . . . sort of doing experiments on a field. It's not the electric field, though, but a field of realities." That was about as far as Fletcher could go – the juiciest morsel he could offer. If Tesla didn't bite, there was nothing he could do about it.

"Realities each propagating with a different wavelength," Tesla mused, "and perhaps interfering with each other. There would be no way to substantiate such a theory . . . unless a person discovered a way to travel from one to another. You say you have done so, and yet there is nothing about you marking you as belonging to a different reality."

"My reality is a lot like this one. You were in my reality, too."

Tesla sniffed and started walking out. "Of course I was. If you have nothing else to say, I suggest you go back to your reality and get a wash and a change of clothes. If you see me again looking as if you have the power you describe, or at least smell less like you have just come out of a swamp, perhaps I will let you dazzle me with the mathematics of the impossible theory of this scientist friend of yours. Like everyone else, I enjoy being dazzled, but I am not as easily fooled. If you are hoping to catch me subscribing to some far-fetched theory so that you can paint some picture of me in the press, you should quit now."

And that was it. Tesla left the hall. Fletcher thought about chasing after him and pointing out the translator headset, but the rush of power that had come to Fletcher was building again and he needed some way to use it – somewhere to go. Before it pushed him back into the void, he focused on the clearing with the gateway, Ethan, and Kaz. He was a lot surer of himself returning than on the outward-bound excursions. Somehow, where he had come from served as an anchor, though he supposed it would stop being so reliable a reference point if he spent a lot of time away.

Back in the clearing, he felt less panicked than the others seemed. From the expressions on their faces, they had been wondering whether they would even see him again. Ethan wore his distress on his sleeve, and might have been a thought away from hugging him out of relief, but Kaz was also stiff with tension ready to burst out with something embarrassing. The hermit who had tried to warn him was the most composed of the three, and was the only one ready to speak.

The asofi spoke with a hiss, but the headsets translated him perfectly. "You are very lucky. The connection could have been more than you could survive. Maybe worse, it may have been just a little more – enough to have you flitting from one world to the next every moment for the rest of your life. Instead, I expect you will have to leave us again soon, but it will be enough time. I do not want to help you, but now that you are connected to the gateway, it is my duty to. Do not make this difficult."

Fletcher had been prepared to surprise everyone with his story about Tesla, and was left stunned by the asofi. So he was going to have trouble staying in any place for more than a few minutes. He knew that. Already, the energy was building again and he would have to release it by jumping again. Was the asofi offering to help him control it? Why was it the asofi's duty? How could Fletcher make it difficult?

"Do not ask questions," the asofi said flatly. "I have been alone here for too long, and no longer have any patience to answer them. I will tell you what you need to know, and the rest is up to you. Do you understand?"

Fletcher decided it was safer to nod than to answer with words.

"Good. Now listen. The reason I, an asofi, am here is because the last keeper of this gate used all his power to stabilize this gate for him to pull me out of the wretched life I was leading before and make me his apprentice, teaching me all he knew as his master taught him. I will use all the power I have gathered over these years to bring my successor here when the time comes. Your friends have told me that they have seen another gate like this on Selparis and met the Makis there, and said that gate did not behave this way. That is because this is a bastard gate. The ancients arranged the gates in a loop to contain the hole between worlds, but this gate is out of alignment. Energy within it builds up and, at the same time, it takes more energy to stabilize it. It constantly tries to find ways to stabilize itself. It has found you," the asofi pointed an accusing finger at Fletcher, "and is throwing much of its spare energy into you. Thanks to you, my work is easier, because as long as this gate can maintain the connection with you, it will take less energy to control it."

Unable to help his curiosity, Fletcher had to take advantage of a gap in the gatekeeper's speech to ask, "is what happened to me the same as what happened to the mages in the ships?"

"Fletcher!" Kaz shouted, and Fletcher remembered too late that this might hint at the secret of the hyperdrive, which he was supposed to keep at all costs. How could he have avoided asking the question, though?

The gatekeeper was quick to allay Kaz's concerns in case they became a distraction. Speaking as quickly as he could without being incomprehensible, he said, "I already know how the hyperdrive works. You do not suppose I could understand these gates without knowing that? Do not worry, I will not give away the secret. It does not matter to me. The hyperdrive was an attempt by the eldrandii and asparii to imitate the ancients, and a very limited achievement. What happened here tonight was not the same as what happened to those mages – they were too far away for this sort of connection. If this gate was stable, there would have been no problem. Because it is unstable, it interfered with them, made them confused, and ultimately drove them mad. In the end, they released all their energy at once, directed at the source of their torment – this gate. Because that energy was different from the gate's energy, the gate released the difference as radiation. Before you ask how I survived the radiation, we asofi are naturally more radiation-resistant and, of course, I do not sit in front of the gate all day. From ancient times, the keeper has lived in a bunker – a radiation-safe bunker – a mile north of here. The gate behaved differently whenever another source of magic was in the region and I kept myself in the bunker for a few days whenever it did."

Fletcher began to feel himself ready to jump again and opened his mouth to say so, but the gatekeeper cut him off.

"It is time again, I know. We will make better use of the time when you return. Make sure you do return. Try to stay to places where you can breathe. For now, focus on controlling where you go. Do that, and I can teach you how to release the energy safely and control when you change worlds. If you find yourself somewhere dangerous, you can return immediately – you have more than enough energy for that without risk – but if it is safe, stay until the energy forces you to return. You must try to keep the cycles as slow as possible. Do you understand?"

Fletcher nodded and started to think about where he should go. It was easier to think about whom he wanted to meet. Someone who wouldn't be repelled by his stink or clothes. Maybe someone who would be interested in him and wouldn't brush him aside or treat him the way adults often treated teenagers. He couldn't pin down a specific person, but his subconscious pulled out a file from his memory and he jumped again.

27

Deduction

Fletcher had never appreciated how much Earth in the nineteenth century had captivated his imagination, but now that he was here again, he recalled all the stories he enjoyed that happened to be set in this period. He couldn't really say he liked the stuffy clothing or the restrained manner, but the age came into its own in those who defied expectations, like Tesla. Fletcher's bad experience with the scientist hadn't really changed his mind about the man – a man who stood on the thin line between technology and magic.

Now what, though? He was standing in the middle of a dingy street, probably in England from the way people were talking, but he didn't see anyone that he could recognize.

"Now here is a case that would put a lesser man to shame," a voice behind him said, "but I dare say no one else would even recognize it as one."

Fletcher whirled around to see a man who, though formidable in stature, looked every bit the ordinary gentleman, dressed in shirt, tie, vest, overcoat, and well-pressed trousers. He had a distinct smell about him that Fletcher couldn't identify, but might have rivaled Fletcher's own stench. Fletcher saw nothing else noteworthy about him. But he had noticed Fletcher.

The tall man continued in matter-of-fact tone tickled with an occasional twist of arrogance. "At first glance nothing more than a street urchin, his clothes underneath the dirt are not pure cotton, but of a blended material so finely manufactured that the best tailor in London would not be able to match the precision of the stitching. The soil on the trousers itself is of interest, since its color can be found nowhere else in London, or indeed anywhere in England, except on this one boy. The band across the head is easy to miss because it blends in with the hair, so its purpose must be functional rather than ornamental, but what function? Covering one ear and having a subtle protrusion extending near the mouth, its purpose has to do with speech and the ability to understand it. Since the boy is not from this country, he must have traveled far, so the likely purpose of the instrument is a translator, but to have a machine that can translate between languages defies imagination. Yet, what other explanation is there? As nowhere in the world can such technology be found, we must conclude that this boy hails from a very distant place indeed."

The man paused for affect, and possibly for applause from some invisible audience. Or maybe Fletcher himself was supposed to express wonder at his ability to conclude so much from a glance, in which case the man was out of luck, because Fletcher was all out of wonder for one day. The way the man had run through the litany of observations eventually reached the literary department of Fletcher's brain, and he finally realized the man's identity.

"S-Sherlock Holmes?" Fletcher said incredulously. Another part of the mind thought, "so that's what tobacco smells like. How did they stand it?"

Holmes smiled, pleased at the recognition. "So I am not unknown where you come from, then."

"But you're not real."

The smile remained, but took on a condescending edge. "Do you think yourself dreaming or hallucinating? Otherwise, you cannot escape the conclusion that I am real, if the word has any meaning at all."

"But, in my world, you're a character – you know, in books." Fletcher accepted that different outcomes could lead to different realities – that was the whole point of alternate realities. But how could a work of fiction become real? There couldn't have been a point where Holmes either did or did not really exist, could there have been?

"And in my world, you cannot exist at all, yet I have no trouble believing you are real because you stand in front of me. It is a matter of method. People do not to trust their senses because they do not really think about what they see and what they experience. With careful observation, not only of what is easy to see, but of everything in front of you, and then the application of a well-tuned method of deduction to those observations, you arrive at the truth, or at least eliminate impossibilities. What I said about you was not a guess. I do not even need to ask if I was right."

Fletcher nodded politely. There was no doubting Holmes' abilities, but Fletcher wasn't sure that he needed to be lectured on how to think. Then again, he had appeared here without really knowing what he was doing, even though his own thoughts had brought him here. His normal way of thinking might have been good enough when he was . . . when he was normal. It was definitely not up to coping with inter-reality travel, though.

As if reading his mind, Holmes continued. "Too often people with power and great potential misuse it or squander it simply because they did not rein in their own minds. Scotland Yard has all the power it needs to make every potential criminal reconsider because of the near certainty of arrest. Why should any case come to me, when I lack any authority or official power?"

Holmes paused for Fletcher to supply the answer. Since Holmes had been so obliging to speak to him, he did his best to keep the exasperation out of his voice when he answered, "Method?"

"Exactly. Because with it I produce reliable results while the good men at the Yard flounder."

It occurred to Fletcher that Holmes was having a bad day – or a slow day – since if he had a case, it would have held his focus. The drawback of a methodical mind was that it had to have a problem to solve. Holmes was interested in him because he was just such a problem, and the great detective was lacking any others at the moment. But why didn't Holmes just ask Fletcher . . . of course he wouldn't, since then the fun would be over and he couldn't apply his intellect to the issue of who Fletcher was, and why he was here. While Holmes ranted, he had not taken his

eyes off Fletcher, taking in every detail, trying to find the clues
that would narrow the field of possibilities – a much larger field
than Holmes had ever faced before. At least, Holmes knew that
Fletcher spoke English and with what accent he did – the translator wasn't making any sound as they talked. What else did the
detective see?

An idea struck Fletcher and excited him so much that he
voiced it immediately. "Your method works if you're trying to figure things out, but what if you're trying to do something? You'd
need a different method for that, wouldn't you – if you wanted
to do something right the first time instead of figuring out what
happened after?"

"The fabled perfect murder?"

"No, no. I mean in general. Say someone had power and wanted to use it properly instead of wasting it, but they weren't police trying to figure out what someone else had already done, but
had to do something new. Would someone like that use the same
method as you?"

"Absolutely. The necessary observations would change, of
course. My trade is a matter of fingerprints, blood analysis, and
subtle details about a person because I am interested in where a
person has been and what that person has done. If you, for instance, were to make a habit of traveling, you would be interested
in other details that would ensure that your travel was successful.
Organizing the facts accumulated and using them to eliminate impossibilities in a systematic way would still produce invaluable
results. Of course, I do not exclude the invention of others. The
key is that the way you think should lead to reliable results efficiently. Everything else is secondary."

It's having a mind like a machine, Fletcher reflected, but not
a machine in the soulless, cold, metallic sense. Just that it churns
out the answers like a machine. Could a person really have a mind
like that without losing some humanity? Holmes seemed to be
passionate enough, but in Fletcher's mind, the detective was still
a construction of someone's imagination rather than a personality
that came about naturally.

Fletcher felt the rush of energy building again and decided to end the conversation properly. "Well . . . thank you. I think that helped. It definitely gave me something to think about." Then, as the energy made him feel light-headed, he added whimsically, "say hello to Watson for me!"

He was back in the gateway clearing in subjective seconds, though he had no idea what kind of time passed when he traveled between realities. It was seconds on a Kentak clock and his own clock, but it was centuries for either Tesla or Holmes.

"Where . . . where did you go?" Ethan asked as soon as Fletcher returned. Fletcher wondered what his disappearances and reappearances looked like to them – did he fade out, get sucked into a black hole, or just plain vanish in a single frame? This was no time for those kinds of questions though.

"That's going to have to wait till later," Fletcher said, feeling physically and mentally tired, but also full of a different kind of energy – as if on a serious caffeine rush at midnight. "It's the sort of thing we could spend hours talking about, and I'd really like to have the talk at one go. At this rate, I'll have something new to tell you every five minutes or so."

"Indeed," the asofi said. "You must find a way to release the energy safely without having to use it to jump."

Unable to restrain himself, Fletcher said, "are you going to teach me how to do magic, then?" He waved his hands like a wizard conjuring something. Humor had never been his way of dealing with adversity before, but becoming withdrawn and introspective wasn't really an option here.

"Not . . . as such," the asofi said, the delay between his words conveying the message that Fletcher's last comment fell under the category of 'making things difficult.' "Magic is only magic to those who do not understand it. I will not tell you how to make objects appear out of thin air or any of the things you might call magic, except teleportation, of course, which you can already do."

Fletcher risked making his teacher even more impatient, asking, "why can't I just jump right back here? I mean, instead of going somewhere else? Maybe I could move a few feet or something."

"At last a sensible question," the asofi said. "These two friends of yours have been . . . never mind. To answer your question, no. It is between realities, so the energy is that which takes you from one reality to another. More energy is required when realities are further apart. Traveling from and to this reality covers no distance in reality space, so the energy required is zero. In fact, you cannot use the energy that way at all, or you would be able to travel anywhere without using energy. You could use hyperspace, but without a ship, you would not find it easy to move."

"I don't think I've been to hyperspace before . . . I mean, not like this. Is it farther away than the realities I've been to? How would I get there – just think of hyperspace? I don't really have an idea of hyperspace." He should have spent more time looking out the rec room windows of the *Azar*, he reflected. After asking the question, he wondered if he should have with Kaz and Ethan in earshot, since he didn't really want them to know whether he could go into hyperspace.

"Hyperspace takes more energy than you are burning off every five minutes, yes, but as you slow your jumps you may be able to go there. I do not know how you would take yourself there. That is one of many things you will have to discover yourself," the asofi said, relieving Fletcher of his momentary apprehension. "By watching the gateway, I am developing my own feel for each of the closest realities to our own, which the gateway spends most of its time showing. It shows more distant ones less frequently. You have to understand when I say more distant, they are not distant at all in physical space. The gateway is a one-way window on what is right here in a certain mapping of space."

"I got that," Fletcher said, "like an elevator. But I can go from place to place when I go from one reality to another."

"As long as it does not violate causation."

"But wouldn't that work for hyperspace, too?"

"The first time," the asofi said, nodding. "The first time, you can go as far as you like, but the universe will impose constraints on how you can return into this reality. Enough of that, you need to be told practical things now. There are two ways to dispose of the extra energy – burn it off, or store it more efficiently."

"Where is the energy?" Fletcher asked. "I mean, is it in my

head, or . . . ."

The asofi shook his head vigorously. "It remains in the void between realities. It is yours in that your mind is connected to it. Your mind is a like a thread. By vibrating that thread, you can affect that energy." For a moment, Ethan looked like he was about to object to this explanation, but wisely stayed silent. "Your energy container is a limited size and more energy is flowing in, so either you use the energy, or the container bursts. The mages in the ships always kept theirs very close to the limit, and when they could not maintain control, theirs burst. You are not close to your limit, but you are being forced to consume more than you can handle at a time, so you . . . ."

"Throw up?"

The asofi allowed a brief smile on his grim face. "It seems like you are following this. Good. But there will come a point where things will be more difficult, and you have to gain some practice before then. To slow your jumps, you need to increase the pressure in the container so that the same volume can contain more, and the gateway's input will not affect you so quickly. You can also release the energy in ways the gateway cannot."

Eager to get to the point before he had to decide on his next destination, Fletcher asked, "okay, so how do I do it?"

"It is a matter of playing your mind like a string. You need to both focus it and then make it produce the correct vibration. The traditional way of doing this, and the way taught to me by my teacher, is through . . . you would call them spells, chants, or mantras." His voice oozed with disdain for the last three words.

Or you could play the violin, Fletcher thought, remembering Holmes' preferred means.

"But it is not enough to say them," the gatekeeper continued. "To be effective, they must fill your mind. This is more difficult to do properly than you can imagine. I have spent years trying to do it better so that I have the energy to do what I must. You are lucky – your capacity is much greater from the start, while I began with little more than a normal person. Even an imperfect use of the . . . spells . . . will have some effect. Whether it is enough effect is up to you. Perhaps you do not mind having to go to another world once a day, or maybe you consider that too much. I will teach you two spells now – one to increase capacity, and the other to release. Repeat after me."

The asofi had Fletcher intone the two phrases precisely and, before Fletcher was pulled away again, he managed to wrap his tongue around the difficult syllables sufficiently well to win an approving nod. Before the jump, he tried to find a more concrete destination from his memories, but his mind was still struggling to retain the newly learned, and to him utterly meaningless, words. In the end, he could only focus on the idea of magic.

28

Plans

Sensha could tell by Corcoris' breathing and a slight unsteadiness in his hands when he gestured that he was growing unsure of the situation. They had been unable to communicate with his contact before landing. In fact, no one in town seemed to be picking up on any of the standard wavelengths at all, leaving everyone in the team apprehensive. That Corcoris was now less confident than he tried to appear only made matters worse.

On the bright side, everyone was on alert as they entered town, and weapons were in full display. Even Sensha, confident in her unarmed combat skills, carried one of the automatic rifles supplied by Corcoris, but only because Jaidee was quick to do so as well. When a solid wall of mob confronted them in one plaza, Corcoris' men formed a protective ring around the minister and his human guests, also wisely covering an alley behind them to use as a retreat route if necessary. Sensha kept an eye on what Jaidee was doing, but the engineer was standing with the rest of the humans, backing up their captain.

The crowd decided not to try to rush Corcoris' men, at least for the moment. Getting past that initial threat of a massacre, Corcoris knew it was time for him to step up and take the reins, though Pierce had her people close to the open alley in case the minister was not up to it. Once the crowd quieted enough so his voice could be heard, Corcoris began.

"Where is Kordon the relay chief?" he started. Sensha thought she could answer the question.

"Dead," came the expected answer from a resonant voice deep within the mob. The kentaki parted to reveal one of their own. His skin was unnaturally smooth and, compared to the others, he presented a much more business-like front, but he had a hunted look in his darting eyes and a strange manic twist to the grin on his mouth as he delivered the grim news. "The traitor Kordon is dead, Minister Corcoris."

The crowd broke into a flurry of hushed whispers. They had evidently not known that they were confronting the space minister. Sensha realized there was only one other thing that could have gotten the town excited enough to assemble like this: the arrival of non-kentaki outsiders.

"Sueton?" Corcoris shouted. "What is the meaning of this?"

"The meaning, Minister, is that the people are tired of the Grikorat allowing aliens to have their way with us, destroying our land and impoverishing our people to their own benefit."

"And, as you well know, Sueton, those were exactly the sentiments I asked you to foster here. I am happy the people have been receptive to the message."

"Yet you come here with the aliens," Sueton said haltingly, but in a higher, almost hysterical, pitch. "Are they your prisoners? If so, we will gladly deal with them for you."

Corcoris paused for a moment, starting to appreciate what was really going on, then said, "these are not plani, Sueton, you can see that. They are from Earth, and they are here to help us fight against the plani"

Sueton laughed and turned to the crowd. "We would have believed that if we had not seen otherwise with our own eyes. The beast, the monster that killed Kordon, let the Earth people, like the ones you have here, live. Killing kentaki without mercy, it somehow yields to them. Why is that, Minister? Maybe the plani are not the ones who have plagued us, but these Earth people are. Why take a chance? All the aliens must be removed from our world. Then, and only then, will we be able to gain the world that the space ministry promised us."

Cheers rang through the plaza. While Sueton appeared to relish in this approval, there was unmistakable tension in his face.

Sensha could almost see disgust in the turn of his nose.

Corcoris was almost at a loss. "Beast? Monster? What are you talking about, Sueton? You were sensible. Why have you led these people into this xenophobic madness?"

"I have not led them at all, Minister. They have led me. What am I talking about? I will show you, though you will have to wait until sunset." The words sparked menacing laughter from the throng. "But we will not be able to deal with your Earth people that way, and we will not let them get away this time."

With more irritation than fear in his voice, Corcoris said, "I want to speak with your council of elders."

"I am afraid you are too late there, as well, Minister. They were tried and convicted of treason yesterday."

"But the council is the court of law here," Corcoris objected, paling. Sensha shook her head at his inability to see that the rule of law had broken down completely here. He was still a popular figure – if he had only seen the reality right away, he might have been able to turn things around. Maybe pretending that the humans were his prisoners would have been a good idea.

"The worst of criminals as the arbiters of justice? We could not allow that, Corcoris. We do not understand the sophisticated ways of the Grikorat, but we have our own sense of things here, and we knew what to do when we . . . when we found poison in our midst."

The humans made no mistake judging the way things were going, and were, as one, looking down the clear alley, ready to bolt. Probably the only reason why they hadn't already was the risk of leaving Corcoris and his men to bear the fury of the vengeful town. Even Sensha had some qualms about that, but she wasn't about to risk her life over qualms. In seconds, she was at the mouth of the alley with muscles tensing for the dash, only wondering whether the crowd had already arranged for some cars to chase any runners down. If so, there was really no hope.

Then, with Corcoris' voice growing more frantic behind her, she saw an unmistakable form over the horizon through the alley. She almost didn't believe her eyes. After all, how could it be? But there it was – Rivel's kandar – draining all hope of escape out of her. If she had the measure of the plani captain's temperament right, he would be in just the sort of mood to fire every gun he had at her as soon as he spotted her running. He would still want to keep the humans alive to extract what he could out of them, so it would be best to stay as close to them as possible.

She went to Jaidee to warn the engineer, but saw her already telling Pierce and pointing at the approaching kandar. The ship was drawing some attention from the crowd, as well, forcing even Corcoris and Sueton to notice.

Sensha tried to read Pierce's posture. There was no indication that the humans were going to make a run for it, and Pierce herself looked like she had expected this turn of events. Sensha might have spat in frustration, but had to concede that they were cornered, and between the murderous mob and Rivel, the humans had a better chance surviving in the hands of the plani. But what about herself? There was no reason for Rivel to keep her alive again, not after all this, and he would be itching to let out some anger after Corcoris had outmaneuvered him.

It was the same choice – run and make her own way or stay with the humans. She was getting tired of it. If she was going to stay with them, she wanted some assurances, and had to secure them quickly. She made a beeline for Pierce and, standing right in front of her, stared up into the captain's cold, weary eyes.

"I am a member of your crew," Sensha insisted. "I have earned it."

Time pressing, Pierce gave the matter as much thought as she could spare, leaving Sensha in suspense for a few moments. Eventually, she nodded and said, "all right. As long as this is about what I think it is and not about the hyperdrive."

"I want protection – the same treatment as your officers get. The hyperdrive . . . will not matter if I cannot get off of this planet."

"Deal. Stay close to me. You're my bodyguard for the time being. That'll leave Jaidee free to do what she does best when the time comes."

Bodyguard. Sensha had not expected that, but it was a fair exchange – Pierce would do what she could to keep Sensha alive, and Sensha would reciprocate. Which one of them would have the harder job?

The plani kandar slowed to a hover short of the plaza, then started to make a circuit around it. Once on the side filled with the kentaki crowd, all gazing up apprehensively, it dropped its altitude and positioned itself directly over the throng, aiming to cook the kentaki with the blast from its engines. The crowd immediately scrambled to get away from the merciless heat beating down on them, and soon the chaos and panic was beyond Sensha's ability to take in. She covered her ears to block the sound of the screaming and turned away, looking down the still-open alleyway. In a flash, she and the rest of Corcoris' party were dashing down it, aiming to get out of the city and back to the cargo ship while the plani were still occupied with dispersing the crowd.

Sensha had just enough space in the mad rush to wonder why the plani were so focused on the kentaki instead of the humans before they had the cargo ship in sight and her question was answered. Rivel and more than a dozen plani soldiers were standing with weapons ready outside the plane. The cargo ship crew sat tied up in front of Rivel, who had his gun aimed at the pilot's head. Rivel's free arm was bound in a sling and the left side of his face had severe burns, making his sneer more lopsided than usual. It did not take much to make a plani unhinged, and the humiliation that Corcoris had dealt Rivel was more than enough. Gone were the calculations and subtle manipulations in Rivel's vicious eyes. Sensha kept herself no more than a foot away from Pierce.

"Step forward slowly with your hands up in the air," Rivel shouted. Just in case they thought about running back into the city, the roar of the kandar's engines returned to the scene behind them. Turning back would only get them baked by its thrust, even if it decided not to use its artillery on them. There was no choice but to obey. No one could doubt that Rivel would rather kill them than let them escape again.

Just in case, Pierce gave pointed looks to each of her people, warning them silently not to try anything heroic. They outnumbered the plani, but were faced with a force ready for action and backed up by a warship. Even if they could retake the cargo ship, the guaranteed barrage from the kandar would end their flight in a hurry. The kandar looked a bit battered from its confrontation with the pirate ship, but much like its commander, it had not lost its sting.

Once Pierce made sure everyone on her side was on the same page, she shouted back, "if we come with you, you won't harm any member of my crew or Corcoris' people."

"Yes," Rivel strained to agree, but had his eyes on Sensha.

"Sensha is part of my crew as well," Pierce hastened to add.

Rivel snarled. "No, she is not. We have the crew listing you filed on your entry into Plani space, and I do not see how you can add to your crew when you do not even have a ship."

"She joined the crew between Plani and here. She's my bodyguard."

Rivel barked a laugh. "You have adopted her as your pet, you mean. If she is your bodyguard, she had better not leave your side. My men will have orders to shoot her on sight if they see her without you."

Pierce looked at Sensha, who returned a nod of acceptance. What choice did they really have? They had only managed to get this concession because Rivel's anger had given way to his impatience.

It was odd that Corcoris had not said a word, and Sensha threw a sideways glance at the minister to check that he was still there. He was, but in sharp contrast to Pierce, he looked beaten – casting his eyes downward and allowing his shoulders to slump. After years of laying low, he had decided to play all his cards now in a desperate gambit to outmaneuver the plani, and had been caught out. He had no more aces up his sleeve and his fate now depended on the leverage that Pierce's ace of aces could buy.

But Rivel had different ideas about how the balance of power would play out. Without preamble, almost off-handedly, he said, "I have decided to abandon the proposed trade for information about the hyperdrive, Pierce. It is clear that you will remain stubborn in your refusal to accept my generous offer."

He let the words hang in the air, delighting in the effect.

"Yeah, right," Pierce said, "and I guess next you're going to tell me you'll give me a ship free of charge! We both know how much the information's worth, Rivel, and I bet that if I offered it in exchange for an equal share in your company as you hold, I'd probably get it."

Rivel's eyes narrowed. "Would you make that offer?"

Pierce shrugged. "Don't know. I'll have to think about it."

"No, Pierce. As it so happened, there was always an alternative at my disposal, though it carries more risk and less certainty. As it so happened, you were on your way to it already, so we will simply join you on your course. You can do all the thinking you like on the way. From now on, though, the rules of the game will be mine. I will honor the code of my people, but if I decide that you are no longer useful to me, I will make certain you never leave this planet. I hope your thoughts will lead you to be more cooperative than you have been."

Pierce glared at the plani captain, and kept her eyes on him as the plani searched for and confiscated all their weapons. The kandar landed and the captives were split into two groups – half of the humans and half of the kentaki were placed on board the kandar, while the rest, including Pierce, Sensha, Jaidee, Sean, Corcoris, and Gorenal, boarded the ministry cargo plane with Rivel.

Did Rivel really have a way to bypass negotiations with Pierce? Sensha doubted it. Why would Rivel have gone through all the trouble otherwise? If he had an alternative, then it had to be a low probability chance, and he might still want to fall back on negotiation if it didn't work. As she took her seat on the plane with a guard two seats down keeping a gun trained on her at every moment, she sincerely hoped that was true, otherwise she was going to find it hard to get out of this situation alive.

Eager to increase her apprehension, Rivel loomed over her before takeoff and, with the deeply scarred side of his face far too close to hers, hissed, "This is the third time I have had to capture you and the circumstances have been less pleasant each time. At first, I thought I would simply shoot you on sight, knowing that Pierce would try to protect you, but then I decided it would be far more satisfying to have you there, to have all your little hopes dashed as I get exactly what I was after. For that, to see the look on your face, I am willing to bear with you presence for just a little while longer. Count yourself lucky, young blood-drinker. You will see the day when the plani finally break the monopoly of the eldrandii and become the most powerful species in the galaxy." Not waiting for her to bite back, he took his seat.

None of the benefits of that power would trickle down to the permanent plani underclass, the dribrora, but neither would it hurt her people. Her eagerness to see Rivel fail was personal, and she had been selfish in her desire to see it, but it was time for her to rethink what she needed to do for her people. If she could get some information to undermine him – show that he was violating ISC law, for instance – that would be leverage. If she could get the hyperdrive secret from the humans, that would be valuable, too. Even if Rivel got it as well, her people could use it to bargain with the other corporations.

Could she play the two sides against each other? She doubted it. She found the minds of Pierce and Rivel to be impenetrable. Both of them, on the other hand, were all too familiar with the way she thought, sometimes seeming to read her mind. If she could only fight them physically, it would be a different story. She sat disconsolately. It might be that the best she could do was to cement the growing alliance between the humans and the dribrora, and to take that as a minor victory. If she could return to Plani with that, at least, then maybe it would be an honorable return.

As the cargo plane lifted off, heading over the river and into the badlands, Sensha resigned herself to the mission of helping the humans get back to Earth, and securing some guarantee of support for her people. It was far more humiliating than her original grandiose intent, but with Rivel's guards holding her at gunpoint, she would be lucky to get even that. It was looking more and more as if Rivel had already won.

29

WANDERER

The novelty of jumping from reality to reality had worn off, and Fletcher desperately wanted nothing more than to sleep. The power of the gateway had, only days ago, been confined to playing around with his mind in his sleep. Back then, only in his sleep was his mind not alert enough to keep him firmly planted in his normal reality – what Kaz had helpfully dubbed "reality alpha." Calling this the 'real' reality was growing increasingly silly, since all the realities were equally authentic. Now that the gate's influence was constant, he had to stay awake out of fear of losing touch with reality alpha altogether.

Would that be so bad, though? He had left Newport Station – left the only home he had ever known – intending on taking his chances on whatever worlds he could reach. Now that he could not only go to the stars, but to entirely different realities, why should he tie himself down to this one? There wasn't anything special for him here.

Whenever that thought occurred, he shook it out of his head. He was just so tired. He was getting grumpy and not thinking straight. Sticking just to the practical, there was the asofi who was trying to help him control all the energy flowing into him. Losing that guidance would be . . . well, he didn't have a very high estimation of it right now, but he was sure he would miss it if he lost it. Then there was Ethan and Kaz, standing with him through all this.

Stressed to the limit as his mind and body were, he had to admit that he was making progress. The period between his jumps was approaching an hour, though figuring out what to do in the elsewhere realities during that time was getting troublesome. It hadn't taken him long to appreciate that cuts and bruises gained in one reality were carried with every stab of pain into the next, and what that meant. Having some control, he no longer jumped to places where he would have trouble breathing, but those were not the only dangers in the universe. He was increasingly appreciating how dangerous human beings could be, especially if you appeared out of nowhere dressed oddly and they were of a superstitious turn of mind. More than once, he had to immediately jump back to reality alpha to avoid people accusing him of witchcraft or of being a demon. Other times, strangers – sometimes overtly menacing, other times apparently bright and friendly – would try to take advantage of what they saw as a defenseless and lost boy. He managed to dash away from a couple of them, but he was still not much of a runner in normal gravity, and mostly had to jump back. Each time he prematurely returned, he set his progress back.

One thing he was beginning to understand was that the mages serving as hyperdrives in eldrandii ships were not nearly as imprisoned as they might seem. While the ship was in dock or in hyperspace, they could easily go wherever they wanted outside reality alpha and spend hours away from the ship without any member of the crew being aware of it. Did the engineers really know what was going on in the hyperspace chamber? They themselves admitted that they didn't. The hyperdrive mages didn't need to be fed with tubes or be deprived of social contact or anything of the sort – they could even go out for a pizza, if that's what they wanted to do. Fletcher still wouldn't choose the lifestyle for himself, but he recognized now that the eldrandii were not out of their minds to do things in this way. That assumed his experience was anything like theirs, but he didn't know for sure whether it was. They had probably not gotten their abilities by a chance encounter with a gateway – from what the asofi had said, he was lucky that his own experience had not killed him, and the survival odds using this shortcut were probably too low to risk.

So he was the lucky one, but he didn't feel lucky. He didn't feel particularly alive at this point, either – more like a zombie. His muscles were sore enough to make his movements appropriately stiff and jerky. Pretty soon, he would be stomping around, mindlessly repeating the words the asofi had taught him.

His irritable behavior was beginning to worry Kaz and Ethan – he could see it in their eyes. He was even snapping at Kaz's questions now, all respect for the first officer's seniority washed away in the flood of new experiences. What could any of them know about how he felt? Even the asofi was only repeating things he had been taught.

Nothing was more grating to his senses, though, than Ethan. He didn't blame Ethan for his excitement, and regretted the way Ethan started passing his questions onto Kaz, fearing Fletcher's angry and impatient responses. Now even Kaz refused to ask Fletcher anything more taxing than "how are you feeling?" But Fletcher could see the need to know boiling behind Ethan's eyes, just waiting for a chance to burst out without being fought back. Ethan and Kaz were almost as sleep-deprived as he was, only getting a quick nap while he was away, but they seemed to grow more attentive as his own senses dulled. Ethan couldn't have been more awake if he had been strapped to a caffeine IV. The contrast was tough to take. Fletcher almost wished that Ethan had gotten the ability instead of him, so that the theorist could enjoy himself discovering all he needed to discover. Almost.

A little after noon on the day after they had discovered the gateway, Ethan worked up the courage to make a suggestion to Fletcher, but he kept his eyes carefully away from Fletcher's as the words came out.

"Maybe . . . maybe you could start trying to carry things with you," he said. "I know you're busy with trying to control it, but . . . ." He waited for some sign of whether Fletcher was amenable to the suggestion or not.

Fletcher looked around in exasperation. "What would you like me to take? What would it prove? I mean, I already carry my clothes with me, so we know I can."

"But . . . but we don't know how far away from your body you can alter the field," Ethan said in a rush.

"This is about ships again, isn't it?"

Ethan waved his hands frantically. "No, no. I was just . . . maybe you could . . . bring back something better to eat?"

That caught Fletcher off guard. He had just been thinking about pizza, and the berry-ration diet they had been on was not doing his stomach any favors. Just the thought of a decent meal with lots of meat involved and maybe some chocolate afterwards left him in no mood to argue and eager to jump.

There was only one problem, though. "How will I get it? I mean, I can't be sure that I'll be in a place where they take cards or computer transfers." From the beginning of his excursions, he had a tendency to travel back to more primitive times on Earth – eras that had captured his imagination. His only trips to a contemporary world were to Mars, where everything was designed so idiosyncratically that it was hard for him to get around.

With the hint of a smile on his lips, Kaz cleared his throat. "I give you express permission to steal the pizza, if necessary."

Fletcher laughed for the first time that day. It felt good. "I don't think I'd get away with it. I mean, I'd get away of course, but I'm not really good at that sort of thing, and I'd probably panic and drop the food before I jumped."

"Don't be silly. He doesn't need to steal it," said Ethan with a gleam. "There's got to be a reality where, right now, there's a festival going on with free food. There just has to be, and it shouldn't be too hard to picture it and focus on it. So go there and get as much as you can carry. Fill up a tray or a box, if you can."

And suddenly things were looking up for Fletcher. Why hadn't the thought of going somewhere with a free meal occurred to him? Didn't matter now. He would definitely get the food, then in the jump after that, he'd go somewhere with a free shower, and then maybe a charity store to get some clothes. Actually, he had better get the clothes before taking the shower – he was desperate for the shower to wash the weariness from his limbs, but there was no point cleaning up just to put on grimy outer layers afterward.

He had a mission. The irony of it was so rich that it made him feel light-headed and kept the smile on his face. He was able to go anywhere in an absurd number of realities and what was he going to do with this free ticket at the absolute leading edge of travel technology? Find food, clothing, and a bath – the very necessities of life. And he was excited to do it.

By sunset, he was still eager to get some sleep, but no longer felt completely miserable. Fed, clean, and carrying a thermos of coffee from which he took steady sips, he felt almost civilized. A part of him wanted to go back to Tesla just to take up the fastidious genius' challenge, but there was no point in it. Being able to supply the rest of his companions with some of the amenities of modern life was satisfying, and even the asofi decided to try some of the pizza and barbecue chicken, and seemed to like the chicken though he was dubious about the cheese on the pizza.

The lady at the charity had been very kind and generous – so much so that it made Fletcher embarrassed, since he wasn't, strictly speaking, poor. Still, he had pressed her for clothes for his friends, and she had willingly provided them. Kaz and Ethan each received jeans and a shirt, in both cases a bit too loose for them but still serviceable.

The upward swing in fortune was palpable at dinner, but Kaz still had concerns on his mind.

"How's the radiation, Ethan?"

Ethan rolled his eyes. "Not the radiation again. Look, I've been checking it regularly like you said. It went down ever since Fletcher made that connection with the gate. We can probably deal with staying here a couple more days. If you're going to keep bugging me about it, though, you might as well take the scanner and take the readings yourself. I'll tell you if anything changes."

"The question is, how long will we have to stay here?" Kaz turned to the gatekeeper. "Is there any reason why Fletcher can't keep up his practice on his own while we make our way north? Did you have anything else to teach him?"

The last question ruffled the asofi. "Anything else to teach him? I must know very little to have imparted it all in so short a time."

"I didn't mean any offense," Kaz said flatly. Fletcher knew that this was as close to an apology as Kaz was going to give.

Having made his point, the asofi moved on. "I do not understand the gateway completely, but what I know will take too long to explain to you. As for what the young man needs to know, I cannot say what might be important to him and what will not be. I was trained to tend to the gateway, and was only told of this possibility – not what to do about it. It is so rare for someone un-initiated in magic yet having the potential to come so close to an unstable gateway . . . so rare."

The words pulled him into a moment of thought, as if something had struck him suddenly. After pulling out the memory, he explained to the others. "There was another. He may be able to make what needs to be known clear, but it is hard to say. He did not make the same choice."

"Who?" Fletcher asked. He didn't really want to leave the gateway until he felt completely ready, and that meant getting a full night's sleep for a start, but if someone knew more than the asofi, he definitely wanted to meet the person.

The gatekeeper did not look comfortable with the subject, but went on anyway. "I do not know his name. It is little more than a legend. The story is that, centuries ago, a changeling – a member of the taran species who can take the form of any four-limbed creature of the same mass – had it happen to him. I do not know how it could have happened, since I was taught that this is the only unstable gate. Whatever happened to him, he never gained control of the power, and travels from world to world at the whim of the gateway, taking the form of whatever species he encounters, if he can. He is simply called the Wanderer."

Ethan snorted. "The Wanderer? Really?"

Fletcher gave an irritated look at Ethan, wiping the silly grin off the latter's face. Actually, the title "wanderer" fit how Fletcher felt about his activities the past day perfectly. More than that, the idea that there was someone else out there like him lifted his spirits, though he wondered how to take the fact that the Wanderer had no control over his jumps.

"A shapeshifter able to go anywhere, blending in wherever he goes," Kaz summarized. "It seems a bit too convenient, doesn't it? Sounds like a comic book hero or something you get out of mythology. Don't take the story too seriously, Fletcher."

If Kaz had offended the gatekeeper before, the asofi was beside himself with fury now. "I do not speak except to be taken seriously. It is a legend only in its lack of details. There is such a person – there must be such a person, or we would not know that it was possible. How would I have known what would happen to your friend? Think before you say such things. I have no doubt that the Wanderer exists."

"Even though, living centuries ago, he's probably dead?"

"Dead in which reality?" the asofi shot back.

Fletcher needed little convincing. "I don't have anything except the word "wanderer" to focus on, though. That doesn't seem like it's enough."

The asofi nodded. "Perhaps, perhaps not – only you can find out. He is known by that name more than any other. Focus on that name as belonging to someone who will understand what you are going through. That may be enough."

Kaz tried to raise other objections, but Fletcher ignored those. It was about time for him to jump anyway, and he focused his mind on the Wanderer – just the word and his thirst to find someone who had experienced what he had.

A leap through the void later, he was standing alone on a barren landscape so similar to Kentak's own wastelands that he wondered whether the attempt had failed. A look around the empty scene revealed a figure approaching him in the hazy distance. The glare of the sun on the landscape combined with the dust in the air made it hard to identify the shape, even though it wasn't very far away. At first, it seemed to be on all-fours, but a few seconds later, Fletcher saw that it was clearly walking upright. Was it the shapeshifter that the asofi had talked about? If it really had been on all-fours at first, and Fletcher's eyes hadn't been tricking him, then it sort of reminded him of Avelyn.

Fletcher wondered whether to approach or to observe from a distance. So far, his ability to focus on an idea and travel to it had been spectacularly successful – beyond all his expectations whenever he set out – but he still didn't know why it worked, and not knowing left him with doubts. He also felt exposed whenever his jumps took him to places outside the anonymity of cities.

Before he could think too much about it, he saw that he was facing a human – or what looked like a human anyway – and started walking towards it. More importantly, it had the violet glow around it that marked possessors of magic – the same glow that Fletcher supposed other magic users would see around him.

He didn't know much about tarans and agreed with Kaz that shapeshifting sounded like something from a comic book, but had not thought to ask more questions about them. Wouldn't a species of shapeshifters be able to create covert havoc throughout the ISC, manipulating events to suit their whims?

Finally getting a good look at the only other person on the vast desert landscape, Fletcher decided that maybe the tarans wouldn't pose much of a threat. It was an excellent approximation of a human with a rugged, angular face and a moderately muscular body, but the texture of the skin was not as fine as you would expect on a human. The clothing was a dead giveaway, though. While from twenty feet away it looked like a crisp grey suit with the shirt collar open and a red tie hanging loosely – inappropriate as that was in a desert landscape like this – a closer look revealed that the texture was identical to that of the shapeshifter's skin. In fact, it was his skin, expertly formed to give the semblance of clothing. Convenient, though Fletcher was a bit uncomfortable with the idea that the man was naked – at least his skin was hiding his private parts.

The face had the right feel to it, though. The man looked like he had seen a hundred worlds – maybe even more than that. His face was full of shadows and depth, like the star of an old western, and his eyes were a deep grey that held Fletcher in their sight steadily. Fletcher wondered if the eyes, at least, were natural and not altered by the taran's shapeshifting. The loose black hair looked natural, too, and Fletcher doubted that anyone would go to the trouble of imitating such a fine detail when baldness was perfectly acceptable.

The taran looked at Fletcher curiously, but didn't say a word as they stood a few feet apart. Fletcher felt uneasy under that gaze, as if he was some sort of insect – an intriguing bug, maybe, but not too much more than that. Apparently sensing Fletcher's discomfort, the taran tried to lighten his own aspect by smiling, but it took him a second or two to get the muscles right, and then it just looked condescending.

Fletcher decided that words were probably the best antidote to the awkwardness. "Are you . . . are you the Wanderer?"

The taran thought it over for a moment. As usual in such times, Fletcher wondered about the translator – it hadn't been calibrated to the right language, so until the taran responded, there would be no way for them to communicate. After thinking about it, though, the taran replied in a soft baritone rendition of English. "I wander, but I doubt I am the only one. You do, too, I think. But not for long. Will you walk with me for a time?"

Fletcher nodded, relieved. The Wanderer walked briskly even though there was nothing in sight for him to be eager to reach. Fletcher was thankful that he had gotten so much exercise lately or he would have struggled to keep up.

After establishing his pace, the Wanderer said, "you have questions. I think I am here to answer them." He looked around as if to make sure there was nothing else important that he had to do.

Those grey eyes had certainly taken the measure of him quickly, Fletcher thought. Would there ever be an end to the questions, though? Fletcher didn't think so, but that wouldn't stop him from asking.

"How come you can speak English?"

It was a silly question to start with, since Fletcher knew the Wanderer must have visited Sol system and learned the language there, but the answer came anyway without any irritation. "I always liked learning languages. I pick them up quickly."

"How long do you have between your jumps?"

"Jumps? Ah, I see what you mean. I might be in a place for a few hours or a few days. Sometimes it is longer. It depends on the world."

"How do you decide where to go?"

"Decide?" the Wanderer repeated blankly. "I just go."

"But . . . when you jump, you get taken to something that has to do with what you were thinking about."

Some of the creases on the Wanderer's face cleared. "That is possible, but I have never done it that way. My mind is blank when I travel from one world to another. I have no thoughts."

Fletcher's brows furrowed. "How can you have no thoughts?"

The Wanderer smiled, this time with better results. "How is it you have so many?"

"If you don't think about it, you could end up anywhere. It could be really dangerous. I mean, you can't breathe in most of the universe."

"I have never thought about it, and the universe has never given me a reason to. Perhaps there is . . . an agreement between the universe and me. It does not try to kill me and I do not try to tell it where I should go. Or maybe I have already died a hundred times over, but when I did, the worlds split into one in which I died and one in which I stayed alive, and I am the one that continued living every time. There may be a world in which we are all immortal, though I do not remember going there. Perhaps I will only go there in the end."

Fletcher's mind whirled as he tried to come to grips with this. "That means you don't have any control. You just . . . what about going where you want to go and doing what you want to do? What about freedom?"

"We all go where the universe wants us to go. I long ago gave up the illusion of having any control. I . . . there was a phrase I heard once, what was it? Ah, yes, go with the flow. I just go with the flow."

Fletcher was repulsed at the idea. "I have control, and I'm not giving up my freedom. I decide where I'm going."

The Wanderer nodded. "If you say so. I have only just met you. Maybe you are different." He sighed. "Wouldn't it be wonderful if I finally met someone who was different? That would make for a day to remember."

They walked in silence for a time, but Fletcher was not short of questions. He wondered whether he really wanted to hear the answers, though. This shapeshifter had no interest in going anywhere, so how could he be a guide? There was one question that seemed safe, but Fletcher thought he already knew the answer. He asked anyway.

"How long has it been since you started jumping? In your time, I mean."

"I have lost track of time. I have no idea. I do not even know how old I am anymore. I suppose I must be very old. Unlike with other species, we tarans cannot even approximate ages on sight since we can change our appearance to suit whatever age."

"But don't you have a normal taran form? What does that look like?"

The Wanderer shook his head. "I have not been back to my home world in so long . . . I would need to see another taran to be able to change. I lost the instinct to take that form not long after I left my world."

"Weird," Fletcher said reflexively. Luckily, the Wanderer didn't appear to take offense or even notice.

"Let me ask you a question," he said. "Since you are free to do what you want, what are you going to do?"

Fletcher stayed silent a few steps, but the answer was obvious, "I don't know yet. That's part of what I'm trying to find out. I don't just want to be a walking hyperdrive. I suppose I should use the power to help people. With great power comes great responsibility, right?"

"Is it really power, though?"

Fletcher didn't know what the Wanderer was getting at. "Of course it is. I mean, let's say you could kill someone like Hitler. Wouldn't you do it?"

The Wanderer's eyes turned cold. "As it so happened, I have had that chance, and I did. Not because I thought it would change anything, but because when the universe put me there, it was the only thing I could do. In that reality, Hitler died shortly after Earth's First World War. There are other realities where he never gained any power, and still others where Germany won the Great War and Hitler had no reason to become what he did. But since he is such a villain to you, I would guess that he did not die in the reality you were born in, nor turn away from his most infamous course. Should I go to every reality and try to kill him in each one? It would be pointless, because every time I did, it would create two divergent histories. Every time I did it, a new reality in which he survived the attack would be created. Now tell me, is this really power?"

Suddenly seeing the Wanderer's point, Fletcher fell silent and stayed that way for a long time. Even though he couldn't find a way to undermine the logic, he found it difficult to believe that being able to do something this amazing was, in fact, useless. He rebelled against the sense of powerlessness that the Wanderer seemed to willingly embrace.

"You know," the Wanderer said after seeing Fletcher struggling, "I began this journey in order to help my people. The gateway on our world was becoming unstable because the natural course of our star had brought it out of alignment. Like you, I had the capacity to stabilize it, and I did. I prepared my mind and made that my last choice."

"But there was a reality in which you didn't, and your people might have turned out like the kentaki."

"Certainly, but I was not born in those. And, unlike anything else, this was something I could only do once, no matter how many worlds I traveled to. I could not save the other versions of my world, even if I tried. You, too, have probably saved a world in the reality of your birth. But you have not prepared your mind for the paradox of powerlessness. All normal beings, fixed in their realities, are gifted with the illusion that what they do makes a difference. The two of us have lost that luxury. Even if I did not tell you all this, you would someday realize it all yourself. The question that remains is whether you will be able to come to terms with it. If you do not find a way, it will eventually drive you insane."

Fletcher's mouth went dry. It was a lot to swallow. Did the Wanderer have to lay it all out there like that? He hadn't even thought about how his connection with the gate might affect Kentak, but he supposed that hyperspace ships might now be able to approach without fear, and that the level of radiation on the world would gradually drop. Just when he might have started feeling good about that, up came the possibility of going insane. It would have been better if he didn't understand, but the Wanderer's meaning was now all too clear. Fletcher remembered the point of The

Invisible Man – what would a person do if he knew he wouldn't be caught? He was facing a different dilemma – what would a person do if he knew it didn't matter? Would he just give up on life and waste away or, like the Wanderer, just go with the flow?

So surrendering to the whims of his gateway had been a deeply considered strategy for the Wanderer to stay sane. Intent on rejecting the Wanderer's way, Fletcher needed to come up with his own strategy. Maybe he would have done so naturally over time without prompting – he couldn't imagine himself giving into despair the way someone else might – but now that the problem was in front of him, he wanted to show the Wanderer that he could resolve it to his own satisfaction. But how?

"There has to be a way," he mumbled. "I can't just give up like you have."

The Wanderer nodded. "I do not think you can. Not yet, anyway. It would be unusual for someone your age. My way is the only true way, but perhaps you will be willing to accept a small untruth in exchange for your sense of free will. A small lie." He held his thumb and forefinger apart an inch to indicate how innocuous the falsehood would be.

What lie? Fletcher thought about it. This wasn't a problem for people stuck in a single reality, so . . . so he had to pretend he was stuck the same way. But how could he do that when he was being forced to go from one to another every hour or so? Even if he slowed the pace down, it would still happen.

Wishing he could just sleep on it and wake up with the answer, he forced his mind to deal with it, and imagined some of those precious gears snap back into place with the extra strain. With a tentative smile, he snapped his fingers and said, "I think I've got it."

"Yes?"

"I'll adopt my reality. I'll . . . make up a rule that I have to go back to it. That's the lie, right? I don't really have to go back, but as long as it's home and I stick to it, then what I do there . . . it matters, right?"

"It matters because you decide it matters. That's right. Believing it will be harder than saying it, though."

"I understand," Fletcher said solemnly, making sure the words didn't sound flippant. He only hoped that his life in reality alpha would be busy enough to distract him from the truth.

"I would not have said so much if I did not think you could handle it, so you can take that comfort, for what it is worth. Is there anything else you wished to ask me?"

"Just . . . is there anything else I should know? I mean, I have this asofi gatekeeper who's helping me to keep the energy under control. Since you don't . . . but do you think there's any spells or stuff like that which he should teach me?"

"As long as you control it to your satisfaction, I think you will quickly know more than the gatekeeper does. Only the creators of the gates will know more than you do."

"Who were they? I guess you haven't . . . have you met them?" How had he not managed to ask about the mysterious "ancients" before? He supposed he had just assumed that no one would know anything about them, or would make up more than they knew like they always did when talking about "ancients."

"I have. Only briefly, though. They were very gracious, and apologized for the trouble their gates had caused. Unfortunately, they had not built the things with an off-switch, and trying to tear down the system would have created havoc throughout the galaxy and across many realities, so it was safer to hope that the instructions they left behind would be enough."

"What did they look like?"

The Wanderer barked a laugh. "You are asking a shapeshifter? They looked quite normal to me, but I would not know if their forms were as ephemeral as my own. But then, I do not remember seeing any creature, sentient or not, that I would not call normal."

"Oh," Fletcher sighed. He'd take the apology, though. It was nice to know that they cared. "I guess . . . that's it, then. I think I have to go back."

The Wanderer stopped in his tracks and turned to look at Fletcher, once again appraising the young man. "I will leave you with this, then. Be careful about how you try to help people. If you teach a man to fish, you can be sure of the result. If you work what looks like a miracle and feed a thousand people, there is no telling what might happen next. I think, though, that even if I said it to you a hundred times, you would still get yourself into trouble. That being true, try not to take it more seriously than you have to."

Fletcher grinned. "I'll try not to, but it's tough when everyone else takes it seriously."

"Yes, it is."

The surge of energy reached a peak and Fletcher caught one last glimpse of the Wanderer walking away from him, continuing on his way with firm strides, before closing his eyes and focusing on his return destination.

30

The Forest

No one was eager to step outside of the cargo ship. Something about the edge of the forest, only a few paces away from where the cargo ship had touched down, took all the courage out of them. Even Sensha, whose physical training included survival in strange forests and jungles, didn't like the look of the plants, though she would not have been able to say why. Maybe it was the unnatural way the light died only a few feet into the growth. Maybe it was the way the trees stirred in unpredictable ways, contrary to the direction of the wind. Sensha had always felt as if forests had a sort of honesty about them – something you could never find in the artificial forest of the cities. This one, though, felt as though it was telling a lie. The way the trees huddled together made it seem as if they were sharing an unpleasant secret that they would only reveal to visitors when it was too late.

The humans had a different reason to hesitate.

"Those trees look a heck of a lot like oaks, don't they?" Sean said, voicing what the rest were thinking. "Damn tall ones, too. What do you suppose they're doing here? I didn't think it was the sort of place that would have oaks, or anything that would look like them."

"Ah, you must be the perceptive one," Rivel said, eyes fixed on the forward view with deep distaste. "We have known about this place, have wondered about it, but did not dare go in."

Sensha sniffed in contempt for their cowardice.

Rivel caught the sound and its meaning, and turned to snarl

at her. "If I didn't know you would use it as a chance to escape again, I would take that to mean you were volunteering to go first. This is no ordinary forest. Further out, the plants are more suited to the planet and its environment, though even they are probably alien to it. Here, it is as the human said. So, tell me, why are trees from Earth growing here?"

He aimed the question at Pierce, but she ignored him. The smile on her face and glint in her eyes told everyone that she had a pretty clear idea of the answer, though.

Rivel had an answer of his own. "Whatever you found on Selparis could only be found by humans. We on Plani have access to the ISC records going as far back as . . . well, far enough to know about the . . . what you call the Atlantian colony on Earth, its colonization of other worlds, and its demise. Here, I think we will find more of what you found on Selparis."

Through a fierce smile, Pierce said, "if you think we're going to help you there . . . ."

"You have no choice, Pierce. You want to see what is here as much as I do. I have waited for a long time. I could have sent my people into the forest earlier, but the risks . . . this situation is better. I admit that, even now, I do not dare step out of this ship first, since I have heard all sorts of reports from this region suggesting that this place has defenses. So, that leaves us with the question – who first?"

Pierce stared at Rivel levelly, as if defying the plani to recommend one of her people. Since she had already been ruled out, Sensha wondered who Rivel would target, and what sort of point he would try to make with the selection. Her eyes followed his as they drifted toward the kentaki onboard, ultimately falling on Gorenal.

"We really have no use for our local friends anymore, do we? But in deference to the fact that we have commandeered . . . ah, I mean borrowed his ship, we will respect the person of the honorable minister. However, his mission commander has failed miserably, repeatedly getting captured, and should be punished. Or perhaps we should say given the opportunity to improve his record? So, Gorenal, right-hand man to the space minister, would you like to demonstrate your bravery and defy rumors of your ineptitude? You can pretend to be mission commander, if you would like."

Gorenal's brows furrowed. "I do not think I would, though I do not see what the problem is."

Sensha sighed. From the very beginning, Gorenal had struck her as lacking in imagination. The fact that he could look out at the forest and not be the least bit daunted by what it might hide . . . but then, what did a kentaki know about such things, anyway?

Rivel had found a soft target, and decided to cajole rather than threaten. He took pleasure in the manipulation. "That is admirable. We are all here quaking in fear, and you, so courageous, see no problem. Please, then, help us to set aside our fears by showing us that there is really no danger."

Sniffing contemptuously much as Sensha had, Gorenal replied, "this is all foolishness." He turned to Corcoris and said firmly, "give me the word, minister, and I will find out what is or is not out there. It is better than letting this plani continue to taunt me, and I would rather volunteer than be forced out at gunpoint."

Setting hard eyes on Gorenal, Corcoris said coldly, "if you want to volunteer, do so."

Gorenal had been hoping for words that would inspire more confidence, but went ahead, anyway. He gave a curt nod to Rivel, who then arranged his men around the hatch, ready to fire at any intruder when Gorenal opened it. Sensha saw an opportunity while everyone's attention was on the hatch, but chose to sit still, conscious of her deal with Pierce. What happened next made her thankful of the agreement that tied her down.

Nothing lunged at Gorenal when he opened the hatch, but no one had really expected an attack right away, and the tension remained at its height as he took the steps down to the ground. Standing on the bare ground without apparent incident, he turned back to those huddled in the cargo ship and gestured around him.

"It is quite peaceful out here, though the wind is incredible," he said.

Then he yelled and grabbed his right foot and everything started. Before he could explain what he felt, he cried out again, hands slowly moving up his leg as they tried to stop the pain from proceeding any higher. Eventually, his hands were at his throat and he collapsed. On the ground, a grey liquid spilled from his mouth and as it flowed, his body diminished, sinking as if into quicksand.

Horrified as she was at the sight, Sensha recognized the nanobots immediately, and remembered her thoughts at seeing the liquid in Orek's secret room. Things were finally coming together, and maybe there was something here she could use. For now, though, she had to make sure that neither Pierce nor herself became nanobot fodder, and that was going to be a real trick with Rivel's mood so unbalanced.

After the stunned silence passed, the grim smile returned to Rivel's face and he said, "it looks like the reports were right, after all."

The puddle began to take shape and the plani aimed guns at it, though without any confidence that their weapons would do any good. The nanobots first took the form of a carnivorous beast, but after examining the situation with a sweep of its eyes, the beast took the form of a human girl in clothing far too thin for the chill.

Rivel's manic smile widened. "So now we see the truth. It would seem as if Earth has a lot to answer for, Captain Pierce. Until the ISC can determine how to hold the relevant parties responsible, you can consider yourself arrested as the representative of Earth on Kentak for violation of the Nanotechnology Convention."

Not seeing that it changed the situation, Pierce ignored Rivel's point and aimed to turn the tables. "Did you know that was going to happen to him?"

"I suspected. But what about you, Pierce, you must have known. Here we have a nanobot colony attacking sentients and taking a human form. Plani was on a known ISC sanctioned mission to explore Kentak . . . ."

". . . but not to take it over . . . ."

". . . but what was Earth after? What were you doing here, Pierce? Overseeing the culmination of Earth's handiwork?"

Pierce almost lost control of her temper. Instead, she spat back, "as if you really believed we caused any of this. You yourself said you thought this was another Atlantian colony."

Sensha added, "just because they take a human form doesn't mean the nanobots aren't controlled by plani. After all, would it not be your sort of plan to use nanobots to take control of this planet, and program them to take human form so you could blame the humans for it?"

"No, it would not," he said flatly, though he seemed to take some pleasure in the idea. He turned to the nanobot female waiting calmly outside the ship. "Now that we have all the accusations out of the way, maybe we should talk to it and find out whether it intends to kill us, as well."

Within a few minutes, the important details of Avelyn's programming were clear to everyone on the cargo ship, though no one was eager to step outside to test the nanobots' honesty.

"Just the kentaki?" Rivel mused. "That is rather inconvenient. I am afraid, Pierce, that one of your people will have to go out next."

Pierce sighed. It had to be done. "Any volunteers?"

Sensha was not at all surprised when Jaidee stepped up, but her eyes went wide when Rivel agreed and moved out of the way to let her descend from the hatch. Rivel was supposed to have dossiers on the *Azar* crew, so how could he not know how dangerous Jaidee was? Catching the expression on her face, Pierce caught her eye and put her forefinger to her lips. Sensha didn't know what the gesture meant, but understood that Jaidee had been something of a secret weapon for Pierce until now. She smiled back. This was going to be fun to watch.

The humans exchanged knowing nods when Jaidee bolted into the forest, changing directions with every step to dodge the barrage ordered by the enraged Captain Rivel. Seconds after she had set her boots to the soil, she had disappeared, and Rivel was left fuming. The failure was his own, though, and he wisely did not say a word until he cooled down. He had few men at his disposal, and too many prisoners, so he didn't dare say anything that might damage morale or diminish the faith his men had in him.

After composing himself, he quipped, "are all your people professional sprinters, Pierce?" He grinned to the other plani to show that the loss of Jaidee, while certainly annoying, was no real problem. "At least we can be assured that the . . . I suppose it is technically a cyborg . . . is truthful about its programming. Shall we go?"

He assigned two plani to guard the kentaki, and marched everyone else out of the ship. They kept their distance from Avelyn, who continued to watch the scene passively.

Rivel acted less afraid of the nanobot than the others, but Sensha was sure it was nothing more than an act. He walked up to it confidently and said, "Can you lead us to . . . to your home, I suppose? To the center of all this."

Avelyn turned to the humans, who were bunched together behind their captain. "Do you wish this?"

Sensha was stunned at this deference paid to the humans. Did that mean the nanobots really were of human make, or were the plani even more intent on fooling everyone than she had guessed? She hadn't registered the talk about Atlantians because she knew very little about the legend, irrelevant as it had been to her life until now. Whoever they were, it was from their remains that Pierce had retrieved the hyperdrive technology.

If there was some sort of . . . cache hidden in this forest, Sensha wondered whether she might be able to pick up something valuable. Not the hyperdrive, which would occupy all the humans and plani, and her people would have trouble using anyway. Maybe something a bit more direct, like an advanced rifle. She looked hopefully at Avelyn, who embodied how advanced the material in the forest might be. If she could gain control over a cyborg or android like Avelyn – something that could turn itself into a death-dealing puddle – her mission would be a great success.

Pierce was uncomfortable with the attention Avelyn was giving to her and her crew, shifting uneasily under the robot's gaze before answering, "yes, take us to whatever the Atlantians left here."

Chin held up triumphantly, Rivel organized his people so that they could keep the humans in check, and the group proceeded into the forest. Avelyn was oblivious to the fact that the humans were captives and under duress. Would Pierce have been able to order the robot to kill the plani? Avelyn had said that she was not programmed to attack plani, but that still left the chance that she would obey an order to do so. There was no need for Sensha to wonder why Pierce didn't at least try, though. The humans were too soft-hearted for that sort of thing. If only she had control over the nanobots . . . did she look enough like a human to try? No, not to a computer. Still, the image of Rivel melting away in a puddle of grey goo cheered her up.

The forest was designed to hide a secret. It was dense, tall, and difficult to penetrate. Avelyn walked lithely across the terrain and Sensha came close to mimicking her, but the rest struggled across the deliberately uneven ground. There were no animals – no creatures taking advantage of the abundant resources the forest had to offer. It was, in its way, sterile. It even lacked the rich natural aromas of a forest, so that even though the trees were technically organic and alive, they might as well have been plastic, because their existence depended entirely on the nanobots tending to them, and not to a functioning ecosystem.

There were similar, though smaller, growths on Plani around the main rail lines, where the greenery dampened the roar of the trains traveling at close to the speed of sound. Those, too, could not survive without a host of automated systems tending to them, and were a haven to all of Plani's misfits – including the dribrora.

Soon they started to encounter signs of what this forest was a haven to, but not in the way they expected.

"Captain," Sean said, looking with dismay at the ground, "there're bits of metal debris in the soil. Tiny shards that're sort of hard to see unless they catch some light, and there's not much of that in here. But they're there. Why . . . ." He left the question unsaid, but Sensha's mind filled it in, anyway – why should there be any debris and why hadn't the nanobots cleared it up?

Soon it was more than just the odd sparkle, but larger pieces of metal or composite materials strewn haphazardly, making it even more difficult to keep up with Avelyn. Sensha eventually decided to take the blow to her pride and stopped attempting to match the robot's agility. Some of the debris was sharp enough to stab right through a misplaced foot and while she could distinguish the dangerous spikes despite the dark, there was no point taking any risks when moving too far forward of the pack would draw a threat from Rivel.

"I don't like the look of this, Captain. I don't think whatever landed here managed to do it intact," Sean said. "You don't suppose . . . maybe these are from the *Azar*, do you? Or maybe one of the other ships that got destroyed in orbit?"

Rivel shook his head. Too dismayed by the scraps in the path to speak sharply, he said, "This looks more like something big – much bigger than any of our ships – disintegrating in the last phases of descent. It may be the remains of massive reentry shielding . . . or it may be that whatever it was crashed on landing." Sensha could tell that he was losing hope in this expedition. He had suffered a series of defeats recently, and was probably primed to be pessimistic.

Looking at the robot Avelyn, though, there must be enough of an infrastructure left of whatever had landed here that the nano-bots had been able to continue functioning. In any case, if something like Avelyn could come out of it, there was certainly still something worth fighting for in the rubble, even if it wasn't what Rivel and Pierce were after. And the more chaotic the interior was, the easier it would be to quietly sneak off to find something of interest while the others were preoccupied.

Through an hour of walking, the remains stayed smaller than half a foot in size and generally more than ten paces apart in a remarkably uniform spread.

Suddenly, Rivel stopped, bringing everyone else to a halt, and he asked Avelyn, "how much more of this is there? How far is it to the center?"

Avelyn looked back demurely and, though it might have only been Sensha's imagination, derisively. "At our current pace, it will take us between two and three days, depending on how quickly you tire."

There were gasps all around. As usual, Sean was the first to put the thought into words. "We're talking about a whole colony ship crashing down, then, aren't we? Basically a whole city breaking apart on impact."

"Much is undamaged," Avelyn reassured, in a softer tone than she had directed at the plani captain. "And we have rebuilt all that we were programmed to."

"That's a relief," Sean said, rolling his eyes.

"Shall we continue?" Avelyn asked Pierce. Pierce looked first to Rivel to see if he had any more questions. If Rivel was deject-ed, Pierce looked as if she was riding high. After all, she already had the information he wanted, and if he had trouble accessing the information from these remains, her bargaining position would improve tremendously.

Rivel started moving again and Pierce nodded to Avelyn. They continued to make their way through the massive forest grave-yard.

31

CONVERGENCE

After another day at the gateway, Fletcher had managed to get some sleep between jumps, and decided he was ready to move on. On the trip back to the river, he even indulged Ethan's need to know about practically everything he had experienced. When the discussion turned to his encounter with Sherlock Holmes, he finally got a chance to throw a question back at Ethan.

"I didn't get to ask the Wanderer, but why do you suppose I was able to meet Holmes? I mean, he's just a character in a story, right?" Fletcher asked.

"Well, where did Arthur Conan Doyle get the idea from?" Ethan suggested. "I mean, if Holmes is a real person in another reality, maybe Doyle just saw into that reality somehow." Seeing that Fletcher did not look convinced by this, he went on, "or . . . or we can think about it in terms of energy. Everyone's got a bit of field potential just to be sentient, and if you put millions of people together and they spend some time thinking about the world of Sherlock Holmes, then maybe that's enough energy to create the reality."

"Maybe?" Fletcher didn't know which explanation was worse – they both seemed iffy.

Ethan put his hands up. "Well, if we had the theory down . . . ."

"Yeah, yeah, I know. You'd be able to calculate the answer. You could tell me exactly how many people and how long it would take, right?"

"Person-hours," Kaz murmured, paying only sporadic attention to the conversation. Fletcher didn't know what the first officer was thinking about, but could read the worries in the lines on the man's face. Something about the way he had spoken threw the other two into a thoughtful silence, and all three travelers grew introspective.

It was past noon, and Fletcher was an hour away from his next jump. After his meeting with the Wanderer, he had mostly kept to a single other-reality destination – a calm, private room with an amazingly comfortable bed, an alarm clock, and a lock on the door. He was nowhere near to catching up on sleep yet, but he was doing better.

He had tried not to think too much about his exchange with the Wanderer, but in the quiet moments it crept up on him. This time, he remembered thinking about the hyperdrive mages and the freedom they might secretly have. What tied them to this reality? That was easy to answer – their duty to the ship. He supposed that was why they allowed themselves to be used that way in the first place – to maintain a firm tie to this reality so they wouldn't risk wandering the universe aimlessly. They must be told that sort of anchor is necessary in their training.

What was that training like? Repeating words constantly to draw in and control the power, Fletcher supposed. It didn't strike him as much fun. Was it worth all the effort? Working hard to gain the gift in the first place, they probably valued it a lot more than he did. Even after a few days of hopping from reality to reality, he had trouble grasping that it was him doing all of it, and he wasn't watching a movie about someone else when he went through his memories.

None of his talk with Ethan involved his personal feelings about the experience – it was all data collecting. Kaz, oddly enough, had shown more consideration for Fletcher's welfare and how he was doing, but now seemed distant in his thoughts, so Fletcher kept it all to himself. Should he try to talk about it? He didn't think Kaz could say anything that would help – nothing beyond empty consolations and a supportive hand-on-the-shoulder.

In the past few days, he had almost forgotten how tedious their journey on Kentak had been. Now, back on the long walk, he wished he was able to travel in hyperspace to close the distance to the river. It would take less than a second – could he judge the time right, or would he overshoot? He thought he knew from the initial phase when he was taken to various realities in his sleep which one was hyperspace, but there were other problems. For instance, what would stop him from ending up in the middle of a hill or a tree? It was easy on a spaceship, since space was mostly empty of major obstacles and safe jump points had been found ahead of time. So, even if he had a pressure suit of some kind, there was a lot to think about before he could do anything more amazing than bring back free pizza.

The boredom made him more amenable to Ethan's desire to experiment, and in his last jump out of reality alpha before sunset, he finally agreed to take a ration bar with him – except he wasn't supposed to hold it. Ethan placed it on the ground four feet away from where he stood, and when he jumped, he focused on bringing it along with him to his alternate reality bedroom. Dubious about the chances of success when Ethan had proposed the experiment, he was pleasantly surprised to find the bar with him on the wood floor after the jump. It was good to know that a lack of confidence didn't affect the result as long as he focused properly. He thought about eating the bar to celebrate, but knew that it would be better to perform the experiment again on the way back, so he dusted it off and placed it on the bedside table before setting the alarm and taking his nap.

Ethan actually hugged him when he came back with the bar once again sitting on the ground a few feet away. He squirmed out of it, but was almost as delighted as Ethan was. No longer afraid of being trapped on a ship and used as its engine, he relished every way his ability displayed some usefulness. Without that, what was the point of going back and forth?

They spent the night still half a day's walk from the river. During the course of the night, Fletcher made two more trips to his bedroom, each time taking along a ration pack placed further away from him – first ten feet away, then twenty feet. Each time, he had no trouble, and on the twenty-foot trip, he decided to eat it, after all. Returning without it to Ethan's shock, he let the researcher despair over the failure for a minute before explaining.

"Bastard," Ethan said, not entirely appreciating the humor, though apparently forgiving Fletcher for making him the butt of it. Kaz got a rare chuckle out of it, though.

By dawn, Ethan had thought up a way to exact revenge on Fletcher.

"I want you to take me with you next," he said.

"What?" Fletcher shouted, unable to believe his ears. Just to be sure, he added, "No way!"

"Why not?"

"It's too dangerous. I mean, I haven't taken anything living yet."

"Except yourself."

"Yeah, but . . . what if our brain waves get scrambled or something? I mean, this is supposed to be my . . . my mental energy taking me there and back, right? I don't know what will happen if I take something else that can think."

"But the mages that work as the hyperdrives do it all the time. We know it works."

Though his view of those mages had changed, Fletcher still didn't like being compared to them. "I'm not the same as them. I didn't get trained like they do. Maybe they need some special spells – I don't know any of that. This isn't space, either. There's all sorts of stuff that could go wrong. On my last jump, the ration bar actually landed outside my room – I had to unlock the door and go outside to get it once I figured out what happened. What if it had ended up in the middle of a wall, huh? What would happen to you? This isn't space – there's stuff around."

"You'll just have to take me somewhere without much stuff around."

"I'm not doing it," Fletcher said, shaking his head firmly.

Kaz stepped forward. "It's early in the morning, and we have to get going. I don't like the idea any more than Fletcher does. You're not a lab rat, Ethan, and I'd rather have Fletcher bring along one of those first before trying anything on you."

"But we don't have any lab rats."

"I know." Kaz left it at that, and started to pack things up.

They made it to the river by noon despite having to stop for one of Fletcher's jumps – which he made without Ethan, though he had to ignore an earful of protests before leaving. When he got back, he found Ethan in a foul mood, alternating between ignoring him and giving him dirty looks. Fletcher couldn't believe how . . . how teenager Ethan could get. The man was shedding ten years of composure at least. Kaz looked disgusted at Ethan's behavior, and Fletcher guessed they had exchanged some words while he had been away.

Fletcher had to hand it to Ethan – the theorist had a clear idea of his mission, and was completely focused on fulfilling it. Kaz had his mission, too – to find the rest of the *Azar* crew and discover what secrets this planet held – but he was much more subtle about carrying it out. Did Fletcher have a mission? At the start of all this, it had been to get away from his father. Well, he had succeeded beyond his wildest dreams, hadn't he? He smiled to himself. Maybe he could be nice and try to help the others on theirs, but his goodwill would not extend to taking Ethan with him on his jumps. He didn't even like the idea of carrying a lab rat. What if half of his mind ended up in the rat?

Back at the river, they decided to rest a bit and take in some lunch. After another meal of berries and rations, Fletcher made a mental note to bring back something for dinner on his next trip. He would have to try for something different than last time, though, or he might end up in the same place, and he didn't think he could count on an equal measure of generosity again.

It was as he was munching the last of his meal that he saw Avelyn approaching, and almost choked.

"I thought she could only come at night," he said between hurried chews. The other two turned to see, and rose to their feet immediately. Helpful as Avelyn had been, they were aware that she could turn dangerous without warning if something in her flawed programming demanded it. Seeing her in daylight marked a change in her behavior, and any change was worth being wary about. But what could they do if she turned hostile? Nothing really, since they were practically standing on her, and she had them surrounded.

She had an unusual business-like walk this time, too, as if she was in a hurry. Not waiting for any of them to ask why she was appearing in the daylight, she said, "there are others here, in the forest to the north."

"Others?" Kaz said, eyes and voice sharp, "who?"

"There are Atlantians . . . others from Earth," she amended, as if trying to decide whether or not there was a distinction. "And there is a larger group of plani with them."

"Plani?" Kaz said alarmed, barely controlling his voice.

"What the hell would plani be doing with Emily?" Ethan said.

Kaz answered before taking another breath. "Forcing her to lead them to whatever the Atlantians left here."

Avelyn understood that, and her eyes narrowed. "The plani are enemies, then."

Detecting a dangerous tone to her voice, Fletcher said hurriedly, "no, no they're not. Not really. Just . . . please don't kill them, okay?"

She turned to him in what passed for her as surprise, "I cannot kill the plani. They are sentients."

"Yeah, but so are the kentaki."

She ignored that and said, "I must continue leading them if that is what they wish. It is part of my purpose to lead people to the city. The city has its own defenses. But if the plani and those from Earth are not allies, what should I do?"

Caught off-guard by the question, Kaz asked, "you're . . . asking for advice?"

"That is what I am supposed to do when I am not certain about what I should do."

"Good programming," Ethan said under his breath. "If I could make a suggestion, maybe you could lead them there very slowly – stall them so that we can get closer."

Kaz looked at him in surprise. "What good could we do? They're probably armed and they outnumber whoever Emily's got with her. I don't think the three of us would make much difference. The captain's probably trying her best to avoid an open fight that could cost lives."

"We could get guns, though. Fletcher could get whatever

weapons we want."

Horrified at the thought, Fletcher insisted, "I'm not going to kill anybody, and I'm not going to help you do it, either. I just told Avelyn not to kill them. Seriously."

His excitement dampened, Ethan replied, "it was just a thought."

Kaz sighed. "Well, stalling them isn't such a bad idea, anyway. Could you do that, Avelyn, just as much as you can without raising their suspicions?"

Avelyn said, "I will do that."

"Could you tell us anything about the people from Earth – their names, maybe?" Kaz asked.

Avelyn rattled off the names she had caught in passing, including Pierce and Sean, then added, "there was also another person from Earth who ran from the group at the start. She follows from behind in hiding."

Kaz smiled. "Good. That's Jaidee. I was hoping she stayed with the captain this time. That's one ace up Emily's sleeve. Don't interfere with her, Avelyn."

"I will not."

It struck Fletcher that the list of humans left one possible ally out of the picture. "Was there a plani who stayed close to the captain? A plani girl?" he asked hopefully. "She's a dribrora – a vampire."

Avelyn nodded. "Yes, she was different from the other plani – an enemy of theirs."

"Good," Fletcher said, not sure why he was relieved to hear that Sensha was all right. A look at Kaz gave him the impression that the first officer was less enthusiastic about her.

Avelyn cocked her head, as if to sniff the wind, then said, "I have to go. As you get closer to the city, I will be able to come to you in daylight more often to guide you through the forest." With that, she disappeared back into the soil.

"That was creepier than usual," Ethan said. "I'm definitely more afraid of her than I am of any plani. Emily's going to want a way to take them down somehow. There's no way she wants them to get the secret this easily."

"Yes, but I don't think that plan will ever involve you with a gun, Ethan," Kaz pointed out calmly. "As far as you and Fletcher are concerned, I'm sure she'd be happier if both of you were safely out of the way."

"But . . . ."

"But we'll try to do something to help them. I'm not sure what, just yet, but I hope it won't involve guns. That gets a lot messier than you've seen in the movies."

Ethan let the jab sink in, knowing that Kaz was right, then replied, "we've got a huge advantage, though. We've got Fletcher."

Fletcher decided not to object. He could see Ethan's point – he could do all sorts of things that the plani would not expect.

"Yes," Kaz said, "but he's also the walking embodiment of exactly what they're after. They'll be glad to have you, too, Ethan, if they find out how much you know about the hyperdrive. I'd prefer it, once we get close to them, if you keep your mouth shut and if Fletcher refrains from doing anything . . . magical. Unless it's to escape from them, of course."

Eyeing them, he waited for both of them to nod before continuing.

"Emily's still got Jaidee and Sean, and they've been through worse than this. I think, with the extra time Avelyn's stalling might give her, she might be able to get the situation under control."

He left it at that, and started leading them up the river again, now with a more urgent pace.

Fletcher sensed more eagerness in Kaz, as if some weight had been lifted off his shoulders. The captain being alive and close by was a great relief, but it was more than that. He remembered how Kaz had acted around Captain Pierce, thinking that the two of them might have had a personal relationship.

Knowing that they would soon meet up again with Captain Pierce made Fletcher feel better about their situation, too. He felt . . . less lost, he supposed.

The plani, though . . . he didn't doubt for a moment that it was Captain Rivel, recalling the confident plani captain and his knowledge of humans. Fletcher wasn't so sure he agreed with Ethan – Avelyn might be dangerous, but she was programmed and therefore predictable in a way that Rivel wasn't. Rivel also had a very definite goal, and could outmaneuver Captain Pierce – might already have done so, in fact. Pierce had once pretended to consider Rivel's offer for the hyperdrive secret. Could she be taking it seriously now that she didn't have a ship?

In the end, that was the question: would they leave Kentak on a ship with an Earth captain or a plani captain? Unless Captain Pierce could pull off a real coup, Rivel might be their only ticket out.

32

Forest Spirit

Three days of wandering through the oak-cloaked wasteland was beginning to take its toll on the morale of the plani team. Instead of maintaining silent discipline, they had taken to whispering among themselves, and it didn't take someone born on Plani to realize that they were less confident than their captain. Sensha knew, too, that just being in a forest – so far away from the familiarity of city life – made the plani uncomfortable.

Worse, everyone was short on sleep and edgy because of it. Night in the forest was loud, as the wind that pervaded throughout the badlands of the continent had its origins here.

As soon as the wind had picked up on the first night, Sean had demanded of Avelyn, "okay, what the hell is doing this? I don't know much about weather, even on Earth, but this is crazy."

"What?"

"The wind! What's with the wind!"

Avelyn had blinked, then answered as if it was nothing special. "The city was meant to run on geothermal processes constructed upon landing. Some of that construction has not developed as intended. This entire forest is little more than a geothermal power plant. The temperature differential is greatest at night, producing the greatest efficiency. The air on this side is the exhaust air. On the opposite side of the forest, air is taken in."

"That's a hell of a lot of power you must be generating."

The matter-of-fact answer didn't stop everybody from suffering through the first night. The plani were worse off than the humans or Sensha, since they had to take shifts standing guard over their prisoners. Sensha needed less rest than the other plani, and took delight in making her wakefulness obvious to unnerve them. She noticed that Rivel barely slept at all, either, though whether he was more concerned about the humans, her, or his own men, she couldn't say.

By the third day, Sean started taking delight in stoking the flames of plani frustration, aiming to drive a wedge between the plani and their captain.

"You know, back home we have all sorts of stories about forests like this," he said as they trudged along. "I think in every culture on Earth, there are stories about forest spirits – secret creatures that hide in the trees. Elves, nymphs, and other sorts depending on the culture. The whole point of them, though, was that they were camouflaged in the forest, so you didn't know where they were or when they might pop out at you. Green and brown, you know? Anyway, they sort of come with forests."

He paused, waiting for someone to take the bait. It was a boring walk, so it didn't take long for a plani trooper to ask, "what were they like, these creatures?"

Sean grinned. "Oh, depends who you ask. Once people started to live in the cities, they started thinking of them as quaint and noble – magical creatures of fantasy. The nymphs were always a bit dangerous, but the elves, they were turned into wise and elegant beings. You ask the people who really had to deal with forests, though – going back to the people who talked about the spirits of the forest in the first place – and there was nothing noble about them. Vicious little things, they'd get people lost in the woods, then attack them when they were confused. Groups of people in the forest like ours would suddenly find they had lost members. A few times, they'd find the people that had been lured away, and what do you suppose they said? They heard strange music, or a voice calling for help, or other things that the others swore hadn't been there. So, they put it down to the forest spirits."

"Nonsense."

"What part? Listen, I'm guessing you've never been in a forest like this one before, or you wouldn't be so quick to say that.

There's something mysterious about any forest, and there's more life in it than you can see at first glance. Can you honestly tell me you've been walking between these towering trees, and you didn't think once about one of them scooping you up and eating you on the spot? You didn't wonder if the branches were more than just in your way, but maybe trying to grab you? And while you were on night duty, weren't there sounds you couldn't account for?"

"The wind was so loud . . . ."

"There were sounds," Sean prodded. "Even with the wind, you could hear voices and footsteps."

"I . . . ."

"Enough," Rivel stepped in, figuring out that Sean had gone beyond conversing as a casual diversion, and was trying to pull something.

Sean shrugged, but kept his smile. Judging from the looks that the plani were giving the trees, he had done his work. With the forest also a graveyard of sorts, it took no imagination to see menace and death in it. Avelyn's ever-eerie manner exacerbated all nervousness, and the plani gave her some thoughtful glances, too.

The first disappearance happened late in the afternoon, and even Sensha didn't notice the plani missing until one of his cohort pointed out his absence. They quickly established that they had seen him only minutes before, and Rivel tasked three of his men to make a circuit within shouting distance while he led everyone else a few minutes back down the path they came. Rivel kept a steady, angry glare on Sean, who smiled back a couple of times, but otherwise pretended not to notice. Sensha saw that the humans had trouble keeping the smugness off their faces. They all knew that Jaidee was now playing the part of forest spirit, and that the plani would get no sleep tonight.

They found the body of the lost plani long before anyone suggested giving up the search. Anyone who saw it, though, instantly regretted the success. Sensha caught only a glimpse through the trees, but that was enough for her. Some of the plani were throwing up, and even the humans turned away in disgust. The body was naked and its flesh was ripped up, as if some wild animal had taken its meal from it. Whatever had torn through the body had done it while the victim was still alive, from the anguished scream still on the face. He had no way to give that scream voice, though – a slash had expertly taken care of his vocal cords.

Rivel's disgust transformed smoothly into rage with barely a change in his expression. "Pierce! Your crew member did this! The one who ran from us!"

"Prove it," Pierce said levelly, eyes meeting his.

"She is the only living thing in this forest that was not with us."

"How do you know that?"

"You know it. And I will hold you responsible for this!"

Pierce blinked. Careful to keep any expression from her face, she asked, "how?"

Rivel chose not to answer, and instead pointed to Avelyn. "You! You probably know every living thing in this forest. Who killed my man?"

With an aloof air, Avelyn said, "I am not an admissible witness for law enforcement purposes."

"Pierce, I bet she would take your order. If your people are not responsible, prove it and ask the robot to tell us."

"You know what? I don't think I will."

"Why you . . . ."

"And if you think she'll take my orders, why don't I just order her to kill all of your men like she killed the kentaki? If you're going to start letting me order her around, you're going to have to think about what that might lead to."

Rivel did think about it. More importantly, his lackeys were thinking about it, and they were quickly getting edgier. First, there was the prospect that a mad human-turned-forest-spirit was hiding in the shadows waiting to attack them with unparalleled vicious-ness. Sensha knew that there was no distinction in their minds between being ripped apart by a forest spirit and being ripped apart by an insane human. Now, on top of that peril, there was the possibility that the human captain could control the nanobots. Their captain had known this was a potential danger, but hadn't shared the knowledge with them until now. Sensha relished the taste of panic and distrust in the air. Whatever Rivel's company

hid in the fine print of their contracts, no plani was ever required
to put their life in danger. Given the death of their comrade, every
single plani had proper cause to walk right back out of the forest
without penalty.

Why didn't they? Did they think Rivel would shoot the first
one that tried in the back? Sensha smiled. This was just too good.

Rivel was no fool, and quickly grasped his misstep in handling
the situation. Looking for some way to regain control, he said, "I
suppose executing a random member of your crew as retribution
would be crass of us, Pierce, so we will wait to exact revenge on
the actual perpetrator when she is caught. Now that we are alert to
the threat, she will not get a second chance. My orders are to shoot
anything that approaches on sight. We will take no chances."

He gave a second look at the body, and decided, "we cannot
leave him like this. Robot or cyborg or whatever you are, can you
build something around him so that we can burn the body?"

Avelyn melted into the soil and a ring formed around the body.
Soon, the edges of the ring rose and formed the edges of a sleek
earthenware bowl with the body inside. Once it was fully formed,
Avelyn returned to her humanoid shape.

Rivel performed the solemn ceremonies himself, laying the
ritual on thick to show that he took the loss of life seriously and
personally. There was no question that the other plani understood
the significance of his display, and were somewhat mollified by
it. That Rivel was making the display meant that he recognized
their concerns and wanted to show them that he valued their lives.
Whether he did or not was another thing, of course, but it was nice
to know he cared enough to pretend.

Sean was not done with the psychological warfare. As they
continued on their way after the funeral, the man was so cheerful
that it even unnerved Sensha. He actually started whistling until
one of the plani men barked at him to stop, and there were times
he was so light in his step that it was as if he was taking a casual
stroll in the park with his girlfriend. Sensha shook her head. It was
almost obscene.

They proceeded in a tighter pack than before and the plani
were on alert. There was no chatter or sign of boredom, and Sean

wisely kept his mouth shut to let the atmosphere brew. Sensha knew that they couldn't maintain the high tension for very long, and once they relaxed a bit after a few hours, Jaidee could pounce again.

"Why is the land on either side of us growing higher?" Rivel asked out of nowhere. Sensha hadn't noticed it before he pointed it out, but they were indeed in sort of a mini canyon, and with the view forward obscured by trees it was hard to tell how steep it would get.

Avelyn stopped and turned. "The city is in a bowl. This is the start of the only entryway. The bowl was meant to hide the city as an alternative to the original program when the outer shield of the colony city fell apart."

Pierce stepped up and, as if waiting for the right chance, asked, "what happened? Why did the colony ship fall apart?"

"Systems failure on landing."

Rivel's eyes widened. "You mean the entire colony ship was meant to land? It was not a failure in orbit? How can something so large be expected to land safely?"

Avelyn stayed silent for a moment and looked like she wouldn't answer, but then something clicked and she started talking. "A number of interconnected hyperdrives placed around the city would generate a field that would jump the city from orbit to a barren and flat location on the surface of this planet. The precision necessary meant a high probability of error, so alternate systems were put in place. When the hyperdrives failed, the bulk of the colony structure was detached from the center and allowed to freefall while the center of the city landed safely using antimatter rockets. Then the terraforming process began. Since the ship no longer had a dome, it was not possible to construct a hill over it to shield it from enemy probes while the colony members established themselves on this world. This method – the forest and basin – was the best option. However, unlike the original plan, it required maintenance, so we have not been able to rest."

Pierce and Rivel exchanged the briefest glance, and Sensha knew what they were thinking. They both wanted to know what their people were walking into and, with Avelyn suddenly forthcoming, they would collaborate to pump her for information.

Taking her turn, Pierce said, "you haven't been able to rest, but why are you attacking the kentaki? That town with the mob . . . I think it was you they must have been afraid of. Isn't that pretty far away from here?"

"In the past decades, there have been sudden spikes in energy, and a reconnaissance system was activated to ensure the safety of the colonists. Instead of finding the colonists and the expected products of terraformation, unregistered life-forms were found to have invaded the planet. We have since begun a program of restoration."

There was a glaze over Rivel's eyes when he said, "oh, the irony. I think I begin to understand this planet finally. This little haven we are being brought into, Pierce, is so cloaked by trees and hills that the radiation levels within must be minimal. Our robot friend wasn't programmed to register the radiation or take it into account. After all these years . . . tens of thousands if this colony ship is really from Atlantis . . . that radiation has transformed the original flora and fauna out of all recognition. It has transformed the residents, too, Pierce. These kentaki are your brethren. And what brought on the first wave of radiation? Almost certainly the failure of the hyperdrives on the colony ship itself." Rivel shook his head in amazement. "Think about it. Does it not all fit together?"

Pierce nodded solemnly, but Sensha scrambled to keep up, and Avelyn looked just as confused. So . . . the kentaki were the Atlantian colonists, then. That . . . was . . . well, Rivel was certainly right about the irony. After so long, the nanobots had lost touch with the people they were supposed to protect, and unable to recognize them, attacked them as unregistered aliens. Could ten thousand years have been enough to change them so much? Or had it been the programming of the nanobots that had developed errors in that time?

From Avelyn's description of what happened, it now appeared more likely that they would find something of value. That boosted the morale of the plani once they grasped the fact, but it also whetted Sensha's own appetite. There was advanced technology here, preserved for their taking. Would the nanobots let her or the other plani take what they liked or would they only allow the humans to? Maybe she could convince Pierce . . . but it was better if she was able to take it on her own and avoid being too indebted to the human captain.

They stopped short of entering the canyon proper as night fell and the highlands on the sunset side cast an impenetrable shadow through which it was dangerous to tread. Tomorrow, they would have to wait close to noon before taking on the canyon, so that the light from the sun directly overhead would give them some sense of the obstacles.

"We have flashlights," Rivel tried to object. "It would be better to camp outside of the city tonight."

Avelyn was having none of it, though. "Your people are the ones stumbling the most. The canyon was not created to be easy to pass. If you want your people to be safe, you will not try to enter it without proper light."

It was a punch to Rivel's stomach, and Avelyn didn't even know it. Even in the dark and unable to see his face distinctly, Sensha could feel Sean smiling.

Avelyn provided them with an excellent campfire that night, but it hardly kept the gloom at bay. Darkness seemed always an inch away, trying to creep closer every time you turned around.

"You must be quite at home in this," Rivel commented to Sensha, pointing at the forbidding blackness all around them. "Creature of the night."

Sensha didn't bother to answer. She wasn't as comfortable in it as she wanted to be, though she had less to be afraid of than Rivel's men did. Still, her night vision only managed to get beyond the closest ring of trees. A few paces more than that, and even her eyes had no idea whether she was looking at another tree or at empty space. Even the humans, who knew that the only danger in the woods was a friend to them, looked claustrophobic.

It was going to be another long night.

33

A Way Out

They hurried north wasting no time, only getting rest during Fletcher's jumps. Avelyn brought back news of the group ahead, including what Jaidee had been up to, and Kaz was anxious to get within range to help should tensions on the plani side erupt into something that the humans could take advantage of. Through some heavy and painful traveling, they were ahead of schedule, and were now less than a day behind Rivel, Pierce, and the rest.

Traveling through the nights had taken a toll on all of them, though, and whatever help they imagined their arrival would bring now seemed an old joke.

"How do you feel about helping them now?" Ethan needled him. "I can't even feel my legs anymore."

"Weren't you the one who wanted to go in like some action hero, guns blazing?" Kaz shot back.

"Yeah, well forget that idea. Put a rifle on me and I'll have to start crawling."

The exertion wasn't anything new for Fletcher, so he found it difficult to sympathize. Quietly bearing the pain ever since being reintroduced to gravity, walking a bit more every day hardly added to the stress he had already been putting on his legs. He was used to dealing with pain, and had no complaints as long as it was the product of his own choice.

Everybody was so exhausted that, even if Jaidee had just walked up to them, she would have had trouble getting their attention. When she snuck up behind Ethan, put a knife at his throat, and whispered, "stop complaining" into his ears, he looked on the verge of a heart attack.

Fletcher recognized the figure as human, but even out in the open, she was so well camouflaged with leaves and dirt on the pants that she looked like a walking tree. There was something odd, though. She seemed to have a faint aura around her, but in the moment of surprise, he didn't make anything of it. Kaz was too tired to grasp quickly what was going on and tensed up, but he soon relaxed and smiled.

"Quit it, Jaidee. He looks like he's going to pass out."

In a blink, she had the knife back in its sheath, and stood placidly while Ethan turned around.

"What the hell! You could have just said hello!"

"Not as much fun."

Fletcher didn't remember Jaidee from the ship – she must have kept to herself – but decided on the spot that he liked her. Of course, after spending so long in the company of just two other people and an assemblage of nanobots, he would have probably fallen for practically anyone who stumbled along, especially if they made Ethan nearly pee his pants.

Kaz looked at Jaidee levelly and asked, "so, what's the plan?"

"I was going to ask you the same thing."

Kaz closed the distance from Jaidee in a few steps and, a few feet away from the engineer, he said, "you mean what you've been doing . . . isn't part of some plan from Emily?"

"No. We didn't get a chance to talk."

"I thought she let you loose to . . . to do what you do best . . . because she decided that there was no chance to make a deal with Rivel."

"I let myself loose to do what I do best because that's what I do."

"We've talked about you doing this sort of thing before."

"So?"

Kaz turned away from her, aggravated. Fletcher couldn't really understand the problem, so he asked what was wrong.

"The problem," Kaz said, trying to keep irritation out of his voice and failing, "is that we might still need to make a deal with the plani, but with Jaidee killing their people in such a . . . way, Rivel is going to be set on getting the upper hand without giving away anything."

"Fuck him," Jaidee spat, "we'd be lucky if he didn't try to kill us the second he got what he wanted, no matter what the deal was."

"The plani don't think like we do."

"Yeah? Well this one does. It's in his eyes. Even if you think he won't kill us, the most he was going to give was a ticket off this planet. Once he got us pinned here, did you really think he'd trade a ship for what we've got?"

"No, but a ticket off this planet isn't nothing."

Jaidee sniffed and said confidently, "we can do better."

Kaz gave her a sardonic look, but said nothing.

"You know something we don't?" Ethan asked, careful not to be too confrontational in his tone.

"No, but she does." Jaidee pointed at Avelyn.

In the forest, Avelyn was no longer constrained in how many places she could appear simultaneously, though she did them the favor of not popping up with a whole group of duplicates – or a whole army. She also didn't bother with a slow approach beforehand. This was her forest, and anyone who walked in it had to assume that she could materialize in their midst at any time.

Kaz looked at Avelyn curiously, and the right question hit him. "There's something in the city that can help us, isn't there?"

Avelyn looked at Jaidee, then said, "if you want to leave this planet, there is a ship. It was made to defend the colony if necessary."

"It still works?" Ethan said, his interest quickly reaching maximum.

"Yes. We have maintained it along with the rest of the inner city."

Ethan took a breath, then asked, "we're talking about . . . this is a hyperspace-capable ship, right?"

"Yes." Avelyn blinked. "Of course."

"But . . . how?" Ethan said, but something about the excitement in his voice told Fletcher that he already knew how. "There's no way a mage could live all this time, unless there's some skewed reality they can stay in where time's mapped differently . . . ."

Avelyn shook her head emphatically. "It has no need for magic. It was a prototype developed by the lead engineer in the city during the journey to this planet. It uses particle acceleration and manipulation."

"I knew it!" Ethan shouted, pumped his fist, and to everyone's shock, hugged Avelyn. Even the robot seemed taken aback, but she stood still and accepted the embrace. Once he let go, he said exultantly to Kaz, "see, I told you! All we needed to do was get the theory right, and we can create the same affect artificially. No need to breed human mages. You're off the hook, Fletcher."

Fletcher wanted to point out that he had never been on any hook, but let it pass. He knew what Ethan meant. With the talk of magic, though, his attention returned to the faint glow around Jaidee and now realized what it meant. He was not the only one in this company who could do magic, though hers was so weak that maybe she didn't even know that she had it. Fletcher decided not to say anything. He now knew what Captain Pierce must have seen in him, though.

"Not so fast, Ethan," Kaz said, looking more confused than ecstatic. "Setting aside the question of whether we can reverse-engineer the ship, we have to get it first. And that's going to be a trick with the plani still having the upper hand."

"I could take care of them, if you give me the order," Jaidee said, with a tinge of hope in her voice.

"No! You and Sean, I swear, you two love creating enemies. Rivel's gone out of his way to avoid harming our people . . . ."

"Not for long."

"But you didn't hesitate to kill his people, did you? Rivel is not just going to lie down and let you take out his force. And if we try to launch that ship, you can bet the kandar will intercept. That's what it was designed to do, after all."

"The ship is armed," Avelyn offered.

Jaidee smirked, but added nothing.

Kaz sighed, then explained, "there's no one on our crew that's trained as a combat pilot, and we'd be at a disadvantage because the controls of the ship will be unfamiliar. That will cost valuable time in any fight. If we want the ship, we're going to have to get it off this planet without risking an interception – either by the kandar or by any other plani ship. We have to have a strategy for getting to Newport Station."

Fletcher kept his mouth shut, but of course the training his father had forced him into had included plenty of pilot simulations – fun up to a point, but grueling if you didn't get food for a few days because you continued to fail a mission. The point about unfamiliar controls was a good one, though, and he didn't want to promise anything he couldn't deliver at the critical moment.

"Any ideas then?" Jaidee asked, implying that she still thought her own solution was viable.

"Our old hyperdrive wouldn't have allowed it," Ethan said thoughtfully, "but maybe this one will."

"What?"

"An in-atmosphere jump. That way we won't have to worry about the kandar."

Kaz shook his head. "Out of the question. We don't know the risks. Unless you have proof otherwise, there was probably a reason why the restriction is placed on all the eldrandii ships."

"But there's no reason to think there's any risk as long as you're jumping to space – you just carry whatever extra matter with you," Ethan complained. "Sure, we won't be going very fast when we enter hyperspace, so we'll have to exit then jump again to get to Newport, but it'll give us enough of a lead."

"I'd rather tangle with the kandar."

Ethan brightened. "Maybe Fletcher . . . ."

"No," Fletcher cut in. He didn't even care what Ethan was going to suggest.

"But . . . ."

"No."

Looking alternately frustrated and sheepish, Ethan said, "well, sorry for being so pushy about things. All I'm saying is . . . we have to use every advantage we've got, or we're not going to be able to get that ship. Isn't that right, Kaz?"

Kaz focused his eyes on Fletcher's and said as sympathetically as he could, "Ethan . . . isn't wrong. I think you should be the one who decides how to use what you can do to help us, and maybe Ethan should lay off of the suggestions, but you have to consider it. You'll think about it, right?"

Conceding the point, Fletcher nodded. He was a part of the team, after all. But it was more of a question of what he couldn't do. He couldn't take anything large into hyperspace yet, and certainly not a ship. Could he bring back weapons? Sure, but nothing that would take down an enemy ship. He knew that he wasn't ready to do anything Ethan might come up with. So, was he just as useless as he would have been without being able to jump from reality to reality? He was tempted to offer himself up as a pilot, after all, just to save face.

"Sorry, I must have missed something," Jaidee said, poking a hole in his thought-bubble. "What's so special about the kid?"

"He can do magic," Ethan offered eagerly.

"Oh," Jaidee said, unimpressed, "is that all? The captain . . . ."

"No, no, not just seeing visions and all that. The real thing."

In an effort to clarify, Kaz added, "we've been having pizza for dinner. Fresh pizza."

"Oh," Jaidee said in an entirely different tone, eyes wide. Looking anew at Fletcher, she said, "nice."

"I . . . I don't just make it appear out of nowhere," Fletcher struggled to clarify, "I actually have to go to a different reality to get it."

"Different reality?" Jaidee shook her head. "Too complicated for me. I'll let you talk that sort of thing over with our wanna-be mad scientist over here. Just get me some pizza. There's nothing good to eat in this forest."

Fletcher cheered up. "No problem. I'm going to jump again in about an hour. You'll have to wait a few hours before I get back, though."

"It takes that long?"

"No, no, but . . . ," Fletcher suddenly found himself at a loss about how to explain it. Instinctively, he looked to Ethan.

Ethan cleared his throat. "Fletcher sort of gets overloaded with the energy. He's trying to control it by putting off jumping at much as possible. When this whole thing started, the energy pushed him back and forth every few minutes. Now he's got it to about every six to eight hours."

"But you could go back and forth quicker, right?" Jaidee asked Fletcher.

"Yeah, but just for pizza?"

"No, in an emergency."

Fletcher shrugged. "Yeah, sure. It just means I'll have to put off widening the gap. I won't suddenly go back to being forced to jump every few minutes . . . I think."

"Let's say there was a gun lying on the ground over there," she pointed to a spot fifteen feet behind her, "and I was coming at you with a knife like this." She drew her blade and started walking towards him. Even though it was just a demonstration, Jaidee was so naturally menacing in her camouflage that it almost made him panic. "Could you jump into another reality, run the distance from where you are to the gun, then jump back and grab the gun?"

"I . . . I think so."

"Do it."

"What?"

"Show me."

As much as Fletcher had resisted similar requests from Ethan, it was hard to argue with Jaidee. She could be very persuasive – especially when pointing a blade at his throat.

He nodded and, as she moved to close the remaining distance between them, he jumped to a familiar reality he knew would be free from obstructions – the same reality in which he had met the Wanderer. Once there, he dashed across the dirt, turned to face where Jaidee would be, then jumped back.

It was eerie, seeing the scene so quickly from a different point of view. The thrill of deploying the energy like this didn't keep Fletcher from remembering what he was supposed to be doing, and forming mock pistols with his hands, he shouted, "Bang!" just as Jaidee was turning around to face him.

Jaidee's eyes lit up. Ethan was grinning from ear to ear, too.

"You might have to do some more of that pretty soon," Jaidee said, "and for real. Are you up to it?"

There was nothing for it – he really had no choice unless he wanted to be irrationally petulant about it. He nodded. What the hell, if he could do it, he could do it.

"Good. You don't have to do any more jumping, but let's go through a few situations so you know what to do, and you don't freeze when the time comes."

Fletcher blinked. "Training?"

Jaidee showed her teeth. "Training."

34

Through the Canyon

With every step closer to their goal, Sensha's urge to tear away
from the pack increased. The narrow dimness of the canyon
heightened the sense that there was something magnificent ahead,
and she wasn't the only one itching to seize the initiative. The
only difference between her and the rest was that she could step
aside and let the humans and plani battle it out between them.
They had no choice but to contend with each other, and that gave
her an advantage.

Something about the canyon made her promise to protect
Pierce a distant memory – as if it belonged to the outside world,
and they were now entering a new, secret world where the old
rules didn't apply. In this new world, Rivel still had an advantage
in weapons, but there was a chance that Sensha could find a cache
somewhere in the ancient colony. In fact, unless these Atlantians
were the most peaceful people ever, there had to be some weapons
somewhere. She could argue that getting to those weapons would
be a fulfillment of her duty to Pierce, not an abandonment of it,
but she wasn't overly concerned about rationalizations as long as
the result was right. She was sure Pierce would feel the same way.

But to find the weapons in good time, she would need the help
of Avelyn, or whatever other ancient systems still operated. It was
too much to hope that the weapons would be lying in plain sight.
That was a problem. Not only did Avelyn make her extremely
uncomfortable, but she had no confidence that the robot would
accept her requests. Would she have to search on her own, barred

from all the locked places that would most likely hide what she was looking for? She was sure that Avelyn could open the locks, but there was scant chance to broach the subject with Rivel close by.

And where was Jaidee? The canyon was too confined a space for her to perpetrate any of her little tricks, but just the anticipation of what the engineer might attempt once they entered the valley made Sensha nervous. The odds were still firmly in Rivel's favor, so whatever the plan might be, it would have to be daring. What if Jaidee was counting on Sensha to play a part? Sensha was on a constant watch for signals and anything that would be obscure to the others yet clear to her, but saw nothing. The humans were also attentive, but nothing about their behavior betrayed that they had seen anything.

Before she could decide what to do, the valley was already in sight. At first, it was just a broad swath of light directly in front of them, the valley captured so much more sunlight than the canyon that it appeared to glow. Once the shapes became more distinct, the awe knocked any other thoughts out of her. The path was lined with a colonnade of unbelievably tall trees – like nothing that existed on Plani, even on its wild southern continent. Visible from such a distance . . . ten of her could fit in the trunk at their base, and they were all at least fifty times her height. To pack them together, and in such neat rows, they had to be artificially maintained. But were they alive? Everything to do with Avelyn and nanobots made that question far more nuanced.

The trees were less surprising to the humans than to the plani. The plani tried not to show their wonder, pretending not to be either moved or afraid when they were both. For the humans, they didn't hide their appreciation, but they looked with familiar eyes. They knew the trees and felt comfortable walking under their shade.

"But I've never seen trees so bare," Sean grumbled. "You should do something about that, Avelyn. These are redwoods, aren't they? Well, I've seen the real things, and there's all sorts of plant-life clinging on to them. There's a whole ecosystem around them."

"An accurate representation was not considered," Avelyn said. "They are functional, preventing satellites from detecting the structures in this valley and acting as part of the geothermal power system."

Sensha had to hand it to whoever came up with this system – even on the ground, it was completely successful. Her eyes had been so focused on the trees, she had missed the comparatively tiny buildings appearing beyond the first dozen redwoods. At first, only a collection of short structures directly in their path were visible, since the canyon walls still limited their peripheral view. As those walls fell away, the broad valley looked filled with all sorts of squat structures, like scattered rocks at the base of the towering trees. And there were more than just two rows of the redwoods – neat lines of them stood throughout the valley, creating a wall of brown behind which little could be seen. Even if there were gaps between their foliage, their shadows covered everything. Sensha was sure that anyone who would go to such lengths for concealment would have taken the trouble of camouflaging the tops of the buildings, as well.

Unaccustomed to voicing her thoughts, she surprised herself when she was overheard murmuring, "who was the enemy?"

Sean gave her a nod. "Just what I was wondering. The guy who programmed the terraformation software might have just been paranoid, of course, but it sure looks as if these people were expecting trouble. Expecting someone to chase after them, though fugitives wouldn't be able to put together something like this." He looked to Avelyn for answers, hoping she would take the bait.

"We were not fugitives," Avelyn said predictably. "There were those who wished to use our knowledge for destructive purposes, and the temptation to misuse the knowledge would continue to be great."

With a hint of alarm in his voice, Rivel asked, "then why were you so quick to bring us here? How do you know we will not misuse it?"

"Because it no longer exists. Most of the knowledge passed with the first generation on this planet, and the rest faded soon after."

Uncertain plani eyes stared at Rivel's back. He cleared his throat and said, "surely they left some records. Are you telling me, in all of these buildings, there is no information about the technology these people use?"

"Yes, but if the technology was deemed sensitive, the keys to understanding the research notes were memorized and not recorded."

The tension among the most disgruntled of Rivel's men exploded. Three of them started shouting accusations at him at once, all in the theme of "you said . . . ."

"Wait!" Rivel shouted over them. He didn't dare to turn around and look at them, though, and instead fixed on Avelyn, hoping that his next question would receive the answer he needed.

"Is there information on the hyperspace drive in this city of yours? Was that considered sensitive, too?" he asked. Sensha was sure that he wished he had asked the question days ago, before they had entered the forest.

"Information on the standard hyperdrive was not considered dangerous, and there are abundant documents concerning it in the engineering section of the library."

Sensha sighed. If Avelyn had been an intelligent ally to the humans, she could have easily ended Rivel's chances right there. Instead, the smirk returned to the plani captain's face, and the morale among his men was fortified. All the work Jaidee had done, chipping away at them, was undone. But it was unreasonable to expect that anything in Avelyn's programming allowed her to lie.

The openness of the valley now provided places for Jaidee to hide as she stalked them. Did the rustle of the wind through the trees also mask her movements? The trees themselves lacked foliage at the lower levels, so they weren't the best help for camouflage, but even an idiot could shield herself from prying eyes behind one of the vast trunks. The plani weren't scouting around anymore, nor paying very much attention to their surroundings at all. Now that the goal was ahead, they fixed on it, already tasting a hard-won victory.

Encircling the buildings, though, was a chest-high steel wall, and while anyone could have easily leaped over it, none of the travelers was under any illusion that doing so without permission would be a good idea. Sometimes walls were placed to keep people out, but they could also be used to indicate a line that should not be crossed – a line defended by unseen weapons.

So they continued along the straight path behind Avelyn, towards an open gate in the wall. Next to the gate stood a female figure Sensha hadn't noticed before. Where had it come from? The answer was obvious – right out of the ground, just as Avelyn had. Sensha looked down and wondered just how rich the soil was with nanobots. How many robotic hands could come out of it and grab her if they decided that she was an enemy? She shuddered at the thought.

It took a few more steps before her companions noticed the figure. When they did, they had sharply divided reactions. The plani relaxed further, probably assuming it was another robot that would guide them to the information they needed. The humans, though, tensed for action, and since they had more experience of these sorts of ruins than the plani, Sensha took their lead. She was already preparing herself anyway, but it looked like this gatekeeper might give her the chance she needed.

As they neared and were able to distinguish its features, the gatekeeper struck everyone as very familiar. When Avelyn took a place at its side, there was no doubt – the gatekeeper looked like Avelyn's mother. The similarities unnerved Sensha, because they seemed so natural. Were they modeled after a real mother and child? With none of Avelyn's intimidating coldness, the gatekeeper was homely and welcoming in her stance and her smile, and Sensha didn't even have to look at the humans to know that this had them confused. It was nothing like what they had encountered before.

Sensha was sure that Pierce had no chance beyond the possibility that she could turn the gatekeeper against the plani. When Pierce tried to play that possibility anyway, or at least aimed to gain some advantage with the assistance of the robots, Sensha would grab her own best hope to bolt.

Jaidee had them all laying flat on a ledge high up on the cliff wall overlooking the valley. Fletcher's face was in a permanent grimace, and the pain from the climb had done a serious blow to his ability to move. Ethan looked like a fallen soldier, sprawled on the rocks in agony.

While the location afforded a view down the road Pierce, Rivel, and the rest walked, it didn't give them much else. There were buildings in the walled city ahead, but with trees and shadows obscuring everything, they couldn't see anything of interest. No spacecraft sitting patiently, waiting for them to board it and escape.

Before the climb, Fletcher had made another scheduled jump, this time to retrieve a listening device Jaidee had described. A small box with a headset attached, its front was filled with buttons and dials to help filter out unwanted noise and to pinpoint the sound of interest. Jaidee now set it in front of her and started tuning it. She was anything but hopeful.

"Gatekeeper looks like she wants to hug all of them," she grumbled.

Fletcher could barely make out the spot down where the road met the city wall that he assumed was the gatekeeper Jaidee was talking about. What kind of details could Jaidee's eyes tease out from that pixel?

"This wasn't what the captain was expecting. The system on Selparis had been homicidal," Jaidee said to Kaz, who nodded to show he understood. Time to start thinking of their own plan.

Considering how aggressive Avelyn could be, Captain Pierce would have naturally planned for a malevolent gatekeeper – one that might at least keep Rivel and the plani from entering the city when fed the right information.

"So . . . what do we do now?" Fletcher whispered to Kaz while Jaidee listened to the proceedings below.

"I'm asking myself the same question," Kaz said, surprising Fletcher with his frankness. "If we see them enter the city without any fight, I guess all we can do is go in and head straight for the ship that Avelyn talked about, secure it, and then see what we can do from there."

"But then the captain . . . ."

"There's no game for us without the ship, and the only advantage we have is knowing that there's one there."

"Aren't we going to help the captain?" Fletcher said, his voice cracking a bit. He looked back and forth between Kaz, Jaidee, and Ethan. Jaidee didn't seem to be paying attention and Ethan looked as dumbfounded as he felt.

Kaz didn't meet Fletcher's eyes when he said, "that's the question, Fletcher."

"Welcome!" the guardian of the gate greeted with arms spread. "My name is Loryn. You have already met my daughter Avelyn . . . ."

"Umm . . . your daughter?" Sean couldn't resist putting the point in.

"As designed by our programmer," Loryn said in a melodic voice that attempted to be motherly but ended up a parody. "We provide different functions. Avelyn's work ends here, and it is my duty to guide you through the city. I can change Avelyn's programming according to the wishes of those within the city – educate her, if you will. She cannot change my programming, but she informs me about those outside the city so that I can decide who should be allowed in."

Pierce nodded to Sean to indicate that he should continue. Rivel made no move to object, not sure of what questions to ask himself and content that the hopes of the humans was fading. Whatever they asked, it would tell him more than it told them, since he had never entered an Atlantian city before, and had less of an idea about what to expect.

"Guide us . . . I guess that means we're allowed in. But why all the camouflage if you're so willing to take visitors?"

"Avelyn's information shows that you fit the profile of those granted entry."

"Really?" Sean gave Avelyn an angry look. "I think she might have missed a few things."

"You are here to access the library. Information in the public library is freely accessible."

"But . . . there's information that isn't?" Sean ventured hopefully.

"Yes. All information concerning heavy weapons systems and other sensitive systems is classified."

"Well, thank heaven for small favors," Sean mumbled. "Now, let's say that two groups of people wanted to enter the city at the same time, but they didn't really like each other. Say, in fact, that they wanted to kill each other, and one of the two groups was Atlantian . . . or at least descended from them . . . and the other wasn't. What would you do?"

Rivel looked ready to interrupt, not sure where Sean would go with the question, but ultimately allowed the question. He wanted to know the rules of the game as much as the humans did. Confident that they were in his favor, he nevertheless gave a nod to his men, and they each took aim at a human.

"Justice in the city was always managed by its residents, as having the law administered by automated systems proved controversial."

Rivel decided it was time for him to take charge. "You know, it seems I wasted a lot of time with you humans. You haven't contributed anything worthwhile to our endeavor, and it looks like I could have walked into this city without you. You know, Pierce, you should encourage your people to be more helpful in the time we have left together, or I will have no reason to give you passage off this planet."

Pierce feigned unconcern – badly. "If it comes to it, I can pay for our way off of this planet. I still have my accounts and plenty of credit, and when has a plani ever turned down hard credits?"

"But there's a matter of price," Rivel held up a not-so-fast finger. "I believe you wisely kept enough credits on your balance sheet to make the down payment on a new ship, but without a ticket away from this world, your accounts are useless to you. So, how much would such a ticket be worth to you? Almost the entire value of your accounts, I would think."

"You . . . ." Pierce snarled.

Rivel held up his hand. "But this is not the time to negotiate. I would rather have my prize in hand first. Maybe then I will be in the mood to offer you a favorable deal. Lead on, Loryn!"

Loryn took it as the order that it was, turned her back on them, and started leading them in. Avelyn stayed outside, glaring at them as was her way.

Eyes sharp for her chance, Sensha saw it just inside the city walls. There was a little gap between the first building on the right hand side and the wall, and the alley produced was completely shadowed. The building was little more than a sentry shack, and in a second, she was on the other side of it, shielded from the sight of her plani guards. She kept running, weaving her way between structures completely unfamiliar to her, hoping that there would be enough of them to discourage pursuit.

She ran at least a dozen blocks before she reached a broad plaza and had to return to the last alley and catch her breath. Was that enough? She looked out at the plaza. What sort of city was this?

Nanobots. They built all this. But why, if the residents of the ship were supposed to leave and settle the planet? Because those residents had to wait in this concealed valley to make sure their enemies had not pursued them, and they decided to make themselves comfortable here first.

Perhaps Loryn had originally been vicious like the computer in charge of the other city the humans had found, but the residents of this city altered her before venturing out. They would have grown tired of the unnecessary security after a few years without any sign of their feared enemies.

Sensha licked her lips. Somewhere in this city, there must still be all the weapons and armor they would have used if they had needed to defend themselves. Information about weapons of mass destruction had to be kept secret, but what about destruction on a smaller scale? Surely Loryn would not mind the disappearance of something like that.

"Where did you want to go?" Loryn's voice made Sensha jump and her heart double its pounding.

Damn nanobots. Loryn had materialized behind her. Sensha checked around to make sure that the others were nowhere in sight, then firmed up her stance.

"Well, now that you ask . . . ."

35

Lost Treasures

"Damn," Jaidee said, pulling off her headphones as Rivel, Pierce, and the rest entered the city. "We're on our own, Kaz."

Kaz nodded. "Lead the way down."

As hard as climbing up had been, down was even more challenging. It was hard to see where the footholds and grips were and, though he tried his best to mimic Jaidee's moves, Fletcher still slipped twice when trying to descend the first few feet – brought back to balance first by Kaz and then, more embarrassingly, by Ethan. The others didn't have any trouble, with even Ethan making it look like a simple hike. Fletcher once again vowed to take his physical training seriously - if he survived this.

But did he really have to put up with his embarrassment? He wasn't sure what would happen if he tried to jump to another reality, walk a few paces toward the hidden city, and then jump back. Maybe he'd find himself safely on the ground, but with his luck, he could just as easily find himself in midair. He could try a reality with a stairwell, but then how would he know how far to go to avoid being either too high or burying himself in the ground?

This was silly. Somehow it had all worked out before, so there was every reason to believe he wouldn't end up dead. In all sorts of jumps, he had always found himself on solid ground. But . . . until he was sure how it worked, he couldn't bring himself to take the chance. Clinging to the side of a cliff made him more survival-conscious than usual.

So, he continued with the rest of them, going down the hard

way. Reaching the ground was like getting back home after a long day. Fletcher would have kissed the solid earth if not for concern about what the others would think of him. He settled on lying down for a bit instead.

They didn't give him much time to recover. Jaidee hauled him to his feet after a look from Kaz. Fletcher didn't object – there was no telling if Rivel himself might find out about the ship Avelyn mentioned, and once he did, his priorities would change immediately.

There was a new Loryn at the gate – well, a new assemblage of nanobots, though presumably the same program acting behind them. Was there any way to be sure? It was once again trying its best to look welcoming and motherly. And it even started with the same spiel.

"Welcome! My name is Loryn. You have already met my daughter Avelyn, and she tells me that you are looking for a hyperspace capable ship."

Kaz and Jaidee looked at each other, sharing the same thought. Fletcher had it as well. Would the residents really have programmed Loryn to hand over a spaceship on request? Now that they were here, it seemed too good to be true. But what could they say? Avelyn had offered the ship, and if she had intended on killing them because they wanted it there was no reason to wait until now. As far as Fletcher could reckon, the worst that could happen was that Loryn would deny them entry into the city. That was bad, but it would also mean that Rivel wouldn't get the ship, either. They would have trouble helping Pierce and the rest of the crew, but their chances of doing that were already low anyway.

They had to take the chance.

"Yes," Kaz said hesitantly. "Yes, we need a ship to get back to . . . to leave this planet. We understand if that's not possible, though. If you need the ship to protect the city . . . we'd be happy if you would just let us into the city so we can make sure our captain is safe."

Jaidee gave Kaz the thumbs-up, and a brief smile of relief lifted his lips. There was no way he could have put it any better. Now, it was all down to Loryn's programming.

Loryn seemed to think it over with a frown on her face, as if weighing different directives. "The ship was a prototype meant to protect the city and, when its residents had established themselves on this world, to provide a way for them to establish alliances with other worlds. Over time, we have gathered enough resources on this world to manufacture a second ship . . . ." But her programming did not let her go any further.

It was clear to all of them that Loryn wanted to say that because a spare ship could be produced, they could have the one that was ready, in keeping with the programming that drove her to try her best to accommodate visitors. But there was the other programming that said the ships were to be used to protect the city and to make contact with other civilizations, and allowed for no other purpose.

Kaz quickly moved to resolve the conflict before Loryn came up with some solution of her own. "Then how about we take the ship on the promise that we will be visiting potential allies? That's completely true."

Loryn's expression cleared. "That would make it easier, yes. But I was only to allow that if the descendants of the city were ready to make this world open – ready to protect themselves."

Here, Fletcher couldn't keep himself silent. Throughout the conversation, the idea that Loryn could change Avelyn's programming had been humming in his mind, and now that the issue of the kentaki had finally come up, he intended to do justice by Kordon, making sure no more kentaki suffered the fate he did.

"Avelyn has been killing those descendants the whole time! They're the kentaki! Your programmers didn't know that the gateway on this planet isn't stable and produces radiation. That radiation changed the people you were supposed to protect into the kentaki over thousands of years, but you've been killing them because you didn't recognize them!" he burst out, avoiding the angry eyes from Kaz. Fletcher had just complicated an already delicate situation.

But Loryn nodded. "Avelyn has relayed your conclusions back, and I have run evolution models that adjust for the radiation, and those models include the possibility that creatures you call the kentaki are descendants of Atlantis. Our original definitions did not take the increasing dose of radiation into account. I have adjusted Avelyn's program with the new model so that she will not kill anymore kentaki."

Relief swept Fletcher's aching body. So, it turned out to be that easy, after all. Mission accomplished. He didn't even need to figure out alien programming – just needed to talk to a better-developed computer than Avelyn. Was Avelyn limited because she was expected to act quickly, while Loryn was supposed to act in a more considered way? That was just Fletcher's guess, but it made sense. He quickly decided to capitalize on this personal victory.

"So . . . so, you see . . . the kentaki have a space program. They've sent missions to other worlds. So they're ready for contact. Can you . . . verify that? It'd show that they think they're ready to make this world open."

Loryn didn't answer directly, but she now had enough information to make up her mind. "You may have the ship. We will begin construction of its replacement."

There was no way to contain the joy at this victory. Ethan jumped and pumped his fist. Kaz shouted something in Japanese that Fletcher didn't understand, but then patted Fletcher on the shoulder as a sign of gratitude. Jaidee smiled. It was subtle, but Fletcher thought he saw some warmth return to her cold eyes. There was also a purple thread of magic that had formed between them, streaming from him to her as if he was some sort of star spewing matter into a companion black hole. Well, he had plenty to spare.

Loryn – this Loryn, anyway – led them into the city. While they had been celebrating, Avelyn had disappeared. Loryn seemed like better company, but Fletcher had the strangest sense that Avelyn was more honest – brutal, but honest. It wasn't that he suspected Loryn could actually lie, but Avelyn's programming was so straightforward and predictable while Loryn's was clearly complicated. That conveyed a certain kind of impression. Fletcher decided that he would have to learn to avoid making the same judgment about real people – mistaking simplicity for honesty.

Fletcher had very little experience of cities – the only proper city he had been in for years had been Dael on Plani – so he didn't have any sense of what one was supposed to look like. He had a vague notion from videos of Earth, of course, but as he looked around, it all seemed normal enough. There were buildings, trees, and streets. He looked to the others to see if there was anything remarkable about the city, but they didn't seem surprised by anything, either. Ethan would speak up if something amazed him.

No mystery where the kentaki got their habit of packing buildings in tight, though. Fletcher looked down the roads at every intersection they passed, and while the roads were numerous, they were all sized for pedestrian traffic only.

There was an unpleasant scent to the wind now – a touch of rotten egg smell. Since everyone else remained silent, Fletcher decided to ask Loryn what it was.

"That is the slight hydrogen sulfide emission from our geo-thermal plant. Do not be alarmed, the levels are well below all risk levels. The concentration is less than ten parts per billion, the limit set by the designers of the recapture system. Unfortunately, since it is heavier than air, the gas remains trapped in this valley. You will quickly cease to notice the smell."

"First radiation, then hydrogen sulfide," Ethan said, pulling out the bioscanner and confirming the concentration of the noxious gas. "Can we get off of this world, now?"

"That's the plan," Kaz said, trying not to sound exasperated with Ethan because, this time at least, he sympathized with how Ethan felt. "How far to the ship, Loryn?"

"Not long. It is at the center of the city, and since this city was meant more as a repository and refuge than a permanent habitation, it is not very large."

That comment struck Fletcher. If it was not a repository, what was in all these buildings? Probably all sorts of messages from the original travelers – each one leaving what they thought their descendants could use. Each building a time capsule. Also, Fletcher supposed that they were all guaranteed a home to return to should the attempt to spread and multiply failed. Since they had not come back, it must have been successful – at first.

Sensha wouldn't have said that she liked Loryn, but she preferred the affable construct to Avelyn. While Avelyn was in all respects a hostile presence, Loryn's persona was amiable and easygoing like the model tour guide. So, in a rare case of dropping her guard, she decided to trust the robot and its programming, confiding in it what she wanted.

To her surprise, Loryn smiled with a touch of mischief and said, "I understand. I think I have exactly what you are looking for. Come with me."

Sensha tailed Loryn for a block, but then had misgivings. "Wait. What is it you are taking me to?"

Loryn blinked. "Exactly what you asked for – personal armor and weapon. You will understand when you see it. It was a prototype that its creator left with the instruction that it should be given to whoever asked for it first. That was typical of the bequests from the residents of this city – each craftsperson left the product of their own work that they did not take with them to any who would come asking for it."

Craftsperson? Sensha pictured bulky ancient steel sheet armor with a sword – the product of a blacksmith's work. Maybe she didn't make herself clear enough about what she wanted, but for now she kept quiet and let Loryn lead on. These spacefarers were advanced enough to create a colony ship – she doubted that they would have wasted space in the ship taking along someone whose only skill was fashioning novelty items. Besides, Loryn had said "prototype," and that meant "advanced."

Loryn led her to a building that was indistinguishable from any of the others, and looked more like a residence with its windows on the second and third stories than a laboratory where technicians would work. A step through the sliding door and a flicker of the lights reversed her impression completely. There was no mistaking that it was a real craftsperson's shop – the tools of the trade and unfinished work were in neat arrays on the left side of the shop floor, while the right side featured the finished products displayed elegantly to entice the visitor. The difference was that the tools of the trade and their products were not only electronic, but more sophisticated than anything Sensha had ever seen.

Some of the products looked like kitchen appliances, but Sensha couldn't be sure.

She shook her head. "It is like the laboratory of a genius. Or a mad scientist. Normally, you would mass produce things like this . . . ."

"The woman who lived here was an inventor famous for her engineering. Even now, we do not have the resources to mass produce these, as this planet lacks sufficient quantities of rare earth elements. This was left as a museum – a monument to a great mind."

And the light made the inventions glitter as if they were gems, but they were only a treasure to someone who knew what they were and how to use them.

"Do they still work?"

Loryn's eyebrows went up in surprise at the question. "Of course. Everything here has been maintained according to specifications."

Sensha resisted the impulse to ask what everything was. There were dozens of little toys – or at least she thought of them as toys for now – and it would take too long to go through everything. She had enemies in this city, and needed to stay focused.

Receiving no further questions, Loryn led Sensha to one of the four doors on the opposite side of the shop from the entrance. None of the doors had handles or any obvious way to open them, so either they slid open automatically or Loryn herself was the key. Wary of being trapped, Sensha decided to stay in the doorway.

She didn't have much of a choice, though. As a single panel of light illuminated the interior, she saw that it was little more than a closet, and even from where she stood, she could touch its only contents once Loryn stepped aside.

It was a jet-black bodysuit. On its mannequin, it looked too big for Sensha. But besides that, it looked too thin to be genuine armor. What could it hope to save its wearer from, when the fabric looked lighter than the clothes she was wearing right now?

"It looks interesting, but what can it do?"

"The armor's primary specifications include the ability to

withstand a million standard atmospheres of pressure – more than sufficient to stop any known projectile weapon – and to insulate from heat energy sufficient to withstand flames. It also reflects or absorbs attacks from most energy weapons."

Sensha blinked at the unassuming suit. "How?"

"Adaptive nanotechnology."

Sensha recoiled. "You mean it is . . . like you?"

"In terms of its construction, yes, but it does not have any artificial intelligence. Its programming is much simpler than mine."

"So . . . it does not decide to do anything. It has set functions."

"Exactly."

It sounded like truly advanced armor – exactly what Sensha had been looking for. Was it too good to be true?

"Would you like to try it?" Loryn offered. "You really will not have a full sense of its capabilities otherwise."

Wary of Loryn's apparent eagerness to see her do it, Sensha nevertheless couldn't contain her own excitement. "But . . . it doesn't look like it would fit me."

"Adaptive nanotechnology," Loryn repeated. "It will adjust itself to your body. You will have to take off the clothing you are wearing now."

Sensha inventoried the clothes she had been wearing ever since she arrived on Kentak, reeking as they were from the sweat of her exertions with creases hardened by dirt from nights sleeping on the ground. She had been in clothing that was even worse for wear during her training, but given an opportunity to take this mess off, she didn't hesitate.

Standing naked, she took the suit off the mannequin, knowing that if she had waited a moment longer, Loryn would have made it melt off the mannequin and stream towards her the way the nano-constructs were programmed to do. If it had done that, she would have run – there was no way she'd let that slime touch her, not after seeing a similar ooze kill Gorenal. So, she held it and pretended it was a normal bodysuit, stepping into it one leg at a time, then pulling on the sleeves, and finally bringing together the centerline contacts.

Once the last pair of contacts – the ones at her neck – were together, the suit shrank to fit her body tightly, and the edges at the sleeves and ankles extended to form gloves and shoes. She turned her head to the left and right to see whether the collar was comfortable, and found that it was completely yielding – there was no resistance to the movement at all. Swings of her arms and fine finger movements felt similarly effortless. It was almost as if the armor was assisting her motions.

Testing this theory out, she started jogging in place, and even as she sped up she felt no strain – or at least much less strain than normal – in her legs. She ran right out of the building and made a circuit of the block. Then another, faster. Still faster, more than twice as fast as she had ever run before, she added random leaps into the air as if facing hurdles, and she might as well have been on a planet with half the gravity. A quarter of the gravity, even.

Finally, she came to a stop back inside the inventor's shop, elated. If her heart was racing, it wasn't because of the exertion, because her breathing was steady. Quite apart from any desire to, she was beaming with delight.

"This is . . . I . . . ," then, still smiling, she asked with a touch of suspicion, "can I really have this?"

"The inventor specified that she wanted it used to protect people. Will you give your word that you will use it to that end?"

"Yes, absolutely. I want it so that I can protect my people."

Loryn nodded. "I detect no sign that you are lying, and that is the only restriction set. It is yours if you want it."

For the first time in her life, Sensha felt lucky. Running her gloved right hand through her hair, she suddenly realized, "what about my head? There must be a helmet."

"There is. However, it was designed to be controlled with the implant. Would you like the implant installed?"

"Implant?" Sensha's alertness suddenly went up to full paranoia mode. "No, I do not want any implant!" Then, reconsidering her initial alarm, she asked tentatively, "what implant?"

"It is the interface that allows you to control the suit with thought. The suit is capable of taking on a wide range of possible shapes. You will have to experiment with it to get a sense of its full capabilities."

Looking at it as clothing, the question hadn't occurred to Sensha before, but now she asked, "where do the nanobots get their energy from?"

"Mainly from your body heat. They can also break down your excrement if the implant is installed. The implant contains a full user manual if you need details."

Every mention of the implant heightened Sensha's uneasiness and uncertainty. It made sense that sophisticated technology like this would be controlled that way – much of Plani's complex transportation infrastructure, including most of the cargo movement at Dael, was controlled by people with chips in their heads. So, why the hesitation? Because even she, with her limited imagination, could picture these robots with their artificial intelligence gradually altering themselves into something their creators had never imagined. Avelyn had already demonstrated this by killing sentients, but what had the centuries and radiation done to Loryn? She could alter Avelyn's programming, so who was to say that she hadn't known what Avelyn was doing – hadn't set Avelyn on that course in the first place? What if this suit and implant was Loryn's way of getting around the restriction that kept her bound to this city – giving her a body to control and roam the galaxy with?

But Sensha had never developed the imagination needed to take that thought seriously. She felt the added strength provided by the suit as she formed a fist with her right hand and punched the air. Then she punched the nearest wall with all her might. The force bent the composite material back to a depth equal to her fist. She felt only the slightest strain in her joints as she pulled back and relaxed – no pain in her hand itself at all.

Loryn frowned and said, "I would appreciate if you did no more damage to this city." She disassembled herself, flowed into the indentation Sensha made, and slowly corrected the flaw in the wall. It took longer than Sensha expected, and she felt guilty at having caused Loryn the trouble. She was about to gamble on Loryn's goodwill, and if it was as forthcoming as it seemed, Sensha would remember the robot fondly for the rest of her life.

Once Loryn formed back up into her bipedal form, Sensha said "sorry, I'll try not to." Then she touched the area of the wall gently, turned around and leaned back on it to see that it was firm, and looked again at it to see that there was no deformation when she did this. Somehow, the suit understood when she was moving with the intent to do damage and when she was relaxed.

Loryn seemed to understand what she was checking. "There is no magic – it is only responding to the tension in your muscles and magnifying the effect. The implant will give you more complete control, so that you can avoid doing damage when you are tense – avoid crushing the people you are rescuing from a disaster, for instance – or to apply the full force the suit can provide when your own muscles are relaxed."

There was no use stalling any longer. Sensha would not forgive herself for not taking the chance – for coming away with a half functioning suit that, while novel, was not sufficient. Perhaps with the implant and all the suit's abilities at her disposal, she would not even need to rely on a trip home from the humans. Maybe she could hijack the plani kandar, and with that platform a plani hyperspace ship. Or, she could use the kentaki – take over Orek's rebels, use them to gain control over the Grikorat and the planet, and mobilize them to help her own people. It would be a win-win situation – the kentaki would advance under her leadership, and her own people could at least come to Kentak to seek refuge from the persecution they faced on Plani. All they would need was some radiation-shielding, an early warning system about those radiation bursts, and a way to grow more appropriate food. She would be useful to her people if this worked, and useless if it didn't.

"All right. Will installing the implant require some sort of surgery?"

"A mild procedure. I will have to sedate you for a little while – about the time you have spent in this city so far – otherwise there's a risk you might go into shock as the implant establishes its connections to your cortex."

Sensha nodded. "Do it."

The city didn't have a spaceport or anything like that – something of that size would be too obvious from aerial reconnaissance. Loryn led Kaz, Fletcher, and the rest down into what she described as a hangar. The building they entered was as plain as the rest, and its interior was almost barren – the floor was clean white marble and there was good lighting, but it looked like an area that people were meant to pass through in a hurry. Directly opposite the front doors was a bank of four elevators. Loryn led them into one of them, and they started their descent.

There was no telling how far down they went, but the journey was smooth and brief. When the elevator came to a rest at the bottom and the doors slid open, the hangar was pitch black and none of them dared step out since the light from the elevator only illuminated a few feet of ground ahead. When Loryn commanded the hangar's lights lit, the intensity briefly blinded them. What they saw once their irises adjusted had them gaping.

"It's red!" Ethan said, delighted.

With relief in his voice, Kaz said, "it's a ship. A real ship. But it's much smaller than the *Azar*. If it's really hyperspace capable, it's the leanest hyperspace ship I've ever seen."

Fletcher had seen the *Azar* at dock on Newport Station, but it was nothing like seeing a ship in a hangar. The dock windows were almost like a screen, making the ship seem more distant and unreal than it was. Here, it was actually possible to go up to and touch the ship – or at least touch its landing gear. They didn't, though. For now, they just exited the elevator and stayed back so that the full magnificence of the ship was in view.

"It only has one body," Fletcher noted. "The *Azar* had two, like most of the other eldrandii ships."

Ethan nodded, noticing the basic difference in the structure, too. "Can't say if it is or not, but it sure looks fast and agile."

"It's the smooth lines," Kaz pointed out. "The eldrandii are great at making their ships slick and atmosphere-capable, but this is something else. I remember seeing a supersonic bomber from the early twenty-first century that looked a lot like this. That plane . . . they said it could maintain a height of a hundred feet above the ground at its cruising speed. This ship looks like it's meant to dominate from the bushes to the stars."

Ethan snapped his fingers. "The *Red Hare*."

"What?" Kaz said, startled out of his appreciation of the design artistry.

"I never liked the name *Azar*," Ethan explained, "and I don't want to leave this one up to the crew like Emily did last time. It's got to be red-something, because it's just so red. And it looks like it can dart this way and that like a rabbit. It came into my head when you said 'bushes'. And of course *Red Rabbit* doesn't sound right at all. Plus, it's a pun on Emily's red hair. Get it?"

Kaz rolled his eyes, but Jaidee said "it's not bad. I like it better than *Azar*, too."

Ethan grinned at this stamp of approval. The atmosphere between him and Jaidee had been tense ever since she put his knife at his throat, but this went some way toward easing the friction.

Kaz shrugged. "Let's get on board the ship first before we think about naming it, all right? Loryn, will you please lead us in?"

36

Confrontation

Sensha had been worried that the implant would somehow change her or affect her mind. It hadn't done so in the way that she had been worried about – her personality was intact, confirmed by a lifetime worth of memories that were similarly untouched. But there was change. She was now aware of a full range of physical abilities never before at her disposal. She could extend a blade from her glove – or indeed, from any point on the suit – at will. If she chose to see them, she could monitor her vital signs and the energy capacity of the suit. Ordering the helmet to extend from her neck and around her head, she could extend or narrow her field of view with a thought, giving her panoramic view at will.

And she was only getting started on the process of discovery. What she thought of as her body wasn't what it used to be, and now encompassed a much greater array of tools, all of which only magnified the benefits of her training. Within an hour of having the implant in place, she realized that she would be unable to take the suit off – it would almost be like abandoning a pair of limbs. Fortunately, its creator had designed it to be an integrated part of the wearer's existence so that there was never a need to re-move it – sweat and waste were absorbed, the material was porous enough to allow the skin to breathe and the suit could transmit touch sensations as desired. Sensha even saw in the guide accessible through the implant that the creator considered how a person could make love while wearing the suit. Eccentric, but in a constructive way.

She was lucky. This was cyborg lite – unlike members of elite military forces all around the galaxy who had permanent modifications made to them, Sensha could take off the suit, and the implant would just be an inert chip in her head. She always had the option of going back to being as she was, even though there didn't seem to be any advantage to it now.

Perched on the roof of the building opposite to the city's data center, she had a more pressing reason to feel lucky. She was about to get her long sought-after revenge on Rivel. With her helmet on, his men wouldn't have any idea what was attacking them, leading to some tactically beneficial confusion. She would show Rivel her face, though. She wanted to see the look in his eyes as life drained out of them, making sure he understood who had wrought his doom. Without that moment, revenge would have no meaning. But not before she used him to get off of this planet. Her bloodlust would have to wait, or she could find herself emotionally satisfied but physically stranded.

Rivel had assigned four men to guard the entrance to the building. To counter her, he would have only thought two necessary. He was more concerned about what Jaidee would do, but Sensha doubted that four would have been enough to stop the human warrior. Of course, now she had the clear advantage over Jaidee and could probably take out a dozen of Rivel's men before one of them managed to get a shot off at her – presumably a futile shot, but she hadn't tested that aspect of her new abilities yet.

But she had to make sure that she could keep the humans safe. With her new abilities, there was no reason their lives should be at risk as she cleaned up the mutual enemy. And after Pierce had done so much to avoid conflict, to make sure her people stayed alive, how would the humans take it if Sensha went in indiscriminately and got some of them killed? With his prize in hand, Rivel would probably be willing to deliver them back to Earth whole with only token remuneration in return, and they knew it. She needed to offer them the same result if she wanted them as future allies, and powerful as she now was, the hope she could bring to her people would require more than she could provide directly. More than ever, she saw that clearly.

Could she remove these four guards without putting Rivel on alert inside?

Just as she was thinking about it, though, there were shouts from inside the building that drew the attention of the guards. Might the humans have actually made a move? Could Jaidee be in there?

But no – it looked like the humans were being dragged out of the library by the plani, and it was Rivel shouting. Through her helmet's audio augmentation, Sensha could hear every word.

"There is a ship, and the humans have taken it. The robot failed to mention this to us before, but now we know, and it will lead us there. All of you be prepared for a fight, but take care with the prisoners. They are our leverage, and without them, the humans may turn the ship's own weapons on us if it is possible to do so," Rivel ordered urgently.

The balance of power had shifted, and Sensha stood stunned on her rooftop perch. If the humans had a ship that could take them away from this planet, that changed matters drastically. She could eliminate Rivel outright. But should she do it now, with them rushing to wherever this ship was?

She shook her head. Too many questions. Since there would be support near the ship, it would be best to wait to see what that situation was like. The longer the gap between the fight and her departure from this planet, the more that could go wrong.

She needed to move ahead and take up her position before Rivel and the rest got there.

"Loryn!"

"Yes?" the artificial intelligence formed behind her.

"I need to get to this ship before they do."

Loryn turned herself into a bird, flew onto Sensha's shoulder, chirped, then started flying. Sensha didn't need much effort to keep up, and they easily outpaced the hurrying plani and their hostages.

Kaz had allowed a glowing smile onto his face as they stepped into the command center of the *Red Hare*, but the news from Loryn wiped that out.

"It suddenly occurred to the plani captain that there might be more than just records, and he asked whether there was a working sample anywhere. I had to tell him the truth," Loryn confessed. It was odd for her to be apologetic about following her programming, but she explained, "I should not have told him that you were already here. I misjudged the situation."

They didn't waste time arguing with her, though none of them was sure what Loryn's motive was. Fletcher guessed she might have thought the two parties would want to meet once they each found what they were looking for – Kaz had floated a reunion with Captain Pierce as an excuse to get into the city, after all – but he was cautious about assuming anything when it came to Loryn. She just seemed too clever for a computer – clever enough to justify all the careful handling he would give to a human with her powers.

Jaidee went to hunt for weapons immediately, but Kaz set his focus on the ship's controls.

"Loryn, I need to learn how to get this working. Are there any defenses? How do we get out of this hangar?"

Fletcher looked at Ethan, but there was no sign of action from that quarter, so Fletcher decided to take Jaidee's lead and began to search the ship. At least it would be good to get the layout of the ship down to have some advantage in a fight. He kept an eye out for crate-sized spaces where he could hide safely. At a size disadvantage to pretty much everyone, he would at least prefer to have surprise on his side or a refuge if all else failed.

"Umm, Fletcher?" Ethan had remained silent so far, and his sudden decision to speak startled Fletcher.

"What?"

"Do you really think the plani are going to try to board the ship and fight us for it?"

"That's what we're getting ready for."

"But they have Emily and the rest as hostages, right? They can't hold them and try to attack us at the same time. They have to use the hostages to get us to give up the ship."

Fletcher could have slapped his head. Why didn't he think of that? The excitement of having a ship to leave this planet on and then the panic of hearing Rivel had caught up to their plan had left him in a daze. Did Kaz realize what might be coming? Fletcher decided that it was best to check, so they rushed back to the command center.

They found Kaz in a surprisingly good mood, and didn't have to wait long for him to explain. "This ship has an onboard A.I., so we can control the ship verbally. In fact, a single person could control the whole ship if necessary. The A.I. is necessary for the hyperdrive."

Ethan shrugged. "I could have told you that."

Kaz didn't bother with that comment, and instead read the look on Fletcher's face. "What is it? They aren't here already, are they?"

Fletcher gave Ethan a glance and Ethan repeated what he had said.

Kaz understood what Ethan was getting at only a few words in and cut him off, shouting, "Ai!"

"Yes?" a soothing feminine voice came out of the bridge speakers.

"Where's Jaidee – the other member of our party?"

"She is on her way back to the command center."

"Good, thank you." Kaz went silent, trying to come up with a counter-strategy for the hostage situation.

Ethan never let a thought go unvoiced, though. "Calling an A.I. 'Ai' sounds like the kind of thing someone who speaks English would do, not some ancient Atlantians."

"It asked me what name I wanted to access it with, and I was in a hurry," Kaz murmured offhandedly, indicating by his tone that he didn't want to talk any more about it – or about anything.

Jaidee's arrival cut off any further comment Ethan might have inadvisably made. She handed Ethan and Fletcher handguns and Kaz a rifle-like weapon similar to the one she carried, then noticed the troubled look on Kaz's face. "Commander?"

"We need a plan to counter Rivel using Emily and the rest to make us give up the ship. Any ideas?"

Jaidee frowned. "I'm no good at that sort of thing, Commander. This ship is defensible. If you want me to go out there to attack

Rivel from the rear and try to free the captain and the rest, I doubt you'll be able to hold the ship without me if Rivel decides to try to take it right away."

"There's no question about that," Kaz said, though he gave a questioning look at Fletcher. It didn't look to Fletcher like a serious suggestion, though.

Actually, Fletcher had since come up with an idea of his own. "What if we could get a message to them somehow? You know, through Loryn. Then they could maybe make a move at the same time we do."

"Sounds risky. And I don't think Loryn will be able to make any signal to them without getting noticed by Rivel or his men."

"But we can try."

Loryn had already materialized after the first mention of her name, so Kaz asked her if she could send a message to the others without being noticed by Rivel or his men.

"There is the one plani who seems to be on her own – the one named Sensha. I would not be able to speak to the others without everyone noticing."

Jaidee's eyebrows went up. "Sensha's on her own?"

"Yes. I led her to prototype nanoarmor when she entered the city, and she is now in the elevator descending to this hangar. She asked me to lead her here ahead of the others."

Kaz nearly jumped as he said in a choked voice, "she is! I . . . get a message to her immediately to say that we are holding this ship and that we will need her to distract Rivel's men so that our shipmates can join us here. Does she think she can do that on her own?" Kaz's voice trailed off on the last words. He had no idea what prototype nanoarmor could do, but all Emily and the rest needed was fifteen seconds' worth of distraction to make the dash to the *Red Hare*.

There was a pause as the Loryn with Sensha asked the question and got the answer. "She was planning to do that already, but she has a condition. She wants your word that you will not leave without her."

"Done. Tell her she has my word." Kaz turned to Jaidee. "You saw Sensha in action. What do you think?"

"Prototype nanoarmor . . . ."

"Good or bad?"

"Both. First good, then bad."

Kaz nodded. "We'll let Commander Raiz deal with the second half of that, I think."

The mention of Raiz made Fletcher suddenly worry about what might happen to him if he went back to Newport Station before he reminded himself that no one could keep him where he didn't want to be anymore.

Kaz was revved up and in full commander mode. "Ai, how long before the ship is ready for launch? Please state it in terms of how long we've been aboard this ship."

"Procedures will require one-point-two-three longer."

Jaidee shook her head. "More than fifteen minutes. That's too long."

Kaz sighed. "But it's a lot quicker than the *Azar* could have managed at its best, and this ship has basically been mothballed for millennia."

"How much longer before Rivel and the rest arrive in the hangar?" Jaidee asked Loryn.

"They are here."

Wanting to keep a line of communication open with the crew members in the ship, Sensha decided to ask Loryn to shrink to some small gray animal and perch on her shoulder, which the robot did. The result was a three-inch long creature that Sensha found disgusting, but this was no time to object. She quickly set her suit to match the grays of the wall and hid on the side of a massive pipe opposite to the hangar entrance. It was difficult to gauge how well-concealed she was, though the camouflaging feature on the armor certainly seemed to get the colors right. The hangar was barren of any obvious hiding spots – except for behind the ship, of course.

The red ship caught and held Sensha's interest until Rivel and the rest arrived. Eldrandii designs were famed for their beauty and streamlining, but Sensha had never found their dual bodies visually appealing. This one was something else entirely – a design that suited her. For the first time in her life, she imagined herself in command of a starship, but that was such a far-fetched idea that she didn't take it seriously. Yet.

The humans must have done their best to delay Rivel and his men, because they arrived later than Sensha expected. Sean in particular had a bloodied and bruised face. The plani all looked undamaged, so he probably avoided fighting back to ensure he didn't spark a more serious confrontation.

Just as her heart started revving up and her muscles tensed for battle, Loryn whispered in her ear, "Kaz wanted me to tell you to wait as long as possible before attacking."

"Wait as long as possible? What is that supposed to mean? Why?"

"I do not know what it is supposed to mean, but he says the ship needs time to ready for launch."

Sensha did not like this new requirement, but there was no way around it. "Tell him that I want to know as soon as the ship is ready."

The negotiations started with Rivel facing the sealed ship a few steps ahead of the rest of his men. If Kaz was willing to abandon Pierce, he could just keep the ship sealed and launch once it was ready to do so. Sensha was lucky that the first officer was attached to his captain, or she would have no escape from this planet either.

"Whoever is in there," Rivel shouted, "we have your captain and much of your crew. If you value their lives, you will surrender that ship to us. In exchange, we will let you all go free. We will even give you passage back to Earth."

Kaz's voice came through the ship's external loud speakers. "This is Kazuhiro Kamiki, first officer of the *Azar* . . . and now the *Red Hare*. You've got what you came here for. You were willing to trade the price of a ship for it before, so I don't see why you don't return our crew to us and let us take this ship in exchange."

"But what have you and your captain given us? Rather than helping us, you cost me the lives of many members of my crew. If you had cooperated from the start, you would have been better for it, but now I cannot let you leave this planet without paying a price. It would set a bad precedent. That ship is my price for your safe passage back to Earth."

"The way I see it, plani captain, we're in a position to return to Earth whether you like it or not as long as we have this ship."

"Only if you're willing to abandon your captain," Rivel pointed out. From his tone, he was enjoying this exchange, but only because he didn't realize Kaz was simply delaying.

"Let's say that I was willing."

"Let us not. I know your dossier, Commander. You're not going to leave this planet without Emily Pierce."

Rivel looked back at Pierce with a sneering smile. Sensha couldn't see the expression on the human captain's face, but imagined it was carefully impassive.

Kaz conceded Rivel's point. "But this leaves us at an impasse because I don't trust you. I don't believe that you'll take us back to Earth. What's preventing you from leaving us stranded here?"

Suddenly all levity was wiped off Rivel's face. "You question my word? Ask your captain. I have been straightforward with her from the very start. It is not my fault that she never accepted my proposals." He looked to Pierce.

Pierce shrugged and said, "don't look at me to help you in your negotiations. You plani are supposed to be good at this part."

Rivel growled something at Pierce that Sensha couldn't pick up, then shouted with an added intensity at the ship, "I have kept your captain and crew alive – take that as a sign of my integrity. If I had wanted to kill them, I could have done so at any time."

"You kept them alive because you knew you could use them as bargaining chips like you're doing now. I bet you were getting ready to order your men to . . . dispose of them . . . before you heard that we had taken this ship."

With a sharp and sudden motion that Sensha wouldn't have thought him capable of, Rivel brought his gun to Pierce's temple. Sensha jerked in surprise and had to force herself still, and while some of the humans and even the plani had similar reflexive reactions, neither Pierce nor Sean moved at all. "And how about if I dispose of them anyway and order my kandar to destroy this red toy of yours as soon as you try to take it out of this hangar?" Rivel didn't waste any time and murmured what was undoubtedly the order to the same effect on his comm link. The kandar was on its way – how long before it was in position to intercept? Not more than a couple of minutes. So much for avoiding that.

There was no response from Kaz, so Rivel went on. "You see that there is no reason for you to be obstinate. You are not going to get the ship either way, but if you hand it over, your lives and the lives of your captain and crew will continue. I do not believe you will act on a vindictive motive – sacrificing your own life and the life of others simply to keep that ship out of my hands – so you know what you must do."

Before Sensha could wonder what Kaz's next move would be, Loryn tapped her ear and said, "Kaz says they are ready and that you should start the attack. Once the enemy is distracted they will open the ship to allow the other humans in. I will not intervene, but ask you to avoid killing the other plani so that I can heal them after the fight."

"Have you told them to avoid killing me?"

"No."

"Then tough luck for them."

37

Endgame

"That's . . . incredible," Ethan said, watching through the bridge display as Sensha took down three of the plani guards before any of them could start firing at her.

Kaz didn't waste any more time on the bridge, ordering the ship opened and ramp lowered. Jaidee was at his side, armed and ready to cover the rest of the human crew as they escaped their plani captors.

Surprised that Kaz wasn't telling him to hide or get somewhere safe, Fletcher followed the two of them to the ship's entrance. He didn't really know what he was doing. He certainly wasn't ready for a fight, nor did he see how he could help at all, but it just seemed right to stand with Kaz and Jaidee in case there was something he could do with his . . . powers.

At first, even Jaidee and Kaz didn't look like they had any idea what to do. "Maybe we should keep the ship closed and let her finish them off," Jaidee said with evident awe in her voice.

"Too risky. They're already shooting wildly, and I'm not counting on Sensha to keep our people safe while she gets her revenge," Kaz said.

Sensha had blades in each hand and relied on the profound speed and agility her suit afforded her to do the rest. Shots hit her, but didn't seem to do any damage or slow her down at all. The plani were screaming in horror from this new unknown menace, but they were also keeping close to their hostages. When the humans started trying to break away and board the *Red Hare*, the plani were close behind – running even faster since they were the ones facing imminent death.

It didn't take very long for Rivel to read the situation, see the entrance of the *Red Hare* open, and to directly order his people to swarm the ship. With half a dozen of them already down, they didn't need any convincing, and now they were neck-to-neck with the humans. Any stragglers were getting picked off by Sensha, but the front of the rush was aiming to crash into Kaz, Jaidee, and Fletcher with no way for the three of them to shoot back without hitting their own people. Soon, they had to clear the entrance because the plani were taking shots at them.

"Should have shut it," Jaidee said.

Fletcher rushed to the bridge and shouted to Ethan, "we're going to have company!"

"Bad company?"

"Yes!"

"Crap."

"Just follow me quickly." Fletcher headed straight for the mess hall/storage room as the first signs of struggle at the entrance of the ship echoed throughout its corridors. He opened a large closet-like cabinet and told Ethan, "get in."

"But what about you?"

"I'll take care of myself. Just make sure you stay low in there. That way the counter over here should block any stray shots. There's nothing to block high shots."

"Good thinking. Thanks." Realizing that any more time he wasted could put Fletcher in further danger, Ethan got into his hiding place without another word.

Fletcher had no intention of hiding, of course. Trusting that all the handgun Jaidee had handed him needed was a pull on the trigger to fire since there were no other obvious safety mechanisms on it, he put his back to the wall next to the mess hall door. He hoped the wall would be enough to keep him safe from shots fired in the corridor on the other side, and waited to attack any plani that wandered in.

The first plani didn't so much wander as fly in, skidding on the floor right to the back wall before slamming to a stop. Captain

Pierce entered next, walking backward since she was no longer concerned about the foe she had dispatched and knew there had to be others intent on taking her down. She spotted Fletcher in his position and nodded approvingly. "Wondered where you were. How've you been?"

"Fine," he said. He probably didn't look it – even the new clothes he had procured on one of his jumps were now dirty and tattered from the climbing. But even though Pierce looked better groomed and her clothes were cleaner, the strain on her face gave away more inner turmoil. She also didn't have a gun, so Fletcher offered her his.

She waved away the offer. "That's all right – he doesn't need his anymore," she said, gesturing to the unconscious plani. She moved to get his weapon, but Fletcher didn't think to move in front of the doorway to cover her as she crouched down to free it from the body.

"Don't move another inch, Pierce," shouted an all-too-familiar voice from the corridor, "drop that weapon and put your hands in the air."

As Pierce complied, Fletcher held his breath. There was a chance Rivel didn't know he was there.

"Boy at the side of the door, I want to hear you drop your gun and then see you slowly move back to stand beside Captain Pierce. Any deviation from this and I will kill her."

Fletcher didn't know if he could really pull the trigger without hesitation if he tried to shift to another reality to get behind Rivel, but this might be his only chance. If he did what Rivel asked, his fate and Pierce's would probably be in the shaky hands of an unhinged plani.

So he jumped to the familiar desert reality as he had practiced with Jaidee and made the move that would put him just out of arm's reach from where Rivel's voice seemed to be coming from in the corridor. The corridor was tight and if not for the practice, there was no way he could have been confident that he would return to the *Red Hare* in the right place.

He came back right where he wanted to be, with Rivel's back to him, and pulled the trigger.

His breath caught in his throat when he realized that nothing had happened. Rivel heard the click of the trigger, though, and snapped to face him, bringing his gun around as well. Facing the wrong end of the gun and Rivel's wide panicked eyes with nowhere to run, Fletcher chest constricted and his heart sped.

Fletcher's sudden materialization through the wall left Rivel confused for just long enough for Pierce to tackle him to the ground, disarm him with a twist, then knock him out with a punch to the face that concussed him against the deck of the ship.

Pierce looked at Fletcher with eyebrows raised in question and a soft smile. "Later on, you're going to have to tell me how you did that."

Fletcher couldn't respond or even smile. Head swimming and knees buckling, the strain of the jump combined with the shock of the gun not firing and nearly getting killed by Rivel hit him, and all he could do was think "oh, no" before he could no longer resist gravity. Pierce caught him before he reached the ground, but couldn't prevent him from blacking out.

When he opened his eyes next, he could still hear intermittent shouts and weapons fire, so he couldn't have been out for long. Pierce had placed him behind the counter in the mess hall, right next to the pantry where Ethan had been hiding.

Ethan wasn't hiding anymore, instead standing guard over the still prone figures of Rivel and the other plani Pierce had knocked down. He peered over at Fletcher and said excitedly, "that was amazing! Glad to see you're all right. I didn't think you'd use your ability, but you did it! You saved Emily's life."

Could Ethan know what had really happened? No, Fletcher decided. He probably popped out of the pantry to help Pierce, freeing the captain to continue supporting her crew in the fight, but didn't know the details of Fletcher's embarrassing failure and the fact that the captain had really saved him. Not feeling like explaining it or talking at all, Fletcher stood up. The sound outside the mess hall had died down and both Ethan and Fletcher were momentarily startled by one of Pierce's crew poking her head in to check if everything was secure.

After the coast was clear, all of the plani with some life in them were brought off the ship, tied up mostly with strips of their own clothing, and left in a corner of the hangar where they would not get fried by the *Red Hare*'s launch. There were five of them – the rest were dead. Thanks mostly to Sensha, there were no casualties on the human side.

"Shouldn't we take them along as hostages?" Ethan wondered. "There's still that kandar."

Pierce shook her head. "Rivel found out the hard way that keeping prisoners isn't usually worth it – especially on unfamiliar territory. And for now, this new ship of ours is unfamiliar territory. Besides, we can always pretend we have Rivel and the rest hostage if we think that will keep the kandar from shooting at us. It won't, though – the plani don't have the same kind of loyalty to their captain that we do – especially when their captain has clearly lost the fight. The plani in charge of that kandar has to be thinking that everyone is going to get a promotion with Rivel out of the way, and he might be able to take Rivel's place if he plays his cards right with us." Then, seeing Ethan, Kaz, and Fletcher all together, she added, "nice to see you're all safe, by the way. We'll have to catch up once we escape the kandar."

"Nice to see you, too," Kaz said, but if he had more to say to Pierce, his words were preempted by Sensha's approach.

Sensha had her helmet off and blades retracted, but still looked formidable in her new suit. Worn out though he was, Fletcher had trouble keeping his eyes off her delicate curves.

There was nothing else delicate about her, though. "Captain Pierce, I have helped you and your crew."

"Yes, you have," Pierce replied, sounding wary of where this was going.

"I demand you allow me to execute Rivel."

"I can't let you do that."

"I can do it whether I have your permission or not, and no one here can stop me."

"So why are you asking for my permission? Rivel insulted you and mistreated you, Sensha, but he didn't kill you even though he could. I think you realize that, and there's a part of you that realizes there'd be no purpose to killing him – not when he's defenseless like this."

"And what is the purpose to showing him mercy except to leave a potential enemy alive?"

At Pierce's side, Kaz offered, "anyone can seek revenge – it takes someone superior to grant mercy. This way, you show you're not afraid of him."

"He gave me mercy to show his superiority – now look where he is."

"But that's because he wasn't better than you. Are you better than him?"

That gave Sensha pause, and Pierce filled the silence. "We need to get moving. I say you don't do it, Sensha, but I can't stop you if you decide to. You helped us, so whatever you do, we'll take you off of this planet to wherever you want to go. Now, everyone on board! Loryn, get the hangar open."

Fletcher followed everyone else rushing to board the ship. He didn't really want to know what Sensha decided, anyway – he had already pulled the trigger on Rivel, and wasn't prepared to judge her one way or the other.

Sensha stood over Rivel. She had pictured this victory so differently before, but now it was just as Pierce had said – killing Rivel felt meaningless, since she had thwarted him.

Clenching her fist, she felt the power her suit gave her. She now had a responsibility to focus her efforts on saving her people, and to waste no time on other pursuits.

She could still take a small measure of revenge on Rivel without killing him, though. She knelt down and sank her teeth into his neck, drinking enough of his blood to satisfy her thirst, but not nearly enough to kill him. Her saliva promoted clotting so he wouldn't bleed further from the wound, but the scar would remain as a reminder to him that she could have killed him, but chose not to. She turned her back on him and was the last to board the *Red Hare*.

"The *Red Hare*?" Pierce repeated in surprise as the ship's engines heated. Fletcher had joined her, Kaz, Sean, and Jaidee on the bridge, though he wasn't sure that he belonged.

"Ethan's idea," Kaz mumbled.

"No kidding. Nice pun, though I'm not as red as I usually am." Pierce ran her fingers through hair that was a patchy mess of red and black. "What are you doing in the captain's seat, Kaz?"

"Sorry about that, but the captain's seat is also the pilot's seat – this ship is meant to be controlled by one person. We haven't found either of our pilots, and I guess our shuttle pilot is still with the shuttle that brought you down to the planet, so that leaves me as the most qualified person to pilot this ship against the kandar."

"No offense, Kaz, but you're . . . ."

"I've at least had some time to get familiar with the controls and the ship's computer. I've named the computer Ai, by the way."

"You would. Way to think outside the box."

"Do I have your permission to continue, Captain?"

Fletcher once again thought about mentioning his own training, but it wasn't as if he had any real experience outside a simulator, and Kaz had a point about being familiar with the controls.

"I don't see any choice. Are we ready to move out?"

"Yes, Captain."

"Instruct the crew to buckle up, then take us out of the hangar."

The bridge had half a dozen peripheral seats in front of displays, but none of them had belts, harnesses, or anything of the sort. Since no one was trained to manage the stations anyway, Fletcher took the seat closest to him. Captain Pierce sat to his right.

The hangar had a long and slightly inclined tunnel that eventually led out of the side of a hill. Kaz instructed Ai to launch the ship, but had his hands on the controls ready to override if events demanded it. At first, they were just taxiing, but halfway to the tunnel exit the engines started increasing their acceleration so that, by the time they were out with nothing but sky in front of them, the ship needed only a few seconds to go supersonic.

Having no information about where the *Red Hare* would exit from, the kandar wasn't hovering in wait, but it was on their tail before they had gained much altitude.

"Do you think you can outrun them?" Pierce asked, looking at the display Ai had automatically put up for them. The units and lettering were meaningless to them, but it was easy to see which numbers represented the velocities of the two ships and to judge the situation by comparing them.

"Eventually," Kaz said. "They're heavier and bulkier than we are, so the atmosphere will keep them slower than us. We're within their weapons range, though. I told Ai to execute evasive maneuvers if she detects anything, but there aren't any other countermeasures on board. Should make it impossible for their main cannon to get a shot at us, since that's meant to take down objects with set trajectories."

"Will Ai warn us before . . . ."

The answer was no. Everyone suddenly had their left armrests digging into their abdomens as the ship banked sharply.

"Holy hell!" Sean shouted. "This thing turns like a fighter jet!"

Out of the corner of his eye, Fletcher saw Pierce caressing the armrest that had just stabbed her. She must be warming to her new ship, because Fletcher felt like punching his own armrest back. His stomach was still in pain.

He was better braced for the next two sudden turns, but he was starting to feel sick.

"Once we're in space, it'll be a matter of how quickly we can get a good hyperspace vector," Kaz said. "I already figured some of that out before the fight, and I'm trying to do the rest now. The kandar doesn't have a hyperdrive, so we'll be free once we're in."

"Three missiles detected," Ai reported.

"I was hoping they'd forget about those."

"Ai, can you shoot them down?" Kaz asked.

"Missiles approaching range . . . firing."

The display showed the plani missiles trying to evade the shots from the *Red Hare*'s tiny rear turret, but Ai dispatched two of them within a couple of seconds. The last was destroyed close enough to rattle the ship from its explosion, but not enough to do any damage.

Sean shook his head. "This ship practically flies itself. Kaz was the right guy to control it, Captain - all it really needs is a nav officer to tell it where to go."

"And I've got it." Kaz announced over the intercom, "prepare for hyperspace jump in ten seconds."

"Are we out of the atmosphere?"

"The density will be within safe limits in five, four, three, two, one."

The forward view changed to a plot of their hyperspace trajectory as the mildly disconcerting sensation associated with entering hyperspace washed over everyone – everyone except Fletcher. For Fletcher, it was much milder than what he experienced with his own early jumps, before he had adapted to his new ability. In his first trip through hyperspace since his encounter with the gateway on Kentak, Fletcher now knew that he would be able to return to hyperspace whenever he liked, and in some sort of spaceship, to travel through it freely.

38

Raiz

There was running water on the ship, but no showers. Bathtubs, yes, but with so many buttons labeled in an indecipherable script that they looked dangerous. Everyone managed to get cleaned up, but they had no spare clothes to change into and Fletcher didn't dare jump to get them some while in hyperspace, so the only one who looked properly clean when Pierce, Kaz, Sensha, Ethan, and Fletcher gathered in the mess hall for a meeting was Sensha in her nanosuit.

There would be other meetings with the rest of the crew, who wanted to know about the future of Pierce's freetrading enterprise, the sort of compensation they would receive, and what sort of rescue mission would be mounted for their still-missing comrades, but for now there were pressing decisions to be made.

"The main issue is where we should go," Kaz said. "We're inbound to Earth space right now, but I'm not sure it wouldn't be best if we diverted to somewhere else first."

"Why?" Ethan asked.

Fletcher could offer at least one answer. "Well, I don't think I want to go back to Newport Station yet. I don't think it's been enough time."

Ethan shrugged. "But there's no way your father could keep you from going anywhere or doing anything you like now, right?"

"Yes, but . . . ."

"That's one consideration, but not the only one," Kaz said. Turning to the Captain, he explained, "I don't think Commander

Raiz will let you keep this ship, Emily. They'll want to figure out how its artificial hyperdrive works. If we dock at Newport Station, we put the decision completely into Raiz's hands."

Pierce shook her head dismissively. "It'd be illegal for him to take it without compensation. To me, that means a new ship."

Fletcher blinked. "You don't want this one? I mean, its hyperdrive doesn't need a person to be trapped in the back for it to work, you don't even need a crew to control it, and it looks great." And Fletcher would have liked it himself, if he had the choice.

"But it's not very practical," Pierce said. "Even if I could keep it, I'm a trader, and this ship doesn't have much of a cargo hold, and it's short on passenger quarters. If I was trying to fight a fleet of warships, I'd love how maneuverable it is, but that's not what I do. But Kaz, why do you think Raiz wouldn't be up for a fair trade – ship for ship?"

"I think he's not going to be in his usual good mood when he finds out that the plani have the hyperdrive secret, that's all. Unless you're going to tell me that Rivel didn't send any information to that kandar."

Pierce sighed. "Not no information. Probably just enough. There was nothing about this artificial hyperdrive, though – I guess because it was a prototype designed at the colony. The plani will still have to rely on mages even if they figure out the theory. That still gives Earth the advantage, even if you don't include the two year head start we have."

"But I think Raiz will wonder whether we deliberately let it go this way instead of fighting Rivel earlier. You're the one who argued with him that we should leak the information out somehow. So, did you plan it to go this way?" Kaz asked, eyebrows raised.

Pierce stretched and leaned back. "You know, just a year ago you wouldn't have thought me capable of it."

"You've changed. Are you capable of it?"

Pierce shrugged. "Probably not, but if you're not sure, then Raiz won't be, either. You know me a lot better than he does."

Sensha couldn't keep silent at this. "You . . . you considered giving it away . . . to him?"

With a warning glance that showed she wasn't intimidated

by Sensha, new suit or not, Pierce said, "let's not forget who I am and what I've done for your people, right? And I don't think you've come away from this too badly. You wanted to get the hyperdrive secret, which wouldn't have benefitted your people at all, and won't benefit the regular plani either – not for a long time. Instead, you got that suit, which you might be able to use to help the dribrora. You could be . . . sort of a super hero to them. But that leads us to another question – where do you want to go?"

Diverted from her outrage, Sensha thought a moment. "I would want to return to Plani . . . eventually. But before I do, there is a dribrora colony on Earth's moon. I would want to go there first. I also want to speak with Commander Raiz to negotiate for the data we obtained from the computers of Rivel's conglomerate."

"I think that's doable. What about you, Fletcher?"

Caught a bit by surprised at being asked, Fletcher still didn't need more than a second to come up with his answer, "Mars."

Pierce looked to Kaz. "You have Mars connections, right?"

Kaz nodded. "I know a friend who could help Fletcher out. We could also arrange to meet Raiz at his place."

"Let's do that, then."

And just like that, Fletcher was going to be living on Mars. Shortly before they exited hyperspace into Sol system, Pierce stopped by the quarters he and Ethan now occupied, and shooed Ethan out to have a word with him. They sat facing each other on the floor.

"So . . . Kaz filled me in about everything that happened to you. Sounds like you went through quite a lot. Are you all right?"

Fletcher shrugged. "I don't know. I guess so. If I think about it, it all seems really weird. Jumping seems . . . natural now, though."

"You haven't had to release the extra magic while we've been in hyperspace?"

Fletcher shook his head. "I think I can go for more than a day without being forced to do it now, and I didn't want to try doing it in hyperspace. It should be like anywhere else, and I'm sure I could get back to the ship just by focusing on it, but . . . I guess I'm a bit tired after everything, anyway."

"We all are. And the energy isn't going down the further away we get from Kentak?"

Fletcher shook his head again. "Totally the same."

"What do you think about living with Kaz's friend for a while?"

"It's better than Newport Station, as long as his friend doesn't know my father."

Pierce smiled sympathetically. "He doesn't. From what Kaz says, he doesn't get out of his dome much. But you're going to have to decide whether you want to tell him about your abilities."

"I'm not going to tell anyone who doesn't already know," Fletcher said firmly.

"It won't be easy keeping it from everyone."

"Probably easier than explaining it."

That seemed to satisfy Pierce. "Commander Raiz . . . could be a trickier issue. He already knew you had some potential, and he'll want to talk to you alone. Do you plan to keep it from him? It will be easy to explain it to him – I think he even expects it."

Sensing that the captain had a recommendation, Fletcher asked, "what do you think I should do?"

"You should be honest with him. He was the one who helped you get onto my ship. I think you owe him the truth, at least."

"Okay. Can I ask you a question?" The words suddenly stumbled out as the thought struck Fletcher.

"Shoot."

"Ethan told me that you can do . . . I don't like to call it magic."

"I don't either. Yeah, I can, but nothing like what you can do. I just get vague hints about what's going to happen. If a researcher got their hands on me, they'd barely be able to conclude it was something more than good intuition."

"Are there actually a lot of people who can secretly do magic?"

Pierce blinked, then laughed. "You mean, like some sort of secret society?"

"No, no! I . . . ."

Pierce patted him on the shoulder to put him at ease, then looked straight at him and said, "I think you know that there's one other person I've met who has potential, but doesn't seem to be aware of it."

"Jaidee."

"And except for her, you're the only other human I've ever met who gave any hint of it. But I think that there must be thousands of people who, if they just got out to worlds like Eldrand or Kentak, they'd find out they were able to do some unexpected things. You'd still be the only one to get zapped by a trans-reality gateway, though."

Fletcher snorted a laugh. "I wonder if people knew about me whether they'd all start going to Kentak trying to have the same thing happen to them."

"Oh, yeah, I can just picture all the crazy passengers with more money than they know what to do with. Too bad for them that this is the only hyperspace ship that's totally safe in orbit around Kentak. Unless what happened to you really stabilized that gateway, which we can't be sure about."

"It's a cool ship. Are you really going to give it up to get one of the eldrandii ones again?"

Some uncertainty clouded Pierce's face. "I'm lucky to have come away from that planet with anything at all. Commander Raiz owes me a lot for this mission, but what I can negotiate beyond that all depends on his mood and how badly he wants this ship. This ship looks beautiful and it's technologically advanced, Fletcher, but it's not useful to me."

Fletcher paused, then said, "okay, but could we get some fresh clothes before meeting Commander Raiz?"

Lacking a shuttle, the relatively small *Red Hare* landed directly on the surface of Mars a half mile away from a minor settlement near Kufra crater. Kaz's friend, Komura Tatsuya, took out a truck with room in the cargo bed for four passengers, and brought with him three bio-suits including one fit for a young man. Only Pierce, Kaz, Fletcher, and Sensha would leave the ship to meet Raiz in Komura's home, and Sensha's suit was already pressurized, containing a carbon dioxide-to-oxygen converter in the helmet that could operate for more than the time they would need.

When Sensha mentioned the feature of her nanosuit, Pierce commented, "I really wish I had picked up one of those."

"There was only one. It was a prototype just like the ship," Sensha said in a defensive tone, as if concerned at the very thought that someone else in the universe might get a suit like hers.

The *Red Hare*'s entrance had an airlock system. First Komura entered, placing the bio-suits inside, then the chamber was pressurized and Pierce, Kaz, and Fletcher each stripped out of their Kentak-worn clothes down to the underwear, and put on the bio-suits. It was the first time Fletcher had ever worn one, but his father had drilled him on how to put it on correctly. Still, Pierce looked him over to double-check.

They were silent on the way into Komura's home, skimming across the red soil, following the trail Komura left on the way out to them. With its inhospitable atmosphere and barrenness, Mars seemed even more alien than Kentak, even though it was in Earth's backyard. Some of Mars had been terraformed, but Kufra crater was still under development – not quite the frontier, but still a challenge for all settlers.

Komura's dome covered his farm, but he actually lived underground. He drove the truck directly into a garage adjacent to the dome, then pressed a garage controller to first seal the place, then pressurize it. After that, he took off his helmet, then signaled that they should do the same.

"Tatsu, I thought you'd be able to afford a pressurized truck by now," Kaz chided his friend.

They got to see Komura's face properly for the first time, and the man stood about five-and-a-half feet tall and, despite a strong jaw and lines on his face, looked a few years younger than Kaz. His buzz-cut black hair gave him a vaguely military air.

"Why, just so you can be comfortable? It's not worth it – only the ones with the suitports can keep the dust out, and you can't carry much cargo or extra passengers in those." Then, as if getting something off his chest, he said, "Kazu, why did you have to bring all this nonsense on me? That man's a maniac!"

Kaz smiled. "Commander Raiz is here, then?"

"Yes, and he's commented on everything – *everything* – in my home in the last hour. I'm just a lonely farmer, Kazu – I'm not used to these hyperactive government boys visiting. Are they all like this?"

"No, just him."

"Well . . . come along." He led them down a spiral ramp and then through an airlock. The next room had six stalls. "Each of you can pick one. Spray yourselves down but leave the bio-suits to me. I've put clothes in each stall and they are one-size-fits-all except for the boy's. Where's my new tenant?"

Fletcher stepped forward but stayed silent.

Komura looked him over. "Scrawny . . . but keen eyes. Well, you'll get some muscle on you here – don't think the low gravity will save you. Your clothes are in the last stall on the right."

After his experience on Kentak, Fletcher didn't mind the idea of putting on some muscle, but was a bit apprehensive at Komura's brusk attitude and snap assessment of him.

Everyone was in blue jeans and white tee-shirts – except Sensha, of course. Fletcher's fit well, but the one-size-fits-all didn't work well for either Pierce or Kaz – being loose but short for Kaz and the right length but tight for Pierce.

Giving them a wince of sympathy when he saw them, Komura said, "sorry. Short notice." He then led them through another heavy door into his underground home proper.

Before they could even take a look around, Raiz greeted them with open arms as if welcoming them into his own home. "Ah, come in! The air is wonderful in here. Komura-san grows plants in here that not only help clean up the carbon dioxide but also give it a fresh smell. You must all be tired – there are some comfortable couches over here."

Komura sighed and gestured for them to follow Raiz. To Fletcher, Raiz didn't seem particularly upset about anything. But did that mean he would be willing to strike a favorable deal, or was the commander just hiding his true feelings to disarm the people he would soon be negotiating with?

Still, Fletcher couldn't help but like the tall and lanky Raiz. Dressed casually in trousers and a polo, the commander gave all the feel of being in his twenties while looking like he was in his thirties, but really he had to be more than fifty. He certainly didn't have any grey in his full head of black hair, but was that because he was naturally youthful despite all the worries he must have or because he cultivated the image and took special care to maintain it?

Once they were all seated, Raiz wasted no time with pleasantries before getting to business. "Pierce, I've heard reports about your ship on your flight into Mars. Is it what I think it is?"

Pierce gave Raiz a coy smile. "Come on, Raiz, you know it is. You wouldn't have come all the way out here otherwise. And before you ask, there's only one of them – it's a prototype – and Rivel didn't get any information that would let him build one. He might have gotten data similar to what we got on Selparis two years ago. Now you tell me – did you know the *Azar* would be destroyed in Kentak orbit?"

Raiz kept his smile. "Please, Captain, I wouldn't do that to you. I don't blame you for being suspicious, though. Now, I hope you understand that you can't keep that ship."

"It's called the *Red Hare*."

"Is it? It's hare as in the rabbit? That was your friend . . . Ethan's idea, was it?" Fletcher's jaw dropped. Raiz certainly made sure to know the people he was dealing with. "Well, it's as good a name as any, Captain, but our scientists need to do research on it."

"Well, I need a ship, and according to the law, I've got a ship. If you want the *Red Hare*, you know what I want for it."

Raiz leaned forward and got serious, keeping his tone business-like and brisk. "The eldrandii are getting more and more reluctant to sell us anything, putting all sorts of new requirements on even standard equipment purchases and antimatter engine overhauls, much less a whole ship. In the time they'll take to process the request, they'll find out the ship is going to you, and probably find out what you're giving us in return, and that will be the end of the deal. Now, since no one else can build a ship for you, what do you suggest?"

"You mean you came with nothing to offer? Should I have done a deal with the plani, after all?"

"There is . . . an Earth Force supply and personnel transfer ship a lot like your *Azar*, except a bit older."

Pierce straightened up. "Go on."

Raiz cleared his throat. "But Earth Force marines aren't exactly the most conscientious passengers, and the ship has taken quite a bit of wear-and-tear over the years. Its interior and electronic systems need a complete overhaul, but because the Council has been cutting the Earth Force budget for decades – all sorts of fearmongering about how the force could be used to undermine national sovereignty and that sort of thing – we don't have the money to do it."

"You're saying I'm going to have to put up the money to fix it up? That's no good. You already owe me for the mission to Kentak and the Council has to accept some of the liability for the mission. I own the *Red Hare*, and while I like the sound of getting a supply and personnel ship like that – nice and roomy for the jobs I usually pick up – I want the replacement refit to my specifications at the government's expense."

"But the Earth Force budget . . ."

". . . isn't the Council's research and development budget, which is huge and not controversial. And the *Red Hare* will be going to R&D, not Earth Force, isn't that right? So that's where you'll get the money."

With all the delight of a salesman who had met his match, but nevertheless felt he was coming away with a good deal, Raiz grinned. "You're getting better at this, Pierce."

"And I want a look at the refitted ship before I sign away the *Red Hare*. None of that marine wear-and-tear, antimatter engines up to spec, and everything."

"Of course. I will bring it here after the refit, to save you the trouble of transferring to Newport Station with the *Red Hare*. Bringing that ship to Earth space might generate rumors too quickly, and it's well-camouflaged on the Martian soil. The Earth Force comes with two cargo shuttles, by the way."

"And those will need overhauls, too, right?"

"The ride down wasn't too uncomfortable, but I decided to use the better of the two. I'll have them cleaned up for you. Anything else?"

"We still have people on Kentak, but the *Red Hare* is the only ship that can orbit the planet safely. We could do it like the plani did by just sending out the shuttle and then leaving the system, but that puts more people at risk."

"And the plani are still on the planet ready to get some revenge against you," Raiz pointed out. "I think the scientists would like us to gather some data on the *Red Hare* in action before getting their hands dirty. If you'll be willing to loan it to me while spending some time here on Mars waiting for the work to be done on your new ship, we'll get some troops together and do an official rescue mission to Kentak immediately. I've already filed the paperwork with the ISC. I think it might be a good idea to establish a permanent presence there – give the kentaki an alternative to the plani."

Pierce relaxed, shaking her head in amazement. "As usual, you have it all thought out. Using the rescue of my crew as a pretext to get involved on Kentak."

"Just stealing a good idea from the plani."

"But I also want compensation for my crew members, who've been subjected to extraordinary danger and . . . ."

"That," Raiz held up a finger, interrupting her, "is your responsibility, Captain. I think the credits I was already set to pay you for the mission will be more than adequate to cover it – enough to pay each of your crew members for a full year. Agreed?"

Pierce shrugged. "Just make sure to prioritize the rescue of my crew over whatever else you might be trying to do on Kentak."

"Done. Now," he turned to Sensha, "about that suit of yours."

"You cannot have it," Sensha snarled.

"No, of course not. But I was wondering if you would mind me doing some tests on it – no one else but me, and just for a few minutes while we're here."

"I do mind."

Raiz's mouth was left gaping for a couple of seconds before he was able to gather himself. Clearly, his charm wasn't working with Sensha. "Maybe we should start over. What do you want?"

"More land on Earth's moon for a colony of dribrora refugees and free passage for them from Plani."

Raiz looked like he was going to choke on air. "Free passage for . . . how many?"

Sensha blinked. "How many . . . would you be willing to provide it for?"

"I see. And I don't own any land on the moon, nor would I be able to transfer the land the government owns. The existing dribrora colony was provided by a private enterprise in exchange for the technical expertise that the dribrora living there would provide."

"Private enterprise . . . ," Sensha repeated with distaste on her lips.

Raiz cleared his throat. "How about this. You have information on a number of plani conglomerates, I believe. Do you still have the data with you?"

Sensha took the card out. Since the data only involved Rivel's competitors and he had bigger targets, he had not bothered to demand it back from her.

"I will have to decrypt what you have there, but once I do it might be of interest to our own corporations on the moon, and maybe they'd be willing to trade substantial lunar territory as well as passage for dribrora. My price for handling the decryption and negotiating with those corporations on your behalf is that I get a copy of the data, as well. That will be unavoidable anyway. Just to make sure you understand – Earth's moon is barren and airless. Habitation modules are available and there's plenty of work, but it's still a dangerous environment."

"I understand. But we will be treated fairly there – that's what those already there have said."

Raiz nodded. "Your people seem to fit in very well."

"And when you negotiate . . . on my behalf . . . ."

"I always try my best to get the best deal possible," Raiz reassured her. "It would tarnish my reputation to do anything less, and I'm still hoping that you will reconsider about the readings on your suit. I'm not going to press you on that point now, but since we have a further deal to make, you know that I will try my best on this issue."

Sensha didn't know whether to trust him and turned to Pierce. "I . . . . ." She wanted to ask for Pierce's advice, knowing that Pierce had at least dealt with her fairly, but couldn't come up with the words.

Pierce understood nevertheless. "I'll consider that part of my agreement with you, too, Raiz. After all, I took Sensha on as part of my crew and played a part in getting that data out of Rivel's company. If Sensha is in any way unhappy with the results of the trade, she can contact me and I'll take up her side. Since it's part of the deal for the *Red Hare* . . . ."

"We'll include whatever bargain I can strike with the lunar corporations in the agreement before you officially turn over ownership of the *Red Hare*," Raiz nodded, then cast hopeful eyes at Sensha. "Will you agree to that?"

Sensha nodded.

Raiz clapped once and said "excellent." Turning to Fletcher now, he said, "I think maybe the two of us need to have a word. Komura-san, could we have the use of your spare bedroom? I suppose that's where Fletcher will be staying?"

Surprised at being suddenly addressed after being left completely out of the discussion and not even having a gap in which to offer drinks, Komura answered, "Y-yes, of course."

As Raiz led Fletcher away from the others, Fletcher could hear Komura whispering hoarsely to Kaz. "What the heck was all that about?"

Fletcher and Raiz both sat on a futon unrolled on the floor that was already decked with sheets and a fluffy blue quilt. From what Raiz had said, it would soon be Fletcher's bed. He had never slept on the floor on a futon, but it was unbearably inviting after all the nights he spent on the ground on Kentak.

Fletcher looked at Raiz expectantly, but even though the station commander met his eyes, it took him some time to decide how to begin.

"I didn't know what was happening between you and your father, and wouldn't have looked into it at all. It was only because an asparii saw you when you were sneaking to that bookstore, noticed that you had magical potential, and mentioned it to me that I started to get curious about you. Otherwise, I wouldn't have paid any attention to you." Then, just to make clear that he was apologizing, he added, "I'm sorry."

It took a moment for Fletcher to decide what to say. "There's no reason you should have known."

"I'm supposed to know everything that happens on my station, and if I had not been so distracted by what's been happening on Earth the past few years, I definitely would have noticed earlier. Your father controls the largest private human fleet – just the fact that he left his son on my station alone while conducting his business in other systems should have . . . anyway, how are you doing?"

Fletcher blinked at the track-switch. "Fine."

"I'm sure Captain Pierce has already told you, but I arranged for you to get aboard her ship. I picked her because I trust her and thought that being around her would be your best chance to realize some of your potential. But the other side is that her ship was the most dangerous one I could have picked. I hope you don't mind that I . . . ."

Fletcher once again chose his words carefully. "Thank you for helping me, but I don't want anyone else . . . setting me up like that again."

Raiz smiled. "Well, it will be up to you to make sure they don't, and I think you're better prepared now. About your abilities . . . ."

Fletcher had agreed with Pierce about being honest with Raiz, but now that he had met the commander, he was a bit more cautious. "I'm not sure I want to talk about them. I don't really understand them yet."

"I need to know as much as possible so I can protect you."

Somehow, Fletcher wanted to avoid giving away the fact that he could jump between realities and could therefore protect himself. He was catching on to the fact that information was a valuable commodity – especially around Raiz – and it didn't look like the commander had anything to give him in exchange. "You said this was going to be my room. That means that you're not taking me back to Newport Station. That means you didn't get custody of me from my father, right? So . . . are you really going to be protecting me?"

"The evidence I have of your treatment is not admissible in court because of the way I gathered it," Raiz said grimly, "and your father has shown how powerful his word is and how difficult it is to win a case against his lawyers through innumerable lawsuits and corporate actions. I can at least make sure that any hints about your whereabouts will be cleaned out since most communication goes through Newport Station, or I can warn you ahead of time if I think your father knows and maybe arrange another little escape for you."

Grasping the subtext of all this, Fletcher grew indignant. "You're only interested in my . . . my potential, though. That's why you want to know how much potential I've got before helping me – to know if I'm worth it."

"No, I . . . ."

"Then you'll just have to help me without knowing anything about my abilities."

Raiz barked a laugh, then stood up. "A speculative investment. Well played. It's a shame Komura is so dull, but I suppose you've had enough excitement to last you for a while." Then with a touch more menace in his smile, he added, "and somehow, even here, I think you'll be an interesting person to watch."

www.ingramcontent.com/pod-product-compliance
Lightning Source LLC
Chambersburg PA
CBHW062003170626
46813CB00001B/25